The Gnat and the Elephant

A world free for the taking, and the faces around Wexley worried about stocks. Blown up and projected across the fine windows watching Chicago's blooming skyline, the visage collective pooled their vast industrial, technological, and people powers to whine about how detonating a stadium filled with Paragons was bad for business.

"You signed up for this," Wexley spoke over a rant he hadn't been listening to. "Every one of you knew what Zhan-Yo wanted. Now it's here and you're looking at the opportunity like it's going to kill you."

"Apparently it might!" said Akash Reddy, worldwide provisioners purveyor, his grocery chain all too annoyed by Paragon price regulations.

A few weeks ago, Akash had been right there calling for a revolution. Now the man had sweat on his brow and eyes darting around the camera, reading about one disruption after another to his precious perishable cargo.

"Stability isn't a common trait in revolutions, Akash," said the man's opposite, Adriana, a spit and vinegar woman, some fashion magnate Wexley had ignored up until today's meeting, when she'd decided to stand on the right side. "We know what comes at the end of all this."

"Do we?" Akash countered. "I thought we wanted a negotiation, a chance for equity between all of us. How is that possible now?"

"It was never possible," Wexley said, projecting from his desk. A small line in the surface near his elbow reminded him of the time, how much he'd rather be anywhere else. He stood, a signal this dull affair would be brought to a close. "We do, however, have a chance at something greater. Why share what we can have for ourselves?"

Not his best ending, but Wexley didn't give the assembled heads a chance to dispute it. With a wave, Wexley sent the call into the digital dustbin, giving him back his skyline. One marred in seconds with a new ring.

"Allow it," Wexley said, moving to the room's center. The coming power play demanded something more than a desk and a chair. "Adriana, where have you been hiding?"

The most interesting person on the meeting fuzzed back in, though her straight lips and frozen eyes showed she had zero interest in playful banter. Fine then. Wexley could do without.

He had for a very long time.

"Don't excuse what happened on that call for patience," Adriana said. "I'm not defending you for my health, or for yours. The stadium was a disaster."

"It was not my idea," Wexley said, grimacing as he did so.

Leaders shouldn't grovel, shouldn't make excuses.

"And?"

"I don't know where he is," Wexley answered. "If he's still alive, Zhan-Yo hasn't tried to contact me. His accounts are frozen, his cards tracked. Either he's dumped every connection he has, or the man's a victim of his own success."

"Which leaves a very important company without a leader."

Wexley strode towards Adriana's head, the projection making her neck-up picture as large as Wexley's body. Nevertheless, he took on the huge stare without a flinch.

"There isn't a vacuum here. Our plan continues." When Adriana didn't interrupt, Wexley allowed himself to move on. No major test of wills today. "As the Paragons regroup, we will approach them with an offer to share power."

"A return to democracy, as Zhan-Yo wanted?"

"A return to proper leadership, as we all deserve. When the Paragons refuse, we'll be left with no other choice than to ratchet up the conflict."

Outside, the shimmering spring sun flickered as a dark oval crossed by the windows. Bigger than a pod and kept aloft by humming jets, the machine didn't notice Wexley's scowl, didn't feel his urge to reach out and slap it from the sky.

"How will you do that?" Adriana asked. "Another bomb? More innocent lives fed to your campaign?"

Wexley followed the drone, walking along his windows as it floated by, "Zhan-Yo went for bombast. I prefer results. Which presents a problem, Adriana."

"What?"

"Results are expensive."

"As if you need the reps."

Wexley gave the woman a nod, "Too much from any one company's accounts would be noticed. The Paragons might be in trouble, but they are not dead. Not yet."

If Wexley's mordant words bothered Adriana, she didn't show it. Instead, she continued her trademarked stare, making Wexley wonder just what she was looking for.

"Tell me what you need and you will get it," Adriana said. "I can work on the others too. But Wexley, we gave Zhan-Yo a long leash because we knew him. You, we don't. Damage us, and you will get no second chance."

Again, Wexley went with the humble nod.

"If this doesn't work, Adriana, I doubt I'll be alive to ask forgiveness."

Wexley canceled his afternoon, sweeping from the office in a rush after the call. He stood at the elevator's front, seeing everyone who had to slide around him as the lift took its journey down to the first floor and beyond. All those people giving him nods, smiles, believing their toils would give them their paychecks, would give them satisfaction. They depended on Wexley, and while he didn't depend on them, he would save them anyway.

In the not too distant future, these people carrying their files, checking their Tamas to see what new regulation the Paragons deployed today, would find themselves freed from their genetic chains. Opportunity would once more live within their efforts, not with DNA's random luck.

The elevator reached the parking deck's lowest level, well beneath the streets and deserted. The designers had built the structure for a society that no longer existed, with cars dominating the streets. Now everyone took trains, buses, pods as the Paragons limited traffic in the city. The empty concrete rows nagged, efficiencies lost as buzzing lights left a ghostly glow on the gray.

One space sat occupied, however. Backed into a corner, a black van bedecked with corporate logos. Its tires were flat, but Wexley made sure the van sat ignored nonetheless. If anyone asked him, Wexley declared the vehicle Zhan-

Yo's, entrusted to the garage for safe-keeping while the fugitive leader fought for his dreams.

Nobody dared ask why Zhan-Yo's van had its locks tied to Wexley's Tama, why the van's charge cable stayed plugged in if it wasn't going to be moved. Taking one last look around the garage and confirming its emptiness—rumbles came from above as those few drivers made their lunchtime exodus—Wexley swiped and tapped a particular code on a particular program. Cameras dotting the garage would blink into a preset roll, one showing a lonely van with zero humans, zero activity.

Anyone watching, anyone wondering why Wexley had disappeared from the tape, would know better than to ask. If they didn't, then Rhimes would solve the problem in a permanent fashion.

His invisibility attained, Wexley popped the van's rear doors. There, cleaned and pressed, polished and perfected, sat an array Wexley had left alone for several days. Ever since that tracker, Kat, had attacked him on some rooftops not all that far from here. Wexley had adopted a discretionary stance, had waited to see if his enemy might make some mistake.

Enemy.

Wexley laughed, a low chuckle as he traded his business suit for its more lethal partner. Kat Collins, a famed tracker in Chicago but nowhere else, had about as much to do with Wexley as a gnat did with the elephant it landed on. She'd disrupted his game, had clued in the Elementals to their true threat.

And when he'd made her an offer any sane human, any *normal* human would take, Kat had rejected the overture and put a fatal end to a whole strike team in the process.

The woman wasn't a threat to Wexley's operation. No,

definitely not. But she annoyed him nonetheless, had brought Wexley near his own demise on that roof, Paragon drone approaching. Insults like that couldn't be left standing, or they would expand like a gas, taking up all the air in Wexley's head until nothing remained but boiling vengeance.

The bullies in grade school had felt the same. His first manager, delivering workplace edicts like some half-assed dictator, had felt the same. Countless bad dates, frustrated dealmakers, and unfortunate passers-by had pushed Wexley the wrong way and, as a result, had to be cleansed.

Not always dead, though the weapons Wexley slotted into the suit's belt and thigh holsters were capable of such an outcome, just repaid. Wrongs righted, scales evened, whatever term you chose. Once Wexley had done that, once he'd put Kat in the same way she'd put him, then that pressure would be gone and he would be able to focus once again.

Focus on Adriana, and the plan whispering in his mind.

"What's her status?" Wexley spoke into the mic as he walked Chicago's streets heading west. Cloaked in a thick ankle-length trench, head covered by a deep blue knit, Wexley looked like somebody to avoid. When eyes caught a flickered hilt, the long gun's barrel showing from its back strap, people swerved far away. "I'm curious."

The words hit with vague precision, meaning everything to their target and nothing to the listeners. And there were always listeners.

"Off the board," Rhimes replied instantly, though Wexley hadn't scheduled a call, hadn't done anything except flip his Tama to a certain channel and started talking. "There's a meeting going on now, something's pulled them all off the streets."

"We don't know what?"

"Feed's been dark lately."

Wexley took in a deep breath, feeling the chill air lace his lungs. Around him, a growing crowd waited for a light to change and offer a chance to cross to the other side. Chicago's early spring had black snow clinging to life along the streets, muddy puddles like genetic soup that'd give way to new life in a month. Water dripped from the raised train lines up above, mingling with the steady whoosh as tires melded with wet asphalt.

Blocks away, a particular sound bounced between the buildings. One that would've made Wexley smile if he cared to. The protests at the Paragon's Chicago headquarters continued apace, a rage against the violence in the city, violence Wexley himself played no small part in perpetrating. Disorganized and decimated by Mynx, the North America's lone remaining Champion, Chicago's own Paragons lacked a strong leader, lacked organization.

Another shadow floated by above, the drone washing its scanners over the crowd as the light changed and feet began their shivering shuffle. Without heroes on the streets, the drones filled the space. Unlike a Paragon, with their powers and their personality, the drones operated on a brutal scale. They offered little understanding and harsh results, giving the protestors more ammo for their fights.

Such a tragedy.

"What other options do we have?" Wexley asked. "I'm near Michigan now."

"Early for you, isn't it?"

"I pay you for your competence, not your opinions."

"If you want my competence, you'll value my opinions."

Wexley grinned now. Ah, how novel it was for anyone to stand up to him. Rhimes had earned the right, though.

Had powered Wexley from one scheme to the next, even if the man had failed to bring Kat to heel.

"Then what would you recommend?" Wexley said, feeling a breeze and turning north.

While Michigan Avenue itself felt too clogged with visitors, the streets alongside the famed way offered up enough buzz. Life happened here: people, ordinary people grinding out a living without pretensions. They sold their gadgets, fitted their suits, or cooked up the salivating smells now embracing the air. None needed a Paragon's protection, none needed some super-powered monster to demand their loyalty.

Chicago had thrived for centuries without their interference, and it would again.

"I'm assuming *no* isn't an option?" Rhimes said, doing nothing to hide a sigh.

"I'm already out. Calendar's cleared."

"Then there's a loner. Looks new too."

"Perfect."

Rhimes beamed the coordinates, the construction site popping up on Wexley's Tama and, fifteen minutes later, at his feet. The building looked like a new condo structure, advertising an urban farm as a central core. Fresh produce every day, all year long for buyers. Wexley snapped a picture, figuring he might look into a move if the building delivered on its promise.

A fence girded the site, with a sole entry gated by a Tama lock. Rhimes delivered again, sending the right codes to Wexley's device and letting him scan in. He left the door ajar behind him, stepping into the shell. Outside walls paneled over with protective plastic served to cut Wexley off from the street, from any prying eyes.

No insulation would mean nothing to hide any noise. This would have to be a quiet affair.

Not a problem.

"I put out the alert," Rhimes said. "You want back-up?"

"Will I need it?"

"No."

"Then you have my answer."

WEXLEY WATCHED as the Paragon picked his way into the building. The young man sported the Paragon's trademark blue and white outfit, built up to provide winter warmth. Going by the clean shave, the close cut, this one had bought into his job. The Paragon even stopped at the sight of Wexley's hulking coat, curled up over his long gun in a reasonable fake for a sleeping person, and reported the find.

"Looks like it might be homeless," the Paragon said, loud. "The gate was open. Construction crew might've left it that way."

Hoping, maybe, to wake up the vagabond. Spark a conversation and get the person out from the site, enroll them in some plan to turn them from a ruffian into a Paragon-produced person. How nice.

Wexley relaxed into the moment, letting Adriana, the countless to-dos clogging his productivity apps fade away. They would be waiting for him after. Now, now was about nature. The predator and prey instinct driving the Earth's primal species into combat with themselves.

The Paragon received his marching orders and went towards the coat. Any hesitance vanished with the perceived solution, the certainty that came with a clear objective. Wexley moved too, rolling his feet as he stepped from behind his chosen wall.

He made no sound, and the Paragon took no notice.

"Hey, sir, you hear me?" The Paragon said to the coiled coat as he approached. "You alive under there?"

Wexley slipped the small baton from its holster. Thumbed the switch activating a nub on the weapon's end. Step after step took him closer. The Paragon kneeled over the coat, reached to move it away. Wexley could dash forward now, hit the Paragon from behind and end the struggle before it even began.

But why ruin the fun?

Instead, Wexley watched as the Paragon shoved the coat aside and took a long look at the rifle beneath. The Paragon brought his hand to his chin tapped twice. Wexley waited, wanted the turnaround, that sweet moment when the Paragon realized he'd been set up.

A hand landed on Wexley's shoulder, spun the man around. The Paragon, somehow, stood behind him, wagging a finger.

Damn powers. Turning a good fight into a random grab bag.

Wexley swung the baton, blinked as the weapon swiped right on through the Paragon's form as if Wexley had attacked some colored fog. When the baton came out the Paragon's right side, Wexley stumbling when his swing hit zero resistance, a kick took out Wexley's right knee.

Wexley fell forward, pulling into a roll to buy himself some distance. The move let him feel out his knee, judge that no tendons had ruptured, no caps dislocated. Healthy enough, Wexley pushed himself up, sweeping the baton around behind him as he rose.

"What're you doing, man?" The Paragon, all two of him, asked from a safe meter away.

"What's it look like?" Wexley stared at the two copies.

He'd seen powers like this before. Paragons that could duplicate themselves, or make images. But the copy had put a real hand on Wexley's shoulder, had been solid for a moment and like air the next. So what were the rules for this one?

The gun on his thigh called to him. Wexley pushed the urge away. Any gunshot would bring drones, and while Wexley didn't fear a single Paragon, those metal monsters would tear him apart without much effort.

No, this battle would be close, soft.

"I'm telling you now, you should drop that thing and give it up," the Paragon said. "I know you're dressed like you're some big shot, but the squeeze is on. My friends are coming, and they will not like it if you're not listening to me."

"Five minutes," Rhimes said in Wexley's ear, listening in on the conversation. "The protest is slowing down Paragon dispatch."

More than enough time, then, so long as Wexley didn't play the banter game.

Taking two quick lunges, Wexley stabbed the baton at the Paragon on the right. Like before, the tip went in and found nothing, though the Paragon recoiled away. His mirror image took the opportunity to swing in a punch, a blow Wexley blocked with his left forearm. The hit felt solid, so Wexley whipped the baton left, trying to score a shocking tap on the Paragon's shoulder.

Again the baton struck nothing, and the blocked blow on Wexley's forearm vanished too. Wexley caught his own stumble as the Paragon backed away, the right image ducking low for a gut shot. Rolling the baton in his right hand, Wexley jabbed it back down, hitting the right image's shoulder just as the Paragon's punch hit Wexley's stomach.

Nothing, no ripple, no ache from a socked spleen. The right Paragon flashed to nothing as soon as Wexley nailed a hit. The two sides danced back a step, the Paragon holding a frown, hands up and ready on both bodies. No longer the cocky fighter but a wary adversary.

Wexley took the clue and advanced, the running clock ticking in his head. He feinted with the baton, darting towards the right image but sliding his right foot in the process, ready to lunge left. The Paragon fell into the same response, leading in with the left form. Betting that he'd solved the Paragon's riddle, Wexley turned the baton and stuck the left body.

This time, the baton bit in, its flash lighting up the shock on the Paragon's face. Those wide eyes mingled with twitching muscles as the Paragon collapsed to the ground, the image on the right disappearing as if someone had turned it off.

"One trick," Wexley said, flipping off the baton. "That's all you had." He knelt down, reached for the Paragon's neck. A hold, a twist, and this one would be dealt with. "At least yours will be quick."

"No time," Rhimes voice cut in. "They'll be on you. Leave."

Lucky kid.

Wexley broke to his feet fast, dashing towards his jacket, the long gun, and slipping them on, returning to his disguise. As he slipped on the knitted cap, Wexley left the building, sparing no look, no word for the Paragon lying, breathing and beaten, on the concrete floor.

2

Gin and Tracking

Shorts, a doubled-up t-shirt to fight the London chill, and new sneakers etching a blister into her heels as she pounded pavement through Hyde Park's stately greens. Celice caught idle glances as she ran, late afternoon urbanites heading for a pub, a restaurant, or just home. Water splashed with every contact, doing Celice a favor by making people clear from her path.

And letting the man, also jogging, as he did every day around this time, stay in sight.

Celice had left Mynx's meeting room in LA, ditched the sob-fest and went to work. If the Champions wanted to play the PR game while the man responsible for detonating a stadium went free, that was their choice. She made a different one.

Her Paragon access let Celice yank the footage from the prison break, where a goon squad busted Zhan-Yo from Mynx's supposedly secure facility. That fancy floor-wide elevator and Mynx's drones hadn't done crap, but at least the Champion had top notch surveillance. Celice absorbed the recording on the flight from LA to New York, then, back at Bastion, she pulled the data on every face she could find on Mynx's cameras.

Zhan-Yo's adopted crew didn't comprise criminals, up until the break-in anyway, but instead people with large holes in their past. Paragon records, compiled with ruthless thoroughness, broke down their lives into nuggets Celice devoured while surfing the sky from New York to London.

She'd picked the European city because damn near every one of Zhan-Yo's group had bought tickets and departed that way in the weeks since the explosion. The flights had come at different times, from different starting points—these people weren't total novices to spy-craft— but the same destination made it easy to trace.

Easy, at least, for a super-powered group covering the planet with its all-seeing enterprise.

The man took his usual left, heading towards the park's east exit. Celice followed, maintaining distance and taking the occasional cross-cut along a muddy detour to throw off any ideas. Her zigs and zags moved her parallel to the man, kept him within eyeshot. He hadn't deviated yet, and Celice had no reason to think he would.

Another workday, another routine.

Reaching the park's end, the man did a double-check for traffic. London played the same game as other Paragon-controlled cities—meaning, every city—and held back cars for broader transit, giving way to mag-lev rail, buses, and vans. Nonetheless, this deep in London's heart, randomness abounded, with wealthier citizens taking their cleared pods for jaunts or specialty transports delivering their desires. Enough, anyway, that the man had to wait several long heartbeats for a truck to roll on by, batteries whirring and misty water spraying.

Celice caught up, hung a few meters back. She paced, feet pounding the walk without moving, trying to seem every bit the impatient runner not wanting to stop. Her Tama, tied to her left wrist, vibrated. Another call, another message, another request from Mynx's Paragon peddlers trying to find where Celice had gone, what she was up to.

As if the Champion didn't have better things to do with her time.

An older gentleman standing to her left shifted his umbrella to block the now-drizzle from landing on Celice's already sweaty, short hair. Beneath his cloth cap, the man gave her the slightest nod. Celice returned a tight smile, kept her feet going. The truck motored on by and the group shuffled forward.

If any one place had surveillance capacity matching the Paragons, London was it. Cameras littered street corners, giving a person with the right permissions access to scan the city from a desk. Celice, holed up in a rented apartment, called in favors and digitally scoured London's streets for a match.

And now that match ran along ahead, passed stores shutting for the evening and others opening. Shifts changed, laughter mingled with shouted conversations, and Hyde Park's nature lost its scents to kitchens warming up for dinner. The park's simple clarity likewise fell to ad banners and brighter city lights, a sensory shift Celice tried to ignore as she treaded after her target.

Too close.

Her father's words whispered in Celice's mind. Aegis had it right. Those meters splitting Celice from her objective weren't enough. If the man bothered to look behind, if he felt Celice's eyes crawling his back, searching out any possible weapons hidden in his baggy track pants and loose jacket, he'd catch her out against the shambling, coat-covered crowds.

But her father didn't know everything. He'd preach one

stealth lesson after another only to fall back on his fists the minute something didn't work quite right. An easy instinct when Aegis could take a thousand hits and not feel a one.

Celice, though, couldn't fall back. Not here, when intersections and alleyways split off every other second. If the man's route through Hyde Park remained static, he took different options off this street every day. Celice suspected he always circled back to the same destination, but she never found the evidence, not for so many long hours watching fuzzy footage.

Celice bit back a laugh as she worked around a soggy tour group: Aegis wouldn't have spent a minute on the recordings. He would've hit the streets, pulling rank to get what he wanted or smashing through enough walls until he found it.

The man broke right, a casual turn onto a thin alley marked by dumpsters and dripping fire escapes. Celice approached, slowing into a walk, hands on her hips as if her jog had caught up with her little lady lungs.

You're unarmed.

The shorts, the t-shirts, the shoes left little space to hide a weapon. Celice had left the apartment without planning to get in a fight. Look like a runner, figure out where the man went whenever he ditched the streets for London's alleys and then retreat back home to prep the next stage. Now that she'd come this far, however . . .

Turning the corner, Celice spotted the man halfway down the alley. He leaned on a drain pipe, one leg lifted up into a stretch. People shifted along behind her, one bumping Celice forward into the alley's mouth. The man didn't turn around at the scuffle, hadn't seen Celice at all, but she had nowhere to hide if he did.

No way to act casual.

Aegis would like this part. Celice could retreat, could

dip back into the crowded press and make her way home, regroup and try again. If she'd been running this like all the Paragon ops she'd supervised over the years, Celice would've pulled the plug. She had time then, she had time and super-powered fighters on her side.

Another night spent without progress in that apartment, with its bare walls and sparse furniture and gin bottles washed down with lime and little else . . .

Celice picked up the jog, heading down the alley with a smile spreading, a harmless someone who knew they'd be seen.

"Sorry," Celice said when the man heard her footsteps and turned her way. "The streets are so crowded, saw you came this way and thought maybe it's a good route."

"It serves," the man said, holding his stretch and waiting for Celice to go on by.

Make the first move.

Waiting let the enemy take control. Celice ground her left heel, turning in the alleyway and delivering a sharp kick to the man's stomach. The sneaker connected, air blowing out as the man's eyes bugged and his lungs evacuated their contents. The stretch and his single-legged stand meant the man should've fallen to the ground, should've given Celice an easy avenue to a pin and interrogation.

Instead, the man kept his hand on the pipe. The hold let him drop the stretching leg, his feet getting their grip as Celice stepped into a follow-up jab right where she'd kicked. Another wave at the man's stomach and she might get him nauseous, might bruise a kidney and take him out quick.

But Zhan-Yo didn't hire scrubs.

The man knocked away the attack, coughing as he did so, trying to suck in air. He back-pedaled, looking to buy space, give his longer reach a chance. Celice couldn't let him, so she pressed ahead, using the man's bulk as a big target. This time, she varied her strikes, blinking hands and elbows high and low, looking for a vulnerability.

Her opponent took the hits when they came, blocked the ones he could, still recovering from the kick. His stance, growing straighter and more settled by the second, showed Celice's hits to his shoulders, to his knees, and one good nail gouge to the cheek, weren't doing enough.

The swing came off a block, the man slamming down his left elbow to deflect a jab then thrusting the fist right at Celice's eyes. She jerked aside, but not far enough, the blow catching her right temple and sending her back two steps. A bruise there, for sure.

And more to come, going by the man's brawler posture. He had his hands up, feet on their toes and bouncing. Worse, a gleam played on a face ready and eager for the fight.

"Don't know who you are, where you came from, but you picked the wrong alley today," the man said, accent placing him as a Canadian Northwoods product.

Keep him off balance.

"Nope, you're the man I'm looking for," Celice sprang the words with a spirited smile, an earnest look that threw the man for a fractional second.

Long enough.

Kicking through a puddle, Celice sent dirty drops raining at the man, following behind them with a sidestep to the right. Her rival pushed through the trick, trying for a long-reach hit that depended on Celice sticking to the ground, like a normal fighter might.

But Celice, daughter of the world's foremost Paragon, wasn't a normal fighter.

She planted her left foot and jumped, heading at a hard angle towards the alley wall. The leap brought her so far right that the man's swing fell short, his follow-through bringing him right into Celice's rebound. Her right foot touched the wall a half-meter up and Celice kicked off, reversing direction and punching forward with the added momentum.

The man couldn't get his own swing back in time to block, taking Celice's shot right on the chin. His turn to stumble. Celice kept on forward, staying on her own feet after the wall jump and using the chaos to grab the man's left leg, twisting it as he recoiled. An undignified plop followed, the tracksuit hitting sopping ground. The man's head came next, cracking on the cobblestones.

Celice leaned over, ready to lay an elbow on the man's neck if he tried to rise. His eyes, though, were clouded and closed, and no longer read reality. Instead, Celice planted two fingers on the man's neck and watched his chest. A pulse beat, the lungs worked their magic. Not dead, unconscious for who knew how long.

"Hey!" A woman shouted at the alley's head, and Celice looked back to see an older couple standing there, watching the evening's improvised entertainment. "What's going on here then?"

Who knew how much they'd seen, how much they'd believe, but a simple excuse would work for most people: The average person wouldn't want their daily comforts disrupted by Paragon business or bloody street fights.

"He slipped while we were practicing," Celice called back. "Get an ambulance!"

She turned back to the man, running her hands through his jacket, looking for something, anything. Getting a Tama off a wrist would take time and tools she didn't have here, and the sheer stillness on his face seemed to mean consciousness wasn't coming back soon.

In the man's left pocket, she found a crumpled receipt.

Coffee, pastry. In the right pocket, a keychain. Only someone paranoid would resort to locks that couldn't be hacked. Celice, keeping low, fingered the two copper-colored keys. She could take them, but then the man would know, Zhan-Yo would know they'd been stolen.

"How's he doing?" came the woman's voice, closer now, excited at being involved. A look confirmed the two were heading down the alley towards Celice. Interlopers being interlopers. "We called, help's on the way!"

Angling her own Tama, Celice captured the keys in three pictures. As the couple came close, Celice stuffed the keys back into the man's pocket and stood up, painting a worried picture across her body.

"Thank you," Celice said as they came close. "I'm thinking he knocked himself a bit hard. I'll go meet the ambulance, if you can watch him?"

The couple, doing their saintly duty, agreed without a second's suspicion. Celice broke off towards the alley's entrance, slipped into the passing crowd, and vanished as a siren's wail broke London's evening peace. Overhead, a drone's dark cloud drifted by, preceding the ambulance call with its own inscrutable eye.

Once, those machines would've filled Celice with hope, with the flush that came with real power in a world that valued little else.

Now, she kept her head down and felt the drizzle turn to rain, the chill fighting off the first pangs from her battered temple.

THE SHOWER WASHED away the grime, and real, dry clothes calmed her shivers. Letting her hair flop free hid the grim circle near her forehead, but Celice couldn't find much else to enjoy about the apartment. Acquired through an ad, paid for with reps from accounts Celice and her father maintained, she'd bought the prior owner's furniture too. The pieces had a lifeless look to them, pleasant enough but without any memories to make them whole.

Bastion, the giant tower in New York that'd been her home for years, held more sentiment in its steeled walls, its glimmering appliances all monitored by advanced AI than this cramped studio on London's west side. At first, Celice treated the space like a hotel room, a temporary abode meant for sleeping, hygiene, and little else.

Then the hours stacked up. The days went by, filled with surveillance and watching tapes on her computer screen with nothing but a small courtyard and walls outside the window. Pubs and coffee shops offered escapes, but any outside venture brought risk some Paragon would catch her, that Mynx would get a drone hunting her down.

Celice felt the buzz again now, the regular call from the local Paragon office. They knew she was in London, maybe knew where she lived. Celice stared at the white glow on her Tama offering a comeback. She could say the words, move right into the facilities here, join back with the team and hunt Zhan-Yo with their help.

But that would mean distractions. It would mean following Mynx's orders, or the Champion running Europe. She'd go from the main player in her own efforts to an accessory. And when they found Zhan-Yo? The Paragons would hold a trial, would show him off to the world and try to paint him as some awful figure.

Zhan-Yo deserved a bullet to the head. Fast, fatal, and finished.

Then, when her father's killer had been wiped off the board, Celice could go back to the politics, the games, the scrabbling for Paragon power.

Swiping on her Tama, she found her pictures. Sent

them over to her computer. The keys themselves held nothing on them except a name, the locksmith that'd made the copies. The next step.

Sitting back on the couch, Celice looked at the dark television bordered by plain, flowery art. Tea waited in the kitchen, along with leftovers from a lunchtime curry adventure. She could find some movie to put on, revel in the day's success. The man didn't have her name, didn't know why she attacked him. She wouldn't be in danger yet.

But a win deserved a celebration. This was London, and even if the world had itself in conniptions over the LA stadium bombing, the people here knew how to have fun.

And Celice could use some fun tonight.

3

Team Dreams

The alarm showcased every difference between where Calvin used to be and where he was now. The logo on his Tama, the Paragon *P*, radiated professionalism. Clean, blue, and white, the logo vanished into a call for Calvin to respond to a missing Paragon in Chicago's north Loop. Not that Calvin would—the alert would go out to other area Paragons and drones, hardly just Calvin—but the ping nonetheless contrasted with the dripping warehouse where he stood.

The stain-coated concrete floor beneath his feet echoed with the sturdy walls as ragtag anomalies tested their abilities. Right now they squared off, two at a time, engaging in teamwork. Each one had to see how they could use their abilities to benefit the other, and vice versa. Something about bonding, about understanding the true power of the team.

Bumper sticker nonsense.

Calvin itched at his neck where his jacket, an impulse buy with his new Paragon reps, rubbed. The warehouse had zero heat, and while Chicago seemed to be emerging from its frozen hibernation, chill still owned the air. The warehouse's broken windows, glass standing like teeth in a jumbled maw, let in breeze aplenty. A breeze that brought more than cold with it.

"Yo," Calvin said to Farrah, beside him, a hard-edged fighter who'd kept her own abilities a secret while barking orders at her charges. "Did we really have to choose this place, or does the burning trash help somehow?"

"Keeps you motivated," the woman replied, not veering her look away from the fighters. "The faster you get your exercises done, the sooner you can leave." She waved forward. "Speaking of which . . . "

"I'm a Paragon. I don't need this."

"Beth said otherwise, and what Beth says goes," the woman replied, noting the Elemental leader running Chicago's show. "Join in."

"I don't have a partner."

"For this, you won't need one."

Shaking his head, but holding to that early departure promise if he played their games, Calvin gave himself a five meter distance. He faced Farrah, who seemed to be watching the others and ignoring him.

"So what're we doing then?" Calvin called.

"Everyone!" Farrah shouted, her voice carrying through the warehouse. "Calvin here believes Paragons don't need teamwork."

"Not what I said."

"Remember what happened when Aegis left his team behind?" Farrah continued. "Not even a legend can go alone! We Elementals are smarter and stronger when we work together. Anthony, Della, show us what I mean."

All the others in the warehouse circled up, watching as the two named Elementals, both in scrappy spring clothes, squared up opposite Calvin.

"I thought these were team drills?" Calvin asked.

"Sometimes proving the *why* is as important as practicing the *what*," Farrah replied. "Go on, Elementals, teach him a lesson."

With all the eyes on him, Calvin did what he knew how to do: he shrank inside himself. Put up a wall and looked for an exit. The people surrounding him weren't his friends, weren't his partners in some fight against Wexley, the Paragons, and a world falling apart. They were just more bastards looking to use him.

His hands, as they always did, felt the current embedded in the black leather gloves on his skin. The leather's slick pull tugged at Calvin, waiting to be embraced. The gloves themselves were nice, warm. Not ones he wanted to ruin.

So as Anthony and Della put a few meters between themselves, making a triangle with Calvin as the far point, the Paragon took off his gloves and stuffed them in his coat pockets. When he did, the air came alive around him. Dust, the chill, and other airborne chemicals teased Calvin, suggesting they could be snared and redirected, stretched and employed.

What did Farrah expect Calvin to do? Fight these two? Anthony and Della, both, had years on Calvin, but that didn't mean much when abilities came into play. Every anomaly had their own curve, from when their gifts first appeared to when, or if, they petered out. Calvin's showed up near his twelfth birthday, along with fuzz on his face and a crack in his voice.

Back then, he'd rolled with the new sensations, considered them another tool in a growing box filled with one foster family escape after the next. Lately, Calvin had been adding more dangerous lessons to that box, ones perfect for the plucky anomalies squaring up against him now.

Anthony went first, the long-haired bar bouncer taking one stride before jumping into the air. Della made a face, like she was blowing up an invisible balloon, and Anthony's leap sent him high enough to touch the warehouse ceiling. Calvin watched as the man twisted in the air, plummeting towards Calvin with a fist held forward, a punching comet crashing to Earth.

When he fell, Anthony's body grew. Every part enlarging with the man's speed, doubling and then tripling in size in the milli-seconds as he dropped. One punch would come with far more kilos than Calvin could take.

So the target moved.

A dash forward brought no progress, Della's refocused wind-tunnel pressing Calvin back and ticking out his time. Not good, but that's why Calvin always operated with a back-up plan. When he started running, Calvin's right hand dropped to his jeans, holding to the denim. His left hand went up over his head, the sensation running electric through him.

Above him, a thin blue webbing sprang forth, expanding up and out, melding with the air to build a blue-white net. Anthony slammed down, barreled into Calvin and drove him into the warehouse floor. The net robbed the crashing man of some momentum.

Not enough.

FARRAH STOOD over him when Calvin's eyes opened, a knowing smile splitting her face. Around them, sounds showcased a return to the drills Calvin had interrupted.

"Get the point, Paragon?" Farrah asked.

Calvin's headache demanded whatever answer would get him away from these brutal people as fast as possible. He'd agreed to tangle with the Elementals because Kat asked him to, because she'd wrapped her life up with these half-way heroes in ways Calvin never would with anyone. Another bad move added to the long list Calvin had been writing since coming to Chicago.

All for a convention, a damned comic convention that'd been ruined by Kat's pursuit.

"Yeah, I get your point," Calvin said, sitting up, shutting his eyes for a long breath to shake off the nausea.

"Looks like Anthony hit you hard. Should we get you checked out?"

"Anthony would've killed me," Calvin said, dishing a cold glare Farrah's way. "The hell you trying to teach these people?"

"A Paragon wouldn't hesitate to kill any of us. I will not teach them otherwise."

"I'm not here hurting anybody!"

"Beth says she believes you. That's enough for some people," Farrah said. "You come here, you refuse to join in what we're doing? Now I have to wonder why you bothered."

The implications lay heavy in her words, that smile long dead. So Farrah held the same standards everyone else did: anyone outside your group was an enemy until proved otherwise. Why should Calvin expect the Elementals to be any different?

"The Paragons took me in," Calvin said. "They didn't ask questions. They saw what I could do and offered me a contract. You tried to kill me. I'm starting to see why you're losing."

He stood all the way up now. Anthony's hit probably had Calvin concussed. What a wonderful present. Calvin ran through a mental inventory, tallying up his possessions, his reps to spend. He'd never had much, and now what he had sat in a storage locker in the Paragon's Chicago headquarters. It wouldn't take long to head that way, take it out, and maybe get the Paragons to send him somewhere new.

Somewhere without all this drama.

"Then you're seeing why we can't take chances," Farrah kept at it. "Everyone here's going to lose someone. Probably soon. We're not playing a little game. We're not running around the streets at night scaring people. This is a real movement, and with all that's happening right now, we have a real opportunity."

"Not one I'm helping with. Next time you decide to start something? Maybe don't fight with the ones on your side."

This time, Farrah didn't stop Calvin from walking out. The man felt eyes on his back, ignored them. Kept his head up and his mind spinning until he left the warehouse, the breeze picking up without the walls. Only then did he connect the chill crossing his legs.

Where he'd worn thick jeans, Calvin only had shorts, and those hanging in tatters halfway up his thighs. Some anomalies had abilities that could take what they needed from anywhere, anything. Calvin's ate his clothes.

What a great damn day.

SEEKER MADE IT BETTER, as the dog always did. The big, white fluff attacked Calvin as he came into Kat's apartment. The place, patched up from Wexley's attacks, served as an air mattress home to Calvin while the Paragons lurched through the disaster in LA. The world's governing group had been leaping from one emergency declaration to the next with Mynx, the nominal local leader, fumbling around in the spotlight.

Calvin had to give the engineer Champion some credit though: at least Mynx stuck around. She took beatings every day in front of cameras and off screen as the Paragons kept throwing out new processes, new names, and new ideas as if hoping memos alone could return the Paragons to some stable state.

So Calvin dodged the drama by crashing with his friend.

"Right, Seeker?" Calvin said, scratching the dog's ears as he hunted down a new pair of pants. The bus ride back here had been an exercise in ignoring stares, but Chicago had enough people that someone wearing ragged shorts on a brisk March day wasn't the weirdest thing. "We're just hanging out here, letting the world figure itself out."

The idea felt a little odd, considering Kat and Calvin had, not long ago, escaped assassination attempts by some dude who, according to Kat, had power and reps in infinite amounts. Calvin wanted to take Wexley and teach him some proper respect, sure, but the lets-go-get-him vengeance slipped away as the Elementals urged caution and the Paragons spun into confusion.

Calvin pestered Kat day by day to get her gear together so the two of them could go CEO hunting at Wexley's office. Between them, Calvin figured Wexley wouldn't stand a hope's chance in hell of getting away, and with Calvin's Paragon connections, he could bring in drone support too. Blanket the tower in guns and good times.

"But no," Calvin said to Seeker, stuffing his toothbrush, the Tama charger, and some clothes into a pack. "Everybody wanted to take a breather instead because they're all scared."

Scared of what Calvin didn't know, but Beth had been real firm. If Kat and Calvin moved against Wexley without her approval, the Elementals would consider them enemies. And, with that tattooed miracle worker bearing Kat's survival in his ink, going rogue would mean a quick death all around. 'Course, as Calvin pointed out night after night, they could hit and run the sniping bastard and Beth wouldn't have to know.

"But Kat's gone all gun-shy," Calvin said, and Seeker woofed. "She doesn't want to lose her new friends, man. I get it."

Calvin didn't, really, but pretending to understand how families worked was a fun little game he played with himself. Made things seem less lonely.

Seeker cocked his head, bright blue eyes staring at Calvin while the dog's tongue hung loose and wet from his mouth. A ridiculous look that had Calvin cracking up as he slung his pack over his shoulder. He'd miss Kat, sure. Even Gordon, that moron, who nonetheless tried to help. The dog, though, would be the biggest regret.

As if sensing his own thoughts, Calvin's Tama buzzed. He glanced at it, saw Kat's name and, above it, the time. Late enough in the afternoon now that her meeting might be done.

"Hey," Calvin answered the call.

"That's it? Hey?"

"It's what I say?"

"How about what Farrah's saying, then?" Kat answered. "I didn't get everything from her words. Did you kill someone, or did someone almost kill you?"

"They double-teamed me and I didn't kill'em because I'm a nice guy." Calvin ignored Seeker's huff. "Farrah wanted to prove a point. She did, and now I'm done."

"Not yet you're not. I need a drink and a chance to vent."

"Can't you call your boy Gordon?"

"He's got his own problems."

Calvin snorted, "So I'm your back-up."

"Sorry, I thought I was talking to Calvin, grown man. Not a child."

The pack slid off Calvin's shoulders as he grinned. Kat always had a way of insulting him into a good mood.

"Where you thinking?" Calvin asked. "And there better not be any Elementals in this place, because I swear . . ."

"You swear what?"

"Don't make me say it." Calvin could hear Kat's own grin through the phone. "It's not polite."

"Then tell me in person. I'm getting into a pod now, which means you're already late."

Kat's taste in bars ran to the gutter, not that Calvin could complain. Beverages at Kat's joints tended to be cheap, so Calvin's new Paragon pay covered all the booze the man cared to drink. Which, since his life had been on the line basically since the day Calvin had graced this Earth, veered hard between a glass and a gallon.

Calvin knew *Carver's*, though. Remembered the steps down into the basement bar, remembered the near-vacant warehouses and stores slopped around with spacing that suggested the planner in this Chicago district hadn't been paying attention. The place had a few office escapees snagging an early out before heading home to their lives, drinking and catching baseball's early season games.

The dark walls bore gouges where bar fights and thrown stools left their scars. On the floor, currently blocked by tables and chairs, sat the loose outline where a ring would form later. In that very same ring, Kat had first played Calvin into nearly revealing his powers. His *anomaly* self. Breaking out there, in that crowd, would've felt oh so good for the second's surprise Calvin would've won off Kat, followed shortly by a fist flurry as a drunk, angry crowd vented its anomaly hatred out on him.

"It's not that bad," Kat said when Calvin sat opposite her, two amber ales in his hands. He passed one along the smooth table to the tracker. "They don't know who you are."

"That you have to say it makes it bad, Kat," Calvin said, trying to find a way to get himself comfortable on the metal, cushion-less chair.

"Yeah, well, no place is perfect."

"This one's a long way from it." Calvin raised his glass. "But the drinks *are* cheap."

Kat clinked his glass and they indulged. Calvin catalogued the feeling in his left hand, gloveless and holding the beer. The glass twinkled, an edge waiting to be sucked up and exploited. Calvin could turn it into a lance, a knife, or twist it into some sort of constellation. His right hand, resting on the table, picked out the paint and the plastic beneath. Both had options, both could be yanked up and split into . . .

"You there?" Kat said. "Or did I just explain today to a brick wall?"

Calvin shrugged, "They hit me pretty hard."

"Sounds like I need to talk to Farrah."

Kat didn't do the whole concerned thing very well.

"Not a kid," Calvin replied. "I can handle it."

"Oh, is that what you were doing, packing up back at the apartment?"

"You saw that?"

Kat waved her Tama, "Hi, you know what year it is? Cameras everywhere, buddy. Tap told me you were in and I checked."

Tap's name killed the spying-on-you vibe Kat's words created. The apartment's AI offered up inane forecasts about the weather, promising good and bad beach days for Chicago coupled with pithy slogans on taking life slow, feeling the sand, breathing in the sea. The surfer bro setup made a fun first impression, an eye-rolling twentieth.

Another thing Calvin could ditch without a moment's regret.

"I'm tired of sitting around," Calvin said. "If we're not going after," Calvin glanced around, saw nobody paying attention, but hid names anyway, "that guy, then what are we doing here?"

"Meetings, apparently?"

Kat's tone and her subsequent return to the beer brought Calvin a little hope. Maybe she was getting tired too.

"I'm saying it's taking too long," Calvin continued, pushing his position. "I guarantee you he's not waiting for us to come his way, but people like him, they don't forget either. He's gonna find us one day, and it's not going to be good if we're the ones getting surprised."

Kat sighed, "I asked Beth about it again today. She's still saying no. I think she wants the Paragons to engage first, wait for both sides to get bloody, then sweep in and claim the win."

"Win what? A city on fire?"

"Ask her. She's not telling me."

Back to the same impasse. Back to the same rut.

"Kat. I'm not playing here. I'm done with this. Either we go after this guy, or I'm getting on the next Paragon flight to somewhere he won't follow. Are you with me or not?"

For once, Kat didn't wilt under the moment. Didn't offer up some excuse about how the Elementals would come around eventually. Instead, she raised her glass again, clinked it on Calvin's.

"Screw it. I'm with you. Let's go get him."

4

Discharged

She'd never been more thrilled to set a tray on a table. Cassidy lifted away her trembling hands and watched as the fruit cup—juicy orange—and the buttered toast stayed level. No falling away onto the plastic or the stone patio beneath. She flashed a tentative smile to her left, where Ano stood ready with the broom. He nodded, then slipped back inside the cafeteria.

Overhead, palms waved in the constant sea breeze. Colorful birds Cassidy didn't know pecked through long, lush grass surrounding the five-table patio, an offshoot from her current home, the lie that'd brought her back to life.

The loose shirt and pants, both white and both fished from the center's spare parts bin, billowed around her, letting air in and around everywhere. The wind brushed skin cleaned by showers, snuck into a mouth with teeth brushed, played in growing hair that'd had a mirror's attention. Cassidy didn't cough from a dry throat, her tan a more natural bronze than the scorched hue it'd kept for years.

And the orange juice? Every day Cassidy bit into these cups and felt rapturous joy in the succulent sugars, in the crisp toasted bread. The soups and pastas in the evenings, too, paraded Cassidy down memory's flavors, each new one an old friend welcomed with gusto.

The meals helped hide everything else. Helped to hide the *wrong*.

The Void. That'd been her name, and the reason for it lingered, a mental scab waiting to be picked so that, again, she could embrace what nature gave her. When the urge rose, as it rose now, Cassidy employed the one weapon she had left.

Grief.

The last time she'd used her ability, she'd enabled an escape attempt from Mynx's, from the Paragon's, prison island. Throwing up her black holes to block drone attacks, Cassidy had burned herself out. Somehow, she'd lived. Somehow, she'd woken up here, anonymous and free.

Her friends paid the price for that freedom. She saw them in flashes, gunned down on the ragged ship serving their escape or blown overboard as the ocean swarmed the sides, everything falling apart. If Cassidy hadn't been there, if she hadn't gone with Thane's ridiculous idea, they would still be alive. They would still be spending long island days catching fish and swapping stories by beachside campfires, scraping together an existence apart from the world.

The thoughts dimmed the pulse, muted the crackle in her mind. Another inner battle won. Cassidy gave her toast a grim smile. What a victory, to use the dead to stop making more.

"You're looking well today," Reva, the center's resident psychologist, sat across from Cassidy without the latter's approval. "This makes three, doesn't it?"

"Three?" Cassidy, done with the fruit cup, went in on the toast. The bread, pre-cut into nice triangles, had gone cold during her reflection, but Cassidy's appetite didn't care. "Three what?"

"Days that you've been up and about," Reva said, with an infinite, tender patience. "You're doing so well."

Cassidy caught the question hanging. Did she remember anything yet, like her name? Her family? The brain scans hadn't shown any severe trauma, though Reva claimed Cassidy's muscles had been wrung out, her very bones thinned by extreme stress.

"Am I?"

In a life that now seemed imagined, Cassidy had been a teacher. She'd taught young children, playing word games, spinning tales to help them learn. Falling into the same routine with Reva had been . . . had been easier than Cassidy expected. Reva seemed to *want* to trust Cassidy's answers, and now the doctor leaned forward, big eyes behind bigger spectacles.

"You are, Jane," Reva replied, using the center's pet name for Cassidy. "We have so many patients here that, when they arrive like you did, never find their way again. We know they'll be with us until they say their last good-bye. But you, you're getting better day by day."

"I'm glad you think so."

"Don't you?"

Cassidy did, in fact, feel better. Her body, though sore yet, felt more and more like herself. She'd gone from being exhausted every waking moment to, now, looking beyond the center's fencing. Somewhere out there would be a plane that could take her home to her family.

And to the Paragons that would put her right back on that island.

"I do," Cassidy said. "Soon, do you think I could leave?"

Reva sat back, crossing her arms on her lap, fingers clasped. "There are certain milestones we need to consider, Jane. First, your name. Who you are and where you came from. We can't very well let you walk away from here without knowing where you ought to go, can we?"

"Is that your decision to make, or is it mine?"

Reva's look didn't shake with Cassidy's tonal transition. "It is ours to make together. When we all feel you have a plan to take care of yourself."

Silence fell as Cassidy ate her toast. To say she had a plan would be optimistic. As much as she wanted to see her family again, Cassidy didn't have any reps, she didn't have any transportation, any documentation that would get her on a plane, boat, or anything else. She didn't even have a Tama, the phone sitting on Reva's wrist.

The center, too, would want to know who they'd brought in. With the Paragons in control, Cassidy wouldn't have to worry about paying for the time spent here, but the center would have to file something. Cassidy would have to give them a real name eventually.

Or . . .

Overhead, a jet rumbled by, leaving a white gash across the blue sky.

"Reva," Cassidy said. "How is my friend doing? Better?"

Reva shook her head, "Not as well as you." She brightened. "He did open his eyes today. For a full minute. I believe he listened as I spoke to him." Another pause, another shift in tone as Reva focused in on Cassidy. "Do you remember who *he* is?"

"It's foggy. I recall snatches."

They'd done this dance before, starting when Cassidy

first woke up. Reva wanted information and Cassidy didn't care to provide it. She'd asked to see her friend before, but Reva always refused, saying it wouldn't be good to disturb the man. The line, though, always left room on the end, as if Reva had been making an offer.

"Snatches of what?" Reva asked.

Her tray clean, Cassidy matched Reva's look. The urge to suck in that energy, pop a void that would swallow the psychologist whole raged up as Cassidy took in the doctor's stare, the slight upturned lips pressed together. Not a blink in sight.

Reva *knew*.

Cassidy shouldn't have been surprised. On the island, surrounded by anomalies all either bashing each other to bits or forming gangs for protection, there hadn't been much need to lie. A teacher convincing second graders to believe in a fairy tale wasn't quite the same as deceiving a provider about your own amnesia.

But just because both knew they were acting, didn't mean the play couldn't go on.

"If I saw him," Cassidy said, "I might remember more. You said his eyes opened? He must be getting better."

"It's a risk. But you've both been here for days already. Your vitals signs look good. I think we can make a visit. What do you say?"

"I say I'm done with lunch, so let's go."

THANE, great foe of the Paragons, tyrant whose name polluted the news with dire proclamations of unstoppable rage, lay withered beneath clean cream sheets. His head, a splotched ball with skin stretched loose over it, splayed its stringy gray locks like a desiccated halo. From what Cassidy could tell, Thane's eyes were indeed open, though their narrow slits didn't focus on anything in particular. Instead, they stared through the room's window out into a blooming, altogether pleasant, flower garden.

Reva stood in the doorway, an orderly just outside, while Cassidy went in. Thane did look awful, but with anomalies, and with this one in particular, appearances told little of the story. Cassidy paced around the bed, circling to where she could look directly at Thane's face.

"You don't seem concerned?" Reva asked.

"Should I be?" Cassidy said as she knelt down, searched those eyes for something, anything.

"He's awake, but hardly alert. We are feeding him by tube, because he doesn't respond, doesn't attempt to meet his basic needs."

Thane stayed still. His eyes didn't focus on her. Shallow breathing escaped those dry, cracked lips. Cassidy didn't know how they had made it off the breaking raft, how they'd survived to this island, to this center, but the past didn't have to direct the future.

She could break away here. Either use her abilities or her smarts to get free from Reva and the center. Then Cassidy would have no chains, would be able to find her way back to her family.

Her hand reached out almost without thought and touched Thane's shoulder. Palm down, a soft grip. She felt the slightest shudder as Thane's heart beat. He'd crashed into Cassidy's life, literally falling from Mynx's plane and smashing into the island. In a rapid, aggressive assault on the fragile society that'd formed among the captive anomalies, Thane bashed and broke the bonds apart.

But he'd brought Cassidy along with him. Had promised her, if not the world, then at least an adventure and a chance to see her family.

Cassidy didn't know how she'd survived the escape, but she could guess.

"So?" Reva asked.

"It's coming back to me," Cassidy said.

"What do you see?"

Now, what to do? Walk out of here? Thane looked so thin that Cassidy could probably lift the man and carry him. Doing that while creating voids to stop orderlies and the police and, eventually, the Paragons?

No. She would need help.

"We were on a boat. Caught in a storm," Cassidy said. "He and I were passengers."

"Your names? Do you know them?"

Cassidy looked up from Thane, gave Reva a frown and shook her head, "Not yet."

She moved her hand down from Thane's shoulder, onto his chest. On his side, with his back to Reva, Thane's body and its cloaking sheets hid Cassidy's motion from view. Or at least, Cassidy hoped so. Because what she did next was decidedly not kind.

"Then keep going," Reva said. "You're both on a ship?"

Cassidy pinched. Squeezed tight with her nails against Thane's loose skin. Pinch and move, pinch and move. Trying to get a reaction, and not seeing one.

"On a ship," Cassidy said. "We were getting blown around. At first we were on the deck but then we had to go below. Captain's orders."

"What was the ship's name? The captain's name?"

Cassidy shook her head. Pinched again. Still nothing. Reva wouldn't let Cassidy keep playing like this much longer. The made-up memory would only go so far before Reva would catch her in another lie.

"Strange that you're having such a hard time with the

names," Reva said. "Amnesia like yours isn't usually so specific."

The urge was always there, always hungry. Cassidy bent to it, let it funnel through her fingers.

"I'm sorry," Cassidy said.

"Oh, it's not your fault."

The void left Cassidy like a cold shock, traveling out to where Cassidy's fingers sent it: right into Thane's side. Heat flushed Cassidy, as if she'd stepped into a furnace, while Thane's body lurched, a gash opening in his side where the hole tore a spot. The sheets hid the mark, but not his jerk. Reva said something to the orderly, something Cassidy should've caught, but she had her attention on one thing:

Thane's eyes, fully open now, locked on hers.

"Cassidy," Thane said, the word starting as a whisper and ending as a growl.

His skin tightened as muscles previously atrophied surged with newfound strength. Like a shirt being pulled taut, Thane's wrinkles vanished. The splotched marks fled, though the hair remained scattered as Thane's body grew.

The center's bed sagged. Some alarm gave a weak squeal before dying, before the frame cracked. Cassidy stood up and away, watching Reva as the latter, mouth open, saw Thane become who he needed to be.

"Stop," Cassidy said as Thane hit his midpoint, well over two meters tall and looking like a truck. Cassidy had her weapon, but she needed Thane sane. "Stay with me, Thane."

"You hurt me," Thane said, pulling himself off the wrecked bed and standing tall. The loose gown that'd cloaked his diminished form clung to Thane now like a bad bathing suit. "Why?"

"Who, who are you?" Reva interrupted, talking to Thane's back from the doorway. "Anomalies?"

Thane looked at the doctor, rumbled a low and threatening noise.

"Reva," Cassidy said slow. "You need to leave us now. Please."

"Leave?" Reva glanced behind her. "I need security right away. And sedatives for John Doe here."

"No sedatives," Thane said, turning all the way around now. "Do as Cassidy says."

Reva, damn her, wasn't one to get intimidated. She stayed in the doorway while an orderly behind her handed over a drawn syringe, ready for use.

It wasn't Cassidy's job to protect idiots from themselves. It was her job to get away from here, with Thane.

"We're leaving," Cassidy said, flicking her hand behind her. The current traveled down her arm, the heat flashed through her again, and Thane's window cracked. The glass broke and vanished, a wall chunk coming with it. "Thane?"

Reva's advance stopped when Cassidy created her void, and it full on ended when Thane ripped the bed frame up and rolled it towards the doctor. With impressive reflexes, Reva back-tracked through the doorway as the bed slammed into it, blocking the way.

"Hold on," Thane said, lifting Cassidy and putting his arms around her in a tight hug.

Leading with his shoulder, Thane barreled through the weakened wall. Trampling through the flowers, Thane ran from garden to grass to fence. Looking over his back, Cassidy saw orderlies push aside the mattress, saw them stream into the room to watch as Thane bashed through the center's barrier.

None drew guns, none tried to catch them. A smart play.

"You brought me back," Thane said as he ran, jumping into a forested hillside. "Thank you."

Cassidy felt branches catch her hair, snag her loose clothes, but she didn't stop Thane. Soon enough Reva would understand what she'd seen, make the connection. Thane had said he'd gone on one of his rampages not long ago, so even if Reva couldn't place him, one of the orderlies or the Paragon sent to review the security footage would.

They had to get distance by then. Had to disappear.

"I wanted to walk away," Cassidy said as Thane barreled down the hill's other side. "I could have, but I had to know. Why are we alive?"

Half running, half stumbling as Thane went along, the man didn't answer for a long time. Cassidy would've pressed him, but Thane wasn't one who spoke according to anyone's pace but his own. The trees gave way to grasses, to a steep drop that Thane cleared with a long leap. Cassidy's stomach ran up her throat as they fell, as Thane scooped her around so his back landed first.

They hit the green grains hard, the rocks and dirt flying up and over them as Thane kept the roll going till their momentum died away. Cassidy, her back on warm, wet sand, stared into an angry face, one wanted across the world for countless crimes.

"Why are we alive, Thane?" Cassidy asked again.

"Because I could not allow us to die." Thane gazed out over the crashing waves. "I remember swimming, you in one arm while my legs kicked for hours. Days, maybe. I was so desperate to save you, so angry at what Mynx and her drones had done. When we washed up, I had nothing left."

Thane stood up off her, brushed the sand from his shoulders. Cassidy joined him, the rocks scraping her skin. Thankfully, the beach appeared deserted, but neither had clothes, neither had reps or Tamas. The circumstances pushed away Thane's confession, or rather, Cassidy let it fade. She'd rescued Thane to pay a debt, and now they were even.

"Thank you," Cassidy said.

They stood there together, watching the waves. Feeling the sand between their toes. Just like back on Mynx's island. Waiting for a chance, for a possibility.

"I want to see my family. I need your help for that."

Thane nodded.

"You will get it," the anomaly said. "You will have all my help and more. But first, we must find out where we are, and how to prevent the Paragons from catching us again."

When Thane's hand drifted out, Cassidy's was there to meet it.

5

A Little Misdirection

Post Paragon, Wexley burned the afternoon and evening away back at the office, and then his apartment. Utilizing his Tama and connected monitors with single-minded efficiency, he tore through the reports, the messages, the calls needed to keep Zhan-Yo's company, Ziran—now Wexley's in every way that mattered—going. Even as he whipped through spreadsheets and blessed sales presentations with his approval, though, Wexley savored the fight from hours before.

That he hadn't completed the coup de grace hardly mattered. Instead, Wexley played and replayed the widening eyes, the shock that'd shivered through the Paragon when the hapless anomaly realized not only that Wexley had him figured out, but that his powers wouldn't help him. Wexley measured his victory by how his opponent *knew* that loss was coming.

The Cabernet on his counter could not compare. Neither could the dismal news reports crawling through Wexley's spare moments, with anchors running harried statistics about protests, Paragon deaths, and the shudder rippling the world's markets. Interspersed between it all came Mynx's voice, clipped in from her press conferences promising stability, promising protection.

Promising her drones.

For what could be a better solution to Paragons dying in the streets than merciless robots enforcing subjugation?

Zhan-Yo hadn't mentioned the precise steps for his revolution, hadn't given Wexley a map to follow, but the man, tucked into an emerald robe softer than silk, figured he had to be walking the right path. While Zhan-Yo made all the major moves, Wexley would continue consolidating power, bringing companies to heel through methods financial and physical. Thus far, a success.

But with Zhan-Yo vanished and the Paragons reeling, Wexley would have to step up and take his boss's place.

"She's giving us cover," Wexley said, speaking into the Tama. "The opportunity is here."

"A gladiator drone's not a Paragon working alone, Wexley," Rhimes replied. Background noise leaked through whenever the man spoke, a restaurant's rumblings. "You can't walk up to one and expect it to surrender."

"Oh, I don't want it to surrender. I need it to get angry."

"Angry?"

On his television, a chromed—like nearly everything in the apartment—set pressed back into the wall, the view flipped to show Mynx's giant facility on the west coast. The Champion called it her Factory, the place all her drones were born.

"I want you to play this out with me, Rhimes, because I think it's important my people understand the why." Wexley had read that somewhere recently; motivation among one's employees improved if they were part of the mission. "What happens if a gladiator drone believes it's under assault?"

"It fights back?"

"And what happens to the people assaulting it?"

Rhimes chuckles, "Don't think you want to know that, sir. It's not pretty."

Wexley slapped the big, glass dining room table dominating the apartment's center. Heard the flat sound, but Rhimes, the man's grainy visage on the Tama, clearly did not. The lack stopped Wexley's triumphant conclusion before it started. Caused Wexley to take another blinding look around his flashy, utterly empty, apartment.

"Where are you, Rhimes? Right now?"

THEY BUILT the plan over midnight, changing early cocktails for water and coffee as the date crept forward a digit. When the restaurant closed, the pair shifted to a nearby bar, one that would make a seamless transition to breakfast when the appointed time arrived.

Wexley and Rhimes, settled on stools next to one another, had their Tamas out on the cherry wood bar. Rhimes produced a notepad from somewhere, sketching out the steps with a blue ink pen co-opted from a bartender all too happy to take the extra tips. Every few minutes, Rhimes touched his Tama, sending out orders to a twenty-four-seven squad ready to work for the reps.

There were no TVs here, and while the jazz band had long since stopped playing and the after-theater crowd left for home, enough stragglers and polite lounge music hung around to give the spot character. A perfect place for plotting.

"Three hours," Rhimes said when the notepad filled

up, when the glasses had their latest refills. "You ready for this?"

Wexley nodded, running his fingers up and down the chilly glass. The ice inside bobbed, reflected the golden lights overhead. He'd have to get back to the van, swap from the hasty going-out collection and into the body armor. Collect the weapons and get into position. The anticipation shoved away sleep's fog.

"And you, my friend?" Wexley said. "Are you ready?"

If Wexley left his gear in an unmarked van, Rhimes kept it slouched about his person. The man approached every activity as a potential ambush, had since the moment Wexley met him. Rhimes didn't suffer much poking at his history, choosing instead to let his loyalty speak for him, and in that, Rhimes hadn't wavered.

Sure, Wexley could hold things against his lieutenant, like letting that damn tracker get away alive, but one mistake didn't mean throwing out all the progress they'd made. Rhimes ran Wexley's own outside group, gathering and training mercenaries and lost souls to do what needed doing to return power to, as Zhan-Yo put it, the people.

Wexley wouldn't even know where to find a replacement.

"You had me guarding Zhan-Yo," Rhimes said. "Failed there, and he got away. You had me try to take that tracker. Failed there too. Most people in my work don't get third chances. I won't let you down."

Wexley planted a hand on Rhimes's shoulder as he stood up, "I know you won't." Wexley squeezed. "You can't. If this doesn't work out, the drone's going to kill you, me, and everyone else."

. . .

DAWN CREPT OVER A GRAY SKYLINE. Wexley crunched the last snowy bits on his chosen roof, looking over apartment buildings bordering neighborhoods bordering highways. Lake Michigan looked frosty this morning out east, visible as Chicago's ever-present horizon. Spread out on rooftops around him, and walking the sidewalks below, Rhimes's team did their work.

Wexley listened in on the squad chatter, trying to parse the lingo. Working alone had its benefits: Wexley never had to worry about someone else, and his missing formal training never made itself clear. Rhimes had offered, back in the bar, to lead the operation, and Wexley had passed that baton.

But Wexley had to see this show for himself, had to be ready to step in and make sure this particular race reached the finish line. Anything else would be catastrophe. Anything else risked losing Adriana and her reps.

With his back to the roof's edge, Wexley removed his rifle from its case. The rounds he slotted in today would leave a big bruise if they hit a person, but if Wexley struck something conductive? Then a real show would start.

The question wasn't whether Wexley or the other three packing the same rounds would hit the drone, but whether Mynx had built in some defense. Whether the drone would get the shooters before they took it down. Rhimes had wanted time to do intelligence work, to see if someone could get a gladiator's specs to know exactly what would work.

Wexley didn't have any more time to give.

"Target approaching west," Rhimes said, the words cutting off all the other conversation. "Upon engage, go silent."

Another wrinkle. The drones would scan and try to intercept any words beamed through radio frequencies when the attack started, a useful trick to track coordinated action. At least, that's what the Paragons claimed the tool was for. Wexley figured the drones used it to pinpoint who to kill.

The gladiator loomed larger this morning than in days past. A pick-up truck's size, the blue and white-painted machine coasted above the homes like an innocuous blimp, jets glowing along its arms and legs. Unlike those bobbing transports, the gladiator had sharp edges ready to deploy weapons and worse.

In the street below, a woman approached a crosswalk. She slowed her jog to match the gladiator's approach, allowing the machine to get overhead as she reached the street's center. Wexley took a deep breath, let the exhale drain away his nerves.

The crack started the game.

Wexley swiveled, keeping his rifle hidden behind the roof's raised lip, and watched. The crack came from the walking woman, a straight up shot from a small weapon, one she stuffed into her waist-bound pack in the second after pulling the trigger. The gladiator drone reacted precisely as programmed, dropping from its height after the harmless shot to drape the woman in its shadow.

A deep, commanding voice boomed out orders to the woman, demanding her to lie down, surrender herself. Instead, the woman protested, shouting denials and backing away. Wexley nodded as he watched the performance: here, a civilian out for a casual early-morning run getting harassed by the very things meant to protect the public.

Anyone reviewing the camera footage later would learn the truth, but that would take hours, days, or, if Wexley and his crew succeeded in downing the drone, never.

The gladiator parsed the woman's protesting as resistance and its various plates, joints, and limbs rotated, snapping into a standing pose. Six arms, two legs, and varied weapons confronted a jacket-and-shorts runner in the middle of the quiet street. Her shouts picked up volume, the gladiator gave another loud call for her to surrender.

Lights flicked on in houses, in the apartments. People awakening to the disaster in their own neighborhood. The woman, noticing the response, gave herself up, cowering on the ground with her hands over her head. The gladiator approached, its steps rattling the road. It declared local authorities had been notified, that the woman would face charges for what she'd done.

"But I didn't do anything!" came the woman's reply.

"She didn't do anything!" Rhimes echoed, popping out from his parked car halfway down the block. Arms and armor cloaked behind a large, puffy white jacket, Rhimes walked towards the drone. "I was sitting here the whole time."

The gladiator told Rhimes to stay back, that this wasn't his affair. Wexley gave the drone some credit for attempting to negotiate, but Rhimes wasn't done. They needed the drone to strike first, so all the Tamas taking video now would catch the clear fault.

"Nah, I'm not staying back while you hurt her," Rhimes said, coming close to the woman, putting his arm on her shoulder. "Let's get going. We can't let the robot take you for nothing."

The gladiator drone raised an arm, the open hole in the thing's palm a clear barrel leading back to some magazine, some round that could turn Rhimes and the woman to ash. This time, the drone's warning left no ambiguity: anything other than immediate surrender would lead to harm.

Rhimes didn't stop.

He lifted the woman, and she played her part, moving herself behind Rhimes, putting his back and its big jacket between her and the drone. A drone that'd finally reached its limit.

The shot came quick, loud. It blew into Rhimes's back and crackled with a blue burst, a sign the drone wanted to stun more than kill. Rhimes collapsed, burying the woman in his burnt jacket.

"Now," Wexley muttered, keeping his mic turned off.

Everyone knew the trigger, and the other eight people with parts in this play started their scene. From other rooftops, from other streets, they came running. Those down below came with household weapons, old rifles and shotguns scrounged from cellars, ones that could claim to be family heirlooms, protected from the Paragon's routine firearm purges. They would be caught on video, the fearless citizens coming to save their own.

Wexley sighted the drone in his scope and triggered the first shot. The round streaked in, slamming into the gladiator's neck and snapping like a lightning bolt breaking a tree. Others followed, crashing into the drone from surrounding roofs. On the ground, the five citizen fighters took more standard means, blowing ineffective rounds into the drone's thick armor.

The drone itself took the first salvo and kept standing, though its weapon arms dropped limp to its side. Sparks flared from an eye as the drone lurched, its left arms sweeping towards three of the approaching fighters and spraying out a yellow fire. The burning acid caught Wexley's team square on, driving them back and prompting more, not feigned, screams.

"That's a new trick," Wexley said, lining up and taking another shot.

Mynx kept her drones shifting through variants, always

keen to keep her enemies on their toes. Before Zhan-Yo, those enemies had largely been the Elementals and other rogue anomalies, ones taking out their frustration with the Paragon program or succumbing to an ability that rotted away their sanity. This time, the drone dealt with a small swarm, coordinated and ruthless.

Wexley paired his attacks with the other shooters on the rooftops, hitting the drone in different sections, frying those components one at a time. Its left and right leg shorted out next, causing the drone to collapse to the street. Rhimes, his jacket and the armor beneath doing its job, pulled the woman away as the drone planted its face into the concrete.

Wheeling free from his hostage, Rhimes yanked a small bat from inside his coat. Lifting it up in both hands, he ran at the drone, like some strange modern Viking. The gladiator wasn't quite done, and Wexley saw the small spikes spring up along the drone's back. He didn't know what those spikes might do, but Wexley plugged another round into them anyway, satisfied as blue lightning sprayed.

Rhimes struck with the bat, a banging hit followed by another and another. To Wexley, from above, every hit looked like a man's enraged battering. According to the plan, Rhimes whacked away at the gladiator's communications apparatus, bashing and breaking in the drone's ability to get reinforcements. Hopefully, too, the hits would ruin any chance for those reinforcements to track what would happen next.

Tires squealed as a dull gray trailer truck romped into view, turning onto the street and backing up towards the dead drone. Wexley, his rifle hidden but within an easy grab should the drone find a second life, watched for open doors, for curious watchers. If the first part had been an easy swing for public support, this would make things more dubious.

How many random walkers would have a truck on hand to snag a drone? What innocent person would try such a thing?

But those were minor snags. For now, the people on the ground, wiping off the acid attack, worked with two more from the truck to hook a winch up to the drone. A button press later and the big machine screeched as the cable dragged the drone inside the trailer. The door slammed shut, a lock clicked into place, and tires kicked back into action as the truck, its trailer lined with signal-jamming metals, careened away.

Wexley took a long look around the horizon, noticed several other black forms screaming their way. Drone reinforcements.

Time to go.

"CASUALTIES?" Wexley asked Rhimes an hour later, back in a suit and in his office, enjoying a coffee and a bagel with skyscrapers all around.

"Light injuries," Rhimes replied. "Nothing more than that. Expected better from the machine."

"You put together a good team." Wexley glanced at his calendar. Full up, and already late for the next meeting. "Is it safe?"

"Nobody's going to find it. We're starting in right away, as ordered. I'll keep you updated on progress."

"Remember what's important. We need to know how they're controlled. Everything hinges on that."

"On it."

"And I want to see it," Wexley said. "Up close. Tonight?"

"Tonight. You let me know, boss."

Wexley let Rhimes go, leaned back in his chair. The shower had left his hair a little wet, but otherwise he showed no signs that he'd greeted the day firing electrical rounds at a homicidal machine. Nobody would know what he'd done.

He swiped back to his calendar, found a dull session in the early afternoon that wouldn't need him. Wexley could dump that one. Could give Adriana a call.

He had a story to tell.

6

Supper Spying

The restaurant rose above her, a waterfall effect climbing from the street-level bar up through several dazzling stories filled with decked-out diners. Celice, snacking on what could, would, be the first of several appetizers, paid casual glances to one pair, on the second story, as they embraced their red wine with gusto. A night off for these two, a night on for Celice.

As it ever was.

The mirrored bar counter made the tracking easier, the surface kept sparkling by obsessive bartenders who mixed cocktails and wiped glass at the same time. To her left, Celice saw one patron stand only to have his plate, drinks, and all his evidence cleansed in barely a breath. Another body stole his stool too, starting a whole new game.

Central London at its efficient finest. Celice mellowed the vibe with a slight sip, the all-day-drinking beer fizzing on her tongue and sliding past without offense. She had no desire to put much alcohol back tonight, but sitting at a bar like this for however long it took her targets to eat dinner and not ordering a drink might attract the wrong attention.

Not that she minded the slow-paced stakeout. Celice had burned the day tracking down the keys and their maker, a scowl-faced man with an accent nigh unintelligible, but who seemed happy enough to point at photos Celice showed him of Zhan-Yo's gang. She bought up some candies the man had on the counter in thanks, sucked on them as she ran through security footage outside the lockmaker's shop.

She'd found the identified targets quick: two men going in with reps and coming out with keys. Connecting camera to camera, Celice traced them far enough till they slipped into alleys and vanished. Keeping focus on that same alley as the hours spun by on fast forward brought the two targets back into the picture.

From there, like the jogger in the park, Celice traced out a route, found where they frequented, and followed the two to this lovely establishment. That she drew disapproving looks for her street clothes—Celice didn't go out for tactical, potentially violent encounters dressed in, well, dresses—didn't matter. They'd let her in with visible relief when Celice motioned towards the bar, and there she joined with a few other scrubs to enter the evening with a proper meal.

Aegis would've hated this whole game. Celice played with a deconstructed salad, a tomato sitting center surrounded by sparse greens, a dressing splash, and a cheese cube. Her father would have climbed the stairs, stomped through astonished diners without giving a damn and lifted both criminals from their chairs before carrying them out into a gruff and rough interrogation.

"You're new," said the character who'd stolen the seat next to Celice. A patchy jacket, full on bowler cap, and an addiction to flannel marked him as a similar outcast. "How d'ya like it?"

Celice analyzed the man's face. Fuzzed, reddish, and with wrinkled eyes, one with a notch off to the side that suggested a prior encounter with a knife, or maybe a glass bottle. Not a face matching Zhan-Yo's associates.

"You can rest that hand there," the man said, turning back to the bar. He raised a finger, and in enough time for Celice to move her hand from the gun's hilt inside her jacket, a highball glass splashed with something appeared. "I'm not here to scare you."

Questions abounded. What random Londoner would know a hand inside a light jacket meant a gun's presence? Who would sit next to the only woman in the bar that didn't look like she belonged there and start making directed small-talk?

"You know how to speak, then?" the man continued. "Or is this going to be a one-way conversation?"

"I can talk," Celice said, feeling stupid as she spoke the words.

"Ah, good. Was getting worried there, my looks have never been much for stunning, see."

He tossed out a wink.

Celice shook her head, glanced back at her salad for a reset. In the bar counter's reflection, she saw her targets still sat, their wine bottle getting low, their meals delivered. They could be wrapping up, or another bottle might signal an hour more. She'd have to watch.

"What do you want?" Celice asked the man.

"Your company for a drink, maybe a second," the man said. "Nothing more than that."

"Doubt it."

"Which part?"

"The second."

The man put back his beverage, halving its contents

into his mouth and licking his lips with a smacking sigh. He leaned in the bar chair, sliding an arm over its back as though he sat in an old saloon and not London's fineries.

"I see how you might be thinking that way, me just coming up in here and acting like your best friend," the man said. "How about we square it up? Start with the names, go from there. Benny's mine, local to London all my life."

A dozen fakes sprinted through Celice's lips. She could've been a Sarah, a Leslie, or a Monica. Could've jaunted through a history Celice had never known as if it'd been her own, but Benny's crinkled eyes said they saw more than the man was letting on. She had enough threads to untangle without adding a whole new identity into the mix.

"Celice," she replied, ignoring Benny's hand with a nod instead. "Not local to London all my life."

"Oh, the accent gives you away," Benny said with a short laugh.

"Does it?"

"It's neutral, has no history," Benny replied. "Like you wandered in here newly made. But you walk like a Yank, and that's what I'm assuming you are."

He emptied his glass, signaled for another while Celice ate the tomato centerpiece, trying to decide how to play the encounter.

"What else are you assuming about me?" Celice said.

"That you're not here by chance, much as I might like it to be so." Benny touched his hat tip at the bartender replacing his whisky. "And that you aren't quite as confident as you're pretending."

"That's a lot for someone who never knew me till five minutes ago."

"I'm a quick study, and you're treating that salad real slow."

"I'm not hungry."

Benny nodded, as though Celice ordering a far-too-expensive salad when she wasn't hungry made perfect sense. Celice checked the reflection again. No second bottle. One looked to be paying a check, but the blur didn't make it clear. She chanced a look up, found the table, confirmed the act.

"You ever been to this city before?" Benny asked.

"Plenty," Celice said, raising a hand for her own bill. "Not for a while, though."

"Changes fast, this one," Benny said. "You'd think the old girl would hang around for a while, take a breath, but she never does."

"I'm sure."

The two targets upstairs stood up, slung jackets over their shoulders. A bartender slapped the bill near Celice and she paid it without looking. Instead, she turned towards Benny, keeping one eye over his shoulder towards the restaurant's exit.

If Benny had one use right now, it could be as cover. Her targets might notice someone watching them, but two people in conversation at the bar? Not a chance.

"What do you do, Benny?" Celice asked, trying to place the last time she'd used small talk.

She'd dated, gone out with friends, but being the premier Paragon's daughter tended to put stress on any relationship. Celice had one when Aegis died, a good one too, but that fizzled immediately. She didn't have time for weekends at the cabin or a night out on the town when Aegis's killer was free. The whole song-and-dance seemed so pointless.

"Help people, mostly," Benny replied. "You could say I'm something of an everyman, doing what needs doing and all that."

"As vague descriptions go, that's a winner."

The two hadn't come down yet. A bathroom stop before braving the London chill seemed likely.

"Oh, now don't be getting saucy." Benny took another gulp. "A city like this needs people like me, the grease between the gears."

"Sure."

Benny sat up, giving Celice a knowing look. His eyes had that particular gleam to them, as if Benny had her heart and mind open before him, ready for reading.

"Could be you might need some help?" Benny asked, the jolly jangle snapping away for serious.

"Don't need anything."

"Most people say that, then they take a good look at their lives and realize different."

There they were, marching on out. Not a single glance her way. Perfect.

"Good thing I'm not most people." Celice stood up. "Benny, thanks for the words."

"I've got plenty of 'em," Benny replied, touching his hat again her way.

Benny looked like he had another catchphrase to deliver, but the pair had already left the restaurant. Losing them here would reset Celice's progress, force her to find another place they visited as regularly as this one. She didn't hustle, not quite, but Celice made it onto the sidewalk only seconds after her targets.

London hit tonight with the same raw weather as yesterday: cold, rainy. The streets shimmered black while lights smeared in water. Conversation and music blended with tires in swampy gutters, but the air carried pleasant dew with every breath. Celice did a casual look around, slow enough to seem like she was double-checking her intended direction.

Her targets headed towards a nearby square, statues looming over a busy roundabout. Celice padded after them, noting a gladiator drone coasting by overhead. The people bustling around her saw the machine too, some breaking out a conversation about a story coming from Chicago. A drone like this one attacking a pedestrian before some local heroes took it out.

That part had Celice a little confused. No way some courageous neighbors could take out a gladiator, especially one that'd malfunctioned enough to go after some random runner. She almost felt sorry for Mynx, who'd no doubt have to scramble after this problem too. At least, so Celice had seen, Mynx had Mila there to help.

The South American Champion always had a chirpy, bright look on things, one that Aegis enjoyed and Celice found annoying. Maybe because Mila could turn a mortal wound into a tiny scratch, but the Champion always seemed to downplay danger. Play up the benefits. Aegis would wave at Mila's approval as if her support alone ought to convince the Paragons to do some dangerous operation.

Never mind how many anomalies might die right there in the field, without Mila near to heal them.

The targets hustled across the street into the square, Celice following behind with bodies in between. The rain picked up here in the open, the droplets lancing hard. People clustered under umbrellas, and Celice wavered on popping hers: an umbrella required a hand to hold, a hand that might be better freed to defend herself.

But her prey made their own move, launching black

umbrellas into the air over their heads and clearing Celice to do the same. She glanced down, pulled out the umbrella from her jacket pocket, and sprang its dull red covering. With the rain blocked, Celice looked up to find her targets again. Around her, the crowd split away for the Underground or other crossings, leaving wide lanes across the slick wet stone.

And her targets were in none of them.

Two seconds to open her umbrella. That's it. No way they could've vanished that fast, not without running and drawing all kinds of attention. Celice turned in place, doing a quick once-around and—

There. Heading straight towards her. Umbrella discarded and hands inside his jacket just like Celice's had been when Benny sat down. The man didn't have an idle look to him, this wasn't some fluke chance.

She'd been made.

Two choices, three seconds to make one: fight, or run. Fight, and maybe Celice wins, maybe Celice gets arrested, maybe Celice dies. Run and she gets chased, loses her leads, and now Zhan-Yo knows she's scared.

You know what to do.

Yeah, she knew. Celice swung her umbrella down as the man closed the gap, settling the umbrella's grip into her left hand. She stepped forward, swinging her left arm back as Celice pressed the retracting button on the umbrella's handle. The red rain shield shrank back, clearing the way for Celice's punch into the man's chest.

Celice struck a sweater's fabric, but rather than soft skin beneath, her hand hit a vest's hard artifice. She'd worn enough bullet-proof armor to know how the things felt, to know these two hadn't come to the restaurant expecting a lazy night out.

Not only had Celice been made, she'd been set up.

The punch rebounded, sending a jammed finger jolt through Celice's hand. The man swept the retracted umbrella aside. Celice figured a gunshot was coming, a quick finale to the evening's show.

"Don't try that again," the man said. Up close, he had the look of someone who'd been surfing the sunlit countries for a long time, bronzed and clean-shaven. A no-nonsense type Celice would've ignored, that her dad might've adored. "It won't work out well."

"How many are you?" Celice asked, leaving her umbrella low, trying to count the strides to the Underground station near the square's edge.

"Enough," the man replied. "We know who you are and why you're here."

"Then where's Zhan-Yo?"

"You don't get to meet the boss till he's sure you'll play nice."

"He killed my father."

The mercenary, in utterly typical fashion, didn't show a single emotion. As if the man confronted fatherless daughters seeking revenge every day. Celice wanted to know if, somewhere, there sat a school for people like this, where they were fed some obscure diet and taught to ignore distress so their leaders could profit.

"He's offering you a choice," the man said. "You either leave London and forget about us, or you hear what he has to say. Peacefully."

"How about option three, where I take you all apart one by one?"

The mercenary tilted his head, as if talking to a little girl, "You know how that goes. You're not your father, Celice."

"Didn't say you could use my name."

The mercenary didn't reply, just stood there accepting

the rain. Celice wiped the water from her own eyes. Felt the cold seeping into everywhere. Thirty minutes ago, this whole thing seemed so promising. On her own, leveraging her skills without the Paragons helping out, tracking down her father's killer.

That's how these stories went, right? The daughter wins the day, delivers justice?

"I want to see him," Celice said. "Zhan-Yo."

"Then you agree? No weapons. We'll send a car."

Details. Celice could use her hands and feet. Without a gun in her hand or a knife in her holster, she could still take out Zhan-Yo before the man's guards interrupted.

"Done," Celice said.

"Good choice." the man pulled his umbrella with that hidden hand and popping it open. "We'll be by." He started walking, heading past her. "For what it's worth, I admired your father. He was a good man."

Celice glared at the mercenary's back as the man walked away, shoes squelching on the stone. A good man? Her father was so much more than *a good man*. Aegis had—

You didn't fight. You should've fought.

They would've killed her. Celice hadn't seen the rifles in the dark, but no doubt they were there. Zhan-Yo's crew ran a dozen deep. She didn't have Aegis's powers, she didn't have Paragon back-up.

You're making excuses.

Celice wavered. The rain kept coming and she wanted to add some tears to it. Would have, if a hand didn't land soft on her shoulder. Another pressed the button on her umbrella, popping it open again.

"You know," Benny said, his bowler cap catching the water and splashing it like a duck's feathers. "It's fun to take a shower in the rain, sure, but I'm guessing you'll be happier back at your own place where the water's warm."

Celice blinked at him, "What?"

"There's a pod there." Benny pointed to a waiting orb pulled up on the curb. "Was going to take it myself, but you look like you might need the ride."

And, despite her father's disappointed voice in her head, Celice took it.

7

Entrance Exam

The disaster saved Calvin from another training session showdown. After yesterday's rumble in the warehouse, the Elementals had the moxie to ask Calvin to come back, a request Calvin ignored until the Paragons solved the problem for him.

"I've never seen someone grin so much," Kat said as they rode the train towards Chicago's northern burbs. "You really didn't want to go, did you?"

Unlike yesterday, Kat and Calvin had their go-suits on. Kat's silver cloak settled over her gadget-stuffed suit and pants, while Calvin sported the Paragon's blue-and-white uniform. The pair looked official enough to send bystanders on the train scattering away, leaving them their own pod corner with which to watch the passing buildings on a gray March day.

The two had taken their long night out into a slow morning, playing in the park with Seeker and getting their caffeine on. Kat ran through a reply to a message from Gordon—the tracker had disappeared off to LA for an emergency conference with Mynx—while Calvin cleansed last evening's alcohol with a run along a nearby creek.

Altogether, given the chaos that'd plagued them over the last month, it'd been a forgettable, wonderful start to the day. No gunshots, no anomalies throwing killer powers at him . . . Calvin could get used to it.

"Look," Calvin said, "I don't want to show them up, you know? Yesterday Farrah pulled a trick, but today I'd have to come at them with the real me. I'd make some enemies."

"Sure."

Calvin let his head fall back against the glass window behind him, the ever-present tingling in his hands making him want to spin his leather gloves into a leather blanket. The transformation would ruin the gloves, though, and despite his newfound employment as a world savior for the almighty Paragons, Calvin's rep account remained thin.

"You're talking like you don't want to be here," Calvin said. "Might be I'm recalling wrong, but an hour ago you were real excited to join up."

"All the Elementals want to do is talk," Kat replied. "It's like, hey, can we get a bunch of really strong, really cool people in a room and mutter about timing all day?"

"Timing?"

"Beth has it all in her head that the Elementals can make their move and carve out their own little world. The Paragons will let them, see, if the Elementals stake their claim when the Paragons don't have the power to resist."

"Like that'll happen."

Kat didn't answer, and Calvin squeezed open an eye, looked her way. Unlike the anomaly, Kat had her Tama up, hand swiping through some news.

"Kat?" Calvin asked. "We still talking here?"

"Uh huh."

"What'd I just say?"

"Asked if we're still talking." Kat didn't turn away from the Tama, so Calvin sat up, took a closer look.

Blistering headlines showed Mynx, the only Champion left in North America, trying to instill some confidence in the region and the world. Burning hour after hour between news conferences and meetings with other Paragon leaders, the article suggested, had Mynx running on less than fumes, and she stumbled over lines, names, and had just canceled the day's remaining slate. Furthermore, the article speculated South America's Champion, Mila, stayed at the Factory now just to keep Mynx afloat.

Though the reporter did note Mila remained in LA whenever Mynx left, often remaining hidden for days at a time. Some new drone in development? Helping some Paragons back from the brink? The article offered speculation, little answers, and a brutal photo capturing Mynx, head down, fleeing a podium.

"Looks rough," Calvin said, returning to his windowed rest.

"That's it?" Kat said. "Looks rough?"

"What?"

"Aren't you a Paragon? Shouldn't the fact that your whole organization's in disarray concern you?"

Calvin snorted, "I'm a Paragon because they pay well. If they go away, I'll go back to doing what I've always done."

"Nothing of consequence?"

"Says the tracker sitting on a train. Don't see you catching any dangerous anomalies."

Kat put the Tama down, kneaded her hands into fists, "That's not important right now."

Calvin could agree with that. Ever since Wexley and his thugs made perforating Calvin and Kat with bullets a priority, the two put distance between their careers and keeping themselves alive. Both played with the Elementals because the rogue anomalies offered them common cause against the killer CEO and his murderous band. Kat, too, used any off hours not spent drowning meetings in bourbon trying to find Wexley's traces, figure out a way she and Calvin could track the man, get some revenge.

The pair had a file now, a growing one. Kat had background on Wexley, had his office and his normal working hours. Probing the man's office building would be the next step, try to see how hard it was to get an appointment on Wexley's calendar. Kat, given her reputation and Wexley knowing who the hell she was, had been prepping Calvin for the task.

Calvin would walk right in, smile at Wexley's secretary, then enter the office. He'd have one hand brushing a metal cuff, the other reaching out to shake Wexley's hand. Then, right when Wexley came close, Calvin would turn that cuff into a razor sharp needle and deliver a mortal move to the man's throat. Follow-up as needed before making a break for it, with Kat waiting down below.

It all sounded easy, but Calvin wasn't exactly an assassin.

This world, though, tended to turn people into what they never expected.

The train dumped them off into a quiet neighborhood. A business smattering near the station dwindled into home after home, a quaint place that made Calvin itch. The midday dog walkers were hard at work, their furry charges lunging at each other and the occasional jogger daring the crowded sidewalks. Coffee-spiced air breezed by.

With Kat next to him, Calvin followed his Tama several blocks towards a few pop-up apartment buildings, older ones sticking around in a red brick formation, as if fending off the surrounding homes. Paragon signs came up early, with pods bearing the Paragon's logo squatting in street centers. Local police joined them, most looking to be chatting with confused civilians about what'd happened earlier.

Calvin's order stuck him with perimeter duty. Walk around, look for signs anyone might've missed, and reassure the public that their anomaly guardians were on the case. At least the day, despite the sun dodging behind the clouds, carried some warmth. After a simple check-in with the Paragon in charge, one whose name and ability Calvin didn't bother to remember, he and Kat set off on the walkabout.

"Looks like someone's a star," Calvin said to Kat as they started up the sidewalk near where the drone had been knocked down.

"I've brought in a lot of anomalies for the Paragons here," Kat replied. "Don't be jealous."

"Jealous? That guy wanted your autograph. No thanks."

"To my autograph, or my fans?"

"Is it going to hurt you if I say both?"

Kat rolled her eyes. The move drew attention to her suit's functions, the full-on visor and face mask so far undeployed but resting near her temples in case an emergency arose. If Calvin wanted to be jealous of something, that suit would be the source, not any fawning from some Paragon clock-puncher.

The drone's crash site sparkled with yellow tabs. Paragons and police dropped the flags, which Kat explained were about marking evidence. Calvin watched as the tracker stalked from one to the next, treating each one as if it might be the key to unlocking anything and everything. Most of the tabs seemed to be noting bullet casings, and a few highlighted broken metal bits. One lighted near a small blood stain.

"See anything?" Calvin asked, then swept a dramatic turn around the street, the homes, the apartments. Beyond the gathered officials, nothing stood out. "Cause I sure don't."

"It's because you're looking for big things, not what's important."

"Hey."

"This one, for example," Kat said, pointing at a tab near her foot. Calvin came over, looked at what seemed to be another dull dark shell. "The shooter missed with this one."

"Cool?"

"For us, yeah." Kat knelt down, waved her hands around the shell like some host illustrating a prize. "See how there's no damage to the pavement here? See the patterns on the shell?"

"I'm listening."

"This isn't a bullet fired from some desperate person defending themselves. These rounds deliver a shock. They'd take that Tama you're wearing and turn it to scrap."

Calvin wouldn't call himself a detective, but he could trace lines like this, "So you're saying the drone didn't get stolen by some soccer moms. Real breakthrough, Kat."

"Still saucy about yesterday?" Kat cracked, and, when Calvin decided he didn't have to reply to that, she went on, "What I'm saying is that there's not a lot of groups that'd use these rounds. Police, maybe, but they wouldn't be shooting a drone. The Paragons have their powers, and the drones are on their side."

Setting his sarcastic hackles down, Calvin squatted next

to Kat, "And the Elementals would've told us if they were planning on hitting a gladiator drone."

"Told me, anyway," Kat said.

Couldn't argue with that.

"Which leaves few options, and one winner," Kat said. "The group that blew up the stadium in L.A., the one that killed Aegis? Zhan-Yo? I'd finger him but since he exploded himself . . ."

"Someone taking up his cause, then? Another anomaly hater?"

"Like Wexley?"

Calvin shrugged, "Seems like a leap to go from taking pot shots at Elementals to attacking a gladiator."

Kat stood and Calvin went up with her. She continued the walk around the scene, stopping again at black marks along the street, tires leaving evidence behind. Thick tires too, ones a tad strange to see on a residential road.

"Rhimes tried to recruit me first, remember?" Kat said. "Wexley did too. They had bigger plans."

"Okay, let's walk this path you're picturing," Calvin replied. "We have the big bad and his gangster friends. They come all the way out here and fight some machine, then steal it? Why?"

Kat, looking across the tire tracks, didn't have an answer.

With Calvin stuck on duty, Kat disappeared to do some digging, leaving the anomaly fending off pestering people. Putting on an official tone and waving away interlopers came unnaturally, every conversation an awkward dance between instilling Paragon authority while also keeping things respectful.

In short, Calvin caught a lotta sarcastic flack. Those dog walkers wondered why they couldn't keep their route along the street. Kids came up with inane questions about

Calvin's powers, why he couldn't just fly off and find the drone. And, worse, reporters descending upon the site soon picked up Calvin's own reluctance and feasted on it.

"I don't know, man," Calvin said to another shouted question from the half-dozen Tama-tapping muckrakers around him. He threw a desperate look to the other Paragons milling about, but the anomalies grinned at him, apparently willing to throw their own to the wolves. "I'm here to keep people from getting hurt, that's it."

"Getting hurt? So you're saying there's still danger here?" another one said, her hand perched right above a Tama that would, no doubt, send panic to Chicago's citizens.

Then again, maybe that would buy Calvin a second to breathe. Take a late lunch break.

"What do you think?" Calvin said. "We have a missing gladiator drone, we don't know what the hell happened to it or who stole it. You think that's dangerous?"

Faces looked back at him, waiting for the words. Calvin had seen that look before, mostly from his former foster parents, the school teachers waiting for apologies. Back then, he'd run away. Now . . .

Glancing at his Tama, Calvin held up his wrist, "Sorry folks, have to check on something here. Stay back, will you?"

Ignoring shouted asks about just what Calvin had to check on, the anomaly turned and abandoned the reporters to their stories. He walked right up to the four other Paragons hanging around the crime scene's center, causing the whole group to stare at the newbie together.

"Had enough?" said the site's lead Paragon, a skinny, slick stick called Weed. As inspiring as the man's name was, Weed's reputation held strong as someone who cut through crap to get things done. Calvin felt his own metrics getting evaluated in Weed's look, rated and assigned a proper role. "You hung in there well for a first timer. Lob, you're up next. Keep'em spinning."

"You got it." A gruff dude whose uniform looked like it'd been measured a few burgers ago, marched off towards the reporters.

"Calvin?" Weed asked, squaring up to the anomaly. "You're new, right?"

"Came in as everything went to hell."

"Came in from where?"

A tough question, and not just because Calvin didn't have what anyone could call a home. Anomalies had a legal obligation to register with the Paragons the moment their abilities popped from genetic code to real-world magic, and Calvin, uh, hadn't done that. He'd had other priorities, like finding food and a place to take a nap.

And authority figures tended to treat Calvin like dirt, so signing up with the biggest one seemed like a bad deal.

"All over," Calvin said.

Weed took the words with another studied stare, re-calculating Calvin's place in his squad, "Well, Calvin from all over, thanks for showing up today."

Weed's words and his tone came mismatched. The tingle in Calvin's hands went up, the leather gloves itching to be turned into something more useful, like a whip around Weed's throat.

"You're welcome?" Calvin said, noticing again that Weed's other three buddies had their eyes on him.

"Took the opportunity to review your record as I haven't worked with you before," Weed continued. "Seems like you went off grid for a few days. Haven't checked in at the tower once in weeks, only by Tama?"

"The tower's ugly right now, case you haven't noticed."

"The Paragons need all the help we can get, and you're nowhere to be seen. Where've you been hiding, Calvin?"

"I came when I was called."

Weed glanced at his associates, shook his head, "Tell me, Calvin, does that sound like something Aegis would say? Come when called? We're about taking the initiative here."

You talk to enough people, you see enough, you start to recognize the roads when they re-appear. Calvin backed up a step, took a big sigh. Kat kept pushing him to find a tribe, get in touch with the ones that would accept him, and here was his outfit, looking at him like all those damn counselors, all those officers.

Not only a failure, but a problem.

Maybe on a different day, one where Calvin hadn't been hounded for hours, after a slam-to-the-floor training session at the hands of immature Elementals, Calvin could've found the calm to push back on Weed's bait.

"Aegis is dead, Weed," Calvin replied. "He's not saying anything."

"Smoke?" Weed said to the woman on his left. "Would you be so kind?"

"Already done," Smoke replied.

Calvin looked at her, she smiled a knife's cut back his way. Something had happened, and with anomalies . . .

"All right, Calvin," Weed said. "There's a rule I have before accepting new Paragons into my squad."

"Let me guess. You gotta trust them first, or some stupid thing like that?"

"At least you're not dumb. Cocky, but I can work with that. I need obedience, I need you to understand who's making the calls."

"I'm not a kid. Tell me what to do, and if it makes sense, I'll do it."

Weed took a long step forward from the group, right up to Calvin's face, "Then hit me. Right now."

Calvin tilted his head, "What?"

"I gave you an order, didn't I?"

All right. If this joker wanted to get laid out, Calvin could accommodate. While Weed waited, Calvin slipped the leather gloves off, the tingle switching from leather's tight pull to the air and all the dust floating in it. No way Weed would take the punch straight up—this whole dance had to be some power play, some animal kingdom strut to keep Weed's friends knowing who led the pack.

Calvin could be a team player, but he damn sure wasn't going to be anyone's example.

The right hook came fast, but as Calvin swung, his left hand pulled in the air and Calvin's right launched it ahead, a localized gale flying faster than the fist. Weed's face snapped back, his eyes closing as the wind hit. Calvin's punch followed, dipping to catch Weed's shoulder, spinning the smaller man around.

Weed stumbled back, eyes blinking, shaking his head. Calvin could've pursued, ran into another charge, but the point seemed to be made. Even the other Paragons watching nodded, arms folded. At least a little impressed.

"That good enough?" Calvin said. "Or do you need more?"

Weed straightened, sent his head in a neck-cracking back-and-forth, "They teach every Paragon the basics, Calvin. When you're fighting an anomaly, though, it's better if you take them out the first time."

"I could've," Calvin started, then stopped. He felt something on his hand, a chilled slime. No, not slime: bodies, small, moving bodies. "What the hell is this?"

"We all get our names for a reason," Weed said, not bothering to close.

The tiny creatures on Calvin's hand scrambled up his arm, clawing and digging along his clothes. They didn't hurt, exactly, but they were growing. Every passing second and the collection went from pin-heads to pebbles, dragging Calvin's arm and soon himself down with them. Each and every one of the things looked like a copy of Weed, only with imperfections, some adjustments, like a single arm or a different shade of hair color, and not an ounce of clothing.

Creepy, freaky, and not at all appropriate.

Calvin jammed his left hand down to the street, found the cement and sucked it up. From his right hand, the rock swept Calvin's skin, covering his uniform and knocking the little Weeds off. Still growing, the clones hit the street around Calvin. With his newly armored fist, Calvin went to work, bashing aside the collection as they came at him.

At first, the hits did well, but soon Calvin saw his cement arm had new little growths on it, a new Weed generation spawning right along him again. Bashing these things wasn't going to work. Calvin had to change the game.

Heavy hands picked up the anomaly before Calvin found a new strategy, the first Weeds now standing half Calvin's height and working together to lift the man up. Unlike the Paragon they sprang from, Weed's clones had blank eyes, a nothing intelligence on their faces. They didn't show any emotion, any fear or anger.

"How do you handle adversity, Calvin?" Weed called. "Do you give up, or do you fight until the very end?"

Oh, Calvin was gonna give this guy some pain. Discarding the cement and letting it peel off his arm as the Weeds lifted him high—for a smash to the ground? Calvin wasn't sure—Calvin reached and gripped the clones with both hands.

Every anomaly had to draw their own lines, had to understand what they could live with. Calvin had his, but now, now he was going to make an exception. Beneath his hands, he felt the cool skin, a texture very much not human, and Calvin grabbed it. The Weed on his left broke down fast, its very essence disintegrating as if fading away like a movie scene. Calvin spun that energy to his right hand, wrapping the other Weed in a cage of its clone's matter.

The move dropped Calvin to the ground, where he hit chest first. He had his hands ready, expecting more Weeds to come grabbing at him, but instead the bodies withered. As if sprayed with some terrible chemical, the forms all shivered simultaneously, turning brown, then black, then melting away to less than dust.

Weed stepped forward, reaching out with a hand. Calvin stared at it, saw Weed's serious look and a serious nod, then accepted the offer.

"Impressive work, Calvin," Weed said, bringing the anomaly to his feet. "The Paragons might be the right place for you after all."

Calvin wanted to throw those words in Weed's face, wanted to storm off into, well, somewhere, but his buzzing Tama cut the rage. Kat, calling in.

She'd found something.

8

Past Meets Present

The night on the beach felt like a return to a vanished past, and Cassidy spent far too many minutes watching the waves and shining moon above them. Thane, his rage and its attendant energy spent, collapsed in the dirt without much more than a sigh. Alone, Cassidy wandered through the years spent on beaches similar to this one, staring out at a horizon pocked with floating, monitoring drones.

No drones here though. Birds, clouds, the starlight above occasionally joined by a passing jet. A peaceful ocean view, not a prison.

At some point, the memories became dreams, and Cassidy woke with the water kissing her feet as the tide came in. Together, the two escapists picked themselves and their shredded clothing up, hiking to the jungle line.

"Two refugees," Thane said, his body straddling the line between skinny and strong, "without money, without clothes, without a home."

"With lives," Cassidy added.

"With lives. Time, I think, to make something of them."

"Let's save the big goals till we get a shower, something to wear, to eat."

Thane shrugged, pointed at a coconut up in a palm tree, "I can climb that."

"I didn't escape an island to eat more coconuts," Cassidy said. "And if someone sees you scaling that tree, and we get caught for a damn coconut, I'm going to be very upset."

"Then what do you propose?"

Cassidy's idea led them back into the brush, hiking towards the closest non-natural sound: music. The light tunes, all drums and flutes, bounced through the trees. Shoving aside firms and stepping over roots, scattering spiderwebs and fending off flies, the pair traced the music to a squat house resting right up on the jungle's edge.

A blue-gray single story, the home lacked luxury but oozed life. Children's toys populated a small yard given over to friendly weeds, while the open windows crossing the house's back let the music loose. A small patio had two chairs and an inviting door inside.

Thane didn't stop when they came close, marching on ahead as if planning on a one-man invasion. Which, maybe he was. Cassidy might've let Thane run right along, too, if not for those toys.

One, a yellow and red car, Cassidy had given her own children a lifetime ago.

"Wait," Cassidy said, grabbing Thane's arm. "Give them a little while. They might leave."

"They are not important," Thane replied. "Time is."

"An hour. More than that and we do it your way."

Thane, his mug freshly washed in seawater, sparkled as the sun broke through early morning mist. He tilted his head at Cassidy, studying her. Cassidy returned the look, feeling the urge in her mind wake up.

Potential conflict, potential void.

"You're soft," Thane said.

"Not soft," Cassidy shot back. "Strategic. We march in and hurt those people, someone's going to find out. Maybe fast. Then the island panics. Right now, we're weird runaways, anomalies nobody knows or cares much about. That changes if we kill people."

Thane considered, leaned against a nearby tree and looked out towards the house. Cassidy matched him, using the leaves and a vast fern for cover.

"Did you live in a house like this?" Thane asked.

"We lived near the coast. Oregon. Two stories, touching a forest," Cassidy said. "My kids loved it."

"Did they know who you were?"

"Nobody knew. Not my husband, not my friends."

Back then, the scales had been easy to balance. The life the books, the shows, her parents told her to have was waiting, and it would all go away if Cassidy indulged the urges. If she embraced being the anomaly her blood made her.

The voids showed up in middle school. At first Cassidy thought she'd caught a cold. Then she thought insanity, some mental disease. Until, alone in her parent's backyard, Cassidy gave in. The treehouse her dad had built years before vanished, taking half the strong oak with it. Her parents covered, refused to talk about it at the dinner table, in the car, or ever.

"But you didn't stop," Thane said, and it wasn't a question.

Because what anomaly would? When nature makes you unique, how can you cast that away? Cassidy would play with the voids, sneak off during lunch periods, or later between classes to quiet spots where she could focus.

"The Paragons changed everything," Cassidy replied. "Anomalies weren't shamed anymore, weren't treated as threats. But what was I going to do, give up the life I'd made for myself and run away to play superhero?"

"Live a lie, and lie to live. So many do it. Now, you no longer have to."

Cassidy didn't mention they'd been doing just that, and would be again after taking what they needed from the home.

With time to spare—so Cassidy estimated, neither one had a watch—the music died, replaced by a car's electric whirr and tires crunching on gravel. Cassidy held up fingers, counting to a solid twenty as the vehicle's noise dwindled. Thane took the lead, stalking as close as he could manage to the house before breaking into the yard and closing with the nearest window.

"Empty," Thane said to Cassidy, following close. "Let's go."

A locked patio door proved another difference maker between the two anomalies: Thane wanted to smash through and be done with it, but Cassidy went for discretion, touching the handle and creating a small void to sever the lock. A simple pull swept the door open, and Cassidy didn't hide her grin when Thane went by.

Inside, the two broke into separate routines. Thane raided the fridge while Cassidy hit the bedroom and bathroom, finding a shower and thanking her own luck that the homeowner happened to be a woman and not one too far off her size. They swapped after, Thane finding a husband or boyfriend's outfits stashed in the closet.

Filled up and feeling more like real people, and Thane decked out in a flower-patterned shirt, the two left the house and walked down the road. Scattered homes transitioned into a proper town. People joined them on the sidewalks while cars shuffled past—no pods here, apparently. Without any reps to spend, the two went for the one place that might help them: the town's little library.

Thane navigated the town without hesitation, like a drone heading right for its target. Cassidy dragged. The clinic, nursing home, whatever you wanted to call it had been a slow reminder of what real life was like. Technology, processed food, electric lights . . . all that felt new after years apart. Now, absent the clinic's confines and controls, the noise and rapid-fire stimuli whirled her around.

She looked at everything, seeing signs for fast food Cassidy used to enjoy, glancing at a theater sign-posting a second sequel to one of the last movies she'd ever seen. Corner stores advertised beers Cassidy used to drink, sodas that'd been a fridge mainstay and now seemed like lost treasures.

Cassidy could go into any of them, experience any of it. She didn't have the Paragon chains on her anymore, didn't have a drone hovering over her shoulder ready to shoot if she strayed from the path.

"Here," Thane said, nodding across the street towards the library. "Before we can make a plan, I need to know what's going on."

Before they'd left the prison island, Thane had gone on about some grand future. A struggle with the Paragons that he, with Cassidy's help, would win. The world would be remade and so on and so forth. Cassidy could admire the man's vision, had even bought into it back on the island, but now, as they walked across a street—a street!—Cassidy brought her hand together and rubbed the spot where her wedding ring had been.

Everything Thane had said came before this feeling, this opening. Why would she throw herself back into a fight against forces that'd beaten Cassidy so soundly last time? That had taken Thane and thrown him onto an island jail without much effort?

"Cassidy?" Thane said, and Cassidy realized she'd dropped his hand, was standing in the library's six spot parking lot like a woman possessed. "What's wrong?"

"It's overwhelming," Cassidy said, somewhere between a truth and a lie. "All of this. I didn't expect it."

"I felt the same when I left the Paragon's hold," Thane said. Left was an interesting word choice. Cassidy recalled Thane mentioning a subtle effort to get him broken out, and destruction followed. "The world did not wait for me, but I caught it anyway."

"Is that what happened?"

"The Paragons thought us caged, Cassidy, and we are now free. We have taken the first step, and now the second awaits."

Back on the island, Thane's grandiose language came across as almost endearing: big dreams and big ambitions in a space that allowed none. Here, preaching near signs detailing late fees and weekend hours, Cassidy had to hide a laugh.

As Thane turned back to the library, the Void made a small promise to herself: if Thane decided on a perilous course, she would leave him. This, already, was too much to lose.

Computers came back quick. The little library had four, three still open with the last occupied by a dazed looking man perusing what looked like sports. Thane and Cassidy set up shoulder-to-shoulder, clicking through prompts warning the duo against any illegal, illicit, or immoral activities.

The Internet and all its glory sat before Cassidy, beckoning her to learn what she'd missed. Thane, on her right, didn't hesitate. In seconds he had tabs open by the multitude, his body shrinking and shriveling as Thane absorbed information and pieced it together into something terrible and miraculous.

Cassidy typed in a news brand. Scanned the headlines. Widened her eyes at the articles about the explosion in LA, Aegis's death, Paragons in disarray. Why reinforcements hadn't come to halt their island escape became very clear: who cared about a few prisoners when terrorists threatened Paragon existence?

"I missed a lot," Cassidy muttered.

"We both did," Thane said. "As you can see, the world is in trouble. We can fix it."

"Can you stop doing that?"

"What?"

"Talking like you're a literal god come down to save us. I mean, here I am worrying about how we're going to get lunch and your head's so far in the clouds I can't even . . . " Cassidy let the words peter out. Thane's look went uglier and uglier as she spoke, and the last thing Cassidy needed right now was a punch-out with her only ally. "Sorry, it's just a lot right now."

Maybe her eyes hit the right slant, maybe the teacher in her inflected the proper tone to get Thane off aggression's cliff, but the man nodded and turned back to his screen. Cassidy did likewise, the break slicing the world news and its hold on her away even as its events told Cassidy she needed someone to talk to that wasn't, you know, an anomaly bent on world domination.

Opening up a chat with the other man opposite them, the one so intent on his screen that sweat seemed to be leaking down his face, wouldn't fly. Cassidy could get up and try a talk with the library's sole employee, but the woman appeared head down in a book. Going back to the screen for ideas, a button caught Cassidy's eye, slotted right in the favorites section.

Clicking over to her old email, Cassidy typed in her address, laughing at how easily the password came back to her. She'd changed it every year, her oldest's name and his growing age. Cassidy expected some welcome back alert, some sign that the email provider had noticed her years-long disappearance.

Nothing. Nothing except a million messages waiting for her. Cassidy didn't bother reading them—what could possibly be important in there to someone with no home, no assets, no existence?—but, instead, she clicked right over to start a new email. Her targets swept in quick, defaulted by the provider as if the faraway servers could read Cassidy's heart.

Cassidy's children, their emails created for school so long ago. Her husband too. No, she deleted his name. While Cassidy couldn't fault him entirely for doing what he'd done—calling in the alert, declaring her a danger— she didn't want her first free words going his way.

The Void typed. Sentences flew by and the screen blurred as she fell into what she needed to say, what she wanted to tell. The island, its inhabitants, the fight for survival. And, at last, that she'd escaped. Cassidy hesitated over that last line.

"Do it," Thane said and Cassidy snapped a look his way. Had he been reading? "Tell them you will see them soon. Tell them you miss them, you love them, and every-thing else. What harm can it cause?"

What harm. Thane might have it right, though Cassidy doubted they'd come anywhere near her family in the future. But perhaps her children, likely in college or beyond already, would get some hope they might see their mother again.

Clicking send brought a smile, had Cassidy relaxing into her chair. She felt a hand on hers, glanced at Thane and saw him matching her look. Cassidy nearly asked him if he'd done the same, when she remembered.

"There's nobody?"

"I have many associates who will be interested to know I am alive and out," Thane replied. "I have nobody who will look as happy as your children will to receive the news."

"I'm sorry." Celice couldn't think of anything else to say.

"There's nothing to apologize for." Thane let her hand go, pushed back from the workstation, and stood. "Let's go. I know where we need to head next."

"And that is?"

"The airport."

Thane said the location with so much confidence that Cassidy didn't bother asking what the hell they'd do when they arrived. No reps, no identification, no Tamas meant Paragon laws wouldn't let them on a plane. Either Thane thought they could break their way in, or he had something better in mind.

The pair made it three steps into the parking lot before two police pods rolled up, positioning themselves across the library's entry. The pods, a blue and gold color, didn't open their doors fully but lowered them halfway, giving the officers inside cover. Stun guns came out, their dark black nozzles pointing towards the two anomalies. Not a single one offered up an explanation.

"I'm guessing they found us," Cassidy said in the silence.

"Yes."

Cassidy glanced over at Thane, the man's body swelling up. One word answers tended to be a giveaway that Thane was on his way to rage mode, where his brain would operate on single syllables while his muscles solved the problem.

"You're going to want to leave us alone," Cassidy shouted to the officers. "He's not going to stop if you start, and you won't win."

The officers stayed still, quiet. Thane kept growing. Cassidy looked around for a starting signal while she tapped into that urge, brought the voids to her fingertips. Together, the two could scrap the officers and their pods in seconds, then rampage through the city right to the airport. Sure, the Paragons would catch up to them eventually, but what other choice did they have?

A jingling sound broke the breezy silence, a happy tune rolling up from the sidewalk as a young man in a Paragon uniform, one stretching to hold its occupant, approached on a bike. Wearing a backpack that looked stuffed to the brim, the man strode past the officers, brushed long dark curls from his eyes and took in the two anomalies.

"Thane?" the Paragon asked.

"Yes," Thane replied, balling his fists.

"Cool. And you? I don't know you?" He looked at Cassidy. "A sidekick?"

"A partner," Cassidy replied. "Call me the Void."

"Nice name. I'm Bits, and I'm going to be real honest. There's nothing here that's gonna stop either of you. I sure as heck can't, and those guys and gals down there will try real hard, but it's not going to work out."

"Correct," Thane said.

"So how about we skip all the murder and mayhem and get right to what you want," Bits said. "'Cause I'm gonna guess we all want the same thing."

"For us to leave?" Cassidy said, not quite believing what was happening.

"And the Void wins the prize!" Bits shouted, and as he did, his backpack opened, shooting little fireworks into the sky over his head. As each one popped, metal nuts and washers and screws fell to the ground around him.

Bits did not appear to notice.

"So here's the deal," Bits said. "My friends here will give you an escort to the plane station, then you'll jump on a flight to wherever. I'll tell the Paragons where you're heading, and you all can beat each other up when you land, okeydokey?"

Cassidy heard a soft growl from Thane and decided to cut the big man off before he did something stupid, like destroy a town for no reason.

"Deal," Cassidy said, then pointed at Thane. "But he's not fitting in those pods."

Bits snapped his fingers, and all those washers and nuts from his fireworks flung themselves at his bike, matched by supporting bars, chains, and more from his backpack. Together, they strung themselves along the bike's frame, bulking it up to a formidable size. When the new bike sat ready, Bits threw Thane a curious look.

"Can he ride?"

9

A Gilded Snare

Start the day with shots fired, end it with shots taken.

Wexley put on his best face, a slight uptick on his right lip, eyebrows ever so slightly raised. The elevators opened and Wexley gave his bemused, happy-to-be-here expression to a waiting server pair. One handed him a champagne glass, Wexley returned the gesture with a nod as he went in.

The hotel's ballroom, a glittering space overlooking Millennium Park and its moving statues, had been done up in Paragon blues and whites. Anomalies in action blasted across screens hanging down from the walls, breaking every so often to an In Memoriam sequence for Paragons lost in the LA stadium explosion. If anyone noticed the grim reminder stood at odds to the upbeat music pumped by a jazz quartet squirreled away into a marble-lined corner, Wexley didn't see it.

Tables served as setting places for drinks, purses, and random napkins as guests avoided sitting for mingling's economic mobility. Stylized people drifted about, forming clusters and peeling off like some chemical reaction, one

Wexley took in for a long gaze. His Tama, covered by the suit's sleeve, called to him.

Rhimes, the secured gladiator drone—those were a pod ride away, and far more interesting.

"For someone who's attended so many of these, you look nervous," Adriana said, appearing beside him and clinking her glass on his.

If Wexley's tuxedo played a traditional part for a gala, Adriana's own outfit kept things reserved. Understated and black and perfect for a host. Her expression matched the role, polite smile and big eyes. The ruthless ambition from yesterday's call smothered by society's demands.

"It's been an exciting day," Wexley said. "I'm not in a gala mood."

"Set the business aside," Adriana replied. "It will continue without you for a few hours."

"Will it?"

An honest question. Rhimes and his team were competent enough, but Wexley knew the Paragons wouldn't shrug their shoulders at a disappeared drone. The anomalies would be hunting everywhere, and one might have an ability able to chop through the signal-blocking blanket Rhimes had around the captive machine. Rhimes knew to drop the drone at discovery's first sign, but if that came before Wexley had his time with the gladiator . . .

"Come on," Adriana said. "Let me introduce you to someone interesting. She's been wanting to meet you for a while, and I think you two would have much to talk about."

"And what about us, when do we get to talk?" Wexley asked as he followed Adriana around the ballroom's outskirts.

"Not here, but perhaps elsewhere. Later."

Ah, so Adriana figured people were listening. A

Paragon benefit event, one pulled together by Chicago's elite to show solidarity with the beleaguered anomalies, didn't seem like the place to hunt for those trying to undermine society at large, but Wexley could keep his mouth shut.

Making benign small talk, like anything else, was a skill. Zhan-Yo had taught Wexley that much.

Adriana brought Wexley up behind a taller, older woman and tapped the woman's shoulder. She turned around and Wexley's own defenses climbed to their maximum. He wasn't armed, but Wexley loosened his knees, his muscles tensed, and if he had to, he figured a quick smash-and-slice could turn his champagne flute into a murder weapon.

"Wexley, this is Beth. She's thinking about investing in your business and wanted to meet," Adriana said, before giving Wexley's arm a little squeeze and disappearing back into the ball.

Beth gave Wexley a warm shark's smile. She cradled a highball glass like it was some crystal ball, but otherwise matched Wexley's stare with a soft look of her own. As she did, Wexley felt his own nerves melting away, concerns drifting and dying. What was there to be worried about? This was a ball, well-protected by Paragons and police security.

The Elementals would surely not try and get revenge here.

"I've been waiting a long time to meet you," Beth said, and Wexley noted her previous conversational partners flanked out around him, wrapping Wexley in a neat body circle. "I feel we've seen each other from afar so many times."

Through Wexley's rifle scope, at least.

Wexley almost said the words before catching himself.

His mind fogged, veering between choices. He hadn't eaten anything—had the champagne sips hit him that hard?

"I'm sure we have," Wexley hit upon a line he could use. "Chicago is such a small city, after all."

He laughed at his own joke, while Beth delivered another pleasant smile mismatched with her icy eyes.

"But now we can rectify that mistake," Beth said. "Put things right, if you will."

How could Adriana have slung Wexley, alone, into this trap? Did the woman not know who Beth was? A possibility, and one Wexley had to let go. He had to shake this malaise, had to find an excuse to get away before this turned grim.

"Adriana mentioned you wanted to discuss investments?" Wexley offered.

"I think we're past that. Do you know a tracker by the name of Kat Collins?"

"Heard of her."

"She passed along an interesting tidbit. You may or may not know that some friends of mine have been targeted lately. Targeted in a very vicious way."

"I'm sorry?" Wexley asked. He backed up, felt a table behind him. Beth followed his retreat, while her friends, two thickset men with nary an emotion in their bones, covered his sides. "I'm not following."

"That's because you're doing the shooting," Beth said.

Now. Wexley should've made his move in that second, taken advantage of Beth's triumphant declaration. Instead, Wexley couldn't find his arm, couldn't seem to remember how to tell it to move. He saw Beth's eyes and in them felt a mortal peace.

"I failed," Wexley said, no longer bothering to hide the truth. "I wanted chaos, and I failed."

Beth, who'd shifted the glass to one hand while sending the other towards her waist, waited. Beyond her, the jazz quartet shifted vibes to a bouncier, faster tune. Someone called for more crab cakes.

"The shootings should have triggered a war," Wexley continued. "You should've gone to the Paragons for help, and they would've blamed you for what happened next. Instead, Kat found me first. And Zhan-Yo did my job."

"You wanted the stadium explosion?"

"Zhan-Yo thinks the world can be equalized. I know better." Wexley shook his head. "The evidence is everywhere. When a better form arises, the old species goes extinct."

"A dangerous view."

Wexley couldn't agree more, but his tongue had gone numb. His whole body felt static, an incomprehensible maze that Wexley couldn't navigate. He leaned back against the table because standing no longer seemed doable. His hands fell, his fingers relaxed.

The champagne glass fell, hit the hard floor, and shattered.

Beth took a step back, and into her gap swept servers so intent on removing the shards that they took no notice of their surroundings. Wexley couldn't find Beth's eyes with the servers in the way, and like a river rushing through a dry valley, his own self returned. Lurching to his right, Wexley pushed on the table to give himself some room.

Beth's friend that way, a sturdy man coated in tattoos, gripped Wexley's arm. Wexley stamped his foot on the man's own, grinding his heel. His attacker released the hold with a whispered curse, and Wexley moved on. He scoured the crowd for a moment, looking for Adriana, and saw her meshed with some other group.

She caught Wexley's eye, though, and faltered at the glare he fired her way.

Then the richest, most powerful man in the room, fled.

WEXLEY HAD the coordinates from Rhimes before he hit the pod, was walking through a reinforced warehouse door half-an-hour later. Still in his tuxedo, Wexley drew looks from a squad pulled together to both dissect and protect the captive drone. Slung into a lead-lined shipping container, the drone fit snug as welding lights and flying sparks showcased efforts to take the machine apart.

"Mynx made'em strong," Rhimes said as Wexley walked in. "We'll get there, though."

"How much longer?"

No matter what Rhimes answered, Wexley would give him the time. Already, looking at the jumbled creation before him, Wexley felt power's sweet kiss. A warm glow. Nobody had taken one of these down before, and here Wexley was, the sole victor. Another blow struck against the Paragons and their invincibility complex.

Every second those anomalies didn't have this drone, didn't know what happened to it, was another second Wexley had to bask in his own victory.

"Another day at most," Rhimes said. "After that, this thing's going to be too hot to keep."

"Whatever you need. Take as long as you have to."

"Sir," Rhimes said, voice dropping quieter, though with the hissing, cracking from the welding, eavesdropping wasn't going to be easy. "I appreciate the confidence, but the Paragons will find this thing. When they do, they won't send in a few rookie anomalies."

"I'm counting on it."

"I'm sorry?"

Wexley glanced at Rhimes, "The drone's a trap. It's going to draw the Paragons to wherever we put it. If the right ones show up, then we can end this fight before it really starts."

"Then what're we breaking it apart for?"

"Taking the top means we have to hold it," Wexley said, raising his voice and stepping closer to the truck-sized drone. He reached out, ran a gloved hand over the thing's fine black metal. "You're right. Enough anomalies could overpower us. If we learn how to use these, though?"

Rhimes gave his characteristic slow triple nod. Always the same gesture whenever the man agreed with something serious.

The two escaped the welding noise and went back outside, to the late night docks and their quieter, if not too quiet, churn.

"The Elementals came after me tonight," Wexley said once they stood alone, overlooking Lake Michigan's dark waters. "At the gala."

"I wondered why you left so early."

"Beth, their leader, was there. I don't know how she managed a ticket, but she had help too. Without dropping my damn glass, they would've had me."

"I keep telling you to up your security," Rhimes said, not sounding the least surprised.

Wexley had rebuffed that advice. He enjoyed his runs to the van, the secret stash, and his own independence too much to have a detail following him around. No matter how discrete, security guards could be spotted, which would in turn mark Wexley as someone important. His anonymity would disappear, and so would his favorite hobbies.

"I don't like playing defense," Wexley said. "How can we attack?"

"The Elementals? We already tried that. You just pissed them off."

Wexley laughed, "I scored a few hits."

"For someone so intent on winning a war, a few hits isn't going to cut it."

A fair point. Maybe Wexley needed to stop thinking of the Elementals as a sideshow to the main Paragon threat. Maybe he needed to wipe them away at the same time, or even before. Then again, the Elementals were dangerous. Contemplating sacrificing his own people in a guns-blazing assault had Wexley frowning, watching the moon's reflection and waiting for answers.

A black smudge marred the reflection. Wexley looked up to see a drone sweeping out to inspect an incoming ship, a glistening thing with moonlight splashed all over it. An enemy and an idea in one.

"Rhimes, I know how we can start our war." Wexley gripped the man's shoulder and began spilling the plan.

LEAVING RHIMES TO THE EXECUTION, Wexley found another pod and took it north, beyond Chicago's core and the most immediate suburbs. The pod pulled into a calm, quiet estate with some name so generic Wexley never bothered remembering it. Nonetheless, the staff at the place, despite the hour, were ready for him.

Two, in their scrubs and looking attentive, waited at the entrance for Wexley to leave the pod. They greeted him with a name that was not his, one that Wexley accepted without comment. The dance continued through the lobby, a cursory check-in. Wexley went through the metal detector, and when it went off, he ignored the beeps, as did everyone else. The signs said visiting hours were long over, but not a one said a word his way.

Not that they should, for how much Wexley paid them.

A tall and burly pair escorted Wexley through to the facility's back. He passed by an exercise room, a nice pool beneath huge skylights, and a cafeteria serving snacks to some late-night residents. Few eyes met his as Wexley walked, and he paid attention to none.

His escorts left him at a certain door, beige and plain, with the name *Regina Smith* overlaid across its front. Wexley turned the knob, went inside to the spacious room. Pleasant furniture bedecked with flowered fabrics lay about the space, lit only by a floor lamp trio staking out the corners.

Wexley's target stood center, by big glass windows looking out into a wooded acre.

"The deer come more often in the Winter," Regina said as Wexley came up next to her. "I like being able to see their tracks."

"The mud might work just as well."

Regina shrugged, "The snow is prettier."

Hard to argue with that.

"Why did you come?" Regina asked after several long seconds watching trees shift in the dark. "Are you finished?"

"Not yet, but we are coming closer."

"How close?" Regina looked at him as she asked the question, a spark flaring behind those green eyes.

"They will tear each other apart, giving the world back to us."

"To you."

"To me, yes," Wexley didn't deny it. "But you know this is the right thing. No more families like ours. No more tragedies." Wexley took her hand. "You're staying up with the treatments?"

"As if I had a choice," Regina said, but she didn't add any spice to the words. "It's nice here, Wexley. It's safe."

"That's what's important."

"I know. I know." Regina rubbed his hand. "I wish I could be out there, though. Helping you."

"Too dangerous. You can't."

If his reply hurt Regina, she didn't show it. Wexley looked hard, too. He always did. Regina needed to accept her state. Any sign otherwise would mean an increase in her medications, a tighter watch.

"You're right, of course. I'm happy here, Wexley. I really am."

"Good." Wexley put up a sigh. "Sometimes I wish we could switch places, you and I. The pool out there looks nice."

Regina smiled, "But then you would be the monster."

ADRIANA LIT up Wexley's Tama with messages, ones Wexley browsed well after midnight as the pod brought him back to his apartment. She started out wondering where Wexley had gone—the bathroom?—and escalated to confusion and even a little panic as he refused a response. Wexley leaned back against the pod's thin cushion and browsed the words, looking for a sign.

Had Adriana known the Elementals would be there? She led Wexley right to Beth, right into the trap. The move had either been a calculated hit or an innocent mistake.

If Wexley treated it as an assassination attempt, one Adriana was in on, then he would have to sever ties with the woman and her organization. Her reps would be lost to him, her support with all those other wavering businesses who couldn't see their salvation so close at hand. Without them, Wexley would be vulnerable, his ambitions limited by his allies.

No. Unacceptable. Backing off now would allow the Paragons to recover, would allow the world to fall back into its normal state. Zhan-Yo's catastrophic moves would have been for nothing.

No, Wexley had to hope Adriana wasn't turning on him. He needed her on his side.

He tapped away a response on his Tama, an excuse about a sudden illness. Simple, standard, and an easy escape. Adriana replied minutes later, as Wexley's pod arrived at his apartment.

Liar.

Wexley stared at his Tama, the small screen holding a question. Wexley needed Adriana, so perhaps it was time to bring her into the real fold. Wrap her up like him, so she had no alternative. Change the world, or die trying.

You want the truth? Come and learn.

Events were speeding up, hurtling towards a moment Wexley could never take back.

Good.

Joyride

The message came an hour after the pod dropped Celice. It had an address and a time. Tomorrow evening, late.

Sleep played fast and loose that night, dancing on her fringes as Celice tried, lying in a sparse bed, to capture it. London's lights split her window, casting shadows that always seemed to take menacing shapes. Celice hadn't been scared of the dark since Aegis showed her how to throw a punch, how to hide a knife and a gun beneath her pillow and pull both out in a second's fraction.

Zhan-Yo knew where she lived. Knew Celice was in London, and had the power to kill her without much struggle. A sniper could've picked her off in that courtyard. How easily could they attack her in this apartment now, swamping Celice with overwhelming numbers?

Dreams came with dawn, and Celice picked up a couple hours sleep before, sweaty and chilled at the same time, she forced herself from the bed. The apartment's living room served as a base for a yoga session, stretching herself awake one position at a time. A cold shower coupled with slapdash clothes to get Celice outside, a cool and misty morning breached here and there by London's lamp posts.

With a small gun tucked into a shoulder holster and her knife plastered to her thigh, Celice pulled up the location Zhan-Yo's people sent along and went. Ten hours till the appointed meeting time, but any smart mission started with scouting out the situation. Where would an ambush come from, what were the escape routes, how many civilians might be around?

Hostages or concerns?

Celice didn't have an answer for her father's question. The Paragon way accepted necessary casualties, but this wasn't a Paragon mission. Celice didn't have their cover, so anyone hurt, even killed by something she did would be all on her. Would Mynx or the other Champions protect her from the consequences?

Maybe, but given the mess the Paragons were in right now—Celice read up on the disasters while grabbing coffee from a sidewalk shop—she doubted any Champion would have time or reputation to spend on Aegis's daughter. Not when Celice had disappeared so fast during a moment when the Paragons could've used anyone and everyone's help.

The coffee and its paper cup didn't offer advice on that choice. Neither did the cobblestone sidewalk nor the occasional passing car. Passersby hugged their Tamas. Celice would've done likewise, except the wristlet would have nothing except disdain waiting for her.

Mynx and other Paragons kept calling, kept sending messages. Every missive joined a pile-up, waiting for Celice. Waiting for a mental state she refused to find while Zhan-Yo was so close.

That was the answer. That's why she left.

"I wouldn't have helped anyone like this," Celice said,

crossing into and through another posh park greeting winter's end with dripping green.

"What's that?" asked an older man walking ahead, looking back at her with curious wrinkles.

"Nothing, sorry," Celice replied, then sped up her steps.

Self-pity serves nothing.

Ah yes. One of her father's favorite lines when Celice had been younger, when she'd been prone to depressed bouts going through school with few friends and fewer opportunities. Nobody wanted to risk displeasing the Paragon leader, and that led to endless respectful declines or fake starring roles whenever Celice tried to participate.

Instead, Aegis suggested she sink all those extra hours into training time, into computer skills and whatever else Aegis believed the Paragons could use. And now here it was, paying off. Once again, her father had been right.

Sitting just off the Thames, on a curving edge away from tourist hunts, Zhan-Yo's chosen meeting place appeared to be a discrete restaurant with zero curb appeal. Faded gold lettering across the top named it *Carlisle*, and the scant cream cloth-covered tables inside indicated some attempt at luxury. No menu hung in the windows, no hours pasted on the front door for casual passers-by.

Celice made one walking pass, then circled around for the second, taking off her jacket and tying it around the waist to give a slight change to her appearance. Not that any serious looker would be fooled, but a half-hearted glance from someone inside might be. Whether Zhan-Yo had the restaurant staff in his employ or not, Celice didn't know, but better to be safe.

After last night, she looked at the rooftops too. Apartments filled in the space above the *Carlisle*, the restaurant meshing hard with shops nearby, giving little ground for stealthy ambushes or hideaways. Maybe Zhan-Yo chose the place for that very reason: with nowhere to sneak about, everyone could feel more at ease.

The *Carlisle* didn't provide any evidence, any hints about what was coming. Celice walked away slow, dishing glances back, hoping someone might step out in pursuit, that she could burn off the coffee's spark, the night's lingering malaise with an impromptu interrogation.

The sidewalks remained quiet.

For precisely one block.

A pod pulled before Celice as she neared the next narrow cross-street. She stopped, hard and fast enough for her coffee to slosh over the cup's rim and splatter the ground before her. A blue pod, cheery enough on the outside, glaring passengers inside, but nothing else. Until, anyway, doors popped and two blue-and-white suited Paragons rose up to look at her.

"Celice?" said one, a woman whose hands already glowed an emerald green as she stood on the curb. "You have to come with us."

"That's your opener?" Celice said. "I thought the Paragons tried to be above cliches."

"She's serious," said her partner, a dude who looked skinnier than a stick. "Name's Roger, she's Sydney, and you're in danger out here."

"The revelations keep on coming," Celice replied, falling into her usual comfort. Dealing with Zhan-Yo and his shadowy thugs was new, defying Paragon demands was decidedly not. "Where is it you want to take me?"

Sydney looked up and behind Celice's left shoulder, frowning, and Celice followed her eyes to see a drone coming around the river's bend. Back-up in case Aegis's daughter resisted, or to help suppress an attack?

"It's not far," Sydney said, "and it's safe."

"You keep saying that like it's going to convince me." Celice finished her coffee, tossed it in a nearby waste bin. "How about you two leave me your number, and if I get into trouble, I'll give you a call."

Celice started to walk away and failed. When she went to lift her foot for a step, Celice found her right leg unable to lift. Not numb, not severed, just sealed to the stone beneath it. Her left leg locked the same way. Closing her eyes to take a big breath, Celice opened them and dished a frosty smile at Sydney, her hands glowing a brighter green than before.

"There's no reason this can't be easy," said Roger. "A short trip, that's all."

Gun in shoulder holster. Knife against her thigh. Celice could pull either one, could probably get an attack off before the Paragons stopped her. Spilling Paragon blood, though, seemed like a poor plan. Still, Celice did not want to get in that pod.

Her feet moved. One, then the other. Celice felt like a child, when Aegis would lift her up and spin her around through the air, her limbs utterly at gravity's mercy. Sydney, manipulating Celice, guided her to the curb's edge, and Celice opened the pod's door, leaving a gray fuzzy seat clear for Aegis's daughter.

Don't let them take you.

Celice went for the gun, but her arm had the wrong angle. While her right hand made it inside her jacket, Celice had to turn for a good shot. As she moved, Celice felt her right foot go free, stumbling her step into a fall. Her right hand, closing around the gun in its holster, didn't listen to Celice anymore. Instead, Celice saw her hand leave the gun alone, leave her jacket, and pull Celice into the pod.

"That's not very nice," Celice said, giving up the resistance. "If you wanted me to come, you could've asked politely."

"We did," Sydney said.

Beside her, Roger tapped a destination into the pod's panel. Sitting down, Celice felt her left foot go free. Felt her left hand lock down. Both folded across one another in her lap.

"Neat ability," Celice said.

"Thanks," Sydney replied, then fell silent.

Celice settled into the seat, watching the two Paragons as the pod went along in silence. Nervous energy crackled, and Celice caught Roger's eyes flicking her way every other second. Sydney drummed her hands on her pod door, the green glow waving in the movement.

These two were not cool under pressure.

Why wouldn't they be happier? They'd just taken Aegis's daughter, dropped her in the pod per their mission's orders, and now cruised through London, objective accomplished. If her father's Paragon adventures were accurate at all, witty banter should've been bouncing back and forth. Instead, these two looked like they were about to have a panic attack.

Anomalies could be plenty dangerous when sane. Celice had seen enough reports of Paragons who'd lost control and the disasters that followed. One way to bring someone down? Give them a question they can answer.

"Who sent you?" Celice asked, putting as gentle a spin on the words as she could manage.

"Gatete doesn't want you to die on his watch," Rogers replied, the pod swinging onto an M road heading west. "It's not a good look."

The name flickered. One of Lukas's lieutenants. The European Champion had died in the LA explosion, meaning there'd be a big vacancy at the top. One Gatete might compete for, one that'd be hard to get with Celice sitting dead in his home.

One that'd be hard to get if Zhan-Yo, Aegis's killer, were found to be living under Gatete's nose.

"You know why I'm in town?" Celice asked.

"We have ideas," Sydney replied.

"And instead of helping, you're kidnapping me?"

"Keeping you safe," Roger interjected.

"Gatete gives the orders," Sydney said, sounding about as pleased with it as Celice was to be sitting in the pod.

"Is Gatete going to be where we're going?"

"That's his choice," Roger said. "Not yours."

"It's not as easy as you think," Sydney added.

Celice caught Roger's sharp look Sydney's way. A rift there, one growing and ready to be exploited. Roger, the loyal associate. Sydney, the doubtful ally.

"What would you do, if your father's killer was within reach?" Celice asked as the pod abandoned London's urban confines for towns and train tracks.

"We're all sorry about Aegis," Roger said. "I met him once. A good man."

"A murdered Paragon."

"Who wouldn't want to see his daughter wind up the same way," Roger replied.

Who wouldn't want his daughter to give up, either. Roger's words confirmed the angle: get Celice into a box where she couldn't get hurt, wait till Gatete had his reputation secured, then bounce her out and claim all the credit for keeping the human alive. Celice gave herself good marks on her fighting and spying skills, but she didn't want to try getting out of a Paragon cell.

With her hands stuck, Celice shifted her feet, ready to bunch up her knees as the pod zipped along the highway. Once she had the plan worked out, Celice waited for too many minutes as the pod reached the turnoff, slowing as they left the highway for a cute road through rolling, sheep-coated hills.

A crossing up ahead demanded a stop and gave Celice a chance. As the pod slowed Celice brought up her knees, feet against the pod's front dash. As the anomalies asked what Celice was doing, she kicked hard, cracking the display. She kicked again, until Celice felt Sydney's ability shift. Celice's feet froze, her hands went free.

Leaving Celice able to reach for, draw, and shoot the gun.

The bullet went right where Celice aimed, straight into the pod's center panel, where Roger had put in the address minutes ago. The pod, moving into the intersection, triggered its emergency protections, popping open the doors and rolling to a stop.

People stared from their own pods as Celice, feeling Sydney swap control to her hands, kicked off the pod's floor, throwing her right shoulder into Sydney's chin. The hit knocked Sydney's head back against the pod's headrest, the anomaly's control disappearing.

Sydney's ability needed her concentration. Good to know.

Roger grabbed for Celice's left hand, a move she countered with an elbow jab to the man's sternum. While Roger gasped for lost breath, Celice kicked her way across Sydney, rolling free from the pod.

She stood in a quiet intersection with eyes all on Celice, holding a gun. Grassy hills offered zero places to run, even fewer to hide. The plan freed Celice from the pod. She hadn't thought farther than that.

"You just had to make an ass of yourself, didn't you?" Roger said, standing up beside his door and glaring at

Celice. "Sydney thinks she's concussed, I count at least six people here staring at us."

"That's what happens when you try to kidnap me," Celice countered, keeping the gun level but backing away down the road one step at a time. Roger didn't move to follow. "I didn't come looking for you."

Roger put a hand up, rubbed his forehead. With his other hand, the Paragon spun a finger in a small circle. Odd gestures and anomalies had a way of combining for bad outcomes, so Celice turned heel and started to run.

And hit a big block, a man standing right in the road. A faint violet glow faded around the newcomer's body: Roger's apparent ability showing itself. Celice bounced back, snapped the gun up only to feel the weapon fade. Like snowflakes in a breeze, the gun blew apart into fragments, swirling into a nice, soft pile. Turning her hand over, Celice let the flakes float to the earth.

"Morning, Gatete," Celice said. London's Paragon leader, standing near two-and-a-half meters, loomed over her. "Surprised to see you here."

"Where Aegis went, problems followed," Gatete said. "I am not surprised to see his daughter continues the tradition."

"Proudly."

Gatete looked beyond Celice, "Roger, take Sydney and head to the compound. We will meet you there."

"All right," Roger answered with zero hesitation, a breezy acceptance considering he'd be leaving Gatete alone with Celice.

Then again, Gatete had a strong reputation.

Gatete jumped out from the anomaly ranks early on by being so damn devoted, and having a rockstar ability to boot. While Lukas never said Gatete matched his flare for the dramatic or the dumb, the former European lead always seemed to throw assignment's Gatete's way, particularly hard ones.

That competence merged its way into how Gatete stood now, skipping his Paragon suit for a more traditional sweater, jeans, and sneakers. As if Roger had interrupted the man on a stroll through a library, rather than managing the ongoing Paragon disaster.

"Shall we?" Gatete waved behind Celice, to an intersection now free as Roger took the gunshot car and every observer decided they didn't want to stick around an anomaly conflict. "It's not a far walk, and I feel you and I could use a conversation."

"I'm not here on Paragon business, Gatete, and I'm not going to cause you any problems."

"No?" Gatete said, and Celice found herself walking beside him, two steps to equal his every long one. "But you will attack people on my streets. Spy on them in my restaurants."

"Your restaurants? Didn't—"

"Stop," Gatete said, in the firm, gentle tones of a tired father. While their voices were nothing alike, Celice recognized Aegis in Gatete's exasperation. "Your generation always seems to like picking fights."

"Now there's a stereotype."

"Rooted in reality, I assure you," Gatete replied. They crossed the intersection, heading towards the town proper. "You can guess why I do not want you known on my streets."

"I'm here for Zhan-Yo. I get him, then I'm gone."

"Or he could get you, and then I am in trouble."

"Up till now, you could've argued you didn't know."

Gatete laughed, a jolly rumble, "Mynx told me the moment you'd booked your flight."

Mynx? Celice had covered her tracks well. She'd

bought the tickets with alternate identities, used reps not linked to her account or her father's. She'd avoided cameras, avoided calls. She'd done everything except ditch her Tama, the central connection to everything the modern world had to offer.

The sigh lasted long. Perhaps Celice needed to re-evaluate her incognito credentials.

"Even if you had evaded her," Gatete said, "we would have found you soon enough. Your face is known."

"Uh huh." Celice folded her arms, studied the pretty cross-hatch shutters in the homes as they went by. "So what happens now, you stuff me in a closet somewhere?"

"Not quite. Instead, I believe we can help each other."

"How's that?"

"You want your father's killer. I want Lukas's spot as a Champion. If I help you catch Zhan-Yo, then you will endorse me."

"Or?"

"Or," Gatete said, smiling, "I will, as you said, stuff you in a closet."

11

Detective Work

The plan put itself together over Chinese takeout and background bebop tunes, a musical phase Kat embraced post assassination attempts for some reason Calvin couldn't fathom. Together the pair, plus Seeker, turned Kat's apartment into a mission map: random objects became entries to the docks, with Calvin's prized sneaker serving as the drone's location against Kat's cream carpet.

The tracker found some unusual videos posted on various social media outlets, ones showing the gladiator drone picking on a walking woman before suffering what looked like a coordinated assault. Despite its best mechanized efforts, the drone faltered and fell to an effective ragtag band—Calvin remarked that the Paragons could learn a thing or two from these people—and then most videos cut off.

"Why?" Kat said as they stood near her big monitor. "You'd think everyone would want the victory caught on tape. The aftermath, all the signs showing how dangerous and reckless these drones supposedly are, but it's not here."

"They got scared?" Calvin answered.

"Right, that makes sense. Someone went around and told them to stop the recording or else," Kat grinned. "Guess who wasn't intimidated?"

"I dunno, a dog cam or something?"

"A little kid. Posts under the name BoogerBoy22. He took this from his bedroom window," Kat said, clicking to a different video.

"Was he, like, not in school?"

"This all took place before six, Calvin. When do you think schools open?"

"No idea."

Kat screwed up her face, "Were you not a kid?"

Calvin stepped back, folded his arms. "Not like you."

"Oh, right, sorry," Kat said, letting the edges drop. "But you're telling me you never went to school? Ever?"

"Can we get back to the point?" Calvin shook his left wrist, the Tama on it. "I'm afraid Weed's gonna call me back onto another patrol. That guy's crazy."

"He's a Paragon, what do you expect?"

At Calvin's rolling eyes, Kat went back to the monitor, found BoogerBoy22's video and plopped it up. Shot from a second story window, the angle held a different depiction. Calvin caught bullets coming in from above, clashing against the drone's armor and letting blue lightning flare. The other recordings, taken from the ground, didn't have the same clarity, didn't prove quite so well the damn attack was an ambush.

"That changes things," Calvin said.

"Keep watching," Kat replied. "It gets better."

BoogerBoy22 showed his potential future in the movies by keeping the angle steady, though the kid's muttered commentary, largely repeated exclamations of *oh my gosh* and *holy cow*, revealed room for improvement. As the fight finished, when the other videos cut away or cut off, BoogerBoy22 stayed on it, committed to the end.

A whirring truck squealed into the frame, dropping open its trailer and a large ramp. The swarthy collection of citizens dropped their coordinated attack and turned into luggage loaders, clamping a winch onto the drone and clearing out what debris they could before scrambling into the truck alongside the big machine. BoogerBoy22 followed the whole thing.

"And here's the best part," Kat said.

As the truck's trailer closed, BoogerBoy22 kept the vehicles butt in frame, showing the truck's license plate clear and center. After the truck pulled away, BoogerBoy22 swapped the camera's view, giving a shot of his face.

"And now he goes on for like an hour about what we just saw," Kat said, clicking away. "I tracked the license plate. The truck's registered to a shipping company, one that has its roots right here in Chicago."

"Okay?"

"You know what trackers get?"

"Permission to do whatever they want pursuing innocent anomalies like yours truly?"

"Exactly," Kat said, grinning. "Even better, we get to look at drone footage."

"Wow." Calvin tried to feign enthusiasm, failed to get anything more than an eyebrow raised. "Cool."

"Am I boring you?"

"Nah, this is just what I wanted to do with my evening."

Kat picked up Calvin's mood and sped up the explanation, whipping through footage from a drone cam catching the same truck streaking towards the lake. Kat synced up other drone's surveillance to patch together some good odds about where the truck wound up, and where it still was.

That led to the takeout order, the mapping on the carpet, and a general feel that here, before Calvin and Kat, sat a chance to break this whole thing wide open.

"But why?" Calvin asked, fumbling chopsticks and noodles in one hand. "Like, I get wanting to know what happened, but the Paragons are handling this."

"Aren't you a Paragon?" Kat lounged on her couch, Seeker sitting below and waiting for the occasional dropped orange chicken nugget. "Shouldn't your moral compass be telling you this is the right thing to do?"

"Uh."

"Look, Calvin, I'm not going to tell you how to reconcile being you with being a Paragon," Kat said. "I'm a tracker. A glorified bounty hunter with legal rights tossed my way by a bunch of all-powerful dictators. It's not perfect, but you know, with enough wine and this delicious sauce, I make it work."

"Your point being?"

"Guess how much reps the Paragons are putting up for the drone's location?" Kat had a way of dipping into a scheming smile that Calvin envied, going from sweet to sinister with a second's notice.

"Now I get you," Calvin said. "How much?"

"Enough that I could leave this apartment, and you could get your own place."

Calvin would've been insulted at the implication he'd worn out his welcome in Kat's pad, but the man felt the same way. Kat's couch worked for now, but he could use a real bed. Could use a shower and a bathroom that weren't clogged by dog hair and Kat's skin care armada. Sure, he had a room at the Paragon's tower in Chicago, but wading through protestors and risking assignments by showing his face there made the arrangement seem less like a home and more like a trap.

"So when do we go?" Calvin asked.

"How many more noodles you have?"

"Depends," Calvin replied, glancing at the carton in his left hand. "Give me a fork, we're done in a couple minutes. I stick with these, and it's an hour."

AN HOUR LATER, the two hopped a train heading downtown, buzzing along the mag-levs between rising, lit up buildings shining through the advancing night. Kat had morphed from her takeout-tasting sweats into her pearl-white tracker uniform, while Calvin eschewed the Paragon white-and-blues for a jacket and jeans combo. His leather gloves rested back on his hands, their tingling a whisper he ignored.

They rode the train, crowded despite the drone incident and continued paranoia pounding the press about the Paragons and their plunging prospects. Mynx hadn't managed to reassure people, though she'd declared an imminent trip to Chicago to handle the disappeared drone issue. Conversation floated through the cars about the last time Chicago had a Champion in town.

That'd been Aegis, and he'd died in the city's depths. Not the greatest legacy.

"Mynx might give us the reward herself," Kat said, watching the train's screens and the news chyrons running across them. "How cool would that be?"

"So cool."

Kat rolled her eyes at him, "Someone's stiff tonight."

"It's Weed and all those Paragons, they have me on edge. It's like getting into a club you weren't trying to join, you know?"

"I don't, really."

"Uh huh, like those Elementals? Same deal. We help them, and now we're expected to go along with whatever the hell they're planning."

"Sounds more like you want to go back to running away and living in a scrap heap."

Calvin shrugged, "At least I was free."

"I wouldn't call fleeing from, well, pretty much everyone and hiding in the dark 'free', but it's your life, Calvin. You can run away if you want to."

"Not yet," Calvin said. "I owe that man, Wexley, a punched ticket to whatever his next life is. He shot at you, he shot at me."

Kat settled back into the seat, "Good to know my partner's got vengeance going for him."

"And the reps, Kat. Don't forget those."

The docks rumbled as the two approached, constant tanks and tankers rolling off and on parked ships. Farther south in the city than Calvin had been in a long time, the Paragon plushness gave way to coarser business, just like the far west areas Calvin had called home not all that long ago. Vast streets lit with harsh lights, bordered by warehouses and claimed by trucks motoring back and forth in a constant shuffle.

Kat knew which yard to find, so the two walked along until they came to a familiar logo: the one belonging to the company owning the truck. An orange, leaping tiger. Aggressive for a cargo company, but who was Calvin to critique? He worked for the Paragons, a super-powered organization whose creative marketing involved a stylized 'P' and little else.

A high-standing gate, chain-linked and covered with barbed wire, prevented their entry. Kat didn't let them linger, pushing Calvin forward on the sidewalk past the entrance. Behind it sat a squat hut where someone inside looked to be watching his Tama. Cameras and their red lights loomed from the gate's top. Inside, through the fence, activity made itself evident through shouts, white lights aplenty, and the grind as tools went to work on their targets.

"Are we not going in?" Calvin asked as Kat had them dip into a dark patch between street lights.

"Not through the front door," Kat replied. "We're not trying to fight them all, just confirm that the drone's here."

"Which we can definitely do standing in the dark."

Kat took Calvin back to the plan they'd put together in her apartment. If the gate happened to be shut, not a surprising turn, the next move was to get Kat up and over the fencing. With the tracker inside the dockyard, Calvin would provide back-up while Kat found the drone, snapped the requisite photos, and booked it out. A good plan, except it meant Calvin would pace out here doing nothing.

"Sorry," Kat said, adjusting the gauntlet on her right wrist. "Maybe if you had a useful ability, you know . . ."

Calvin gave her a light push, "Shut up and get going. We'll see who talks trash when I have to save your ass."

Kat gave him a wink, then took a swift run towards the fence. As she ran, Kat extended her right arm and fired her grapple. The rope looped over the fence's top and Kat activated the grapple's draw as she jumped, pulling her into a running climb up the fence's side. As Kat neared the top with all that nasty barbed wire, she jumped, relying on her momentum and the grapple's retraction to swing her up and over the barbs.

Swinging overhead, Kat released her grapple, falling over the fence's other side as the wire sucked back into her gauntlet. Kat rolled as she hit the ground, rising and flashing a quick thumb's up Calvin's way before disappearing into the container maze.

Calvin edged back, putting himself in the shadows between two streetlights. Beyond the dockyard noise and the gentle breeze coming off the lake, the night felt familiar, like he'd stepped back to those earlier years diving in the dirty areas to survive. If he closed his eyes, Calvin could fall into his scrabbling self, feel the questions coming: where would his next meal come from, how about a shower, could he trust the local shelter not to report him to the Paragons?

Cocky confidence did a lot, then, to keep Calvin going. He'd been hunted, yes, but every evasion brought with it the certainty that the next escape would come cleaner. Calvin's ability to wield his power grew savvier, smarter, to where he'd close off hallways as he ran down them, or trap the pursuit in icy, sandy, rocky prisons. Those questions, then, came to be asked without fear.

His Tama buzzed. Calvin glanced at it. Saw two messages. One from Weed, asking if Calvin wanted to meet his Paragon team out for an ad hoc patrol tonight. A team bonding event. Calvin swiped it away, went to Kat's.

She'd sent a picture. The lighting wasn't perfect, and some worker's big body marred the right side, but the black metal in the center belonged to one thing and one thing only: the missing drone.

You got the pic, let's go.

Calvin sent the reply, glanced towards the containers, waiting for Kat to come running back over. Nothing showed itself.

Not that easy.

Not that easy? All Kat had to do was run, jump, and grapple. Hell, Calvin could tear a hole in the fence for her.

Why?

Calvin crossed the street, came up to the fence. Tried to peer through it to see Kat. Yeah, the act might be suspicious to someone monitoring those cameras, but who cared now. The second Calvin or Kat sent this picture along to the Paragons, this dockyard would be swarming with drones and anomalies ready to decimate anyone, everyone involved.

His Tama didn't buzz. No reply yet.

At least, not the expected way: the dockyard's casual ramble broke as cries went up inside, and not the occasional calls for help moving this or that, but the angry, ordered declarations from trained personnel starting a hunt. Calvin had heard those calls before, usually directed after him.

Tracing their target here wasn't difficult.

Calvin tore off his gloves and stuffed them in his jacket pockets, touched the cold metal on the fence with his right hand. He felt the strength in those fibers, the molecules beneath, and Calvin drew on it, sucked it in like a kid would a smoothie through a straw. Only, instead of his throat, Calvin sent the stuff out his left hand, sculpting the fence into a blade with a nanometer edge. Sweeping his newfound sword, Calvin cut a clean hole and stepped into the dockyard.

The containers Kat had gone after lay straight ahead, but the shouts seemed to be coming to Calvin's left, towards a quieter section, populated with shipping containers and little else. Calvin broke that way, the metal sword in his hand clattering to the ground and breaking apart. He hadn't forged the thing, had sustained it by drawing from the fence itself, like a wave surviving on its own momentum.

Lifting his Tama as he ran, Calvin had the thing dial Kat. She might not have the time to tap out a message, but a call could work. The Tama sent its signal out, and Calvin lowered his arm in time to see two men, rifles in hand, break into his path. They weren't looking his way, and Calvin ran right into the leading one, taking him to the ground.

Instinct pushed Calvin's right hand to the dockyard's concrete floor, while his left grabbed the fallen guard's own left arm. The concrete ran itself where Calvin wanted it, sealing the guard's arm in a stoney vice. Continuing the draw, Calvin swung himself around onto his back, drawing the concrete with him and exploding it into a solid shield.

If the second guard didn't know what hit them, the presence of an airborne concrete circle must've cleared things up. That, and his partner spitting out confused curses. Calvin saw the guard raise his rifle, and the anomaly flung the concrete shield up at the man. As soon as the stone left Calvin's grip, it began to dissolve, but not fast enough to keep the second guard from getting concrete kilos to the face. The guard toppled over like his friend, groaning.

"Sorry not sorry," Calvin said, pushing himself out from the divot his powers had made in the dockyard's floor. He reached down to the first guard's rifle, used his right hand to dissolve the mechanisms inside, then picked up the second rifle and aimed it at the first guard's head. "How about you start running the other way?"

The first guard stared at Calvin, confused. Calvin pointed the rifle at the guard's arm, no longer trapped as the concrete's cohesion broke. With a wiggle, the guard freed his arm from the crumbling crud. The man decided not to be a hero, taking Calvin's advice and running back towards the containers.

"Calvin?" Kat's voice came over the Tama. "Where are you?"

"Just having some fun," Calvin replied, breaking back into a run. "Tell me you're already gone so I can leave this place."

"More like I'm surrounded. Help?"

"Where?"

"Just watch."

Calvin jerked his head up in time to see two bright, near-blinding flashes spring up several rows away. Guards, soldiers, whatever-the-hell Calvin and Kat were up against cried out at the light, but follow-up commands came as Kat's attack dissipated. The people that took the drone had been coordinated, competent, and they were showing the same energy here.

Not good.

"You got a strategy, or are we just winging it?" Calvin said, slowing to a creep and hugging a ridged container on his right.

"Break left and we get out," Kat said. "That's it."

Approaching feet told Calvin he'd have friends in a hot second if he stayed on the ground, so he dropped the gun —as if he could shoot the thing with accuracy anyway— and used his hands to mold the container's side. Handholds and footholds led to a swift climb up to the top of two stacked containers. Below, a rushing trio didn't notice the deformed container and kept moving, heading right to . . .

Calvin took it in, heart sinking and blood pumping all in one. Kat stood, no, ran around a clearing between container rows, rolling and jumping between at least ten people trying to take her out. The soft puffs coming from some raised weapons suggested they weren't going lethal, yet. Calvin tried to figure out what was shooting at Kat as she whirled around the makeshift arena, her white cloak flying in the wind.

Darts? Rubber bullets?

Kat matched the attacks with her own arsenal, taking out anyone who ventured close with kicks and punches, the two gray orbs that'd blasted off the blinding lights sitting dead near the space's center. From this high up, though, Calvin could see the perimeter forming, could see more people reinforcing the ways out. The soldiers weren't advancing either, content to pepper Kat from a distance until she tired out.

"You need to go over," Calvin said. "There's too many in the gaps."

Kat swerved at Calvin's words, breaking from a would-be rush at a quartet on the arena's left side for the container stack next to them. Out came the grapple, flinging high and latching on to the top container. Kat jumped, hit the hard metal wall and ran up, projectiles pounding into the spaces around her.

Striking her. Something hit Kat hard in her back, followed by a second impact that bent her hood and slammed her head against the container's side. She fell limp, hanging by the grapple as more shots struck home.

Calvin froze. He could've jumped, propelled himself over to the next stack and maybe climbed it. Come over the top into Kat's arena, thrown himself into the frenzy. He started to do just that, till a new voice called a stop to the shooting. Calm, controlled, a man Calvin recognized walked through the guards into the space, then began gesturing for someone to cut Kat down.

Rhimes. The man who'd nearly taken Kat out last time.

Calvin glanced at his Tama. A message sat from Kat, sent just now.

Run.

12

A Pleasant Flight

The Paragon proved true to his word. Cassidy and Thane arrived at the airport, went in through a back entrance with Bits escorting them every step. Then, with Bits hovering nearby, with security stepped up, Cassidy and Thane sat on a bench beneath a palm-covered overhang among other vacationers. Thane, at least, accepted the circumstances and shriveled himself down during the ride over, embracing a more normal human frame that drew little attention from anyone else.

The anonymity extended to boarding the plane, to the short flight to Honolulu and the connection, which Thane had demanded from Bits on the way, to Thailand.

"This feels like the wrong way," Cassidy said as the pair walked onto their connecting flight.

"It is the *only* way," Thane rumbled. "Going back to North America now would mean attention, and capture."

"Because Thailand won't?"

"You and I are not so well known there. And the region's Champion is recovering from the LA attack. We won't be noticed until we mean to be."

Several passengers around them looked over at Thane as he spoke, confused looks crossing their faces. Cassidy put on a smile, patted Thane's shoulder, "I know, you like to pretend you're important."

Okay, so she wasn't the best at improvising. Thane, thankfully, caught on to the attention and fell silent, using direct glares to turn away eavesdroppers. Neither one said another word until they were secured in their posh, first class seats. An added bonus: nobody else purchased the upgrades, leaving the two anomalies alone in the luxury cabin.

"Bits is treating us well," Cassidy said.

"They are putting us with fewer people." Thane nodded at the empty seats around them. "There could be problems."

"They'd never risk it on a plane."

"Don't assume the Paragons wouldn't kill everyone here to destroy me. The cost would be trivial to what they think I could do."

"Is that their fault, or yours?"

Thane narrowed his eyes as he looked at her, while behind him, through the small window, Oahu rushed by as the plane took off.

"You seem hesitant about our path," Thane said. "We escaped from the island. We have hope and promise now. Is that not what you wanted?"

"I never thought we'd make it."

Saying the words aloud brushed Cassidy a different way. She hadn't believed it, had she? Thane's crazy plan to break free from the island shouldn't have succeeded. It didn't for everyone on the boat except the two of them. But Cassidy had gone along with it anyway, believing, she supposed, that death in the attempt would be preferable to a life wasted away in Mynx's palm tree prison.

"Understandable," Thane said, turning away from Cassidy to the window. "It's hard to plan for the unbelievable."

"You did."

"Yes. I did, when we washed up on that beach, spent and nearly dead, I turned inward."

"You shriveled up and abandoned me for days."

"You handled yourself."

Hard to deny that. Didn't mean Cassidy *enjoyed* what'd happened, being sealed up in a clinic without an identity.

"So what are we doing, then, mastermind?" Cassidy said. "What's this grand plan you worked out lying in that bed all day?"

Settling in like a parent delivering a story to a child, Thane proceeded to spend the next hour, then two throwing steps at Cassidy, the one-by-one moves they would make after landing in Thailand leading to an eventual takeover of southeast Asia followed by global expansion. Cutting, ruthless, and detailed to a degree that had Cassidy asking for more coffee every time the attendants went by, Thane's architected apocalypse seemed masterful.

And vulnerable.

Dazed as she was by Thane's deluge, Cassidy found a weak spot in his schemes and clung to it until Thane finally, mercifully, found an end. With his fingers steepled, eyes shining, Thane concluded with a heavy, triumphant breath.

"See?" Thane said. "We will win."

Cassidy let him bask in the presumed victory. She'd taught her charges for years the exact same thing she was about to throw Thane's way: the big bads in world history, those who thought they could waltz to a win by their sheer brilliance, always made mistakes. Always assumed things would go too well.

"You're sweeping the Paragons away like they're some nuisance," Cassidy said. "You're assuming they won't organize to stop you."

"That's what I saw in the library while you were peddling the note to your children," Thane replied. "The Paragons are in far too much disarray to handle us now. They've even had a drone stolen, just today. Citizens brought it down in a neighborhood. Average people, taking up arms against their oppressors!"

"They'll do the same to you. You want those same drones, Thane."

"But without the idiots in control. Impartial justice, safety, and consistency. That's what this world needs, and what I can deliver."

The plane's captain killed the conversation by announcing the flight's first real meal and Cassidy let the words die. If Thane wouldn't listen to her fears, then he'd have to learn them firsthand. Until that happened, Cassidy might as well enjoy the flight and all first class had to offer.

When the attendant came by, Cassidy switched from coffee to champagne.

THANE RUBBED CASSIDY'S SHOULDER, waking her up. Blinking away a shapeless dream, she followed Thane's look out the window. Land, lush and green, sat far below. They must be getting close.

"Landing soon?" Cassidy asked.

"Soon enough. We are descending," Thane replied. "But there may be a problem."

"What?"

"Let me out and I will tell you."

Cassidy shifted, let Thane unbuckle himself and get past her. He stood in the aisle, facing the curtains blocking their lonely first class cabin from the rest of the plane. Towards the front, an attendant had her eyes on her Tama, not Thane. Cassidy felt the urge spike in her mind, a void waiting on her fingertips.

As if she would create one here, in the plane, where the slightest disruption could cause the whole craft to plummet to the ground. Cassidy didn't know whether Thane, at his most enraged, would survive such a fall, but she herself definitely would not.

"Wait here," Thane said, then marched passed her and through the curtains.

Cassidy sipped at the water, clearing off some of the lingering champagne in her throat. The liquid combination, coupled with in-flight food and sitting for so long had Cassidy feeling like she needed a jog, a shower, and another nap . . . in any order.

Thane came back a minute later, frowning, "The plane is light."

"What do you mean? There were passengers in the boarding arm with us. It was crowded?"

"If more than a dozen sit back there now, I would be surprised," Thane replied. "I am also doubting this plane is heading where we expect it to. The captain hasn't made a single announcement. Nothing about customs, weather, or where we are."

"There's no way the Paragons would've had time to set something up," Cassidy said. "No—"

"They had hours and hours," Thane squeezed back by Cassidy. "We may have Hawaii's every Paragon on this flight, taking us right to an ambush."

The attendant stood up, shook a bottle of champagne Cassidy's way. The Void shrugged, gave the attendant a nod for more.

"What are you doing?" Thane asked, seeing Cassidy's

moves.

"Asking questions."

The attendant approached, reached for Cassidy's empty glass. Cassidy put her hand on the woman's wrist, gripped it tight but not so hard to hurt. The attendant gave her a curious look, one that fell when she noticed Cassidy's grim face.

"Do you know who we are?" Cassidy asked the attendant.

"Mr. and Mrs. Smith," the attendant replied, doing a nice job adding confusion to her voice. "It says so right on your ticket."

"I'm sure it does. Do you know where all the passengers went?"

"All the passengers?"

"If you play dumb with me. I can pop a hole so small in your heart that you won't know what's happening until, slowly, you drown in your own blood." The attendant turned suitably gray. "Answer my question."

The attendant shot a look towards the curtains, "It's for safety. We let them out the back door. Rebooked them onto another flight. With you two, we couldn't risk . . ."

Thane grunted. He'd been right.

"And the ones left? Who are they?"

The attendant didn't say anything because she didn't have to. Cassidy had the woman's wrist in her grasp in one moment, and then felt a different, stronger wrist the next. This one belonged to a new man, one in a teal Hawaiian T-shirt and khaki shorts, looking more like he belonged on a golf course than in a speeding plane with the most dangerous people on the planet.

That he could replace the attendant in a blink gave the man away as an anomaly. Now Cassidy had to figure out the man's ability, as there were a whole lot of ways he could have made the attendant disappear: super speed vanishing her to the plane's back, a teleportation gimmick, shrinking her down to some small size, or maybe he'd been the attendant the whole time and only now revealed his true face.

"We don't want trouble," the man said, "but you're not supposed to be here."

Thane unclipped his seat belt. Cassidy didn't remove her hand from the man's wrist. The voids whispered, wanting to be used.

"A little late for that, isn't it?" Cassidy said.

"We're flying over wilderness. There's not a soul around. You can leave."

"Jump?" Cassidy laughed. "How about you land, we walk out, and that's it?"

The man reached over, pried his wrist from Cassidy's grasp and stepped back into the aisle. "That's not the deal. We open the door, you jump out. Whether you survive the fall is on you."

Now Cassidy unclipped her belt, looked at the cabin-splitting curtains. No sign reinforcements were coming through, though they had to be waiting.

"This is a murder, not a deal," Thane growled. "Move, Cassidy. Let me handle him."

Back on the ground, with Bits and the hapless officers, Cassidy felt they had the advantage. Thane and The Void could've torn up the town with impunity. Here, Cassidy didn't get that same vibe. They'd wandered right into a Paragon ambush. The same people that'd put her into a prison now wanted to shove her out of a plane.

They'd followed the Paragon's directions and were about to wind up dead anyway. Might as well fight.

"He's all yours." Cassidy sat back in her seat as Thane started across.

Except Thane wasn't by the window anymore. The man crouched in Thane's seat, while Thane himself fell through the aisle into the chairs across the way. Cassidy connected the body swapping dots, started to throw a small void at the man, only to find a window and the plane's outer wall in front of her.

Oh, this one would be annoying.

Thane roared and the floors shook. Already scraping the plane's ceiling with his head, the anomaly turned his spit-flying mug towards the Paragon. He swung a fist, and in that second, Cassidy found herself flipped back into her own seat, Thane's hammer-blow coming her way. She ducked forward and Thane's swing went overhead, coming around to crash into the seat in front.

"Control!" Cassidy shouted, only to find herself shoved out of the creaking seat as Thane pushed himself back into the aisle.

The Paragon backed away down the aisle, keeping a light, cocky grin on his face. When Cassidy picked herself up and met the Paragon's eyes, he pointed to the plane's exit.

"There's your way out," the man said. "Or we can keep this dance going."

"Then let's dance," Cassidy replied, dishing her right hand out, a void leaping to her fingertips.

The Paragon flipped places again, putting Thane right where Cassidy's void should've gone. Instead, the man choked, coughed, and died as his insides collapsed on themselves. Cassidy wiggled the fingers on her left hand, facing where Thane had been. A predictable Paragon was a dead Paragon.

"Done?" Thane grumbled, looking at the body.

"Yes," Cassidy said, brushing back hair that'd fallen out of place with all the switching. "But he's only one."

Turning, Cassidy went through the curtain into the plane's main compartment. And dove forward as a bright blue beam burned through the space where she'd been standing. Cassidy felt the heat on her neck, smelled smoke as hair that didn't fall fast enough took a scorching blow. She expected the plane to plummet with the blast, but instead heard Thane's surprised roar.

He could take it.

Glancing up, Cassidy saw the attendant, now with a grimmer look, pounding towards her. As the attendant ran, her feet pulsed with every step, shooting green lines Cassidy's way. Like growing veins, the lines accelerated their approach along with the attendant. What the hell they might do, Cassidy didn't know, so she tossed a void into the aisle's center, then crawled into the plane's middle.

The thrown void tore at the chairs around it, ripping apart fabric. The attendant yelled, and Cassidy heard a hard thump, but the green lines didn't reach her. Thane gave another roar and Cassidy heard the curtain tear away as the monster man careened into the compartment with them. Gripping a seat, Cassidy stole a look at Thane as he tore down the aisle, timing the rush to meet her void as it faded. That blue beam looked to have left smoking char on Thane's shoulder, not that it seemed to matter.

With their attention taken, Cassidy peered over and took a Paragon count. Thane's dozen estimate seemed in line, though they all moved so much it was hard to get a firm lock. Lights and sounds flashed through the back as the Paragons exercised their abilities in constant waves. The blue bolts came from a small man who seemed to hoover up whatever he touched, turning it into that crackling energy. At first, Cassidy thought the man had incredible accuracy, until she noticed a Paragon next to him twisting her hands and bending those beams right into Thane's body.

Thane himself swung and punched, but the attendant, with her feet under her again, seemed to let every swing pass right through her, as if those green veins gave her some protection. Either way, Thane's frustration only grew, and the Paragon attack picked up: the other eight were spreading out, some lancing other projectiles at Thane's back while two more had their eyes on Cassidy.

In an open field, Cassidy might've given Thane the odds to overpower everyone and smash them to pieces. In a cramped plane, where Thane's size only made him an easy target? Even Thane might find himself worn down, burned away.

"Give up," said a woman coming from the left, her hands reaching Cassidy's way with a light purple glow between them. "There's no way out."

Wasn't there?

Flinging her right hand up, Cassidy threw the void, feeling the heat break her into a sweat even as the void tore apart the plane's roof. Metal screeched, wires sparked, and pressure popped, savaging the ears of everyone on board, though not so bad as Cassidy expected. When Thane woke her up, he'd mentioned the plane was descending.

Maybe low enough to fall.

The fighting around her stopped, every Paragon trying to decide how the ruptured plane affected their plans. One person, though, didn't care to consider the change: Thane. As Cassidy warmed up another void, Thane's burning, bruised form launched a Paragon across the plane, smashing into the woman that'd called on Cassidy to surrender. With another hoarse roar, Thane pulled up and tossed chairs at the other Paragons, forcing ducks and dodges.

Cassidy used the distraction, pulled herself back to the aisle on the right and crouched-ran towards Thane. Inside her, she felt the heat building, the pressure sucking at her fingertips as though she'd dipped her hands in lava.

"Hold me," Cassidy shouted as she closed with Thane, as she released the void behind her.

As the plane sheared in half, Cassidy hoped the man, the monster, was sane enough to listen.

13

Whipped Cream and Scheme

Some mornings, the meetings flew by. Wexley handled them on autopilot, adding minimal input and approving employee suggestions without fuss. Not exactly prime CEO behavior, but it wasn't every day Wexley had a prize waiting before lunch.

Rhimes called over breakfast with the good news. The tracker, Kat, the one they'd tried to take out in the snow not that long ago, stumbled onto the disabled drone and didn't get away. Rhimes dismissed the discovery as chance, with Kat likely roaming by hunting for another anomaly. In fact, two guards found and fought another anomaly nearby, though they'd failed to capture that interloper.

Wexley, at the time munching on his standard energy bar breakfast, let Rhimes and his idea slide, drumming his fingers on his glass kitchen table. A tracker with Kat's reputation didn't seem like the type to just stumble on something like the drone. And hadn't she worked with anomalies before?

So Wexley had his assistant clear his mid-day calendar, and now, after this last meeting—something something branding opportunity—Wexley dashed down, caught a pod, and careened south.

Rhimes wasn't dumb enough to keep both the tracker and the drone in the same place, so Wexley only had a mild shock when the pod pulled up near a slapdash diner. Bedecked in chrome and advertising lab-grown burgers and fries, along with fresh daily pies, Wexley took a long time leaving the pod, enjoying the ambience in a parking lot with too many spots for the current age. Childhood trips to similar themed destinations played behind his eyes.

The lunch time crowd arrived in full force around Wexley, pods screaming in with families and working crews, dropping them off in bands to collect their burgers before streaming away again. Milk shakes flowed, grease hung in the air, and order numbers rang over idle conversations.

Wexley pushed—pushed!—the door open, held it for an older woman and her daughter coming behind him, and then continued on past the front counter. Booths clung to the diner's sides, cushion-less seats a ribbon-red color meshing with speckled white tables. Everything had a laminated gleam.

For once, here, surrounded by casual hum and churn, Wexley found his fingers weren't itching for a trigger. His mind wasn't settling on schemes for this and that. Stock prices and sales demos didn't dominate Wexley's periphery.

The diner did what it set out to do: it transported Wexley to a simpler, gentler time.

At least until Wexley went through the staff doors, passed through a buzzing kitchen to an office in the back. Blocked off by a black-painted door, one showing chips and grease stains, Wexley tried the splotched silver knob and found it locked. He looked at the peep hole, another artifact in this camera-driven world.

The dead bolt clicked, the door swung aside, and Rhimes stood with a professional's look about him. Body armor, visible handgun in a waist holster. Wexley assumed a jacket sat behind the door, ready to keep Rhimes's materials hidden from the innocents outside. Rhimes himself didn't look tired, didn't look strung up on caffeine: how the man could seem to work endlessly without rest and ignore the drugs, Wexley couldn't fathom.

As Rhimes retreated, Wexley saw another guard posted inside, this one with a heavier weapon. With his back to the office's wall, the guard ignored Wexley's entry, keeping his eyes locked on the young woman strapped into a cheap office chair. Zip ties, those little plastic vices, wrapped around Kat's wrists and legs, each securing her a little more.

Her suit and its gadgets lay on the office's lone desk, leaving the tracker in a t-shirt and what looked like pajama pants, ones speckled with dogs chasing bones. The outfit looked so at odds with the situation that Wexley laughed before he recovered.

Kat glared at him, her icy blues setting the table for the conversation.

"You know," Wexley said to Rhimes as he stepped inside. "I could really use one of those milk shakes. You want one?"

"I'm good," Rhimes replied.

"How about you, then?" Wexley asked the guard.

"All set, sir."

"Then it falls to you, Kat, to keep me from drinking alone?"

"Strawberry," Kat said, not softening her eyes at all. "Whipped cream if they have it."

"I'll have the same," Wexley said, glancing at Rhimes. "Mediums, please."

The man vanished to carry out the request without another word. Wexley took Rhimes's place beside the office desk. A folding chair sat opposite Kat, but Wexley ignored it. He'd been sitting through all the morning anyway, and looming over his opponents always felt better than an even stare.

"You're not going to butter me up," Kat said, "so don't even try."

"I don't have to. There's nothing I want that you can give me."

Now Kat's look faltered. Wexley would've grinned in another time, but reveling in victory now just seemed gauche.

"I don't understand?" Kat asked. "Why am I still alive?"

"Oh, we will use you. It just won't require your help. All I need is your body, your name, and your reputation."

"Because?"

The fishing question. A move that might bait a mono-loguing villain, but Wexley had other things to do besides discuss his plans.

"I assume you found the drone, and that you told somebody about it?"

"And the idiot gets it on the first try."

The guard stepped forward, looking like he wanted to slap Kat. Wexley held up his left hand, forestalled the attack. Kat could say whatever she wanted: in the end, she was the one tied to the chair, while Wexley had a trillion-rep company at his back.

"Then why is the drone still in my possession?" Wexley asked. "The Paragons wouldn't wait to attack."

"The Paragons are a mess and you know it. They'll come eventually."

So Kat hadn't sent the image, the drone's location

directly to the Paragons. No matter their disarray, the Paragons had sent a team to the stolen drone's attack site, had deployed their other drones around the city to search for their missing friend. Given a target, the anomalies would swarm.

"Did you tell your other friends?" Wexley asked. "I imagine they would want to know. A captive drone might be a valuable tool for the Elementals."

"Going to have to guess on that score."

Rhimes came back in, two milkshakes, both frothing with whipped cream, in his hands. Wexley took them. He leaned forward, put the straw so Kat's mouth could find it. She took a long slurp. Wexley matched. More sugar than strawberry, but still delicious.

"When is she getting in?" Wexley asked Rhimes.

"Evening. Best guess."

"Who?" Kat asked.

"Then move the drone. Move her. Right to where we discussed. Once they're set, release the location," Wexley said, then he turned to Kat. "This whipped cream is great, isn't it? A perfect extra."

"I'm not—" Kat started, but Wexley waved her off.

"I made you an offer. You ignored it. You slaughtered my team. You're going to die, Kat. That's not in question. What I'm eager to discover, though, is how much you will help me first."

ADRIANA MET him later on the lake shore, north of the diner. The wind today, blessed with some sunshine, kissed warm. Wexley even ditched his jacket, the blazer alone providing enough protection. Adriana didn't do the same, cloaking herself in a coat meant for January's icy claws.

"I'm sorry," she opened, stepping up to him in Soldier Field's shadow. "I didn't realize."

"Then you know her?" Wexley asked. "Beth?"

"A name among dozens. We didn't screen people this time. It was a big ball for the Paragons. What's suspicious about that?"

Wexley leveled a finger at her, "You're new to this, so I'll forgive this one mistake. Everyone is picking sides, Adriana. Everyone sees a war coming, and they want to know where they'll be when it starts, and when it ends. That means we have enemies. Smart ones, clever ones, anomalies. There are no more innocents among us."

"What a grim way to look at it."

"It's a perspective that's kept me alive."

"Has it?"

Adriana's raised eyebrow and unfazed look twinged a nerve. Wexley grimaced, turned towards the rippling sapphire waves.

"Enough to do what I need to do," Wexley said. "Are you ready for the same?"

Adriana stepped up beside him. Wexley felt her coat brush his blazer. She stood as tall as he was, her hair let loose to fly in the wind.

"I assume it was you that took the drone?" Adriana asked.

"Not a bad assumption."

"What are you doing with it?"

"You'll see."

Adriana nodded. "Soon?"

"Soon."

"Then when it's over, if you're still alive, give me a call."

The line could've ended the conversation, but Wexley didn't walk away. Aside from the investor calls, those pressure-packed meetings spent trying to convince a wealthy band to stick with a revolution that might undermine their industries, Wexley didn't spend any time with equals. Rhimes and his team were employees, as was everyone at the company. Zhan-Yo had been close, but the man had grown increasingly reckless and, now, had vanished.

Adriana had reps. She had social standing. Wexley didn't know if she could kill a man a dozen different ways like he could, but how much did that really matter?

"Shouldn't you be somewhere?" Adriana asked as the silence petered out.

Wexley waved back towards the office towers to the north, "If you ask my calendar, I ought to be sitting in some beige chair listening to a strategy discussion that will become meaningless if this all works out."

"But instead you're here."

Wexley took the remark, let the wind blow.

"When Zhan-Yo ramped up his efforts, he started missing meetings too. The man became an absent executive, barely present, and even when he showed, his mind was so far off course we stopped asking him questions. I didn't understand it then, but I do now."

Adriana waited for Wexley to continue, though he guessed, by her patience, she knew what was coming.

"When you find what's most important, everything else fades away. I don't care about the profits, the expansions, the new Tamas we're rolling out next quarter," Wexley said. "A few months ago, those were paramount, and this whole revolution seemed like a side hustle. A vicious game that wouldn't ever have any real impact."

"Zhan-Yo blew up a stadium."

"Sloppy, but it worked. The Paragons are lost, and I'm more committed than ever."

"As am I," Adriana took Wexley's arm and nodded him

back towards the street, where a pod had pulled up. "Come with me."

"Where?"

"Does it matter?"

Bold, strong, and intoxicating. Wexley went.

Adriana's pod zipped north, right into the heart of Michigan avenue and the tourist shopping binge that only grew stronger as the afternoon deepened. The pod squeezed into a side street, dropping the pair off by an unassuming store selling shoes. Wexley blinked at the displays, wondering if Adriana had brought him all this way to critique his fashion sense.

"Come on," Adriana said, walking past the store and down a slight alleyway dominated by trash bins and employees on break.

The two were an obvious mismatch with the alley dwellers, and eyes watched the pair with the suspicious respect given to a potential manager, or someone that might penalize the employees for spending an extra minute or two off shift. At least one audible sigh echoed out as Wexley passed by.

Adriana stopped at a moss-green metal door, a brand name her company owned blazed on the outside.

"We couldn't go through the front?" Wexley said.

"Not for what I need you to see," Adriana replied, tapping on her Tama.

The lock inside the door clicked, and Wexley, adopting the gentleman's role, pulled the door open and held it aside. Adriana gave him a nod for his troubles and led the way in. Pasty lights awaited them, illuminated racks upon racks with designer clothes waiting for their chance. Adriana navigated the maze without hesitation, impressive considering just how many rows there were, how deep they went, and how utterly same it all felt.

"If you're trying to show me what you sell, I get it," Wexley said.

"Not quite," Adriana replied. "We're nearly there."

Past the last row, another door waited for them, set into a wall that looked newer than the rest of the building. Again, Adriana pulled out her Tama. Again, she tapped away. And again, the door opened at her command.

Inside here, though, weren't racks. Instead, a single large, humming machine whirred away. Two employees, one working the machine, the other carrying a familiar bundle to a box on the side, glanced up as Wexley and Adriana entered. Upon seeing their boss, they went back to work without a question.

"You make their uniforms," Wexley said.

"At first, only in New York." Adriana went over to the nearest basket. She ran her hand along the silver and blue. "Now, everywhere. I bought every company with a Paragon contract."

"Good business."

"Great business," Adriana said. "Their anomalies burn through so many outfits." She looked at the two employees, gave Wexley a knowing smile. "Let's let them work."

"Why show me?" Wexley asked when they were back among the racks.

"Two reasons," Adriana replied, leading them back towards the alley exit. "First, because I need you to know I'll lose as much as anyone if the Paragons collapse."

A good sign. Trusting anyone without skin in the game was a fool's exercise.

"And two, because we can use it. Ever wonder how the Paragons always seem to know where their friends are? How the drones can find exactly where to go?"

"The uniforms?"

"Exactly," Adriana said. "You have one drone. Turn its

systems inside out and I think you could find every Paragon wearing their uniform, down to the meter."

And if he had all the drones? The Paragons would figure it out quickly, but in those first days, those first hours . . . all across the world Wexley could have a mechanical army conduct a surgical sweep.

"You have a cute thinking face," Adriana said as they went back outside. "I'd like to see it more often."

"That won't be a problem." Wexley took one finger and placing it on her cheek. "If tonight goes well, we'll have reason to celebrate."

"Then you'd better get going," Adriana nodded down the alley to the waiting pod. "I'll catch the next one."

Adriana's send off put Wexley heading south, though he swung by his favorite parking garage and his favorite van first. Rhimes had been sending Wexley the occasional update, and sources within various air traffic monitors and the Paragons themselves—never underestimate a disgruntled bottom-feeder's motivation—confirmed Mynx was now en route to Chicago.

A Champion's personal touch added to the city. Wexley smiled to himself: the last time one had come here, the results had turned out quite well for him.

Armed and armored, Wexley sent Rhimes the go command. The pod didn't take Wexley back to the crowded shipyard, but rather to a private marina on the lake shore. Here, resting in its berth, sat one of Zhan-Yo's few concessions to his wealth. The man had a penchant for frugality, but he'd acquired a speed boat made for surfing Lake Michigan as a sole gift to himself. Something about freedom and how the water expressed it perfectly.

And then Zhan-Yo almost never used it, save when Wexley reminded the man of its existence. Taking a ride out into open water served as a good place to have dangerous discussions. Zhan-Yo's revolution started out there with nothing but light chop for kilometers around. Now Wexley had the keys, and was going to put the final stamp on what Zhan-Yo started.

With the sun settling in behind Chicago's towers, Wexley spun up the boat and headed out into the lake. Four seats, packed with power, water bottles, and, now, Wexley's very illegal weapons, the boat sliced the cold water. Few others were out and about—not a week ago, the lake's ice made it a dangerous decision. A screen over the steering wheel gave the coordinates: ten kilometers south. Another marina there, another dock, and then a short pod ride to the rendezvous.

Going straight by pod would've been faster, but the manual boat ride cut the path for anyone listening in. And besides, the breeze was warm, the sunset beautiful. The lake a shimmering purple gray.

Fighting a Champion meant risking his life. If these were going to be his last moments, Wexley wanted to enjoy them.

Single Malt Strike

Celice approached the meeting place, a quiet pub nestled between an Underground stop and a grocery store, with determined steps and her hands well away from the gun hanging in her shoulder holster. She browsed the sidewalk, the apartment balconies above and around the bar, seeing only a few people out this late. Someone cashing a cigarette, another couple clinking wine glasses amid conversation. Nobody watching her, though. Nobody stalking Celice that she could see.

Well, except for her friends.

Gatete and his team—Roger and Sydney included, albeit after back-and-forth apologies—had her back. They'd deployed to the blocks around the meeting place an hour ago, confirming their locations with Celice while she set forth from her apartment, providing the visual to Zhan-Yo's presumed spies. Celice had her Tama up and ready to call in the crew if Zhan-Yo showed, giving Gatete his prize and Celice her revenge opportunity.

Whether or not she could stab Zhan-Yo with a sword

like the man did her father was a problem Celice could solve later.

Shaw's Girl, set in gold lettering on a black bar over the entry, welcomed Celice through a heavy door. Inside, a long bar counter stretched back to near-front, with a couple tables hugging the spare space street-side. Stools snugged into the counter gave sipping space to a local, loud cluster hollering at some sport on the lone TV. On the right, spaced two-seater tables glowered beneath scrappy old lamps and older Soho playbills hung up on the walls.

Only one table was occupied. A single man nursing a fresh pint. Unlike the locals and their patchwork outfits, this one wore his leather lightly, casting shadows in all the right places to make picking out a weapon difficult. Celice recognized his face as the one belonging to the umbrella ass from last night.

Her contact ID'ed, Celice made her way to the bar's end, raised a finger and found herself with a peaty eighteen year in a highball glass. Celice took the seat opposite the man, sliding her drink along the patched wood and wondering which opening she wanted to take.

There was the aggressive approach, sending a hand inside the jacket and offering the man two quick shots to the skull if he didn't give up Zhan-Yo's location. That'd be satisfying, if unlikely to succeed. The cliched seduction strategy made no sense—Celice didn't dress for that strategy, and the man across from her wasn't some scuzzy politician looking for a power play.

Waiting for Zhan-Yo's guy to call the shots wasn't good either. After getting caught up in Gatete's ambush earlier, Celice needed to work off some energy. Play some offense.

"Where's the important one?" Celice asked, watching the man's eyes make regular treks over her shoulder and out the bar's windows. "Outside?"

"Not here," the man said. An American accent. Did Zhan-Yo employ any locals? "Not going to be, either."

"Then I'm leaving."

"No." The man nodded at her scotch. "I saw what he poured you. That's good whisky. Don't waste it."

Celice gripped the glass, made as if she was going to down the whole thing in a single gulp. Earned a wince from the man, then changed up the raise to a sip instead. The man's obvious relief showed he wasn't a robot.

The conversation cracked open.

"He doesn't want to hurt you," the man said. "Zhan-Yo's in a complicated position. You're a headache he doesn't need."

"And I want Zhan-Yo's head on a platter. You can see the problem."

The man nodded, "My job's to get us through this without another body, so here's what I can offer you."

"Is it Zhan-Yo's head on a platter?"

"It is not."

"Then—"

The man held up a hand, "Look, I get it. I've been in the game a long time. Don't let tunnel vision cost you what's important. At least hear me out. Then, if you want to get yourself killed, we can arrange that."

Celice accepted the offer with another whisky encounter. After the chilly London night, the stuff roared right on down her throat and delighted her stomach with a campfire supernova.

"Zhan-Yo came here after the stadium. You know that, but you probably don't know why." The man gave Celice a beat, and when she gave him nothing, he continued. "Wexley, his right-hand man, took over Zhan-Yo's company. You can't have a criminal trying to run a multi-national organization."

"Really?" Celice raised an eyebrow as best she could. "News to me."

The man laughed. A genuine one rolling right along with a nod. "Point. Anyway, Zhan-Yo's trying to organize a revolution. He wants the common person to take their power back. Anomalies shouldn't have it all just because they have abilities that I don't, through luck."

"I'm getting bored."

"Zhan-Yo tried talking to the Paragons, but they wouldn't listen. Your father wouldn't listen. So he made a desperate play, and then another. Now he wants the ones in charge to talk, to make a deal and re-arrange the world before it's too late."

"Too late for what?"

"You've seen the news, I'm sure. Does it seem like the world's going in the right direction?"

No, no it did not. Celice had tried to block out current events, because looking at the Paragon disarray, watching Mynx struggle to hold North America together while the rest of the Champions fiddled with their own fires only put guilt onto the emotions Celice had to contend with every day she spent alone out here.

That the Paragons needed some spark, some unifying moment was obvious. Mynx's latest press conference settled on some missing drone, trying to rally people around this attack on law and order. Hard to generate sympathy for a machine, though.

"If you're trying to convince me that Zhan-Yo's going to bring the world together after murdering my friends and my father . . . " Celice didn't need to finish that sentence.

"He's not the healer," the man acknowledged. "But, as he told me, he can help the one who is."

The highball holding her whisky was well made. Celice gripped the thing so hard a lesser glass would've shattered.

The audacity, asking for peace now. Asking for the Paragons to bow down and give up.

"Did Zhan-Yo say what he wanted as part of this deal?" Celice asked. "What happens to him in this glorious future? Does the terrorist killer get to walk away free?"

The man sighed, sat back in his chair. His jacket parted enough for Celice to see that, like her, he carried a gun hanging from his shoulder.

"So that's a no, then?" the man asked.

"That's a hell no," Celice replied. "Where is he?"

"Well," the man said, reaching for his pint with his left hand.

The move caught Celice's attention. Up till now, the man had been drinking with his right. She started moving as he did, the man's right hand zipping inside his jacket for that gun.

Celice shoved the table on him. The thing had heft, a sturdy metal base old and unbalanced enough to make a good toppling tower. The table's top pinned the man's arm into his jacket as it drove him to the pub's floor. Celice had her own gun out and ready, aiming at the downed man.

The silence made her press her lips together, sighing all the while.

The group listening to the event on the TV, the bartender who'd doubled her order without another look, all had their own weapons out, drawn on her. Of course Zhan-Yo wouldn't send a single goon in here. This was an all-in situation. Celice either said yes to his terms, or she went down fast.

"Okay," Celice said, raising her gun to the ceiling. "Let's take a breath, everybody."

The cue worked, as six separate handguns, shotguns, and one mean-looking revolver kept their bullets in their barrels. Celice had herself an audience, and she had herself a few seconds.

All the time in the world.

The bartender frowned, his hands holding the shotgun flipping and swinging the weapon like a club into the closest man's back. The target toppled into the next man over, who turned with a shout only to catch the shotgun, now flying through the air, in the face. Two other goons hit themselves hard with their own handguns, knocking themselves out.

Only Revolver kept his head, turning back from the chaos and pulling his trigger. Celice rolled forward, the pistol shot blasting over her head and putting a bullet hole right in an old Les Miserables playbill. Celice came up with a gut punch while her left hand wrested the revolver off to the side.

The man struggled, wheezing after Celice's hit, and tried a knee. Celice elbowed that away, then grabbed the man's jacket and used her lower position to flip him over her back, slamming him down to the bar floor. In the process, her fingers extracted the revolver, snapping it into position, muzzle right at the man's face.

He stuck up his hands, and the pub's door clanged open.

"Another win for the good guys," Gatete announced, leading Sydney and Roger in after him. "As though we expected anything less."

Zhan-Yo's gang groaned around them, but they remembered themselves fast enough. By the time Gatete reached Celice and looked at the beaten bunch, their lips sealed, their hard looks masks to what lay beneath. Celice took a long step back as Gatete demanded the group reveal Zhan-Yo's location.

"You brought reinforcements," said Celice's original

target, who'd extricated himself from the table and now leaned against the wall, hand on his stomach. "Breaking the rules."

"That's rich, coming from the guy with seven friends," Celice replied.

Gatete's entreaties drew nothing from the assembled crowd, and the Paragon glanced over at Celice.

"What do you think, daughter of Aegis? Should we slaughter these traitors here and now, or put them on display first?"

"I think we leave that choice to them," Celice replied. "They take us to Zhan-Yo and we let them walk away."

Gatete gave a half-hearted frown in response, threw another sweeping look back towards his new charges, "The Champion's daughter offers mercy. What do you say?"

"I say Zhan-Yo's not paying us enough to die for him," said the man next to Celice. "The name's Mathieu, and if you want to see the boss, I'll take you right there, right now."

Celice searched the words, the man's stance as he offered to betray his leader and found nothing false in either. Gatete waved a hand towards the pub's exit.

"Then lead the way, Mathieu," Gatete said. "Sydney will ensure the rest of you stay here. If Mathieu takes us where we need to go, then you will be released without harm."

All in all, not the worst negotiation for Zhan-Yo's lackeys. Celice had the impression, from the sparkle in Gatete's eyes and fire when he spoke of slaughter that the Paragon wouldn't mind throwing a few bodies into the street. A claim the Paragon had fought, defeated terrorists in central London would elevate his profile.

Best to attach politics to any action with that one.

Mathieu shouldered his traitorous burden without hesitation, leading Celice, Gatete, and Roger out the pub's exit. His teammates gave Mathieu looks ranging from disgusted to grateful, a spectrum Celice didn't find surprising among mercenaries. In a group picked by reps and reps alone, loyalty had to be a fluid concept.

Not that the Paragons had proved to be much better. Aegis had been lured in and abandoned by a traitor, and Celice figured the LA attacks would've needed insider help. Every organization had rot, but with the Paragons, the usual dissatisfaction might cause hundreds or thousands to die. Aegis used to grumble about loyalty tests in the early days, Apinya and a couple others reading minds and, if necessary, remaking them.

Her dad had been wistful then. Celice kept her own worries quiet.

Outside *Shaw's Girl*, another five Paragons milled around the sidewalk waving along passers-by. Overhead, a gladiator drone hovered, its spotlights washing out the quaint streetlamp glow.

"I don't think you brought enough reinforcements," Mathieu said, taking it all in.

"It's a show," Celice replied while Gatete passed along the plans to the Paragons. "Gatete needs this to get attention, so he can reap the rewards."

"And you?"

"I just want Zhan-Yo."

"Because that's going to solve all your problems," Mathieu said.

"People keep telling me that, and it's getting real old," Celice said. "You going to keep walking, or is Zhan-Yo hiding in this trash bin?"

With Roger and Gatete following, Celice and Mathieu set off down the street. Not before, of course, Celice had Mathieu's several weapons—shoulder and ankle holsters, a knife inside his right sleeve—removed and handed over. Rendering the man harmless seemed to boost Mathieu's mood, as if killing the possibility he could hurt someone lightened the man's conscience: he pointed out buildings as they walked, naming them and their pasts.

"Are you a part-time historian?" Celice asked after the fifth such minor landmark, a home of some old British hero, spawned another story.

"We've been here a while," Mathieu said. "Before you, Zhan-Yo didn't need us doing all that much. Spent a lot of time reading, walking."

"Apparently."

Gatete offered to call a pod, but Mathieu emphasized the footfalls, saying it wouldn't be much farther. And that pods could be traced.

"We're with you," Celice said. "Why's getting traced a concern?"

"As if you're the only ones we're concerned about."

"Aren't we?"

Mathieu started to laugh, sighed instead as they turned onto a narrow side street blockaded in by bricked apartments, "You have such a narrow lens."

"He killed my father."

Mathieu didn't have an answer for that, or chose not to give it. Celice fell into a glower that lasted until Mathieu stopped at an unassuming blue door. He tapped in a code to the lock pad on its right side, then pulled it open. Chai tea's warm and spicy smell wafted out, complemented by a sticky sweet pastry aroma.

Someone hadn't been idle all night.

"He bakes now," Mathieu said with a shrug. "It's meditative."

Gatete laughed, "Of course. Why not? Overthrow a peaceful world and bake a cake in the process."

Celice shook that image away. She wasn't here for Zhan-Yo's hobbies or his self-reflection.

"Let's go," Celice said, and Mathieu executed the order.

Inside and up a narrow, dark wood stair, the group climbed a story and stopped near another door, also blue and also locked with a number pad.

"He'll be inside," Mathieu said, looking right at Celice. "But he'll want to talk. Don't shoot."

"That's not the plan," Gatete said, the laughter gone now. The Paragon leader back to his position. "We are here for a prisoner, not a corpse."

Mathieu, though, waited for Celice to agree before punching in the numbers. With a simple, cheery chime, the lock clicked and the door opened. Zhan-Yo's sanctum lay before them.

A mediocre kitchen swarming, indeed, with mixing bowls, whisks, and an oven overlaid with those fresh-baked buns greeted their first look. Celice, though, skipped past the domesticity to the flatness beyond. A large living room, wood-floored, lay barren, a couch and several chairs squeezed up against the sides. A big window opened on the left, show-casing a park down below.

Zhan-Yo himself didn't hide. He stood near the fireplace at the apartment's rear, wearing body armor and, sheathed across his back, the twin swords he'd been known to use. If Celice and two Paragons bursting in carried any surprise, the man didn't show it.

"Welcome," Zhan-Yo said as the bunch went in, Celice drawing her shoulder gun and leveling it Zhan-Yo's way. The man didn't seem to notice. "I trust Mathieu was a capable guide?"

Zhan-Yo threw a nod at his associate before turning back to the group. Celice had made it to the kitchen counter, but going any closer might risk Zhan-Yo getting in a quick strike while she shot, so Celice steadied her stance there. Gatete and Roger stayed near the door, content to watch from a distance.

That Zhan-Yo obviously knew they were coming didn't faze Celice—she'd tapped into London's surveillance network, and Zhan-Yo probably had his own way of doing the same. Or someone in the bar had sent the word ahead. Regardless, Celice had her target dead center, and her finger rested on the trigger. This close, with Zhan-Yo not moving, she could hit a single, fatal shot.

Revenge would be had, the world would be safer.

But Gatete wouldn't be happy.

"Celice," Gatete said from behind, as if he could read her thoughts. "Remember the plan. His life is not yours to take."

Zhan-Yo raised an eyebrow, "I wasn't aware my life was anyone's but mine."

"Says the man that's murdered so many," Celice cut in. Nonetheless, she slipped the handgun back into its holster. "You're coming with us, and you're going to pay for what you've done."

Zhan-Yo reached up, drew a sword with each hand, leaving them pointing towards the floor and away.

"Come with you?" Zhan-Yo said. "I don't think so."

Celice found herself grinning at the gesture, "I hoped you'd say that."

15

For A Tracker

Chills swept him up and down despite the jacket, despite the heat in the laundromat where Calvin had been sucking down caffeine for the last few hours. Outside the poster-coated windows and across the street sat a strange restaurant that looked like one of those diners from a movie, all chrome-plated and cheesy. He'd even dared to order a burger and a milkshake from the place, just to pass the time.

Kat was in there. Calvin knew because he'd watched them take her. Had followed the trio that'd stuffed Kat into a pod by taking its license number and dumping it into the Paragon's database. Every pod and its destination, right there on his wrist.

It would have been spooky if it wasn't so useful.

He tapped his tingling fingers together, the leather gloves back on. A few people moved around, their chosen machines churning. Calvin earned himself some good stares, but this wasn't a neighborhood where you asked random people questions, and every time he met wandering eyes they turned away and didn't come back.

He wanted to go rushing into the diner. Run up, suck in some concrete and go bashing to the rescue. Only Calvin had no idea where Kat was in that restaurant. How many people were watching her. It wasn't so much the potential for collateral damage that kept the Paragon in check, but how quick he might wind up dead if he tried.

Then the damn pod pulled up.

A heavy duty transport pod meant for freight, the thing had no reason to drop into the diner's parking lot. Taking up two spaces, the pod settled in near the diner's back, away from the afternoon customers streaming in. Calvin watched as its big doors opened up and four new armed and armored bastards leapt out and went towards the diner's back entrance.

Calvin stood up before he knew what he was doing. Action seemed to inspire action. He pushed his way outside, took a chilly breath, and crossed the road. A line six people deep spread away from the diner. Calvin could take a spot there, watch and see what might happen.

But he'd been watching for too long.

Instead Calvin kept on going by, went through the parking lot and the pods inside it. He came up to the last row before the break, the asphalt stretch leading back to where the heavy pod had parked. A door *chunked* open and Calvin bent down as if to tie his shoe, watching with one eye as the pod's crew, plus Rhimes, left the diner.

Kat firmly in tow.

Six on one? Not good odds, but wherever they were taking Kat would probably be worse.

Calvin went towards the freight pod, passing around the last passenger pod in his way, at a casual walk. He heard Kat giving Rhimes and his crew some solid trash talk as they loaded her into the pod's rear seat. Kat's fire perked him up—if the tracker still had her energy, then Calvin could free her first, get some reinforcements.

Bending over—the ol' tie-the-shoe gag never died—Calvin reached and touched the asphalt with his left hand. With his right, Calvin took the rocky feel and passed it through, elongating the energy into a black, rocky spear.

"Hey!" came the first shout from the pod. Calvin glanced up, saw a mercenary heading his way. "What're you doing?"

"Catch," Calvin replied, flinging the asphalt javelin with his right hand.

Throwing full-fledged stone would take strength Calvin didn't have, but he'd stenciled out the asphalt into a thin wedge, light and sharp. The rock needle lodged itself in the mercenary's body armor, sticking out like a strange flag-pole. Rhimes's man looked down at it, confused, and took Calvin's second, smaller needle in the leg.

Now the man yelled, and Calvin broke into a run at the pod's back. Another mercenary popped from the pod's left side, raising her weapon. Rhimes and the other crew piled into the pod, its electric engines whirring to life.

Running. Cowards.

Calvin dragged his left hand on the ground as he ran, holding his right up near his face, spreading the asphalt out in a fanning shield. Bullets streamed in, each one with a loud pop, blowing away the protection faster than Calvin could make it. Flecks pinged Calvin's coat, scratched his face.

Another second and his makeshift shield would fail.

Another second, and Calvin hit the shooter in a running, falling tackle. Keeping his left hand on the asphalt meant Calvin's rush hit the mercenary's stomach, knocking her to the ground. Her legs tangled with Calvin's and he joined her fall, hitting shoulder first as the freight pod, Kat inside, pulled away.

Calvin, his asphalt shield collapsing to dust, scrambled for the mercenary's gun. If he could shoot out the pod's engine he could stop it. The weapon lay on the ground a meter away. Calvin delivered a solid kick to his opponent to get towards it, buying himself some freedom.

A sharp crack blanked Calvin's ears as a bullet skipped off the ground near his head. A glance confirmed the first wounded mercenary had recovered, leaning on one knee and holding a handgun. The man's aim seemed shaky as he fired again, the bullet zipping by Calvin as the anomaly curled back around.

Calvin had no cover, so he had to create some. By diving back on the second mercenary, he put an allied body in the way, desperation giving way to frustration as the freight pod picked up speed.

He'd never catch the damn thing now.

The second mercenary slugged Calvin in the face, a hard hit that sent his brain on a spin-cycle. Pushing Calvin to the ground, the mercenary stood back, breathing hard.

"Clear out," the wounded one ordered. "I can't get a shot with you in the way."

Calvin reached out in that second, grabbed the woman's foot. He pulled, sucking away the leather, the plastic, and shoving it into another spear. Not the most creative, maybe, but Calvin needed damage, and, for that, putting things into points tended to be the best option. The anomaly didn't have much leverage from the ground, but Calvin didn't need it.

When the woman, jerking her nearly bare foot from Calvin's hand, stepped aside, Calvin threw. This time, the strike didn't miss. Two meters, too perfect. The wounded mercenary, now with a nasty shining black spike in his throat, collapsed.

"What the hell are you?" his partner said, pulling at her own handgun.

"I'm just trying to get my friend back," Calvin said, again planting his hand on the asphalt. "You pull that gun, you wind up like him."

The woman hesitated, watching another asphalt spear grow in Calvin's hand, "Or what?"

"Or you tell me where they were going, and then get your buddy some help."

Calvin twitched his right hand as he spoke, feeding the asphalt into wicked barbs and hooks along the spear. Impractical and probably ineffective, they looked sinister in the late afternoon light, the asphalt's shards shimmering. The mercenary made some calculations, came up with the result Calvin expected.

She left her handgun alone.

THE PARAGON TOWER in downtown Chicago was, for once, not mobbed. Protestors against Paragon control had come out in force since Aegis's death and the subsequent drone army flooding the city's skies, while counter-protestors pushed back, shouting statistics showing the years since the Paragons took control had been safe, good, and generally calm.

Calvin edged around the remaining clusters, keeping his jacket pulled tight so the Paragon uniform's silver-blue wouldn't show through. After extracting the locale from the mercenary, he'd gone back to Kat's apartment for a quick change. Now downtown, a back-and-forth journey that ate up two hours, Calvin looked up at the tall, blazing building catching sunset in all its glory.

Already the upper windows had been replaced, the damage repaired from Mynx's fight. Calvin hadn't known the traitors that'd died then—he actively avoided meeting more Paragons if he could. Still, Calvin squinted at the clean-up, at how quickly any sign had been erased.

If he'd been in charge, Calvin would've advertised the traitor's cost. Made it clear that you take the wrong path, it's not going to end well.

Whatever. It wasn't his responsibility anyway.

The quadruple doors, thick glass laced with lines meant to suck energy away from the windows and into heatsinks on the ground, curled open when Calvin tapped his Tama. A little thrill shot through him with the green-lit chime: somehow, Calvin always expected the Paragons to drop him, kick him back to those streets.

"The man of the moment," Weed said as Calvin walked into the four-story lobby, a ridiculous statue and banner array that made Calvin feel like he'd wandered into an award ceremony. Weed and his team stood off to one side, throwing Calvin curious looks coupled with more than one waved Tama, digital clocks showing. "Bold to join us one day and call an emergency meeting the next."

"Not what I wanted," Calvin replied, walking over and keeping his head up. The authority in these places triggered old instincts, made him want to find a shadow to stand in. "A friend of mine's in trouble and I can't save her alone."

"Hear that, guys? Calvin needs our help. Should we give it to him?"

"Who's the friend?" Smoke asked, her eyes peeking out from beneath the Cubs ball cap constantly on her head.

"A tracker," Calvin said. "Best one in the city."

"Name?" said another, a pale dude whose beard went on too long.

"Kat Collins."

Smoke whistled. Weed frowned.

"Not doin' it," the bearded one replied, and when the whole group looked his way, he shrugged. "She's the one that brought me in."

"Kat's brought in half the Paragons here," Weed said. "We owe her, Lob."

Lob? Calvin wanted to shake his head, but held himself to an inside laugh instead.

"You maybe," Lob replied. "You haven't been dragged along on the end of her grapple, gettin' told how your freedom's done."

"I have," Calvin said, drawing eyes back to him. "She caught me. That's why I'm here. She's also saved my life plenty of times, helped me out when I had nowhere else to turn. Maybe she did her job with you, but she's been a friend to me."

The group's fourth member, Particle, the only one whose Paragon uniform showed front and center, snapped their fingers. Calvin found himself locked on them, as if sucked in by a magnet.

"You all wanna think for a minute?" Particle said. "The Paragons are a mess. Mynx herself is coming here tonight, trying to calm everyone down about this drone and stuff. Know what'll help? A good rescue mission. High profile tracker like Kat? Save her from some goons?"

"And the drone," Calvin interrupted, breaking Particle's hold.

"What?" Weed asked, and Calvin shrugged under the foursome's stares.

SNOW-SPOTTED CORNFIELDS SPREAD around them as the pod sped south, well away from the city. A full moon served to illustrate their surroundings in ethereal silver, providing a convenient distraction for Calvin as Weed had the team running through the plan for the fifth time. Making a plan when you didn't know what was going on made no sense, but Calvin chose to keep his eyes outside and say 'yeah' whenever Weed mentioned his name.

The pod announcing their imminent arrival saved the group from a sixth review, with Smoke using Paragon overrides to kill the pod's lights and force a drop-off on the roadside a half-kilometer away from their destination, the coordinates Calvin extracted from the mercenary.

"Remember," Weed said, "they'll know we're coming, or that someone is. Be quiet, be surgical. We're here for Kat, then we call in the reinforcements when she's secure."

Calvin wanted to bring in the whole cavalry, drones and every available Paragon, but Weed talked him off that ledge. First, Chicago's Paragons had to prep for Mynx, and second, the Elementals had been more and more active lately, requiring heavy patrols on the city's west side. The reinforcements would come, but only after Calvin and Weed confirmed the drone was here too.

Without the drone, well, Kat was only a tracker.

Calvin wanted to slug Weed for that comment, but Weed softened the blow by saying he understood it sucked, but Calvin had to remember the bigger picture. The last thing the Paragons needed was a high body count because some tracker had gone in over her head.

So now Calvin crept through wintry stalks instead of charging in, army at his back.

The goal, a massive barn with lights set up all around, didn't exactly hide. As the five left the pod—which moved itself onto the shoulder and settled down to wait—Smoke did her thing, casting a rippling wave around them that

Calvin felt more than saw. Anyone outside looking in wouldn't see much more than darkness, blurs.

Particle played the scout, moving fast through the stalks, their uniform hidden now behind a black tactical suit they'd pulled on back in Chicago. Calvin came second, his own past running through, well, everywhere serving to keep him on Particle's heels. Weed, Smoke, and Lob rounded out the back, the bearded one quitting his grumblings as soon as Weed made the call to rescue Kat.

Calvin kept flinching as they went, trying to get used to the noises around him. His teammates . . . the word felt odd, a situation he didn't know. Not that Calvin had time to get introspective. Kat was the mission, and all that mattered.

Particle snapped their fingers again, lightly, and Calvin's eyes went straight ahead and slightly right. The barn, blocked by some spindly trees, had its doors open. The drone sat inside, clear and sparkling in the light.

"There we go," Weed whispered, bringing up his Tama. "Time to call in the party."

While Weed made the connection, Particle kept moving forward, Calvin right on their heels. At first, the stealthy Paragon threw Calvin an annoyed look, but when they saw Calvin wasn't a total klutz clomping through the brush, Particle put their attention back to where it belonged: the barn, the drone, and the swarm surrounding it.

"This isn't a fringe group," Particle whispered, crouching in a muddy gap between chopped stalks near the tree line. "I don't see any identifiers on the uniforms."

"That's 'cause they're not here to make a statement," Calvin said.

"Then why take the drone?"

"Don't know about that, but these guys prefer a body count."

Particle nodded, "They're way armed. I vote waiting till reinforcements arrive."

"What happens then?"

Particle quirked a small smile, "Imagine a dozen drones blazing by above, torching everything while dropping battle-ready Paragons and you've pretty much got it."

"So everyone dies?"

"We don't take too many prisoners," Particle replied.

"But Kat's right there in the middle. What happens to her?"

"If she's lucky, she lives?"

Calvin shook his head as Weed and the others caught up, "Not good enough. I came to you for help, not to kill her."

"We have fifteen minutes before the strike gets here," Weed said, putting a hand on Calvin's shoulder. "Let's use it."

Calvin met the man's eyes, gave the slightest nod. Maybe Weed deserved a little respect.

Particle took the lead again as the quintet headed into the trees. On the other side, staked out every few meters, guards stood watching out into the dark. Each one wore bulky body armor, the kind meant for stopping both bullets and energy-based anomaly abilities. Long rifles hung from their hands, not the flimsy pistols. Calvin remembered Kat's walk into Rhimes's arsenal: looked like it'd wound up here.

The barn sat in the guard ring's center, and a chair, marked by a spotlight, sat before it, closer to the trees and Calvin. In that chair, head down and looking asleep, sat Kat. Calvin looked around but couldn't see Rhimes or Wexley.

"Twenty," Particle whispered, a tone so soft it sounded like rustling leaves. "Plan?"

Weed took over, putting Calvin and Particle on the left, with himself, Lob and Smoke on the right. They put five meters and a whole lotta strategy between them. Without Smoke's cover, Particle snapped their fingers several times, each one pulling the nearest guard's eyes away. Calvin had to suppress a whistle: Particle's ability had seemed like a stupid trick back in the Paragon tower.

Now? Damn handy.

"Ready?" Particle asked.

"Always am," Calvin replied.

Particle snapped their fingers again, and Calvin's head twisted to lock in on the guard ahead and to his right. Calvin blinked—guess that was one way to identify a target.

"Go," Particle spoke and darted ahead and left, towards their own sap.

Calvin broke into a run, giving up cover for noise. He brushed his hand against trees as he ran, sucking in their bark and launching it with his right hand, wood missiles flying towards his target. The hits bonked off the guard's helmet, prompting a shout as the guard wheeled his rifle around. Calvin swerved right, gripping a tree trunk hard to whip himself back straight and siphoning enough wood to make a heavy club.

The guard found his aim, blinding Calvin with the rifle's flashlight. Meters split the two, the thin trees at the grove's edge not adding much cover. In a second, Calvin would be perforated with bullets, and there wasn't a damn thing he could do about it.

Except the guard didn't fire. The man jerked his head to the right, shaking as he tried to fight the turn. A fight the guard won, just in time to look back and catch Calvin's club right in the temple. The guard collapsed as the first shots fired, bullets whizzing into the air. Calvin dropped next to his victim, one hand on the man's armor and the other spitting the essence back out and over Calvin's jacket.

In five seconds, what'd been a breathable spring accessory had its blue nylon coated with bullet-stopping fibers. Its weight had Calvin working to stand, the guard's rifle in his hands, but when a shot banged into his chest and sent Calvin back to the ground, Calvin couldn't argue with the results.

The guard that'd pegged him ran closer, leveling the rifle for a killing blow. Calvin stuck his left hand in the muddy ground, raised his right, and launched a dirty geyser. The brown grime splattered into the guard's faceplate, all over his hands, and the weapon, buying Calvin enough time to curl forward and pull the guard's foot out from under him. With the man on the ground, Calvin climbed up, caught the guard's flailing punch, absorbed the guard's glove and sent its leather around the guard's neck in a tight vice.

The alarm calls changed their tune as Calvin finished subduing the second guard. At first, it'd been calls to attack the new arrivals. Now, the orders changed to securing the prisoner. Calvin glanced Kat's way, saw only an indistinct blur, as if staring into a deep, rippling pool and trying to see its bottom.

Not blurry, though, was the Weed swarm pouring out from Smoke's screen. The thin man's copies sprinted out towards the guards, who proceeded to cut them down with withering gunfire. Yet, even as the Weed copies fell, more sprang up, smaller and faster than the last. The first ones reached the guards, biting their ankles or climbing up their legs to poke at their eyes, pry hands away from triggers, or pull pins from belted grenades.

Calvin absorbed the explosions with the second guard's body armor, sucked away into a rectangular shield. He waited, wondering when Weed, Smoke, and Lob were going to make their break away with Kat in tow, but nobody left the screen. Weed's manic swarm seemed to be dying out, and the guards would find their composure.

Worse, the clock kept ticking. The drone firestorm wouldn't discriminate.

Again, Calvin ran. This time, he kept the shield up, catching bullets as he hit Smoke's barrier and went right on through. Inside, Calvin picked up a grim situation: Smoke had her hands full trying to figure out the metal binds tying Kat to the chair. Lob bent over Weed, trying to stop what looked like a bad gunshot wound to the man's chest. Kat, for her part, looked either drugged or unconscious.

"Help Weed," Calvin said to Smoke, setting the shield aside, where, without Calvin's focus, the fibers unfolded fast into a blue-black blob.

"You can cut these?" Smoke asked.

"Nope," Calvin said, putting his hand on the first binding, a steel cuff tying Kat's ankle to the chair. "Better."

More bullets blew by, going by over Calvin's head as he crouched at Kat's feet. Sucking in the binding, Calvin whipped the results back towards the bullet's source, a narrow, long steel needle. A pained cry came back, earning Calvin an approving nod from Smoke.

"We need to get him outta here," Lob said.

"Then throw him," Smoke replied as Calvin set to work on the next binding.

"Alone?"

"If I leave, they'll shoot us all, moron," Smoke said.

"Then I'll come back."

Calvin, throwing another spear towards more

incoming fire, glanced Lob's way. What the hell did the Paragon mean?

"Make it quick," Smoke said. "We should be dead already. Particle's doing a helluva job out there."

Lob didn't say another word, but picked Weed up. The ground beneath the bearded Paragon vibrated, a tremor Calvin felt in his ankles. Then, the man leapt high, up and out of Smoke's screen into the night sky.

Anomalies. Never knew what you'd see next.

With Smoke huddling against the chair for cover, Calvin took off Kat's remaining bindings, then broke down the chair and turned it into a makeshift barrier. Together, the trio squeezed in. Calvin heard Smoke's heavy breathing, saw her eyes close tight.

"What's wrong?" Calvin asked, sitting Kat between them.

"Too tired to hold the screen up much longer," Smoke hissed. "And I took a hit in the side."

Calvin saw the red, then, leaking onto the ground. First Weed, then Smoke. How many Paragons was Kat worth? He looked at the tracker, her matted hair hanging over her face, her uniform dismantled and tossed away except for the shirt and pants. Bare feet sat in the mud.

A heavy splash went up as Lob landed, wobbling a little, in between the group. He looked over their way, saw Smoke, and started towards her.

"Get her out," Calvin said. "I'll hold us."

"Gettin' hairy," Lob replied, bending down to pick Smoke up. "Don't know how much longer Particle can keep it up."

Lob rose, Smoke in his arms, and again the ground shivered. Lob crouched, and Smoke's barrier sparked out. One second, the four sat disguised in the shimmering screen and the next they sat in a circle, surrounded by approaching guards with their guns up.

They fired. Lob leapt, bullets following his leap into the sky.

And Calvin jammed his hand into the mud. With his right, the anomaly spat out the earth as he absorbed it, spreading the dirt around and over him and Kat. As Calvin's left hand drew up the mud and the grit beneath it, Calvin and Kat sank further into the hole, every second digging them deeper, Calvin burying them.

But, at least, burying them alive.

16

Sweat Equity

Thane scooped her in the sky. The giant wrapped Cassidy up as they plummeted towards the trees, debris crashing around them. The Paragons might've been among them, or not. Cassidy couldn't know, couldn't care less. She'd sent a message to her family. The only goal, now, was not to die until she saw them again.

"Stay angry," Cassidy shouted, the wind pulling at them as they fell.

Thane roared. A good sign.

They struck a tree, Thane's back driving into a leafy canopy and pushing through the trunk. Branches whipped and scratched Cassidy's legs, face, everything. Then Thane hit the ground, launching dirt, leaves, and who knew what up and around. Cassidy felt the air blow from her lungs, felt her right shoulder snap as she bounced off Thane and rolled across the ground. The pain seared her eyes, prompting stars and a near pass-out saved only by the knowledge that to embrace darkness here was to die.

Instead, Cassidy looked up. Saw falling disaster as the plane's remnants splashed down around them. Mustering her focus, Cassidy threw a void above her and Thane, wide enough to cover them like some mystical umbrella. Engine pieces, chairs, supplies, they crashed into the void and vanished, disintegrated as Cassidy burned herself up.

When the shrapnel stopped, Cassidy still breathed. Thane, next to her, groaned as he shrank back down to a normal size. When she let the void go, the hot sun slammed through the now open spot in the forest, roasting them. Bugs, not ones to let new food go untested, swarmed fast.

And yet, Cassidy laid there. Felt her throbbing shoulder. They were lost in the wild, but they were alive. That would be enough.

"A minor setback," Thane said as they wandered through the jungle. "Nothing more, and nothing unexpected."

Cassidy led, using small voids to cut away anything too thick to walk through. Bugs swarmed, though moving at least kept the crawling ones away. Vines dangled, brushing against her head. Animals cried out in howls and hoots she didn't recognize, and the afternoon's heat coupled with humidity to drain her. Only the dire thought of spending a night out here kept Cassidy moving.

"Because falling from a plane, in which we were ambushed, is a minor setback," Cassidy replied without turning around. Thane shriveled up more, using his wrinkled mind for some inscrutable planning. "I thought we were going to Bangkok, and now we're in some random jungle."

"How many Paragons attempted to defeat us and failed?" Thane said. "We showed them we cannot be taken lightly."

"Tell me how we can convince these mosquitos of the same thing."

"We'll be free of these insects soon enough."

Not from Cassidy's view, as the trees continued on ahead as far as she could see. The ground squished beneath her feet, the shoes stolen from the home on the island already falling apart. At least the other clothes were light, cool. Covered in dirt and torn, but Cassidy had to take what she could get.

"How are you so sure?" Cassidy asked.

"The plane's velocity, direction, and our flight time put us near a sizable town," Thane said, not bothering to explain how he could calculate those things. "The Paragons were descending. There will be an airport here, or a vehicle to acquire, and from there we can make our way to Bangkok."

"Where we'll do what, get attacked again?"

"Most likely."

Cassidy stopped, glared Thane's way, "We barely made it off Mynx's island alive. Now we fell from a plane. We should both be very dead, but you want to press on?"

"Of course. What other path is there?"

"Vanish. I could get back to my family. Be happy for a change."

"Destiny would call. You would find yourself unsatisfied."

Cassidy laughed, went back to walking. Find herself unsatisfied, right. The one time she'd embraced her abilities, chased after a higher calling and Cassidy had lost everything. If the island and its endless days and nights on the beach had taught Cassidy anything, it was that there were better things than pursuing so-called destiny.

Like sharing a breakfast with her children. Like taking a hike and sipping wine on a hilltop beneath a bright blue sky. Or going to a theater and watching some play, even one put on by her son's goofy theater group.

If that group still existed.

Thane proved himself right. He'd directed Cassidy where to walk and chop, and she stepped through the trees onto a spongey dirt road. Tire treads indicated recent passage.

"How'd you know?" Cassidy asked as Thane bent down to study the tracks.

"I heard the vehicle. It passed some time ago."

"What? It was too noisy—"

"The sounds you heard had the truck's among them. In this state, I parsed them out." Thane stood. "See these treads, heading this way?" He pointed at a deeper set, albeit one that looked older. "The truck was heavier there than here. Laden with goods, returning home."

"Or delivering them somewhere and coming back empty."

Thane locked his wrinkled visage on Cassidy, straight on. Would he attack her, declare her stupid? Cassidy felt the voids tingling on her fingertips, narrowed her focus on his heart. Hard to know if a void could take Thane out, but she would try, she would fight if he—

Thane laughed. Cold, hearty.

"I like you," Thane said, "for so many reasons, my dear. You are clever, you are deadly, and your nose wrinkles up in this cute fashion whenever you're focused." He waved at the tracks. "Of course you're right, we are taking a chance either way. However, one thing will be true: so long as we walk along this road, we shall wind up somewhere better than where we were."

Cassidy pushed the urge away, took a long, deep breath.

"Then lead on, smart guy," Cassidy said, "because any place other than this muddy, buggy jungle sounds pretty good."

The village didn't emerge, it appeared. The trees, from one step to the next, thinned out and made way for homes, shops, and the collective community that reminded Cassidy of the island. Twenty-first century mentalities coupled with remote realities, bringing broad streetlights, charging stations, and electric vehicles onto unpaved roads, homes that ranged from prefabricated to junk piled just so. Cooking spices melded with the humid air to drench Cassidy in nose-tingling smells as children shouted, kicking soccer balls in the drier dirt patches. Someone had a sports broadcast blaring on a radio, carrying over everything else.

Everything except the big, bus-sized monstrosity in the town's center.

Coated in Paragon blue and silver, the bus bore its name in the local language, scribed along the side in a script suggesting either a cheap scam or an action hero's imminent appearance. Tinted windows sat above the words, while below, nozzles hung off the side like the ones Cassidy remembered from the firetrucks she'd show her students on field trips.

"Don't worry," Thane said when Cassidy hesitated at the town's edge. "They're not here for us."

"How do you know?"

"The label on the bus." Thane looked at Cassidy as if this should be obvious.

"I can't read it."

"Ah, sometimes I forget . . . " Thane waved at the village. "The bus is the opening salvo in the Paragon's fight to modernize everywhere. Apinya's quest, I believe. It will be followed by changes that will render this village unrecognizable, and utterly dependent on Paragon largess."

Cassidy cocked her head, "You know all this from a few words on a bus?"

"I know all this because Apinya and I developed the

strategy together, back when I was chained to a chair and forced to do what the Champions asked."

There wasn't much she could say to that. When Thane moved to head deeper into the village Cassidy followed behind. At least the bugs didn't seem so thick here with the cook fire smoke keeping them away. A glass of water or three, a shower, and maybe some clothes not caked in mud might be nice.

Who said you couldn't ask for a few creature comforts on the road to world domination?

Thane skipped right by any hopes for such things and went straight for the Paragon bus. Cassidy tried to find a rationale for not sneaking through town and hitching a ride elsewhere and failed.

"What are you doing?" Cassidy finally asked as they neared. The bus itself had its doors open, with villagers going inside and coming out holding buckets. "Was nearly getting killed on a plane not enough?"

"I'm changing the plan," Thane said. "I thought it over during our jungle walk back there. We cannot hide from the Paragons, but they don't appear to have the resources to fight us either."

"Where are you getting that from?"

Thane pointed to himself, "Not long ago, when I escaped their prison, the Paragons sent two Champions, an anomaly horde, and drones after me. Now, we get perhaps ten, and ones who didn't know what they were up against, thrown our way. Why would that be?"

"Because we appeared on an island and left before they could prepare?"

"Kauai is hardly isolated. Drones could've been sent from Honolulu. They could have trapped us somewhere, like the open ocean."

Behind Thane, following a villager off the bus, came a

uniformed Paragon. She went right for Cassidy and Thane, with straight-line steps that showed either suicidal courage or an assurance of victory. The voids leapt to Cassidy's fingertips, and she nodded past Thane's shoulder.

"Our answers approach," Thane said, turning.

Cassidy grimaced at the anomaly's back. Every time she tried to get a bead on Thane, he seemed to slip into another lane. At first, on Mynx's island, he'd been fixated on escape, flavored with some nebulous, almost corny plots about what to do after. Then, on Kauai, he'd been quiet, determined only to come to Bangkok with nary a mutter about what waited there.

Why had she bothered to come with him all this way?

Oh, right, because these Paragons kept trying to kill them, and it helped to have a near-invincible monster on your side.

"Would you both please come with me?" asked the Paragon, slanting her way into English like Cassidy had that library computer: a skill learned but left to languish. "I'm Achara, leading the Paragons here. It would mean much to us if you would come onboard our lab for just a moment."

"Another trap?" Thane asked.

Achara frowned, "Apinya disagreed with that approach, but Hawaii isn't in his jurisdiction. We aren't the same."

"You're wearing the same uniform," Cassidy added.

"And you are wearing the same mud my brothers had on their clothes every day." Achara smiled. "But I don't believe you are here for treats."

Thane looked Cassidy's way, a confidence vote that caught the Void a little by surprise. A concession?

"Then go ahead," Cassidy said. "We'll follow."

Achara nodded, turned back towards the bus. The

mud, Cassidy noticed, didn't stick to her Paragon boots or the uniform at all. Treated with some chemical, or coated with some anomaly gift. Either way, how nice it would be to have a pair.

"Be warned," Thane added, "if you are lying, you will be the first to die."

"Then I'd better not be lying."

The bus appeared larger on the inside than it looked from without, as all but a few seats had been stripped away. Those remaining chairs, bolted in to the bus's floor, centered several large basins, each one filled with what looked like water. The rearmost one seemed murky, polluted, while the middle took on a clearer mix and the closest a level of clarity Cassidy hadn't seen since her beloved, or perhaps loathed, beach back on Mynx's island.

Achara waved Cassidy and Thane to a two-spot bench along the closest container while she moved deeper into the bus near the middle cloudy basin.

"Don't take offense," Achara said, "I have to continue working or they won't have enough clean water for the day. If you like, take a cup and get yourself a drink."

Without waiting for an answer, Achara reached forward and dipped her hand in the middle. The Paragon's eyes closed briefly. The cloud shifted, the brown and murky bits sliding off to one side while clear water split to the other. Once the halves aligned—Cassidy watched this after taking Achara's advice and filling her own cup from the first basin—Achara took her hand out. The basin rumbled, draining away the water and leaving the muddy remnants alone. Outside, children and adults approached the bus with more buckets and bottles, using the nozzles to fill their vessels.

"There has to be a more efficient way to do that," Cassidy said as Achara moved opposite them.

"There is, and it's coming," Achara replied. "Even the Paragons can only lay infrastructure so fast, and this is far from any major center." Again she put on the polite smile. "It's why we flew you here."

"Then you will transport us to Bangkok," Thane said.

He left the second part, the threat, lingering in the silence. If she picked up on it, Achara didn't show.

"Apinya called me two hours ago." Achara went to the farthest basin, the muddiest water. She leaned down, pressed a button on the basin's side. Much like the second one, whose clear water now flushed into the drained first basin, the last reservoir transitioned its filthy contents. "He told me to look up to the sky and tell him what I saw. I said it looked like we were being attacked because the sky seemed to be on fire."

"The jet," Cassidy said, and Thane put a hand on her wrist, squeezed in a way more commanding than affectionate.

A warning, but of what? A water purifying Paragon hardly seemed dangerous.

"The jet," Achara confirmed. "The Paragons survived, of course, or this would be a different meeting altogether."

"But I split one with a void?" Cassidy said. "Nobody would survive that."

Returning to the seat opposite Cassidy and Thane, Achara filled her own cup with water. Cassidy had to admit, the purified liquid tasted like a pure elixir going down after all the sweat, the dirt, the bugs.

"You should know with anomalies what you see isn't always reality," Achara replied. "We would, however, like to find some truth." Achara leaned back against the bus windows, sipping from her cup. "Why did you come here?"

"If Apinya knows where we are, then he can guess

why," Thane replied. "We need a way to Bangkok, Paragon."

"You can buy it with your honesty."

Thane snorted, "Then tell your Champion that we are here because he is. I intend to find Apinya, take his place here, and use this region to start the change the world desperately needs." Thane leaned forward. "In other words, Apinya is weak, and it is time he cedes his power to someone stronger."

Achara nodded, as if Thane had just finished giving his thoughts on white versus brown rice, and looked at Cassidy, "And you?"

"I want to get back to my family without being afraid some machine, or one of you, might take me away in the night or kill me during the day."

"Thane's vision is going to bring you that?"

"Yours sure as hell didn't."

Thane stood, took a cup, filled and downed the contents in a single gesture and threw the plastic aside. "Bangkok. Now."

"All right," Achara stood up to Thane. "You want your ride to Bangkok, I can give it to you. Before I do, however, Apinya has asked for a favor."

Cassidy saw Thane's muscles tighten, those arms and legs begin to expand. She could've reached for a void, could've been ready to throw down, but after the plane, the walk, the heat, she just took another drink of that excellent water. If Thane wanted to tear Achara apart and claim the bus, then he could go right ahead and do it on his own.

Achara didn't do what people tended to when confronted with Thane's monster threat. Instead she poked Thane in the chest. Thane's breath shot out, his head wrinkled, even as his arms and legs grew and grew until he pressed against the bus's ceiling.

"Half and half," Achara said. "It's not usually this drastic, but with you I suppose I'm not too surprised."

Thane collapsed, teetered and fell to the bus's floor alongside the basins. Cassidy wasn't sure why until she saw his crippled chest, tiny and withered, working to feed the massive, oxygen-sapping muscles surging across his body.

"Calm down, Thane, or you'll die," Cassidy said, resisting the urge to comfort the man. If Achara decided to turn this into an actual attack, going after her when Cassidy had her attention divided would be a good next step. "As for you, reverse it."

"I can," Achara said, "but again, Apinya asks a favor. The village has a problem, and I think you could provide the solution. Do it, and you'll get your ride to Bangkok, and Thane can go back to being the monster he wants to be."

Rocket Rumble

The night wasn't supposed to start with a Paragon ambush. In fact, Wexley, waiting in the nearby fields surrounding the barn holding their captive drone, was supposed to be the one doing the ambushing. Rhimes had his main squad in the spotlight, ready to handle the attack when it came, then Wexley, Rhimes, and a few handpicked others would come from behind and unleash the surprise.

Now Wexley had a few members down and an anomaly holding his prized hostage captive beneath a seemingly impenetrable mud bubble.

"Mud," Wexley said again to Rhimes, the man's Tama in dark mode held up between them. "That's what's stopping you?"

"It's real thick," came back the reply, as if that would be a satisfying response. At least the man seemed to realize the dismal effort, because he kept on going, "But they can't get out either. They're stuck, and we took care of the others."

"Took care of?" Wexley asked. "Bodies?"

"They ran," the man replied and Wexley rolled his eyes to the stars. "We hit'em though. I know that much."

"And how do you know that much?"

"Because the grass is red around here, you catch my meaning."

That at least swung in a positive direction. The Paragons needed to suffer a little for the damned incursion or they might come right back to extract their trapped fellows. Not something Wexley needed when the reports from Chicago were saying Mynx had landed. The Champion would get the word soon about the drone, and Wexley figured she'd be coming mere minutes after.

She'd know, of course, about the waiting guards now. Those escaped Paragons would warn Mynx.

"Run the numbers again," Rhimes said. "How many?"

"Five. One's stuck in with the hostage. We hit at least three. The fourth, that one was a nasty piece of work. Couldn't hold a focus on them, and then they were gone. Never got a good look."

Rhimes glanced at Wexley, asking a question: send out a force to find the Paragons? Finish'em off?

Wexley shook his head. The wounded Paragons were probably gone already. The damage had been done. Focus on the main objective.

"Then get back to your setup," Rhimes said. "Stick two on the mud, make sure they're ready if the bubble drops. Otherwise, the operation is still a go. Remember, when the signal comes in, don't expect chatter."

"You got it."

The call clicked off. Wexley unslung his rifle, checked the rounds again. The barrel. Everything shined in the moonlight, ready for its work. He had more packs on his belt, and, like with the drone assault the other morning, full body armor on. A helmet this time too, though right now that hung off his shoulder.

"Concerned?" Rhimes asked.

"Should I be?" Wexley looked towards the barn. "If I'm guessing right, this group targeted Kat. Not the drone. You said someone hit your team back at the diner?"

"On our way out. Bad timing." Rhimes spat off to the side. "Should've stopped and reinforced my team, but I didn't know whether the anomaly had friends."

"You made the right choice. We still have the hostage, and now an extra Paragon."

"Then we're clear to send the message?"

Wexley took a deep breath, enjoyed the night air, packed in with the earliest spring scents. Nature, beginning its climb back from the long winter. Just like him, like his friends, thawing out the anomaly hold on the free world.

"Send it. Let's bag ourselves a Champion."

MYNX DIDN'T MAKE a subtle entrance. Rhimes blasted the message to the Paragon tower in Chicago, hitting every known email address and even convincing a few paid-off people to leave taunting recorders blaring in the tower's courtyard. Each one had a simple message, listing the drone's location and daring the Champion to come get it.

And promising, if Mynx didn't arrive, future carnage.

Wexley had no back-up for this one, no way to carry through on the threat, but with the stadium bombing such recent history, he had to bet Mynx wouldn't risk it.

She did not.

With ten drones flanking her, several carrying Paragons inside, Mynx charged towards the barn. Wexley and Rhimes picked out her lights coming from Chicago, at first appearing like low stars, then low planes, and finally like what they were: black metal monsters gliding through the night.

As Mynx's force neared the target, Wexley, Rhimes, and the back-up five lay low in the field. Overhead, Mynx and the drones slowed and then spread, moving from an arrow formation to a circle. They surrounded the barn, moving in sync like hive-mind insects. The drones changed their running lights to an angry red, making it clear to everyone peace had no part in their performance.

"Beautiful in a way," Wexley muttered as the formation progressed.

"I prefer the one in the barn," Rhimes replied.

Mynx herself took the lead. She plummeted in, her suit smaller than the drones around her, but still bulky and loaded up with murderous measures. Like a close-up comet, Mynx smashed down into the center, right where that mud bubble ought to be. Rhimes's force opened up, their bullet-spewing spray echoing across the fields.

"What if they kill her?" Rhimes said.

"They won't."

"Could get lucky."

Wexley shook his head, raised himself to a crouch and pulled the rifle up to his eye. The scope zoomed him in, let him look.

Mynx, her suit taking rifle fire and bouncing it away like Wexley might a child's toy, seemed to be ignoring the guards. Instead, she clomped right past the mud bubble and approached the captive drone. Wexley frowned, trying to figure out the strategy in charging solo while her reinforcements all waited around the edges.

"She makes machines, right?" Wexley asked. "That's her ability? Machines?"

"It's not advertised," Rhimes replied. "She's not like Aegis. Flashy."

Mynx, her armor apparently impervious to the gunfire, made it to the barn doors. The captive drone sat a scant meter or two away. Her armor expanded, spreading steel wings to cover the barn entrance. Spotlights highlighted the new shield, and blocked Wexley from seeing into the barn at all.

"Tell them to go close," Wexley said, fighting off panic. If Mynx re-activated the stolen drone somehow and flew away, this would all be for nothing. "Now."

Rhimes relayed the command and five guards broke into a run towards the barn doors. Some pulled riot batons from their belts, while others lowered their shoulders like they were going to run over Mynx's armor. As inspiring sights went, it could use some work.

"We might be losing it," Rhimes said. "Should we activate?"

"They're too far. If we miss, then it's over."

"If she finds a way to disable—"

"Rhimes," Wexley said. "Tell the others to fire. I want them shooting at the drones, emergency plan. We go too. Right now."

Rhimes took the order like a good soldier ought: he acted without questioning. Again the Tama came up, again the words came out, and those guards that weren't chasing Mynx raised their rifles, found cover, and fired. The hot crackle again rang out over the fields, sparks flying where shots hit the drones.

Blue lightning where the right rounds struck home.

Wexley raised his own rifle, zeroed in on the closest drone as Rhimes did the same next to him. His fingers found the trigger, and Wexley let loose the first shot. The round streaked into the night sky and slammed into the drone's rear jet, breaking into azure coils and sending the big machine jerking towards the ground.

When the machine rotated around, when the other drones swooped in towards the shooting guards, Wexley almost cheered. The gladiators and the three transport drones couldn't ignore their own programming, they had to neutralize the threats.

"Send it," Wexley said, and Rhimes did.

Wexley didn't see a pop, didn't catch any fireworks or hear any screams. Instead, the drones simply dropped. Already moving towards the guards, the machines barreled headfirst into the ground, into trees, into the mud. They struck the earth and flipped or broke apart, joints not made for a high speed impact.

Any Paragons stuck inside the transport drone's cargo bays would be tossed around, would find those bay doors unable to open.

In less time than it took for Wexley to fire a second rifle shot, all but one of the flying drones had been downed. Beautiful wreckage. He'd have to give Rhimes and his team a bonus.

But to do that, Wexley had to live, and the one drone not caught by the short-wave blast had its gunsights set on Wexley, Rhimes, and their short team.

"Give it everything!" Wexley shouted, pulling on his helmet. Rhimes had his own rifle up, squeezing off rounds at the approaching drone.

Rhimes's shots plinked off the drone's front plates as if the man threw peanuts. Wexley's own second shot didn't fare any better, the EMP shell crackling without effect across the drone's shoulders.

The big machine's spotlights lit, centered on Wexley, Rhimes, and the other five members, each one laying into the drone.

"Cover!" Rhimes called, and the damn thing opened up.

Tiny vents appeared in the drone's joints, and, with little whistles, micro rockets sprayed into the sky, twirling into the air before zeroing in on the team. Wexley dropped his rifle, yanked out the handgun on his hip and squeezed the trigger, snap-aiming towards the star shooting right at him.

And missed.

The micro rocket felt like a stab striking Wexley's chest, shoving him back and off his feet into the mud. He brought up his hands as the thing exploded, heat scorching his armor, wrapping his helmet and head in a fiery flash that died as quickly as it came.

The mud sucked at his shoulders, its cold an opposite to the searing shock seeping through his head to toe suit. The armor clung to him in patches, bare and burned skin feeling the night wind for the first time. Wexley took a breath, fought off the shock long enough to test his limbs. Found them working, found them tight.

Light struck him. White, bright, and focused. The drone lining up another salvo.

Wexley raised his right hand, still holding the pistol. Squeezed the trigger. The gun popped off a round, the bullet streaking towards, hitting, and bouncing away from his target.

"Damn you," Wexley said, and waited to die.

He waited for one blink, then two. The drone's light stayed stuck on him, and for a moment Wexley wondered if he'd actually died before, with the rockets. If this was some sick joke of an entry into a dismal afterlife. Maybe the anomalies, the Paragons, controlled that too.

The light died. The drone fired up its engines, launching upward and then, with a sonic booming speed burst, shot away back north towards the city. Why? What'd happened?

Wexley didn't have the answers, and his body didn't have the energy for more questions. His head dropped back to the mud, the helmet splatting in with a sickly noise.

"Boss, wake up," Rhimes spoke with a shake Wexley felt through the numbing morass clogging his mind. He blinked, saw light, a yellow one though. Where? "We have her, Wexley."

"Who?" Wexley thought he spoke, but the question came out as a wisp, a gasp.

"The big one," Rhimes replied. Wexley waited for a hand to help him get up, but Rhimes extended none, so Wexley made the attempt himself only for Rhimes, with a mother's press, to keep him down. "Don't move yet. I ran a scan but we have to make sure there's no damage first."

Around them, guards hustled. Orders called and responded. Electric engines whirred. A clean-up and extraction in full swing.

"How are you alive?"

"Because I didn't try to shoot the rocket," Rhimes said, huffing a laugh. "Don't know where you found that idea, but don't try it again."

"That was pretty dumb, wasn't it?"

"'Specially when you remember our vests are thicker in back. My rocket bounced off me when I dove, exploded over my head." Rhimes rubbed his neck. "Have a couple new scars to show off, but that's it."

"Remind me to listen to you more often."

"Will do, sir." Rhimes Tama blinked and the man nodded. "You're clear. Might be hurting for a while though."

"Drugs can handle that," Wexley said, sitting up.

Spots flared in his eyes, looking like those drone's targeting lights all over again. With them came a dizzy rush, a dry ache across his skin. Rhimes held Wexley's shoulders as the man looked down at himself. He'd been covered with a sheet, aloe creams cooling the skin where it touched.

"How bad is it?" Wexley asked.

"You'll be hurting. Don't know for how long. A hospital would be the best place for you."

"Not going there. Not yet. Where is she?"

It took long breaths and short steps, Rhimes helping steady Wexley the entire way to the barn. Around them, everyone else scrambled to clean up the site. Any guards not loading up into a transport kept their rifles trained on the downed drones, waiting for any Paragons hidden away inside to break out. The plan called for the Champion's capture and a swift exit. Reinforcements would be coming from Chicago soon, and Wexley didn't have enough mercenaries to survive an open fight with the anomalies.

Mynx's suit lay off to the side, already being picked over by Rhimes's team for vulnerabilities, for things they could steal. Two guards standing pat outside the barn's opening avoided looking at Wexley, though they gave Rhimes nods.

Not that Wexley could afford to care about such tiny things.

Not now.

"We don't have much time," Rhimes muttered as they came in. "Our pod's already waiting."

"It won't take long," Wexley replied. "I just need to make sure."

"Make sure what?"

"That it's her."

Rhimes threw him a quizzical look, mouth and eyes curling in confusion. Inside the barn, Mynx stood, regal even in captivity. Standard dumb cuffs held her hands behind Mynx's back, while someone had been smart and smashed her Tama's screen to render it useless. Her glare would've made Wexley flinch if not for the drugs, the pain, already coursing through his nerves.

Standing before a Champion would always be an experience.

"Mynx," Wexley said. "I'm—"

"I know who you are," Mynx said. "I know what you're doing, and I know you will be crushed."

Wexley coughed, brought up his hand to wipe his lips. Skin came with it, already blistering.

"Great. Don't care. I'll ask this once, and if you get the answer wrong, he's going to end your life right now."

Mynx tilted her head, "He can try."

Wexley bit off a response. He'd read the books, he'd seen the movies. Mynx would play the conversation out, buy time for her Paragons to break from the drones, for more to come in from Chicago.

"Who's Denise Jones?" Wexley asked. "And why did you kill her?"

Mynx didn't have to say a word for Wexley to know they'd caught the right one. He nodded at Rhimes, and let the plan execute around him.

It felt strange to carry out an interrogation in a robe, but Wexley couldn't let his own problems stand in the way. A discrete physician—another person on Rhimes's employ, another reason to give the man a raise—met them at the rural airport hours south of Chicago and pumped Wexley with what he needed to stay awake, to stay numb to the burns. Wexley hadn't missed the grimaces, the doctor's sighs as he pulled one vial after another, one IV bag after another from his truck and handed them to Rhimes.

"Hospital," the doctor finished, telling Wexley straight. "Don't wait. You'll need grafts."

Instead, Wexley boarded the plane. A twenty-seater jet,

already occupied by Rhimes and his most trusted soldiers. And, in a separate, small room towards the back, a captive Champion. Wexley joined Mynx in the room, buckling himself into a seat opposite her couch. He pressed a button on his right, told the flight captain to get moving, then settled in and looked at his opponent.

Mynx had her Paragon uniform on, looking all silver and dignified as she sat on the tan leather cushions. The beige intersected with white throughout the room, making it feel a little like Wexley had stepped into a farm. Two small windows on either side looked out into the airport's blinking runway lights, the plane's starting engines knocking out any other sounds.

For the rumbling take-off, Mynx and Wexley looked at each other. He found Mynx both older and younger than he expected, her skin showing an aggressive care regimen while her posture, the grays nibbling at her hair, and just the *feel* Wexley found looking at her suggested someone past life's breaking point and on its downward slope.

What did she see in him? A maniac?

Looking at himself, Wexley almost laughed. For a man who'd spent the last two decades in suits, whether bullet-proof or three-piece, settling for a scrappy robe and an aloe vat, not to mention the IV hanging from a stand by his hip, marked a departure.

Maybe Zhan-Yo had felt the same when his revolution carried him from the corporate heights to Chicago's dirty sewers.

"I've looked better," Wexley said as the plane leveled out.

"Where are we going?" Mynx asked, straight as a razor's edge.

"I think you'll recognize the place," Wexley said. "It's one I've wanted to see for a long time." Wexley shifted his right hand, tapped a finger on his thigh while Mynx puzzled away. No, he wouldn't wait for her to figure it out. "Mynx, where is Mila? The Champion you've kept away from her home?"

Now he had Mynx's attention. She snapped her eyes to his, that glare coming right back. All the Champions seemed to run hot tempers, all except Apinya, that Paragon of peace and philosophy.

"What do you want with her?" Mynx asked.

"Isn't it obvious?"

"It's an improvement. My machines always wear their purpose on the outside. Now you do as well."

Wexley gave her a nod, "Your machines? I thought they belonged to the Paragons?"

"Not all of them."

"What about the one we took? Was that yours?"

Mynx curled up a lip, "It's no good to you anymore."

"We can repair the damage."

"Not this kind. Your little trick didn't quite work."

Wexley raised his Tama, told Rhimes to get an updated assessment on the drone. While its use as bait for Mynx had been accomplished, the gladiator could still be a potent fighting machine, and Wexley was about to need every weapon he could find.

"You do understand my abilities, don't you?" Mynx asked.

"You have a way with machines."

"Quite a way," Mynx's eyes glittered. "Bold of you to put me on a plane."

"That's nothing compared to where I'm taking you."

Mynx sat forward, scooted to the couch's edge, "Wexley, understand this. Every Paragon on this continent and very soon the world will be looking for me. They will come to find out you did this, and then your company and everyone in it will be taken. The innocent will be shuffled out, but the complicit?" Mynx didn't smile, didn't gloat. "I gave up mercy when Aegis died."

"I don't want your mercy, Mynx," Wexley said, leaning forward to match her move. "All I want is your army."

Blades

Two people enter, one leaves. Standard rules for a duel. Satisfaction went to the victor.

A father avenged.

Celice forgot about Gatete, forgot Mathieu and Roger and all the little pieces in the apartment telling a story other than the one she wanted to believe. The one standing before her right now.

Zhan-Yo had a single blade ready, the other sheathed on his back. He rested on his toes before the fireplace, giving Celice none of the cracking revolution he'd delivered back in Chicago on their first meeting. Then, she'd caught him by surprise. Then, she'd turned his every move against him, had been about to deliver a deathblow before Mynx made a rude intervention.

Death wasn't on the table this time either, but humiliation made a good substitute.

"If we have to play this pointless game," Zhan-Yo said, "then let's get on with it."

Celice replied with her feet, kicking into a run across

the short kitchen, the living room and its spread furniture. Too little space to make much speed. Enough to stop hard.

Zhan-Yo's greeting swing went where Celice should've been. Where she was after the blade passed by. The swordsman tried to bring the sword back, caught a strike to his face followed by a kick to the gut that plastered him across the fireplace. He cleared room with a lazy swing, Celice dancing away and darting back in.

This time Zhan-Yo moved, lurching to his right as Celice came in on the left, leading with another hit. She cuffed Zhan-Yo on the shoulder, drawing nothing from the swordsman except a swirling slash. Celice ducked, felt the air shift above, and heard the blade connect with the fireplace's stone. Another sloppy swing.

"Are you even trying?" Celice growled, coming in again as Zhan-Yo made a predictable cut down.

She reached forward and up with her right hand, caught Zhan-Yo's descending hilt and pulled it towards her, taking the hilt's blunt impact on her shoulder. Her left hand pulled another triple punch series into Zhan-Yo's face, enough to send the man stumbling away. Back towards the kitchen and the watching trio.

Gatete clapped. Roger stared. Mathieu frowned.

Zhan-Yo spat bright red blood across the dark wood floor.

"Are you?" Celice asked again.

"Would it matter if I was?"

Celice reached along her leg, found the thigh knife and pulled it free. Did it matter? Really? Her father demanded vengeance. It didn't have to be fair.

"No," Celice answered.

Again she came in quick, and again she stopped as Zhan-Yo brought the blade to bear, kitchen counter at his back. Zhan-Yo didn't just go in for the feint this time, but stepped forward as he swung, ready to catch a stopping Celice in her trick.

Repetition would kill the cocky fighter.

Celice used her momentum to misdirect, to bounce from her left foot over towards the wall on her right and the couch pushed aside against it. With her right foot planted on the main cushion, Celice jumped back towards Zhan-Yo, coming in at his side as his lunging swing brought him out of position.

Zhan-Yo froze. She had the knife pressed up against his side, point peaking through the man's armor. The filleting would be quick, Zhan-Yo's death would be slow.

"Stop now," Gatete announced. "I believe this show is over, however much I may have enjoyed it."

Zhan-Yo dropped his sword. It clattered on the floor without ceremony, without triumph. "I surrender."

Celice didn't move the knife. Her hand gripped it tight. A little further, another second and she could fulfill her promise to her father. And what would Gatete do, exactly? Attack her?

"You don't get to surrender," Celice said. "Not this time."

She moved, pushed the knife.

And found it gone.

Gatete clucked his tongue as the hollow flakes that had been Celice's knife fluttered down, "Now now. No more fighting."

"He doesn't deserve to live another second," Celice said. "Not one——"

"He will live as long as he needs to," Gatete replied, "because what better way for Zhan-Yo to die than by helping us?"

Celice stepped left, with Zhan-Yo between Gatete and Roger. Zhan-Yo's sword sat at her feet, ready to be flipped up and used. Gatete's ability had to have some limits. Maybe sight was one. Zhan-Yo looked at her, his face a set mask. A prisoner already resigned to his sentence.

Sliding her foot beneath the hilt, Celice flipped the fallen sword up, grabbing the hilt with her left hand and swinging the blade while stepping back, a stroke that should've left Zhan-Yo gutted on the ground.

She never made contact. A clashing ring enveloped the apartment as Zhan-Yo's second blade, drawn from its shoulder sheath, caught Celice's stroke as her attack neared his armor. The two weapons stayed frozen, Celice pushing up, Zhan-Yo forcing the blow back down.

No rage, no anger crossed him. As if Zhan-Yo had defended himself because logic demanded it, rather than self-preservation.

"Why won't you die?" Celice snarled.

"Because it is not your place to kill me," Zhan-Yo replied. "Not yet."

"The man has it right," Gatete said, stepping around between them and lashing Celice with narrowed eyes. "You will stop this, Celice, or I will—"

"You'll what, Gatete? You'll tell the Paragons you kept me from avenging my father?"

"I'll tell them you are a rogue actor causing violence within my city," Gatete said, putting a hand on both hilts and spreading the blades apart. "I will have Mynx come and get you, and make sure she puts you somewhere you won't be a danger to anyone else." With the swords separated, Gatete flipped from discipline to reward, patching in a bright grin to the room. "But I would much prefer we take our prisoner and get him settled. There is a party to plan for!"

Zhan-Yo dropped his second blade and followed Gatete from the apartment without another word. Celice, her stolen sword in her hand, watched. The night had gone so wrong, so right.

She'd caught the man who killed her father.

Then why did Celice feel more lost than before?

Outside, pods waited with more Paragons, including Sydney, who dished Celice a loathing look. With Gatete leading their little group, Sydney gave a short briefing, noting Zhan-Yo's mercenaries had been taken from the pub and sent to the very same place Zhan-Yo would be going in seconds.

"And the reception?" Gatete asked.

"Locally trending," Sydney said, her stare drifting towards Zhan-Yo. "Once we break that we have him, though, the world's going to pay attention."

"I know. We need to maximize this. Get them moving, then let's huddle back at the Tower. No mistakes."

"The Tower?" Celice asked Roger and the Paragon rolled his eyes at her.

"The Tower of London. Legendary prison?" Roger said. "Or did Aegis not teach you any history?"

"He was spending too much time teaching me how to spot an asshole. Looks like I found one."

Roger snorted and joined Gatete as the Champion climbed into his own pod. Two other Paragons relieved Zhan-Yo of his armor and weapons before stuffing him into another pod and joining the man inside. The two vehicles shot off, leaving Sydney, Celice, and Mathieu on the sidewalk.

"Coming?" Sydney said to Celice.

"What about him?" Celice pointed to Mathieu. "You're not rounding him up with the others?"

"Hey," Mathieu started.

"Narrative," Sydney shrugged. "We'll release his picture, say that Zhan-Yo still has an associate at large.

People will see you, send pictures, get scared. Then we'll have a drone catch you, a surprise appetizer at Zhan-Yo's execution."

Celice felt not-so-vaguely ill, like her stomach wanted to reject the Paragons as much as her dinner.

"And kill me?" Mathieu asked, apparently as disbelieving as Celice.

"That part's up to you," Sydney said as her chosen pod scooted up to the curb. "It'll be better if you recant and apologize right there, in front of all the cameras. He'll let you live if you do that, guaranteed." Sydney must've seen their faces, because her own softened. "I know I sound like a monster, and like Gatete's some evil thing, but it's reality, right?"

"A messed up one," Celice said, aware she and Mathieu stood side by side looking at Sydney, a team by chance.

The Paragon presence had sent civilians scurrying for cover, leaving the street and the sidewalks almost deserted save for a dog-walker doing everything he could to keep his terrier away from the trio. A light rain shifted in overhead, drizzling the street and dripping along the windows.

Sydney pointed at her, "You think your father would've had so much success if people didn't pay attention to him? Gatete needs people to know he exists so that he'll get the promotions."

"And you?" Mathieu countered. "You're helping with these sick games?"

"Coming from the man who helped bomb a stadium?" Sydney laughed. "Spare me. It's a raw world. If Gatete moves up, guess who takes his place?"

"Roger, by the looks of it," Celice said.

"He'll go with Gatete and run Europe. I get London and a chance to breathe."

"What a prize for all your principles," Mathieu muttered. "I can't defend what Zhan-Yo did, but at least we had a good reason."

"And how the hell do you know what my principles are? Celice, get in the pod. Mathieu, better get running, You have a few days and then you're dirt."

Mathieu chuckled, took a step back, "You Paragons are so surprised the rest of us hate you, but is it really so hard to see?"

Celice stuck her hand out, took Mathieu's left arm and held it like she would a friend's. The move came quick, an instinct putting itself into action.

"My father built the Paragons," Celice said, moving her eyes from Syndey to Mathieu and back. "This isn't what he made."

"Time—" Syndey started to talk, but Celice cut her off with a single raised finger.

"You get in your pod, Sydney," Celice said. "You take it back to Gatete and Roger and all his friends. He's got Zhan-Yo. He can leave us alone."

Sydney mixed anger and confusion into curiosity, "Us? You and Mathieu?"

To Sydney's credit, Mathieu looked equally lost. The expressions threw Celice for a moment, had her wondering if the decision was the right one. Until she remembered Roger and Sydney had kidnapped Celice not all that long ago, that they were playing Celice and Zhan-Yo to get ahead on their own ambitions.

It wasn't about justice, about making the world a better place. Those ideals might sound cliche, but they were the ones Aegis held.

Ones Celice would cling to in his absence.

"Is that a problem?" Celice asked, leaving no guesses as to what might happen if Sydney made the wrong choice.

"I'll tell Gatete," Sydney said. "You'll have a few hours head start, for all the good that it'll do you."

The Paragon didn't wait for anything else, no chances for Celice to change her mind. Sydney slipped into her pod, Tama up and tapping away without so much as a warning glance back.

"I did not expect that," Mathieu said, getting his arm from Celice's grasp. "I don't need your help either. I'm not exactly—"

"I didn't do that for you," Celice said, taking a turn around and heading down the street. She needed to flag a pod where the Paragons wouldn't see it. "I needed to buy myself some time."

"Time for?" Mathieu said, falling in line with her.

"Figuring out what the hell just happened."

Mathieu didn't reply to that. They walked alongside each other in the drizzle, Celice breathing in the cold and re-ordering her life. Aegis never mentioned much about how it felt when a mission ended, when he'd completed a goal. Celice had spent so many adventures in the background, calling in reinforcements, coordinating Paragons, that every win came on the periphery.

Aegis would celebrate, but, almost every time, he'd call it early. He'd retreat back to Bastion in Manhattan and disappear into his terminals, eager to find the next thing to chase. Back then, Celice didn't understand why her father couldn't celebrate, couldn't breathe easy for a day or three.

Now, walking in the London night without a path forward, sideways, or anywhere, Celice found the reason.

"Where are you going?" Mathieu asked as they continued walking past pubs, shops, clubs, London's late night.

"Aren't you supposed to disappear?"

"That's a trap and you know it."

"Not if you really run," Celice pointed up at a passing plane's lights flashing overhead. "Gatete won't follow you overseas."

"You don't believe that."

True. She didn't. Once Gatete painted Mathieu with Zhan-Yo's brush, every Paragon on the planet would want to find the man and turn him over.

"Then I'd recommend finding a new identity," Celice said.

"Is that what you're going to do?"

"Again, why do you care what I'm going to do?"

Mathieu quick-stepped and blocked Celice's path on the sidewalk, "Because we could use your help."

That stopped her.

"We?"

Mathieu folded his arms, nodded off to the side, beneath a closed parlor's overhang. They'd passed beyond the Paragon presence, and while the drizzle had the streets quieter, London was still London. If Mathieu had some secrets to share, Celice could give him the chance.

"Zhan-Yo figured this would happen," Mathieu said when they both clustered against a closed store's wall.

Mathieu pulled out a cigarette, lit it, but didn't take a pull. Celice understood: cover for standing there.

"He knew I'd lead Gatete right to him, that he'd get captured and staged for a public execution?"

"Okay, maybe not all that." Mathieu mimed taking a drag. "Nobody thinks they can outrun the Paragons forever, especially not after what we pulled in LA."

"Maybe Gatete's not wrong."

"I'm not arguing we're saints, Celice. Hell, we probably deserve bullets to the head. But we're not here because Zhan-Yo's dumping reps in our accounts."

"Buddies, then?"

"Revolutionaries," Mathieu said and Celice laughed, sharp and short.

"Zhan-Yo, I can believe," Celice said. "You, maybe. But all those guys in the pub? They're all itching to overthrow society?"

Mathieu shrugged, "Zhan-Yo made us all swear to it. Whether they hold to that, I don't know, but they've stuck with us this long. Stuck with him."

How many Paragons joined up, stayed with the organization just to be with Aegis and the other Champions? The number had to be more than zero. Might be more than anyone expected.

Then again, with what she'd seen lately, the Paragons had a lot of problems. Her father's world might not be as invincible as it looked a few months ago.

"You still here?" Mathieu asked, dropping an unsmoked cigarette and stubbing it out.

"Thinking," Celice replied, shaking off the introspection. Something for later. "You said I could help. With what?"

"Saving our guy." Mathieu had his hands halfway up as he said the words, as if expecting Celice to thump him. And she would have, might have, except a two-kid-and-mom family passed by at that exact moment. The world seemed dark enough without starting a fight in front of children. "I know what you're thinking. I know you wanted to finish Zhan-Yo off in there."

"Keep talking and maybe you'll dig yourself out."

"I'm not going to try and convince you Zhan-Yo needs saving because he's a good man." Mathieu looked out into the street, unwilling, apparently, to face Celice's hard stare. "What I'm saying is that he's the best chance to save the world your father built."

Celice rolled her eyes. What other response was there?

"Let me prove it to you." Mathieu raised his Tama, tapped in an address and showed it to Celice. "Here's where we've been staying. It's not too far. Come with me and you'll understand, I swear."

"Understand what, precisely? Some new scheme to kill more anomalies?"

"We tried that. Twice. Didn't work. Zhan-Yo's moved on."

"I'm so glad he's seen the light."

"He admits he's made mistakes," Mathieu said. "Can you?"

"Sure. When I let Zhan-Yo leave that apartment without a sword stuck in his back."

Mathieu finally cracked, the stoic facade falling into a sigh at her words. He shook his head, ran a hand along his chin, then turned away from her and started walking.

"Know what happens when revenge is all you think about?" Mathieu said as he stepped away.

"Can't wait to hear this."

"You become a slave to a memory. Come by, and maybe you'll find a way to get free."

Celice watched Mathieu walk away in the drizzle for a block before making her own turn, heading off in her apartment's direction. As she went, she pulled out her Tama, entered in the address Mathieu had shown her.

Just in case.

Night Riders

He stopped when the gunfire did. Calvin didn't know how deep he'd gone, how thick the mud layering above them was. The earth ran rough across his fingers, funneling itself from his left hand and blooming from his right until now, when they sat cocooned in the dark. Calvin's Tama glowed, its eerie blue the sole light.

"What?" Calvin asked—Kat had muttered something he couldn't understand.

He'd kept her body wrapped against his as they burrowed deeper, trying to give as small a profile as possible to Wexley's guards. The more Calvin had to spread it, the thinner the mud would be. The fewer bullets it would stop.

"Get off me," Kat repeated.

"Can't," Calvin replied. "No room."

"What?" Kat squirmed, putting her face towards Calvin's, the Tama's glow showing black, wet soil all around them. "Where are we?"

"Yeah, about that," Calvin went to a whisper, "try not to talk. We don't have much air in here."

Kat caught on to the implications as Calvin ran through their options. He could try burrowing up this time, but unlike shoving mud up into the air, Calvin would have to take from above and put below, a space that was, right now, already occupied by dirt.

In short, he didn't have a good answer for this one.

Worse, if they broke free too soon, Wexley's goons would perforate them.

Kat reached, grabbed, and twisted Calvin's arm so she could see his Tama. Wincing at the tight angle and unable to read what the tracker typed into the device, Calvin watched Kat and tried not to breath. When Kat let go, she leaned back into the tight nook around them and looked up at him.

Thank you.

Her lips moved slow enough for Calvin to read them.

No problem.

He exaggerated the words, figuring he'd succeeded when Kat flashed a small grin.

Just you? Kat asked.

Calvin shook his head, *Team effort.*

Where?

Don't know, Calvin added a slight shrug. He didn't want to say dead, didn't want to say shot. Weed and his crew weren't exactly friends yet, but Calvin would rather not dwell on the idea that he'd dragged his co-workers into a fatal firefight.

Calvin's Tama beeped. Short, shrill. Kat's eyes popped open and she grabbed Calvin's arm again. Grinned.

"Gotta love the Paragons," Kat said, and at Calvin's look, she rolled her eyes. "They'll be here before the air runs out. You think Mynx would let a little rock get in the way of tracking her anomalies?"

"What?"

"Give it thirty seconds." Kat looked up past Calvin's shoulder. "You might get dirty."

"If I live, I'm good with that."

The thirty seconds passed with Calvin buzzing through a short retelling of the attack. All the while, the air went thinner and thinner. Breathing felt like stretching for something in the far distance, lungs working harder and harder for less return.

The ground above shook. Calvin felt his muddy creation buckle, fall onto his back. The weight crushed him into Kat, who managed a muffled curse. His Tama light vanished under rock and dirt, the stuff smashing into him from all sides. Sand went into his ears, some gnarled root pressed against Calvin's lips while something he didn't see, but could feel wriggling, mashed into his nose.

Whatever rescue Kat had found was going to kill them.

Just as Calvin was trying to decide which way he'd rather die—any way not involving the worm writhing on his face won out—the pressure vanished. Moonlight poured in as a metal hand reached, gripped Calvin's back and pulled him out. Below him, Kat took a huge breath before sitting up and climbing from the pit.

Kat's summoned drone set Calvin down next to the barn, in a spot littered with bullet casings. While his eyes adjusted to the light, the sounds told a different story. Some Paragon leader snapped orders, while pounding feet and buzzing engines signaled drones, pods, and Paragons in high numbers.

Calvin felt a hand on his shoulder, looked over to see Particle standing near him. Their uniform held slashes, and they had a bandage wrapped tight on their right arm, but that didn't seem the cause of their worried look.

"That makes all of us," Particle said, not waiting for

Calvin to launch into a debrief. "Weed's the worst. Smoke next. They're already out."

"They'll live?"

Particle kicked at a bullet casing, "They have a chance. Question is, does Mynx have any?"

"Mynx?"

"Where've you been, under a rock?"

Calvin squinted at Particle, caught the ever-so-slight upturned lip. "That's not funny."

"Who's this?" Kat said, brushing dirt off herself as she approached. "This one of your team?"

"Particle," they said. "Rescuing you about killed us."

"Sorry."

"Not as sorry as these punks are going to be. They took Mynx. Some EMP thing knocked out her mech suit and crashed a few drones into the dirt. Ugly, but you kick a hornet's nest, you're gonna get stung." Particle snapped their fingers, forcing Kat and Calvin's eyes towards a pod sitting empty near the road. "That one's yours if you want it. I'll hang here and tell them what they want to know."

Calvin could read lines well enough to understand Particle's point. If something had happened to Mynx, then the Paragons were going to want to know why a small team came in sooner. Would want to know why that small team had waited to call in the firepower. Particle seemed unbothered by the idea of deflecting, meaning Particle could either lie with the best of them or wasn't scared about any discipline.

Either way, Calvin wasn't going to pass on, well, the pass.

THE POD MADE good speed back towards the city, clear top providing a great night sky view. After being trapped beneath the mud, Calvin found his eyes trending up more than anywhere else, digging that freedom. The pod itself stayed quiet save for its engine's mild whir, the occasional bumps and clicks along the road.

"Thanks for coming after me," Kat said as they zipped along. "Being a tracker's a lonely time. People don't tend to notice when I'm missing."

"I'm not used to having friends," Calvin replied. "Figured I ought to keep the ones I have alive."

"Even if it means getting a Champion captured?"

"How the hell was I supposed to know Mynx would be coming?"

Kat laughed, "Don't look so sad. It's fine. They took a Champion. Every Paragon on the planet's going after them. Wexley's toast."

Kat's hair clumped around as she leaned back in the seat. Her white uniform looked more brown than anything, the dirt digging in. Scraps showed where she'd had a rough time, but Calvin didn't see any broken bones, any blood stains.

"What'd they do with you?" he asked. "In that diner? And here?"

"Wexley talked," Kat replied, closing her eyes. "More at me than with me. I was an accident."

"Think we meant to go into that dockyard."

"I mean the capture. We're nothing to these guys. Wexley and Rhimes, that whole operation? It's a lot bigger than you and me."

"Kat, don't know if you remember, but I'm used to being nothing. Prefer it."

"Me too."

When a follow-up didn't come, Calvin looked over to see Kat breathing deep, those eyes closed. She'd had a long day, so Calvin gave her the moment. He tapped the window on his left, a dark, dirty field passing by. With every touch he felt the pod's glass and what he could do with it. Break the vehicle, create a knife, or . . .

He took traces while Kat napped alongside him. Siphoned off the surface with one hand and spun it with the other, molding the glass by feel. The liquid crystals formed at his fingertips and flowed down, melding with their predecessors to make, bit by bit, a surprise.

"We're getting close," Calvin said as Chicago rose up around them. "You ready to wake up?"

"Not at all," Kat muttered, keeping those lids down. "Do I have to?"

"Dunno how long this pod's going to let you stay inside," Calvin replied, "but I think there's someone who'd be very disappointed if you didn't come out."

Kat sat up, smiling. Seeker had that effect on people, and Calvin didn't even consider himself a dog person. For most of his life, the dogs Calvin knew were chasing after him, hunting his smell through forests and fields. The fluffy tank took in Kat's friends like they were his own, and Seeker made one helluva blanket in Chicago's long winters too.

"Calvin, did you make this?" Kat said, noticing the object Calvin held in his left hand.

"Might've. Long ride, and you weren't talking much."

"Sorry. Turns out being a hostage is exhausting. Can I hold it?"

"Should be fine."

Calvin's creations tended to falter when left on their own, because breaking structural integrity to make his own shapes inevitably came back to haunt them. He'd tried to make an extra effort here, though, weaving the glass to support itself, to keep it from getting too bent or stretched.

"It's beautiful," Kat said, holding the glass dog, a rippling, sparkling Seeker. "How?"

"The pod's windows might not be so bullet-proof anymore," Calvin said, and at Kat's concerned look, he put up his hands. "Settle down, I already put in the check request. They'll figure it out. Nobody's gonna get shot in this thing."

Kat nodded, apparently mollified, "Why'd you make this, Calvin? I like it, I mean, but why?"

Not a question he'd thought to answer, but now that it'd been asked, Calvin found a way to respond, "Thought it might be nice to make something that wasn't violent for a change." The pod rolled to a stop outside Kat's apartment building. "I used to do that sometimes, when I spent the night in some dump, or beneath a bridge. Make little trinkets I could sell for some spare reps the next day."

While Kat cleaned herself up from both the dirt and Seeker's frenzied welcome licks, Calvin took his Tama and confirmed Weed, Lob, and Smoke made it out alive. Lob's launches had put them well outside the lit-up ground and Smoke kept them hidden until Paragon reinforcements brought better help.

Smoke pitched in a tough description about Mynx's attack, and the disabling shells used by Wexley's team. Mynx had called off the fire-bombing to save the gladiator, interrogate the leaders, a call that blew up when Wexley's EMP went off. The drones had been downed fast, the Paragons inside trapped. Once Mynx had been secured, the whole force packed up and ran, beating out the Paragon's own reinforcements by mere minutes.

"They played us," Calvin said when Kat had herself put together. "Wexley and his crew. Right from the start when they took that drone."

"He wasn't expecting you, though," Kat replied. "They

didn't think we'd get to the docks either. He's not as clever as you think."

"Then what is he?"

"He's just like all those other idiots who keep clawing for power," Kat said, sitting on her bed while Calvin claimed the couch. Takeout was on its way: stir-fry, available even as the clock edged midnight. "They get so wrapped up in all their ambitions. It's why they all wind up failing sooner or later."

Calvin whistled, "Kat the philosopher in the house!"

"More like Kat the tired and jaded."

"So you don't think he's so clever, what's he doing next?"

Kat, petting Seeker, pursed her lips, sent her eyes to ceiling, then shrugged, "You want me to make a bet?"

"I asked, didn't I?"

"Okay, you take Mynx, right? Set up all this crap with a drone, risk it all to go after this Champion. You don't make a dice roll like that unless it's the winner."

"Or you're crazy." Calvin sat up, stretched. Sitting in the mud pit and the pod hadn't done his muscles any favors. "Like the guy who did in Aegis. He was crazy."

"Is crazy. Zhan-Yo's not dead," Kat said. "Or, if he is, nobody's announced it. Anyway, we can't go with crazy because that doesn't help."

"Doesn't help?"

"Sure. If we think Wexley's acting all random, then we can't predict what he might do, so why bother?"

Calvin laughed, looked at Kat, "Where's this coming from? You a psychiatrist now?"

"I'm a tracker, you moron. How do you think I find anomalies? How'd I find you?"

"Luck?"

Kat wagged a finger at him, "Calvin, c'mon. Wexley

has a plan. So far, I bet it's going pretty well, even with your stunt. Know what else he did when he met me at the diner?"

"What?"

"Drank a milk shake. Dumbest thing. Point being, he didn't give a crap that I was there except to brag. We're small to him, Mynx is big. And what's Mynx got that's hers and hers alone?"

"Reputation? She's a Champion. He gets famous."

Kat stood up, went to the giant computer monitor that served as her tracker home base. Seeker padded along with her, apparently unwilling to let her get away after Kat's disappearance. When the tracker sat in her chair, Seeker plopped on her feet.

"Show and tell?" Calvin asked.

"I thought you didn't go to school?" Kat shot back, pulling up the tracker database. Anomaly names and reps sprang out, showing the feeds into Kat's accounts from the work her marks completed. "Mynx put all this together, a big database for trackers, assisted by drones."

"Right."

"Guess who controls the drones?"

"The local Paragons?"

"Now you're just playing with me," Kat said. "I know there's a brain somewhere in there."

"I didn't go to school, remember?" Calvin grinned, Kat's eyes rolled.

"Most of the drones come from one spot. It's why Mynx is who she is," Kat said. "She has the Factory."

"The what?"

Kat didn't answer right away. Instead, she put her hands on her desk and swore, a slow, long curse that had Calvin's good mood dying away with the word. The tracker saved her colorful language for meaningful moments, and given the subject . . .

"We're not going to be enjoying that takeout, are we?" Calvin said.

They ate it in another pod as the little car swung through sparse late-night streets, searching for an address Calvin didn't care to remember. If they never wound up at the Elemental's headquarters again, he'd be just fine with that. Too many rules, too many self-important anomalies who considered themselves better just because they didn't wear the blue and white.

"You're sure we need them?" Calvin asked. "Because if what you're thinking is right, the Paragons are going to be all up in this."

"The Paragons have leaks everywhere," Kat said. "And they just had their asses handed to them by Wexley."

"You think the Elementals will do any better? You forget we had to help them fight Wexley, like, a few weeks ago?"

"You want to know what I think, Calvin? I'm guessing Wexley's not playing for kicks here. I think he's got a plan to take a lot more than Chicago, and a lot more than a few anomaly lives. We're going to need the Elementals in on this, just as much as the Paragons."

"Okay . . . "

"They're going to die if Wexley succeeds, Calvin. They deserve a chance to fight for their lives."

"Good luck convincing them to do that."

That killed the conversation till they arrived at the cafe that doubled as the Elemental's headquarters. Long-since closed for the night, they found the anomaly watching the entrance sitting on a bench in the park opposite. The man looked lost and confused until Kat repeated Beth's name about a dozen times. That, paired with Kat's clenching fists, spurred the guard into action.

Minutes burned before the cafe's door opened and two other Elementals, rubbing their eyes but otherwise ready to go, led the pair down into a room smelling of thick coffee. A large thermos sat on a table next to a tray holding pastries labeled with the dubious day-old moniker.

"We're not used to hosting at this hour," Beth said, the Elemental leader sitting on a metal folding chair next to an equally scrappy table. Like the others, she'd thrown together a lounge outfit, as though coming from some slumber party. "Excuse the situation."

"Consider yourself excused," Kat said, frowning as Calvin snagged a coffee for himself, along with a couple berry-filled danishes.

"What?" Calvin said as he joined Kat at the table, getting her a coffee of her own after setting his own stuff down. "We're being nice enough to warn'em about the end of the world. Least they can do is give us a donut."

"The end of the world?" Beth said, her eyebrow doing its thing. "That sounds hyperbolic."

"Normally, I'd agree," Kat said. "But not this time. It's Wexley, Beth. He has Mynx."

Beth sat forward, "The Champion?"

"The Champion." Calvin took a long drink from his coffee, followed it with the danish. Delightful. "Like I said, the end of the world."

This time, Beth didn't look so skeptical.

20

The Negotiator

The village's problem didn't live in the village. Achara led Cassidy and Thane—restored over several minutes to his old self—past the scrappy homes, open-air shops, and lunch's sweet-smelling aftermath wafting from kitchens. The jungle closed about them as they reached the village border, save for a well-padded, rocky trail heading up a slight hill.

When Cassidy pressed Achara for more details in the bus, the woman only said that the problem was one the Paragons weren't having much luck with. Not everyone, it seemed, cared to join in with the silver and blue. Not everyone wanted to sacrifice their freedom for the good of the whole.

"So it's an anomaly," Cassidy said.

"In a sense," Achara replied.

"If you want us to succeed, surprises aren't going to help."

"Less a desire to surprise, and more a lack of a good explanation," Achara's gentle expression never faltered, never gave hints that she hid some devastating secret behind that face. "I can tell you that victory here won't mean breaking bones and smashing hearts."

With that description, the trio proceeded up the trail until, nearing the hill's top, Achara fell back. Saying her presence would only hurt Cassidy and Thane's efforts, she chose a sturdy tree, leaned on it, and looked at her Tama. Cassidy figured the Paragon was sending some message to her friends, laughing about how she had two of the world's foremost villains running her errands.

"Think it's a trap?" Cassidy asked Thane, the latter in his middling form with muscles and wrinkles aplenty.

"Definitely a trap. The question is what kind."

"What kind?"

Thane didn't answer, climbing up the trail and cresting the hill. Cassidy went after, again wondering why she'd decided to follow an inscrutable madman to this damned hot, buggy place. The cool water in the bus faded quick when they returned outside, and the jungle's welcome canopy shade came with mosquito clouds whose pestering had Cassidy feeling she'd lost pints to the insects. At least the island came with breezes and few bugs to care about.

The hill's top did what it could to erase Cassidy's frustrations. Baking under the hot sun, a massive, multi-level wood-and-mud structure loomed. Scrap stuck out at odd angles from the building's sides, what looked like old car parts serving as supports keeping the whole place together. Chickens and several goats roamed the grassy yard, taking no notice of the two newcomers. At the structure's top, hanging limp in the windless air, stood a flag bearing a tiger's snarling face, orange and black.

"I would guess we have come to a lair," Thane said.

"A lair for what?"

"Them."

Thane pointed to the building's front door as it swung

open on creaky hinges, revealing a trio that had to be younger than Cassidy's own children. Teenagers, and by the looks of them, not doing so well. Dirt and scratches marred shallow faces and thin bodies, torn and stained clothing hung loose over lanky limbs. And yet, the three, two women and a man, came onto the porch with arms folded and anger firing.

One of the women, her floor-length hair tied into braids, spoke at them. Cassidy didn't understand a word, but she heard defiance, she heard a warning. These kids didn't want visitors.

"They say they will not come," Thane muttered.

"What?" Cassidy said, seeing Thane tapping his chin in contemplation. "Come where?"

Achara hadn't mentioned what, exactly, Thane and Cassidy were supposed to do with the house or its occupants. Did Apinya and his Paragons want these kids destroyed? The idea seemed ludicrous, and Cassidy wouldn't do that anyway. Criminal or no, killing random children didn't fall within Cassidy's range.

Thane might be another matter, if they made him mad enough.

The trio whispered to one another for a few seconds before the woman took the spotlight again, stepping forward. Behind her, in the doorway, Cassidy caught flashes, the telltale reflections off other peeking eyes.

"More kids inside," Cassidy whispered.

"Pieces for the puzzle," Thane replied.

The leader spoke again, louder this time. Repeating the earlier words, but adding another phrase at the end.

"Now she's threatening us," Thane said. "If we don't leave, we'll pay a price."

"Are you going to talk to them? Because I don't think they'll understand me."

"I can't." Thane shook his head, "At this stage, I can understand, generally, but wouldn't know how to speak a sentence. If I get weaker, then perhaps . . . "

On the porch, the three teenagers spread apart, giving themselves a few meters between. Cassidy didn't see any weapons, but she made the connection. If the Paragons wanted these kids, then they were probably anomalies. And that meant anything could happen.

Cassidy put her hands up, high and open. Plastered on a smile she hoped wasn't threatening.

"Please, Thane," Cassidy said. "I don't want to fight these kids, and I don't think Apinya wants us to either."

Thane nodded, and as he did, the man's body shrank. Muscles withered away, his knees bent, and Thane's hair fell out, leaving gray wisps. The teenagers on the porch gawked, the boy looking like he might vomit.

But nobody summoned fireballs, shot lasers from their eyes, or teleported to stab Cassidy in the kidneys.

"Give him a second," Cassidy said, trying out the old English on the teenagers. They snapped their attention to her, narrowed looks suggesting only her tone came through. "We're not here to hurt you."

She tried to put her motherly spin on it, to shake the webs off a style Cassidy hadn't employed in a decade.

When Thane spoke, his voice came out as a rasping whisper. The words sounded right, even though Cassidy couldn't understand him. The teenagers came closer, their leader leaving the porch for the weedy grass, her mouth opening wider as Thane continued to speak. When he stopped, she replied, fast and clear, almost eager.

"What are you telling them?" Cassidy asked.

Thane didn't answer her, but kept talking with the teenager. When the young woman started nodding, then waved for the boy to head back in the house, Cassidy felt a tremor run up her spine. Back on the island, Thane had a way of curling people around to his interests, building a coalition with a combination of impossible dreams and determination.

"Thane," Cassidy repeated, interrupting his latest stream. "What's going on?"

Thane gave the young woman a slow smile, held up a hand, then turned his gnarled self towards Cassidy as if she were an impatient child demanding attention.

"The surrounding villages send their anomalies here," Thane said. "Right to this house. The villagers are scared of them, but they bring food and water, leaving it at the trail here. The cowards can't make themselves murder their own children, but they are too afraid to live with them. I think Achara and her Paragons want to collect the anomalies for themselves."

"And they don't want to leave?"

Thane's smile widened, "The Paragon reputation precedes them. These children prefer their freedom to what Achara promises. They've seen what happens when they tie their lives to adults who think they know better."

Then why would Achara send Thane and Cassidy in here? To see if the kids would kill them? To scare the kids into realizing who might come after them without Paragon protection?

"I think they will come with us," Thane continued, snapping Cassidy's attention back to him. "Several are quite strong, according to this one. With them at our side, we wouldn't need Achara's cooperation. We could force the issue."

"And bring Apinya down on us."

The young woman frowned at Cassidy's words, likely catching the Champion's name. She spoke fast, saying the Champion's name more than once, and Thane's grin grew.

"She says they're not afraid. Apinya is a nuisance who doesn't understand them. We do, Cassidy. We know what it's like to be persecuted by the Paragons." Thane looked at the young woman, spoke to her.

Cassidy saw motion towards the house, looked at it, and found her mouth falling open. At least twenty teens stood on the porch and the grass around it. More stuck heads from windows above. This wasn't some scant few anomalies.

No wonder Apinya hadn't tried to use brute force. Who knew what cataclysms might lurk in there?

"I get it now," Cassidy said, taking a deep breath.

"An unexpected gift," Thane agreed. "I thought we would have to hide, to wait for a chance. Apinya, instead, has given us the instrument of his own downfall. They will come with us, and together, we will force these Paragons to treat us as equals."

"You can't. They aren't fighters, they're kids." Cassidy nodded at the teenagers. "Apinya will kill us, them. I don't want their blood on my hands, Thane."

Thane's grin faded into a set line. He said a few words to the young woman, who nodded and barked a name back at the house. The teenagers parted, until one came out, a boy walking with a cane, one leg looking small. If that bothered the boy, though, Cassidy couldn't see it. Her focus, instead, went to the boy's chest. He didn't wear a shirt, and weaving across his skin, like snakes, were moss-green lines.

"Look at this one," Thane said. "He has a Champion's power. To give him over to the Paragons, another gem in their collection . . ."

Swapping languages again, Thane called across the yard to the boy, who looked younger than the others.

The boy, expressionless, reached with his free hand and

felt among his chest. When his fingers touched one of the lines, it curled up around the point, forming an earthy dot on his brown skin.

Cassidy went blind.

No, not blind. She saw colors still. Shapes, but ones shifting and indistinct, as though Cassidy had fallen into an ink blot test. The jungle's humid air weighed on her, the children's chatter filled her ears, but for all Cassidy could see, she stood in a blank white sea with black clouds around, under, and over her.

Voids leapt to her fingertips, and Cassidy tried to recall where the boy was. It seemed like he'd made some illusion, which meant he stood where he'd been before. If Cassidy could put a void in the right spot, it might—

"Don't," Thane said, his voice coming in from nowhere. "It will end soon."

He spoke again, calling out to the boy.

Without a flash, without a blink, the yard and the house and all the teenagers came back. Most rubbed their eyes, a couple glowed in different colors, abilities coming out when under threat. Nobody seemed to panic, though, even when the boy shifted his fingers to a different dark line. Like before, it swirled around his finger, coalescing into a dark circle.

A coconut sweetness flooded Cassidy's mouth, almost overwhelming, as if she'd stuffed herself with candy. She found it hard to breathe, her body so convinced it was full. Coughs rang out across the yard, and Thane laughed.

"The senses," Thane said. "He can twist any of them to his own desires. Perhaps we could buy them time, break away and start anew deeper in the jungle. Preserve this treasure."

A new sound came from behind, the cracking, brushing

of boots on rock. Cassidy turned to see Achara, flanked by a Paragon squad.

"They are all treasures," Achara said. "They deserve better than this. They need training, healthcare, and a path forward."

The teenagers retreated at the Paragon's appearance, shading back towards the house and inside. The boy with the cane and the dark lines remained, though, standing with the young woman who'd been there from the beginning. They looked determined, they looked small, they looked too young for this.

"Why?" Cassidy asked, putting herself between the Paragons and the teenagers. "Why send us here?"

"To see if you could understand," Achara replied.

"Understand what?"

"That despite the Paragons, the world is not a kind place," Achara said. "We are at a tipping point. Pushed much more and we will fall, leaving anomalies like this. Persecuted, abandoned."

"Feared," Thane added.

Achara nodded, "Thane knows our survival rests in gathering every anomaly we can, bringing them together, and standing united against those that would destroy us."

"And who's that? Normals?" Cassidy asked.

"The ones who attacked us across the ocean. Who murdered a Champion and, now, have stolen another. We show kindness in one hand, and strength in the other."

Thane walked towards the house, tottering in his weak form. Cassidy kept herself turned to the side, pacing with the anomaly while putting eyes on the Paragons. Achara had a steel slate look going that suggested the banter phase of their meeting had ended.

"Convince them to come with us, Thane," Achara said, "and Apinya will give you a chance."

"Weapons," Thane muttered as the pair approached the house. "That's what they're after, what they're always after. The girl there told me as much."

"Told you what?" Cassidy asked while Achara repeated Thane's name.

At a flick from Achara's hand, the Paragons spread from behind her, getting clear sight lines towards the house.

"After," Thane said, "I will explain. For now, I need to tell these children a story."

"A story?" Cassidy asked.

"The Paragons are not some monolith, like any group," Thane said. "If these young ones understand how they can shape the Paragon's future from within, perhaps they will decide not to die without."

The voids hung close to Cassidy's fingertips. A quick gesture or two and she could have a couple Paragons down, but who knew what she'd be going up against. Unpredictable anomalies made every conflict a dice roll, a chance experiment with fatal outcomes.

Worse, who knew what might happen to the children? Would the Paragons try to keep them safe? Would Thane, if he blew up into his raging best?

Thane reached the porch's steps and held a hand towards the boy. The young woman put her hand on the boy's shoulder, holding him back. Thane spoke, the woman replied, hot and angry. Cassidy squared herself behind Thane, facing the Paragons with her arms outstretched.

"Don't make this mistake," Achara said. "Nobody needs to die today."

"Paragons always say that, and it's never true," Cassidy countered.

Achara didn't deny the charge. Her right hand went

up, and Cassidy figured, when it fell, everything would go straight to hell. Behind her, Thane and the two teens continued talking, words flying fast.

"They will come along," Thane spoke up. "Have your soldiers stand aside, Achara. There will be no fighting here today."

Cassidy shifted aside a step, the boy joining Thane at the step's bottom, looking both defiant and . . . relieved?

Achara's smile looked as genuine as Cassidy's confusion.

THE CHILDREN HAD BEEN WORN down, Thane explained. They rambled along a rough rode in a svelte Paragon pod, one designed for large groups and haphazard terrain. Achara and the boy shared the front seats while Thane and Cassidy had the rear. The others would follow, so Achara promised, in the coming days and weeks.

First their parents, their villages had cast the children aside. Brought them to the hillside and the dilapidated house and left them where, the villagers hoped, the anomaly abilities wouldn't destroy their livelihoods. When the Paragons came, they offered salvation in exchange for loyalty, for separation.

"But the kids didn't give in then," Cassidy said.

"They had power, and a home," Thane replied. "I held off many Paragons on my own with a few mercenaries and a good place to defend. I suspect the Paragons also feared the look fighting children would present."

"So they used us to, what, mediate?"

"Exactly," Thane said. "I told the children they would lose everything if they held out, that they could gain some help by submitting now."

"Will they?"

Thane, not quite so wrinkled anymore, shook his head, "I don't trust the Paragons to deliver on anything once a threat is removed. The children will be treated like any other captured anomaly. Sent to training camps, educated and immersed into Paragon doctrine."

"Then why did we do this?"

Now Thane had the confused look, "To get to Apinya. Our goals now depend on the Champion. Everything else is immaterial."

Cassidy sat back in the pod's soft seat, felt the road's rumbles climb up and down her spine. At least in here there weren't mosquitos, and the air conditioning dealt with the heat. The comfort gave her room to think, to wonder just what she'd been doing.

"Back on the island, you spoke about change," Cassidy said. "You spoke about vengeance, but for a better world. You cared. What happened?"

Thane put his hand on hers, and Cassidy started to pull away only for him to grab tight, "I am the same man I was then. On the island, we dreamed. Now, we are doing."

"Smooth words."

"Apinya will have sweeter. When we arrive, we will convince him to see things our way."

"Thane, I don't even know what 'our way' is anymore."

Thane took his hand off hers, put it on the seat between them, a metal patch between the cushions. He patted the silver surface.

"The world is Mynx's island writ large," Thane said. "It's time we brought order to the chaos."

21

Machine Games

They landed outside the city, pre-dawn. Several hours sleep jacked away with energy drinks and stronger stuff. Waiting pods shot Wexley, Rhimes, and their small crew—Mynx jammed in alongside them—towards the Factory. While Rhimes managed logistics, Wexley kept his eyes on his Tama. Thus far, the Paragons weren't reporting Mynx's capture. Burying it behind the better story: that a team had recovered the missing drone south of Chicago.

That drone had little left to recommend it save the scrap making up its skin, but leave it to the Paragons to spin a loss.

Mynx, sitting across from Wexley in the pod, kept her eyes on Wexley and her mouth shut. At first the constant stare made Wexley itch, but he'd dealt with worse annoyances for less benefit. After another hour, Mynx and her glare wouldn't be a problem anyway.

LA's night hadn't given any ground when the pods pulled up at the Factory's main entry. A giant door served as a loading dock, sporting the Paragon's bold blue emblem over its center. On either side towered two gladiator drones, looking newer and deadlier than the one Wexley's team had downed in Chicago. Beyond them, the door itself stood solid and resolute.

Behind that?

Adriana's reply came as the pods parked. Wexley glanced at it, saw the question mark and grinned. He'd sent a cryptic message on the jet, asking her to get the other players ready for a big announcement. They'd be paying attention when the time came, and with their support alongside the Factory, Wexley would have all he needed.

"Mynx first," Wexley said as they exited the pod. "She's the key."

The Pacific air kept its cool, dry and windless in the Factory's valley. Overhead, a few stars managed to fight their way through the city's light, washing up from the south. Around him, mercenaries left their pods, Rhimes included, and checked their weapons. None stepped from the street onto the Factory's entry, per strict instruction.

The two drones standing by the gate didn't react, per their own rules.

"I won't help you," Mynx said as two mercenaries lifted her from the pod.

"Won't you?" Wexley replied, patting his various holsters, making sure he hadn't forgotten something. "I read about your encounters with Dr. Jones, Mynx. How you two worked together before her accident?"

"What about her?"

"Fascinating ideas. Life extension through anomaly DNA? Too bad it didn't work out." Wexley stepped right up to Mynx's face. Let her see that he wasn't joking. "Not too hard to figure out why you were curious. The Champions are getting old, Mynx. Time, a villain not even you can beat."

Mynx kept a fierce quiet.

"But you're willing to fight it," Wexley continued. He wasn't much for monologuing, preferring a gunshot's snap, but he needed Mynx here. Getting into the Factory by force wouldn't work. "So I'll make you a deal. Get me inside the Factory, and you live. No shot to the back of the head, no poison in the cup."

"Liar."

"Am I? When have I lied to you, or anyone? You might not like me, but I tell the truth, Mynx. I have no reason to do anything else."

Mynx shook her head, "I can guess what you're going to do in there. Not happening."

"Even at the cost of your own life?"

"I've cheated death a million times. About time he caught up to me."

Rhimes, standing behind Mynx, held up a single finger. The back-up plan. Wexley glanced towards the gate, those drones, threw Rhimes the slightest nod. Mercenaries closed around them quick, cutting off any straight-on views from the outside.

"What's this, a dance circle?" Mynx asked.

Wexley held out a hand and someone placed the syringe in it. Before Mynx could do anything more than shy away, he jammed the needle into her neck. Pressed down the plunger, watching the watery orange liquid drain away. Mynx stuttered out a few curses, then collapsed into a waiting mercenary's arms.

"C'mon," Rhimes said, voice carrying over the group. "We're late."

The mercenary holding Mynx led the delegation, approaching the gate and the gladiator drones with the Champion in his arms like some martyr. The gladiator drones noticed as soon as boots hit the Factory's entry courtyard, the beige-gray tiles sending some signal to the machines. They did what Mynx's drones tended to do: bristle with weapons, red eyes burning as they watched the approaching group.

"Hands off the guns," Wexley said as the group approached. "We're friendlies here."

As they neared the gate, both drones moved in synchronized motion to block the approach. Shining lights at the mercenary carrying Mynx, both drones stuck hands out, palms up. At the same time, in equally deep and demanding voices, they told the party to stop.

"Do as they ask," Wexley said. "Now, we wait for help."

They didn't need to wait long. Wexley counted one hundred seconds before the Factory's gate shivered and slid open. Behind the drones, standing alone in the huge entry hall, was the person Wexley hoped had stayed.

Rhimes and his intelligence team were earning all kinds of bonuses lately.

South America's Champion split the drones, walking towards Mynx and the mercenaries with furious confidence. Mila didn't have to be afraid with the gladiators at her back. Didn't have to worry when anyone touching her would find themselves immolated, shot, and smashed in no particular order.

Time to take another risk.

Wexley went left, putting himself between Mynx and the approaching Mila. The drones zeroed in on him, a blinding display his raised hand couldn't fend off.

"I know you," Mila spoke first, a meter apart. With the drone's light behind her, Mila looked more like a shadow than a person.

"I suspect you do," Wexley replied. "She isn't hurt. Badly."

Mila tilted her head, looking past Wexley towards Mynx's unconscious body, "There is no way out of this for you. Attacking a Champion ends only one way."

"Then let's play it out, shall we?" Wexley nodded behind Mila. "If you'll walk us in?"

"Or you'll kill her?"

"Faster than the drones could stop us, I'm afraid."

"You would die."

"Like you said, I'm already dead. I'm just choosing how."

With a gambler's mentality, Wexley ran the odds as he spoke. When he and Rhimes had devised the plan that night in the jazzy bar, the list ran long. So many things needed to break their way that Rhimes only came around on the whole idea when he'd gone several drinks deep, the hour late enough to scour away hesitations.

Mila's presence met one measure, and the Champion's relationship to the Factory and its systems was the next unknown. Mynx had to have advanced defenses in place, nasty tricks to pull on people dumb enough to try an attack. Plenty had tried over the years, from rogue anomalies to human factions vying to do, well, exactly what Wexley attempted now.

The difference? He had Mynx. The others always left her as a queen in her castle to be brought down in the fighting.

Could Mila play the same role, masterminding the Factory in Mynx's absence?

"What are you hoping to do inside?" Mila asked, the question's innocence stumbling Wexley for a second.

Did she really not guess?

"I want to see how she does it," Wexley said, leaning on a little honesty to hide everything else. "Once we know how the Factory works, we can replicate it."

Mila shook her head, "You can't run this without her—"

"With respect, let us decide that." Wexley tapped his Tama, looking at Maya. "Clock's ticking."

Gears turned. Outcomes played behind the Champion's eyes. Wexley didn't bother projecting anything other than a straight-faced determination. This wasn't about bluffing anymore, just a deal.

"The weapons stay outside," Mila said. "Drop them."

Hmm. Not quite the plan, but Wexley could roll with it. Rhimes's soldiers could handle themselves hand-to-hand, and if it came down to a firefight, the drones would destroy them all anyway.

"You heard the Champion," Wexley said, uncoupling his own holsters. "Ditch the gear."

Not a single voice raised in protest. Was that because the mercenaries were well-trained, or because they all knew their faces had already been captured by the Factory's cameras? The Paragons would have their identities soon, their bodies not long after if this attempt didn't succeed.

Fatalism sometimes bred obedience.

"Lead on," Wexley said after the weapons clatter died away, an arms graveyard littering the Factory's front.

Mila turned around, walked back towards the Factory's entrance without any stress landing on her shoulders. Wexley checked, made sure the mercenary carrying Mynx had one hand on the Champion's neck. Ready for a snap, so quick that even a drone wouldn't risk a killing shot.

"Don't let go," Wexley warned, then followed Mila.

The guarding drones tracked the mercenary crew as if they were walking into a gala. Wexley kept after Mila, all while trying to take in what he could as they passed beneath the Factory's enormous gate.

Mynx, it turned out, wasn't the world's foremost decorator. The Factory's insides revealed clean steel walls missing art, design, or anything resembling emotion. No signs offering directions stood anywhere. Clean blue-white lighting shimmered off walls, floors and nothing else.

"This is . . . something," Wexley said, catching Mila's ears.

"It's hers," Mila replied, adding nothing else.

Not going to be fast friends, then.

Beyond the loading area, through another two-story tall and wide door, the Factory opened up into its mammoth interior. Carved into the hills, the Factory expanded like some hidden hive, blowing up into levels above and below where they stood, with massive freight lifts sitting like metal leaves near the balcony they stepped onto.

What had been quiet save for their boots now erupted into a tuneless fabrication chorus, with hisses, clanks, whirs, and more combining together into productive static. Wexley saw assembly lines chugging along below him, piecing together more drones in a process that sent the machines higher and higher as they grew, ultimately leaving them off across the space from the loading dock.

There, assembled in rows, sat gladiator drones in glimmering colors. Chicago's black styling coated a few, but more stood in greens and whites, in Paragon blue and a deep red that Wexley recognized from the African factions.

"All the world's protection, right here," Wexley said as the crew followed him onto the catwalk.

"They'll be hunting you soon," Mila said. "We're inside now. What do you want?"

"The heart," Wexley replied, motioning to Rhimes to bring Mynx forward. "I want to go where the drones are controlled."

"We don't—" Mila started, but Wexley cut her off with a raised finger.

"They receive patches like any other computer program," Wexley said. "We know, because we've taken one apart. Mynx must have a way to send these updates. That's what I want."

"Then ask her," Mila said. "Oh, wait. You can't, because she's unconscious."

Wake the Champion and risk turning the Factory against Wexley and his crew, or flail around inside the giant building until they tripped the defenses anyway?

"Wake her up," Wexley said to Mila. "That's your thing, right?"

Mila didn't bother replying. Instead, she went to Mynx and the mercenary holding the Champion. Wexley saw Mila's back, saw her bend over Mynx, and wondered if she was going to pull a fairy tale and kiss the Champion. Instead, faint, glittering lines grew from Mila, pulling towards Mynx like loose spider webs. The filaments burrowed into Mynx's clothes, slipping through seams in the Paragon uniform.

Rhimes called the crew to keep watch on their surroundings, not the show, an order Wexley ignored. He might despise anomalies but that didn't mean their powers weren't fascinating. Wexley walked to the side, getting a view as Mila's webs continued connecting her to Mynx. Of course, Mila's ability would take her own energy, or life force, or something like that and use it to put Mynx back together. So many anomalies ran that way, their gifts sucking away the host's will.

The webs shifted. What had been a loose float in the air became a directed lunge, the points tied to Mila popping off and flowing to the mercenary holding the Champion. Before the soldier could react, those filaments anchored in his neck, his face, and the gap between his gloves and his sleeves. The man shuddered while Wexley reached for a pistol he no longer had.

The soldier dropped Mynx to the floor, then collapsed right along with her.

"Stop!" Wexley said, waving an arm through the filaments, trying to break the connection between Mynx and the soldier. Like some apparition, though, the strands dodged around Wexley's swipes, always maintaining their soft silver ties. "Mila, cut this off or—"

"Or what, Wexley?" Maya said, Rhimes and the rest turning back in now. "You need Mynx to find your heart. This is how you get her."

At Wexley's glance, Rhimes had his arm tight around Mila's neck, ready for a quick snap. The Champion didn't falter, but looked down at Mynx, at her fluttering eyes as consciousness came back while the same fled the soldier.

The Factory's leader awoke. And that presented a problem.

"Not a word," Wexley said, kneeling over Mynx. "You start to say, to do anything, and Rhimes takes out your friend."

"One hostage for another," Mila said, voice tight with Rhimes's pressure. "You're such a leader, Wexley."

"I'm desperate. This is what it takes."

The group burned minutes on that balcony as Mynx picked herself up, Wexley directing another mercenary to keep close to the Champion. Mila's filaments faded away as Mynx returned to life. The suffering soldier didn't lose his own, though the man seemed like he'd be out for some time. Wexley didn't need to order him left behind: that directive had been issued well before the mission began.

An all-or-nothing expedition didn't have room for casualties.

"Welcome home," Wexley said, helping Mynx to her feet. "Now show us the center, if you would."

Mynx looked at Mila. Rhimes had released the Champion from his hold, but he stood right behind her just the same. From that distance, Wexley figured the man had at least three ways to down his charge.

"Did they hurt you?" Mynx asked.

"Threats. Like little children," Mila replied.

"They're like that." Mynx glanced at Wexley. "You want the Factory's heart?"

"That's why you're awake."

Again, Mynx looked to Mila. The South American Champion returned the look with a slow nod. An interesting gesture. Wexley put two fingers out to his right, every mercenary catching the command and spreading out. If that nod had been a signal for an ambush, Wexley's team would be ready.

"Nervous, Wexley?" Mynx said. "Are you as afraid to die as you think I am?"

"We both have work to do before we go, Mynx," Wexley replied. "Let's go."

Mynx didn't argue further, but instead led the group to a nearby lift and set it running down. The open-air platform sank into the Factory's noisy abyss, every level it passed providing a salivating glimpse into the assembly lines that would soon belong to Wexley. Yes, the gladiator drones formed the Factory's backbone, but other weapons, smaller robots, churned from here too. Each one could be tweaked to serve his needs, arming Wexley's mercenaries with the tools they needed to destroy the Paragons.

And secure a better, brighter future.

One level above the bottom, Mynx stopped the lift. Unlike its churning brethren, this floor kept quiet, a cool breeze moving along a teal-lit landing. Glass walls showed server banks beyond, three meter-high black towers, blinking lights in time with one another.

"Everything flows through those?" Wexley asked.

"Don't forget my back-ups," Mynx said, leading them from the platform. "You'll need to take those too if you want total control."

"You'll tell me where they are?"

"Assuming my life is still under your threat, of course," Mynx said. "As you mentioned, I would prefer to live." She put a hand on Wexley's arm, pulled his look to her. "Because how am I going to exact terrible vengeance on you if I'm dead?"

Wexley met the charge with the same ice he'd deployed in so many meetings, so many charged encounters where his career and, later, his life lay on the line.

"I look forward to seeing what a Champion can do," Wexley whispered in reply.

"You won't."

Beyond the server banks, in an otherwise simple, circular room, sat the Factory's heart. A giant terminal with a monitor as large as Wexley's office wall, the place lit up when the crew walked in. The monitor splashed up diagnostics that seemed to cover the whole Factory, giving an at-a-glance look at all the destruction spawning every minute in the place. Destruction that could be controlled by Ziran, by him.

"It's time, Mynx," Wexley said. "Hand it over."

Mynx took a leading step towards the terminal, before spinning back to face Wexley.

"I don't think so, little man. Your game ends here."

As the Champion spoke, the center's walls shifted. Three panels moved aside, revealing smaller, human-sized drones. They dropped down around Wexley and his crew, bristling with weapons, shining their lights on the mercenaries.

Mynx's triumphant grin lasted as long as it took her to notice Wexley's own smile. He waited one beat beyond that, letting the confusion sink in as his team refused to declare any surrender.

"Sorry, Mynx," Wexley said, "but I've got a few moves left."

This time, he flashed three fingers.

Dry Reveries

Cold, dark, alone. A perfect apartment for surfing memories and trying to find answers. Celice, the clock ticking towards bar close, threw her Tama's display to the room's television and sought the past. Coming so close to Zhan-Yo cut a cloak she'd had over her shoulders, exposing the still-bleeding wound left by her father's death.

She told the Tama to start from the beginning, and it obliged.

The compound held a quaint flavor. The Vermont acres acquired by a government intent on maximizing newfound potential in its special citizens. They weren't even called anomalies then. Popular media dubbed them 'heroes', and Celice cherished those earliest memories when delivery drivers, when visiting friends would call her parents as such. A husband and wife couple, with a young daughter.

The branded pinnacle to serve as bedrock for the Paragon initiative.

Not that Celice remembered that much. Assistants with ever-changing names and appearances would come by at all hours to wake her up, take her to the daycare center where Celice would curl up on a mat or play in the dirt outside with other Paragon children while their parents engaged threats throughout the world.

The Tama scrolled the pictures, taken from Paragon archives, showing the daycare center, the sprawling base. Normals and anomalies working side by side back then to . . . Celice looked out the window to the drizzly night. How many times had the words been thrown at her parents in the end? Like accusing knives, the old government said they were protecting the world together.

And how had her father answered?

Oh yes.

We're going to protect the world from you.

Celice had been four then. Eating her dinner as her parents blurred through one phone call after another, voices getting more and more agitated until the doorbell rang, until the lock undid itself and opened to show not one, not two, but a full squad standing armed outside.

Those pictures didn't land in the Paragon archives, but Celice didn't need the Tama's images to bring her back to that night, or the ones that followed as Aegis and the other Champions commenced their swift takeover. Back then, it'd seemed right. Remove the corrupted governments, the ones so bent on throwing increasingly dangerous anomaly forces at each other, and install leadership by the righteous, the strong.

"The arrogant," Celice said.

Her glass held water when she wanted something stiffer. Alcohol didn't make for a good partner in spy-craft, so Celice kept the apartment dry. The Tama blinked. A new place now.

New York, Aegis and Celice's mom moving to the big city as their central command. The Champions in their full stride, embracing adulation as they roped anomalies the world over into the new Paragon organization. Celice rode the elevators up and down, gawked from the rented office tower's top floors at the metropolis below.

Tutors came and went, blitzing Celice through solo classes. In the evening, she would pick apart her parent's adventures, inserting her own ideas, loving their laughter and wishing they would tell her the whole story. Even then, Celice caught the pauses, the gaps. Villains would magically surrender, cities under threat would make it out with little damage.

The Tama exposed those lies. Headlines splashed along showing the Paragon's dangerous rise. Dictators and democracies alike fought back, and found themselves crushed by enemies that didn't follow any rules. Aegis and his Champions were both ruthless and efficient, their abilities making normal combat a trivial game.

Aegis would relay the scores to Celice at dinner or, if an evening engagement took hold, over breakfast the next morning. Every country giving in marked a notch in the win column. Any that hadn't yet given up?

They would see the light.

Benefits followed fast. Celice saw them first-hand as Aegis brought her along to declarations, when he or Celice's mom would give one speech or another vanishing a predatory industry from existence and replacing it with something better, with Paragon protection, or a steady rep stream to keep those kicked from jobs in good financial health. Celice didn't understand it then, but she saw the smiles on those faces.

Looking at them now, on the Tama screen, Celice saw something less than pure joy in those cheering crowds. Those were forced yells, Paragon flags waving with too much snap in the hands, their holders perhaps afraid Aegis would catch them out and declare them not supportive enough.

But the world did improve, didn't it? Celice asked the Tama and the computer complied, swishing away its photos and videos for statistics. Measured in any possible way, deaths around the globe plummeted under Paragon control. Life expectancy went up. Nobody fought over healthcare or budget deficits.

Everything hummed with guaranteed survival, with guaranteed protection, with Paragon-powered guard rails.

"So why am I here?" Celice asked the apartment, getting nothing but outside city noise in response.

If her parents had created such a paradise, then why had her mom died so young? Why had her father followed? Why was she sitting in a dark apartment, alone, wishing she'd killed a man hours earlier?

Every day the tutors continued, unceasing even after her mother's death. When Celice's teenage birthdays came and went, her anomaly abilities making no appearance, Aegis drove himself away again and again. He built Bastion, a spear shoved into Manhattan's heart, only to abandon the building at every turn for one more fight, one more chance to lose himself in heroism.

And she'd helped him, loved doing so. The first call came when she'd turned fourteen, a simple smash-and-stop involving some drug runners that didn't know better. Aegis could've turned it over to the drones, but he wanted Celice playing back-up instead. She'd walked in with him, watching through Aegis's Tama as he dismantled the criminals one punch and kick at a time.

Celice called in the media when Aegis told her to. She called in a Paragon clean-up crew to collect the bodies.

He bought her a bracelet afterwards, a date inscribed on the silver.

"To remember when you became a Paragon," Aegis said, clasping the bracelet on her wrist.

Celice thought she'd been joining the world's guiding light. Had it ever been that way?

The Tama blipped again, heading to the last message on the list. One she'd received before Mynx called with the news on that awful day. Aegis started talking, telling a simple story about his wife, Celice's mother, and times with and without violence. About sunsets and sunrises, love and yearning for a better world for their daughter.

That one message felt more real than anything in this place, than anything going on in the world. Two people in love looking forward to the rest of their lives. If she closed her eyes Celice could even pretend that it'd all turned out that way.

For a second.

"Trig news," Celice said, getting up and refilling her water, grabbing an energy bar. Sleep wasn't going to come tonight. "I need a break."

The Tama's response didn't help. Competing headlines mashed onto the wall-mounted screen. On the left, bold panicked white-on-red declared Mynx, the only Champion left for Pacifica and Atlantis, had gone missing after a fight to Chicago's south. That earned a frown.

But the words on the right? Those earned a curse.

Gatete had gone public days before he said he would. Celice told the Tama to play the Paragon's speech, Gatete wearing the same clothes he'd had on from Zhan-Yo's apartment. In a brief, fiery, and all-too-cocky address, Gatete declared he had Aegis's killer in custody. If those who took Mynx didn't release her by mid-morning London time, Zhan-Yo's head would be falling off.

The Paragons, Gatete said, would not stand for intimidation. For threats.

"Who said you get to speak for the Paragons?" Celice muttered.

"Do you see anyone else doing it?"

Celice shot up from her chair, rolling the glass in her hand up into a throwing grip. The water inside splashed everywhere, cool drips parading down her face as she looked at Benny, standing inside the apartment's open door. With his hands up, Benny came inside, clicking the door shut behind him.

"You going to answer my question, Celice?" Benny said, folding those upraised hands.

The man looked like he did the other night, bowler cap and plaid overcoat, pants and shoes making him look like a blend between a ragged Scot and a dock-working English-man. The pipe hanging from one lip didn't help matters.

"I think you get to start first," Celice replied, "and start fast, before I get something more dangerous than this glass."

"Really, you're going to the threats?" Benny said, though he kept his distance. "After you let Zhan-Yo, the object of your intense obsession, walk with a little scratch, I'd think you'd be done talking big."

Celice boiled up a retort but killed it quick. Benny's jabs weren't important.

"Don't get sidetracked," Celice said, as much to herself as to the intruder. "How'd you get in here, and why?"

Benny tapped his temple up near his eye, "Have my ways, and I'll tell'em to you later, but there's something more important we need to be doing now."

"Which is?"

"Leaving." Benny moved back towards the door. "You saw Gatete's power grab. He's going to want you present and accounted for, willing to say what he wants you to say."

Celice didn't shift a muscle. "If Gatete wants me to call Zhan-Yo my father's killer, I can do that."

"And are you willing to crown Gatete Europe's next Champion too?"

"What do you mean?"

"Aegis's daughter, side by side with Gatete makes one powerful image," Benny said. "Nobody's running up against that."

"You say that like there's someone who'd make a better fit."

"Come with me, and maybe you'll meet'em." Benny looked past Celice to the TV on the wall, now blank. "Or you can keep on going with your pity party." Shook his head at her water glass. "Though I don't think you know how to hold one of those either."

The corridor creaked, wet stone smells sifted up the apartment's stairwell as Benny and Celice made their way back towards London's soaking streets. At Benny's advice, Celice had packed weapons into their usual spots. When she'd asked the man why, he mentioned that Gatete had been known to take what he wanted.

"And what about you?" Celice said. "Breaking into my apartment?"

"Ah, I didn't do any breaking," Benny replied. "You showed me the door code yourself."

"I didn't show you a damn thing."

Benny tapped his temple again as they hit the ground floor. Outside, the building's glass doors gave view into the dark street.

"You've lived your life around anomalies, and you're still no good at figuring them out, are you?" Benny asked.

"They don't make sense, so I've stopped trying," Celice countered, going back into the chill drizzle.

If nothing else, the icy water chased away any exhaustion.

"Can't argue with ya there. Let's go this way. There's an all night place, makes the best flat whites."

"I thought we—"

"I've been seeing what you're doing for a couple days now, and that's enough for me to know you like your coffee," Benny said. "So why don't we set you up to do the right thing first before demanding it of you."

"You've been watching me?"

"Not watching you, not really." Benny laughed off Celice's gut-him-like-a-fish glare. "You have your eyes, right? Except they're mine too, right now. Like one of those little pictures in a picture on the TV."

Benny clarified over the next three blocks, giving his ability a range: unlimited, so far as he could tell, a number: one unsuspecting soul a time, and a start: a simple touch. Then Benny had a movie he could watch when he wanted, an ongoing camera lens in someone else's head.

"Can't hear anything, can't smell or feel anything," Benny said as they sat in a small booth, a dim-lit hideaway under a bridge serving as his miracle destination. As promised, the cream-and-coffee smells poured over heavy, mashing with fresh-baking bread. "So it's not like I'm living your life or anything, but for some light spying?"

"Creepy."

"Do I look like a creep to you?"

"You really want me to answer that?" Celice said, dropping a sugar cube into the frothy white.

From the moment Benny appeared in her apartment to coffee gracing the table, Celice kept scanning him over for answers. That the man was an anomaly added more wrinkles, more questions. Worse, Celice couldn't shake a growing concern that she wasn't all that good at this spy stuff.

Aegis and other Paragons had taught Celice the techniques, and she'd aced anything having to do with computers. But she'd gone from little field work to embarking on a cross-world hunt for the planet's most wanted murderer. Celice's own status and her chosen target guaranteed attention, and maybe she wasn't good enough to handle it.

"You know," Benny said, "I took this job because I liked what your father tried to do. Not what he wound up with, 'course, but the goal he started with."

"What?"

"I'm old enough to remember those early days. Was a kid then, but people were so afraid. Your buddy might sneeze and blow up a block. Aegis wanted to change all that, and he did." Benny tapped his mug on its little plate. "Then he lost himself. They all did."

"Says you."

"You're hiding in an awful apartment, Celice. Don't think that's what your daddy had in mind."

"Not his fault Zhan-Yo stabbed him in the back." Celice raised her Tama, checked the clock. Dawn skated closer. "Your time's running low, Benny."

"Nah. Give it a few minutes. You'll look out the window on your right, there, and see just what I've brought you here for."

Celice glanced that way now, saw a dirty underpass, empty in the streetlights save for a full trash bin.

"Your dad wanted anomalies treated right. Zhan-Yo wants the same for normals," Benny said. "He's fallen, but you could pick him back up. Think about it, Celice. How many would come together, you stand with him?"

"I'm not 'standing' with the man who stabbed my

father. You said this was a job. That you took it. From who?"

Benny held up a finger, and in fewer breaths than Celice thought possible, two new coffees appeared before them. The man hadn't said a word.

"Are you going to answer?" Celice said.

"I shouldn't have to. You followed the trail here, now put it together."

The pieces presented, the caffeine doing its work to counteract a sleepless night, and Celice took aim at Benny's challenge. Facts arrayed themselves on the table at her hands, imaginary boxes filling in with details and sliding against one another.

An anomaly, one who knew Celice had come to town. Not in any uniform and seemingly unknown to Gatete and his band. Not working with Zhan-Yo either, or Mathieu would've mentioned the man. Or, at least, not working directly with the murderer. At the same time, sympathetic to the man's views, but not a lone wolf.

Only one organization had the resources and the attitude to fit these pieces together.

"You're an Elemental," Celice said, doing nothing to keep the accusation from her voice. The damned anomalies only drove chaos into the world. "Which means I have nothing to say to you."

"Because?"

"You know why."

"I'd like to hear you say it," Benny leaned forward, steepled his hands. His beard's bottom snarled in his coffee's foam.

Celice stood up instead. Pushed away the coffee. She'd wasted enough time here. Gatete had an execution in a few hours, and while Celice might not like the approach, seeing

Zhan-Yo's head roll would be satisfying on some deep level.

Benny didn't try to stop her.

The pod, waiting outside the diner's entry, did. Roger and Sydney stood beside it, thick jackets laying over street clothes and looking none too patient. Bags sat under their eyes like they probably did beneath Celice's.

"Ready?" Roger asked when Celice came outside.

"A free ride?" Celice replied. "How nice."

"I wasn't talking to you," Roger said. "Traitor."

"Traitor?"

"Elementals, conversing with Zhan-Yo's associates?" Sydney shook her head. "Sad to see Aegis's daughter turn her back on the Paragons."

"She *is* a normal," Roger said as Celice took a deep, lung-filling breath.

Streetlights splashed golden glows on the wet cobblestones at their feet. The cafe's white-lit sign glowed overhead, and London's first traffic rumbled across the bridge. Coffee's svelte smell hung thick. All in all, a beautiful setting to deliver an ass-kicking to these punks.

Sydney went first, the green glow taking her hands and locking Celice's to her sides. Roger reached into his jacket, pulled out a knife and went right for a clean stab. Celice danced back, but Sydney released Celice's left hand for her left foot, locking Celice up mid-move and sending her to the ground.

"Hardly fair guys," Celice said, trying to push herself up only to lose her left hand again and plop back down.

"Tragic," Roger replied, the knife coming in low.

Benny blew through the doors, barreling into Roger and rolling them both to the ground. Water splashed as the pair struck at each other, Sydney keeping Celice's hands pinned. She tried to work her feet, get them back under her, then gave up on that idea: the slick stones made an unassisted stand impossible.

So she crawled. Rolling forward, Celice pushed herself towards Sydney. Roger's knife flashed and Benny cursed.

"What're you doing?" Celice said, kicking her feet to get towards Sydney. "This isn't you, or what you believe in!"

"This is the world your family created!" Sydney replied, retreating a step to put the pod at her back. "We survive, Celice, by doing what we need to."

"And by losing who you are!"

Sydney laughed, a dire bark, "Says you."

As Benny yelled again, more painful this time, Celice slipped on the stones. Felt her face hit hard as Sydney swapped limbs again, swept Celice's legs away. Worse than the pain, though, came the understanding.

Her father's world didn't want her.

23

A Tracker and An Anomaly

Beth pumped Kat and Calvin for details, filling out the last few hours until Wexley's plan and its success came through clear. As they spoke, Calvin couldn't believe he'd failed to see all this in the moment. If he, Weed, and the others had told the Paragons about what waited around that barn, then Mynx might've countered the ambush.

Then, instead of sitting in a sparse cafe basement as the night ticked into bar hopping time, Calvin could be out celebrating or, more likely, taking a deserved night's sleep.

"You did well," Beth said, cutting off Kat's free-wheeling descent into strategy. The tracker had swung the conversation towards a rescue mission, a signal sent to the LA Paragons to get them to hit the Factory hard. "Both of you. This turned out for the best."

"What?" Calvin asked as Kat's mouth hung open, apparently unable to leap to the new track.

"You saved yourselves, and you let the best case play out for us. I can see from your faces that this isn't what you expected to hear, but understand: if Wexley and the Paragons can destroy each other, we will only benefit."

Beth's words murdered the room. Kat still seemed stunned, but Calvin turned that old, untrusting wheel. Everyone had it out for themselves, and why would the Elementals be any different?

"Did you know, I tried to destroy Wexley not two nights ago?" Beth said, sitting behind her desk, white lights aglow from above. No windows showing Chicago's night, a claustrophobic detail that had Calvin's neck itch. "Secured an invitation to some charity event and nearly had him. He's an awful man, with far too much power."

"We know," Kat managed. "That's why—"

"But even awful men have their uses. Aegis, for another example. Wexley and the other Champions can fight each other while the Paragon rank and file lose their way. We can offer them a home, someplace new."

Calvin snorted. He couldn't help it. Every time Kat brought him by these Elementals, they thought they were the baddest of the bad. A big player ready to break out and grab the world in their hands. He'd seen both sides, though. Been in the Paragon's tower in Chicago, touched Mynx's drones up close.

And he'd been in that damn warehouse getting tossed around by anomalies playing at being heroes.

"You find destiny funny?" Beth asked, in that same tone Calvin's old schoolteachers would use whenever he'd get bored in class.

"I find it hilarious," Calvin said. "You think you're gonna waltz right into that tower and get the Paragons to help you? Do that, and you'll find yourself back on the street or buried beneath it in five minutes flat."

Beth stiffened. Again, just like those schoolteachers. Someone not used to getting talked back to.

"You're not understanding," Beth said, fighting into her standard calm and using her ability to project it. Calvin felt it as Beth looked at him. Like getting hit with lounge music and a sweet toke all together. "The Paragons are a menace. We need to be free from their control, and that will not happen until they are broken."

The thing about Beth's calm, though, was that it worked way better when you didn't know what was happening. Calvin teased out Beth's blanket, peeled it off his personality like he might shrug off a sneeze.

"Then you all prance in, declare anomalies free from anything, and we get what? A big party in the streets as the normals see all these half-assed gods with no rules?" Calvin said, standing up. "Kat, I think we're done here."

Kat glanced up at Calvin, frowned, "Beth, I don't think this is what you want."

"Oh, it very much is," Beth said. "When I first met you, I wanted your help finding Calvin to make our own ranks stronger. I wanted his help to knock the Paragons from their perch. This might not be how I imagined our rise beginning, but I will not let the moment pass."

Moving her eyes past Kat and Calvin, Beth nodded towards another Elemental at the door.

"Let everyone know," Beth continued. "We're beginning the takeover. Right now."

"Takeover?" Kat asked.

"You said the Paragons are scattered, their drones are down. It's time we take their tower, and come into the open. All the world's anomalies are waiting for us."

"Can tell you that's not true," Calvin muttered, then glanced Kat's way. "Think we'll be leaving now. You seem set on the whole conquering the world thing, and that's not really my play, so . . ."

As he spoke, Calvin slipped the leather gloves off his hands, embracing the stale air's feel, the particles he could pull apart. Nothing terribly deadly he could grab here—

tiny coffee grains wafting around didn't present many options—so Calvin hoped the warning signs he read on the Elemental faces were an overreaction.

But the way the door locked when the Elementals followed Beth's order to spread the word, the way Beth wore a weathered smile, the trap-like feel in the room all came together say things in the cafe were about to get rough.

"I hate it when I wind up helping the wrong people," Kat said, pushing back her chair.

"Then you must have hated being a tracker for so long. All those anomalies you put in chains." Beth sneered. "Sit down, both of you. You've played your part tonight."

Calvin ran a quick count. Three Elementals in the room, counting Beth. Kat had her gear on, which made her at least an anomaly's equal. A little surprise, and they might have even or better odds here.

"Okay," Calvin said, sitting down and drawing a *what the hell* expression from Kat. "Can we get some coffee then, if you're keeping us here?"

The hope one Elemental would leave to get some vanished when Beth used her Tama instead, a mug appearing in seconds while Kat stewed. Beth stayed on her Tama while the coffee arrived, tapping out messages to whomever.

Calvin took the hot mug in his left hand, felt the ceramic burn his skin, caught the raised eyebrow from Farrah, the Elemental trainer who'd handed it to him.

"Sorry we didn't work out," Calvin said to her.

"What?"

Calvin sucked the heat from the mug, sent it in a searing blast straight into Farrah's face. The Elemental staggered back, screaming, as Calvin whipped the ice-cold mug and its contents right at Beth. The Elemental leader's ability didn't seem like it'd be much good in a fight, but better not take chances.

Footsteps came rushing up behind and Calvin went forward, planting his right hand on Beth's desk and feeling its thin metal. Beth, cursing as she picked coffee off herself, seemed occupied. Sticking his left hand behind him, towards the rushing steps, Calvin stripped the metal and sent it spearing back. A stiff, strong impact juddered down Calvin's makeshift weapon, and when he looked 'round, Calvin saw Anthony, ability-enlarged with his sprint forward, staring at the metal spike coming from his chest.

"Sorry," Calvin said, letting go as Anthony stumbled, then fell to the side. "Wasn't trying to kill anyone today."

He would've felt sorrier for the anomaly, except, you know, they'd bought full in with Beth's plan to screw up an already busted world. Calvin's pity was in short supply, and besides, the Elementals had people who could bring a man like Anthony back from death's brink.

A bang jerked Calvin's attention towards the room's sole exit, where Kat stood over the dismembered lock. With a yank, she creaked the door open to find two more anomalies waiting outside.

"Mind letting us leave?" Kat asked as Calvin moved to reinforce.

"You will not!" Beth called from behind the desk.

"Stay down, please." Calvin grabbed the chair he'd been sitting in, snapped his left wrist to send a splinter series back towards Beth. She yelped and did as Calvin asked, diving beneath her desk.

Farrah had no such concerns.

The Elemental trainer hit Calvin with a waist-high tackle, dragging him to the ground. As he hit, Calvin tried to turn, get a grip on Farrah so he could start siphoning away what made her, her. Instead, he caught air. Saw

Farrah running at him again, as if she'd never taken the tackle in the first place.

This time, she kicked at Calvin's face, a blow he blocked with quick hands only for stars to erupt from his skull as something smashed his head. Rolling away, Calvin caught Farrah's shape approaching again. What the hell was her ability, anyway? How was she moving so fast?

He felt the concrete floor beneath his hands, and Calvin pulled its strength, sent the hard chemical compound racing around him as Farrah ran in. She struck, hitting the blocking concrete. A split second later, Farrah re-appeared back on the approach, this time angling for Calvin's kidneys, then stopping as those, too, disappeared behind a thin concrete wall.

"Hiding?" Farrah said, settling back as Calvin completed his shield.

"Nah, just waiting for a friend."

Behind Farrah, Kat, dashing back from the anomalies at the door, whipped her wrist and sent two silver orbs flying forward. They struck Farrah in the back, drawing a look from the anomaly at what'd just smacked her. Calvin closed his eyes, laced concrete over his face to be safe.

Kat loved this trick, and why not?

It always worked.

The flash bled beyond Calvin's closed lids, but when he popped them open and let his concrete barrier fall, the room appeared normal. Well, normal except for the writhing Elementals on the floor. The two new ones had chased Kat into the room before getting their retinas blazed by the orbs, and they joined Farrah in rubbing their eyes, trying to get some vision back.

"Time to go?" Kat asked, picking up the spent orbs and heading towards the exit.

"Way past time," Calvin replied, heading by Farrah.

He thought about giving her a shove, maybe sealing an ankle in concrete, but why waste the energy?

"It won't matter," Beth called out as the pair left. "You can't stop this now!"

"She's a dramatic one," Calvin said, the cafe door shutting behind him. Kat already had a pod signaled on her Tama. No other Elementals presented themselves in the early morning dark.

Even so, Calvin turned and put his hands on the door, molding and twisting the glass, metal, and plastic to seal the door to the glass windows around it. The Elementals could smash through the glass or take a back exit, sure, but they'd have to think about it first.

"She's bullshit," Kat said. "Like everyone else."

"So now you're seeing where I come from."

"Trust no one, the world's trash? Guess so."

The pod trundled near, sliding into the curb. Its door slid up and back, presenting two fine seats. Slipping inside, the two set the pod on a careening course towards the Paragon tower downtown. On the way to the cafe, Kat had her head back catching a nap. Now it was her turn to press her face to the pod's window, staring out into the city night.

Calvin ran through a dozen cocky lines, ready to double down on society's crappiness. Every faction just wanted power, so putting trust in any would set you up for disappointment.

"I've been alone for so long," Kat said, Calvin more watching her reflection in the glass than her face. "Beth and the Elementals seemed to offer something different. A team that didn't have the Paragon's whole . . . vibe. I'm not trying to take over the world, Calvin. I *like* hanging out with Seeker. Walking the parks, eating takeout. But every time I try to relax lately, it all goes to hell."

"Preach," Calvin replied.

"Don't you feel like that? You're, like, *the* wandering anomaly."

"Me? I'm not wandering anywhere. I go where I want, and people always seem to have a problem with it. That's the thing, Kat. We're too important. Nobody's gonna leave us alone."

"We're too important?"

"Yep," Calvin stretched his arms, laid them across the pod's back and shook his head. "We're so awesome everyone wants a piece."

Kat laughed, returned to her window gazing. Calvin watched her, not quite sure what to say. Here they were, streaking in to warn the Paragons that Mynx's Factory might be under attack and, now, that the Elementals might be out for blood. A tracker and a runaway anomaly trying to keep the world together.

As crazy as it felt, Calvin could look back on too many nights like this burned away hiding in scrapyards, using his abilities to break the locks on motel rooms and steal what he could, and doing it all alone. Those all had the same edge as tonight, a balance where things wouldn't be the same in the morning, but at least Calvin wouldn't be falling off that edge solo.

At least, when dawn came, he'd have someone to share it with.

"Hey," Calvin said. "Thanks."

"Thanks?"

"For not going with Beth back there. Like you said, they seemed to be your friends."

"They were my friends, but so are you."

"How'd you choose?"

Kat turned away from the window, looked at Calvin. A slight smile graced that hard face. "Are you kidding? Once you share the fighting floor at *Carver's*, that's a bond you can't break."

Calvin slid his arm down, landed on Kat's before he realized quite what he was doing. His hand found Kat's, cold fingers snaring together. All those lonely years broke apart in the electric touch, and Calvin *felt* Kat's essence as he would the dirt, the glass, the anything. She flowed through, in pieces and as a whole, the rush suffusing him.

He'd touched people before, had twisted their bodies to save himself, but not like this. Never like this.

Kat coughed and Calvin looked up, saw wide eyes, an open, stunned mouth. In a second, Calvin had his hand free, started to apologize. Then he noticed the red. Leaking through Kat's suit, pooling on the seat around her.

"What the hell?" Calvin said. "What's happening?"

Kat tried to say something, but only blood came up through her mouth, pouring over her chin, and the Tracker slumped forward. Ice flared inside Calvin, his thoughts flying through options. First aid? The pods all had kits, but this didn't look like something gauze and bandages could fix. Kat needed better help, needed a hospital.

Needed Paragon assistance.

"Pod," Calvin said. "Emergency, closest hospital. Now!"

The command kicked the pod into action, the lurch throwing Calvin back into the seat. Kat's seatbelt kept her steady. The blood continued pooling, but the pod's burst helped knock away the panic. Paragon training kicked in, one step after another, meant to keep the anomalies alive in dangerous situations.

Calvin punched in the rapid sequence on his Tama, a five digit command that activated his own Paragon medical emergency beacon. He unclipped his own seatbelt and tore off Kat's cloak. He had to get to whatever was hurting her, had to find the source.

Beneath the cloak, the red staining made it clear the wound came from Kat's stomach. As the pod careened around another corner, Calvin pressed his hand to the darkest, warmest area above her waist. Picking at the fibers, Calvin siphoned away the uniform, piling its cloth and plastics in a useless heap on his right.

A bullet hole. A bad one, right in her gut.

And Calvin knew, then, why Kat was bleeding out in front of him. Knew who was responsible if she died that night, right there.

And who would pay.

"Stay with me, Kat," Calvin said in between curses. He pressed his left hand against the wound, put his right on the piled plastic, and started drawing the fibers back. "Don't let them win."

Remaking the uniform, Calvin sealed the wound, laying the cloth, the thick material on tight right around the hole. Kat might be bleeding inside her body too, but Calvin couldn't do much about that. He had to keep her alive, had to keep her heart beating.

Just a little bit longer.

24

Real Food, Real World

The sprawl welcomed them with a rainstorm. Any sunset vanished in the gray downpour, though Cassidy figured she'd trade beauty for the water's cooler temps. The pod wound through increasing traffic, with cargo pods meshing in to create a slow moving river heading into Bangkok. The city's sky-stealing buildings twinkled, drawing Cassidy's open-mouthed awe with their heights, their curved sides joining together many meters above ground. As if half the city decided it would live above the other.

"A curious decision, isn't it?" Thane said next to her. "Guess who began the effort?"

Thane asked the question with his usual slow venom.

"The Paragons?"

Not that Cassidy had any idea, but with Thane, anything bad seemed to trace to the anomalies.

"Hardly," Thane laughed, "The Paragons aren't architects. A woman proposed the shift. She lead the plans, convinced the companies in question to spend their reps on these massive structures. Impractical, but beautiful in their way."

"She just convinced them?" Cassidy pointed at one they passed on the right, which seemed to have four zig-zagging towers coalescing in a ball at the top. "To build something like that? How?"

"Bribes, threats," Thane mused, his eyes sparkling as he spoke. He'd seemed much happier since they'd convinced the orphans, since they joined the Paragon patrol heading into town. "She didn't use any, because she could twist their minds with a pen."

"So there was an anomaly involved."

"Of course. Anything she wrote down, once read, would become the most fascinating idea to the reader," Thane said, shaking his head at some memory. "The things she could get people to believe, to sign."

"And?"

"Not every enemy the Paragons destroyed died in a fight," Thane said, that smile falling into a sigh. "Apinya changed the rules. No more paper copies. Tamas became the norm, and nobody used paper for anything. Last I heard, she does well enough for herself, wallowing in some mansion down south."

"What a terrible fate."

"To be stripped of your power, your purpose? I would consider that a terrible fate indeed."

Cassidy threw Thane what she hoped was some signifi-cant side-eye, "Terrible fate indeed? Ever since we left the island, you keep going on like some maudlin prophet. Talk normal."

"I spent decades tied to a chair in an underground facility, Cassidy. When I get angry, I become an unstop-pable monster. When I'm happy, I shrivel up into a wrin-kled, fragile shell. Nothing about me is normal."

"You, me, and everyone else."

The pod brought them right to the Paragon's headquarters on the city's western side, across the river from the Grand Palace. Apinya had some decorum, because he'd made his throne a svelte, smooth sister to the gold-and-traditional opulence. The Paragon's blue P glowed in the deepening evening, a small light against Bangkok's overwhelming sparkle.

Achaya and the orphans left first, whisked into the headquarters while four other Paragons, all uniformed up and looking way too serious, kept Thane and Cassidy beneath an entry overhang. When Cassidy asked, the Paragons declared they'd be allowed in when Apinya decided and not before. Thane, being Thane, went and stood in the rain, turning his face up towards the droplets and letting nature pound away.

"Does he normally do that?" A Paragon boy that couldn't have been older than fifteen asked Cassidy. The boy's appearance and accent marked him as a local, though the other three could've been from anywhere.

"Thane doesn't *normally* do anything," she replied, folding her arms and rolling her eyes. "He's dramatic."

"He's also slaughtered dozens," grunted an older Paragon, his English smooth and practiced. "Thane deserves death."

"I'd like to see you give it to him," Cassidy countered.

"Apinya's ordered otherwise," the older Paragon said, "or I would."

"Your Champion's protecting you from yourself."

Achaya appeared back at the building's quad doors, calling for Cassidy and Thane to come along inside. Thane, soaking wet, went without a word, and Cassidy stepped on after him, dodging the puddles.

"When the time comes, don't die defending a killer," the older Paragon said to Cassidy's back.

The Champion sat on a well-cushioned chair in a

maroon room, buried in robes and blankets despite the mild temperature. Artwork coated the walls, paintings framed and placed near each other in cascading rows. Overhead, hanging lanterns flickered with what seemed to be real flame, echoing their shadows and warmth throughout. Incense burned, a nose-stinging fragrance that unraveled Cassidy's nerves as she breathed.

"All local," Apinya spoke, his well-worn voice a thin reed. "As is every piece on the walls throughout this building."

As she came in further, pairing Thane on his approach, Cassidy noticed something else. Two IV bags hung from poles next to Apinya, their tubes leading back to the man. A tray stood by him, with a black ceramic tea pot and lemon water. Dragon fruit, its white and black-speckled inside, splayed on a plate. Hardly the imposing, impressive array fit for a Champion.

"The attack in LA was worse than I expected," Thane said by way of a greeting. "I'm sorry so many were lost."

"No, you are not," Apinya countered. "You were never one for sorrow or mourning."

Thane did not deny it, instead gesturing towards Cassidy, "This is the Void."

"I know who she is," Apinya said, looking Cassidy's way. With the low light, she had a hard time reading his face. "Mynx treated you too harshly, Cassidy. I apologize on her behalf."

"Not accepted. She can apologize herself."

"That may be hard to come by. It seems Mynx has been taken by an enemy to us all."

Apinya followed up that nugget with more details, ones Thane scooped up with analytical interest. Cassidy could see Thane's mind working, its increasing speed evident as his body weakened next to her. Apinya seemed to key into

Thane's interest, the two falling into a banter that left normal conversation behind in a linguistic blur Cassidy had neither the interest nor desire to follow. Like being stuck at a dinner with two old friends and their stories, Cassidy knew this conversation wasn't for her.

The Champions, the Paragons, and their political power plays didn't matter so long as she could be free, so long as Cassidy had a chance to get back to her family.

"Do you have a computer I could use?" Cassidy announced, pouncing on a quiet beat.

Apinya did, and Achaya directed Cassidy right to it. A loaner office, without windows and socketed away in a spare slot on the first floor. Beneath two spirited jungle paintings, surrounded by moss-green walls, Cassidy used the provided Paragon login and found herself once again exchanging messages with her family.

Except, this time, her children answered Cassidy's replies instantly. Morning in Pacifica, what the Paragons labeled North America's west coast, meant her kids were having their coffee, stumbling around getting ready for school.

She had them call in sick, had them connect through the Internet's magic to pop up on her screen in crystal clear video. Up until the instant her son and daughter's face appeared, Cassidy didn't believe it would happen. Something would get in the way, a technical glitch or an attack by Paragons. Mynx, captured or not, would send in her drones to take Cassidy back to the prison island.

But no. There they were, somewhat bleary looking, smiling through the camera. Cassidy's breath caught as she picked out the features, the eyes, the hair, the freckles on her daughter's cheeks. They'd grown older, yes, but they were still hers.

Words flew faltering at first but picked up speed quick.

Cassidy drove the conversation, excavating details like an archaeologist at a fossil-filled dig. She learned about passions, caught hobbies and quirks. Favorite colors, sports, and songs.

The spaces opened wider as the conversation went on, gaps Cassidy's children kept circling around. The initial rush falling into lurches as everyone realized how much remained untold, how much had been missed.

And when Cassidy tried to talk about the island, about the collectives formed between the anomalies, the back-and-forth fighting, scrabbling over resources while drones watched on the horizon?

Her children shook their heads, said 'wow' and 'that sounds awful'. They looked at her differently now, the same expressions they'd held when the Paragons first came for Cassidy. She wasn't their mom, but an alien, someone who did things, who had things done to them that these two normals—she'd asked that straight away: no anomaly powers—couldn't understand.

The call cut.

The program redirected back to a different face, one Cassidy both knew and didn't know. He'd raised their children, had been Cassidy's partner, and when he'd found out, he'd damned her to the island. Filip had aged worse than Cassidy, gnarls climbing his large cheeks and pushing back a peppered hairline. Stubble ran rampant, hiding in chin folds that'd grown over the years. A black turtleneck hid anything else, the webcam showing a cream wall behind his head.

"Stay. Away." Filip's voice had a tired anger to it, a dragon trying to rouse from its sleep.

"Always so polite," Cassidy countered, swallowing the bile that surged in her throat. "How did I stand you for so long?"

"You lied."

"Nope, never did. You never asked if I was an anomaly. It didn't affect us."

"Until it destroyed everything we'd built."

"Your fault."

Filip reached out, gripped his camera's either side, as if he wanted to strangle her, "Your damn blood. You should've stayed on that island, Cassidy. It would've been better for all of us. Don't call again."

This time, when the call died, it didn't come back. Cassidy immediately tried another, found the number blocked. What a bastard.

The change had been immediate that afternoon. One minute, a happy family in their prime. The next, Filip losing his mind. Despairing that his young children might be anomalies. That his wife could tear him apart without a second thought.

Who knew what broke him, but Cassidy didn't get a chance to say goodbye and for that she'd never forgive the man.

Cassidy needed a restroom, needed some water. After those, provided without comment by two Paragons—the young and old one from before—waiting outside the small office Cassidy had borrowed, the Void went back to Apinya's hall. Getting back to her family still hung as a priority, but Cassidy needed to figure some things out first.

Namely, who she was: a mom, or Thane's partner in his quest to reshape the world?

Before the call, Cassidy had drifted towards the former. Skate back to the past and find her family waiting, ready to disregard the in between and embrace Cassidy's return. Now? Their mother had a criminal's label, would never hold a normal job again. She couldn't walk onto the soccer field, go to a parent's weekend at her kid's college without drawing the wrong kind of attention.

Thane, though, didn't offer any better ideas. He and Apinya were still going at it, splashing conversation back and forth, colleagues deep in their own world. Cassidy caught Thane throwing lines outside the room's entrance about some multi-faceted propaganda scheme to turn people's trust their way and decided she couldn't handle that. Not right now.

Instead, with those same two Paragons trailing her, Cassidy made for the building's exit. Rain drummed down outside, but umbrellas lay handy in a bucket at the entrance. Cassidy took one, popped its Paragon-blue shield with a button, and strode towards the nearby river. Bangkok's lights confronted the stormy twilight, her shoes splashing with every step.

Back on the island, when storms struck, the anomalies would retreat inside the few huts on offer. Some would have abilities to lessen the impact—Cassidy herself could create voids to catch hail—but otherwise they rode out the typhoons like they did everything else: with bland ennui. Tomorrow would make another day, with more fish to catch, more trees to grow and cut, and now more huts to repair.

Here, Cassidy could return to the building, could find a hotel and disappear from the weather. She wouldn't have to fix anything the storm damaged. Food would be there in the morning, so long as Cassidy had the reps to pay for it.

Speaking of . . .

"You two know somewhere I could get a good meal?" Cassidy asked the Paragon pair shadowing her.

"How's your spice tolerance?" the young one piped up, the old one just glared.

Three bowls stuffed with lab-spun beef, eggs, veggies

and spices set atop metal tables mere minutes later. The chosen place, a thin line stuffed between offices, hid beneath a huge overhang where cooking pots spilled onto the sidewalk, letting the savory aroma draw in anyone walking by. Daw, the younger Paragon, dug into his bowl, splattering hot sauce on top the steaming mix. Kamnan glowered, choosing to pick at his food with the chopsticks while keeping one eye on Cassidy. She matched Kamnan's slower stance, feeling her way around the meal even as her stomach protested the pace, demanding more food now.

Cassidy pushed back: getting indigestion here, now, would be rough.

In fact . . .

"Is Apinya putting us up somewhere?" Cassidy asked.

"Don't know," Kamnan answered, and Daw, egg hanging from his lip, frowned at his counterpart. "Not our call."

"So you're babysitting me till when, then?"

"Morning," Daw answered faster this time. "We're going in shifts."

Cassidy laughed, "We get twenty-four hour protection, huh?"

"You could call it that," Kamran replied.

"There a reason you're all upset, while he's having fun?" Cassidy asked, two bites later.

"He's missing his own family," Daw said, drawing yet another glare from Kamnan. Daw threw on a joker's grin. "He's lazy. Bangkok hasn't seen much action, so he's soft."

"Daw," Kamnan growled.

"Sorry," Cassidy offered. "You can leave if you want."

"And let a killer run free in our streets? I will not."

Killer. The word should've hurt Cassidy more than it did. Maybe she didn't want to let Kamnan under her skin, maybe she'd been called a villain long enough now that the label didn't bother her anymore. Kamnan's implications matched her own dismal perception: Cassidy wasn't free. Would never be. She couldn't get on a plane and go after her family. She couldn't choose to go back to school, go visit someplace new. She'd traded the island for a bigger cell, with better food.

Cassidy turned to her chopsticks for comfort, delving another bite from the bowl. And another.

And another.

Her chopsticks hit the bowl, and only the bowl, before Cassidy stopped. She felt eyes on her, glanced up to see both Daw and Kamnan staring her down. The former blended confusion and worry, while the latter showed stern resolve and nothing else.

"It's been a hard decade," Cassidy said, shoving the bowl away and standing up.

The other two didn't look finished, but who cared. They could get more anytime they wanted. Cassidy had other, more important problems, and solving those started outside. The rain continued, but Cassidy didn't let that stop her. She left the umbrella too, though Daw and Kamnan popped theirs.

She went into the street's center, the pods streaking around her as algorithms performed to perfection. Everything in its place, except Cassidy. Imprisoned, yanked along, forgotten and forbidden.

"I'm done," Cassidy called back to the two Paragons. "Tell Thane and Apinya they can do whatever the hell they want, but I'm done."

"Done with what?" Daw asked.

"All of it."

The voids kissed her fingertips, waiting. They called her a villain, a killer. Her kids still called her mom.

She wouldn't find out which she was here.

25

A Taste of Victory

Wexley went right at Mynx in the Factory's innermost center. The small room, lit by monitors and overhead globes, pressed everyone together, close enough for a surprise. His three finger flash curled into a straight-handed kidney shot. Mynx doubled over and Wexley took advantage, using his left hand to grip her throat and push the Champion back against those monitors. Around and behind him, Rhimes and the team broke into their own action, taking drone fire while deploying skills Wexley hoped they had.

Wexley didn't expect them to defeat the drones, or to hold off an attack for long. He had a different bet, one that depended on the body he held before him.

"Call them off," Wexley said, pressing Mynx against the screens. He brought his second arm up into her stomach, helping to keep her feet off the ground.

Mynx stared at him, eyes bugging out. Veins pulsing as her body tried to cope with Wexley's grip. She couldn't talk, but Wexley didn't need, or want, Mynx to get involved.

Behind him, a soldier cried out. A drone gun fired. Rhimes shouted more orders. A metal hand fell on Wexley's shoulder, heavy fingers digging in.

"Reeves, isn't it?" Wexley said, holding Mynx tighter. If he lost his grip on her, Wexley would be dead before she hit the floor. "She dies if you don't back off. Follow your programming."

"And how would you know what my programming requires?" The drone's vibrating voice buzzed in Wexley's ear.

But, aside from that sound, the other fighting stopped. One soldier cursed to himself about a wound Wexley couldn't see.

"Call it a hunch," Wexley said. "All the stories have AIs protecting their owners."

That, and Mynx had a history of saving herself above everyone else. What happened in the LA stadium explosion? Oh, right, Mynx had shot herself up above the stadium in a protective shell while everyone else suffered down below. What happened in Chicago when she'd been near death?

Drones floated in from everywhere to rescue her.

"Then what do you propose?" Reeves asked.

Wexley opened his mouth, about to talk, when he noticed Mynx's eyes go glassy. He knew how to hold a choke, knew that he hadn't cut off all the oxygen. Which meant Mynx might be trying something different.

So he went tighter. Mynx gasped, her eyes went back to Wexley, narrow and angry. Like they ought to be. Wexley smiled right back. Amazing how fast the nerves went away once he'd crossed the line. Everything hung in the moment, but Wexley could only move one way.

"Save the anomalies. Protect them," Wexley said. "All of them. You understand how."

The drone stayed silent. Wexley had no idea if the AI could actually come to the right conclusion, but he used sound logic. The kind a machine would know, would take to the farthest extremes.

"She'll die otherwise," Wexley added.

"Human promises are fickle," Reeves replied finally.

"They are all you have."

"Reeves, don't listen to him!" Mila called, before a soldier silenced her.

Wexley felt the drone's hand pull off his shoulder, heard the clack as the drone took a step back. Preparing for an execution? Maybe, but any shot could risk striking Mynx. Wexley couldn't stop now, couldn't flinch.

"Make your choice," Wexley said.

Reeves announced his decision with a dwindling whine, the drones slumping around the soldiers as the AI killed their power. Wexley tightened his hold on Mynx just enough, then, for her eyes to roll back in her head, the Champion to slip into unconsciousness.

No sense giving her a chance to override Reeve's very good decision.

"Now," Wexley said, handing Mynx's body over to a waiting mercenary and shaking out the soreness in his arms. Holding any body that long had his muscles tight, aching. "Reeves, let's discuss how we can keep our beloved Champion and her Paragons alive."

The plans flew together fast, Wexley acting as a guide while Reeves, pulling secrets from the Paragon vaults, orchestrated the next steps. Mynx, apparently, already had an island reserved for criminal anomalies. There were others like it, sanctuary spaces that could be made into isolated homes for the Paragons. They would be kept away from civilians, brought food and medical supplies.

The anomalies would have their chance to live in peace, while the world could do the same.

Wexley gave Reeves the blessing, told the AI that the Paragons wouldn't see things his way. The drones would need to be weaponized, would have to be persuasive. Any anomaly that resisted, well, they couldn't be allowed to risk all the others, could they?

Small sacrifices for the greater good.

And Mynx?

Wexley walked the mercenaries holding Mynx and Mila down to the Factory's most secure medical space. Mila moved under her own power, a mercenary's hand on her throat to remind her that free speech had its consequences. Mynx came by carriage, one strong man cradling the Champion like a child.

This far down into the rock, the Factory dropped its high tech pretensions. Instead, Mynx went with a natural look: stone serving as wall and ceiling, albeit decorated with lights. No artwork offered itself, and with the Factory's omnipresent hum silenced by the depths, the space felt unnerving, mysterious.

"This is supposed to be for healing?" Wexley said as they went down the sole corridor. "No garden? Koi pond?"

On either side doors split off leading to infrastructure. Signs labeled things like the furnace, server rooms, and water control. All the nuts and bolts Wexley would hand over to his company, and those who stood with him. The leaders whose faces had doubted him back in Chicago would throw themselves at Wexley now, wanting to secure their place in the new world.

A new world, Wexley had to admit, that'd come easier than he expected. A captured drone serving as bait, one overconfident Champion, and now the biggest weapons on the planet were Wexley's to control. Probably a lesson in there somewhere, one Wexley could dig for when he had a minute to breathe.

Reeves directed them to the corridor's end, an ocean-blue room with three tanks inside. Each one looked large enough to hold five people, standing at least four meters tall. A thick, teal water filled two, while the other pair were dark and empty.

"I had them prepped for your arrival," Reeves said.

Wexley frowned at the second tank, "Mila doesn't need one."

"The Factory does not contain holding cells. To keep her safe, I request that you put her inside."

"Hear that, Mila?" Wexley said, turning to the Champion. "Reeves wants to keep you safe. Isn't that nice?"

Mila's reply would've made Wexley's mother blush. It made him laugh. The idea, the very idea that a normal like him could drive a Champion to talk like that . . . Wexley had faced a god—no, two!—and came away victorious.

Her words were nothing now.

Reeves opened up the two tanks, their tops hissing. On the room's right side, special suits waited for anyone so lucky to be entombed. A drone that seemed all gleaming arms did the honors, handling Mynx first with soft care as it slipped the suit and its zippered limbs around the Champion. Wexley might've been afraid Mynx would wake up, except he'd had Reeves deliver sedatives from Mynx's own private stash.

Even Champions needed help sleeping sometimes.

The drone extended its top two arms like some growing plant to put Mynx in the chosen vat. The Champion sank slow to the bottom, bubbles rising up around her. A peaceful look settled on the woman, certainly the most calm Wexley had ever seen on the Champion.

"Perhaps I'm doing her a favor," Wexley said to Mila. "She looks happier now, doesn't she?"

"You ought to give it a try," Mila countered.

"I might. There are extra tanks."

Wexley frowned when he realized the third tank had a darker bottom, had water marks around its base. Gesturing for Mila—pushed by a mercenary—to follow, Wexley went over to the empty tank. Definitely damp, although down here, who knew how long water might last?

"Was this in use?" Wexley asked Mila.

"You think I'm going to tell you anything?"

Wexley straightened, put a hand into a fist. He wasn't much for beating up on prisoners, but Mila had been a frustration all day. And she'd be going right into a healing tank.

"You will not," Reeves said, the AI's voice coming from the arms drone. "We are protecting the Paragons, not hurting them. Touch her and our arrangement comes to an end."

"Of course," Wexley replied, letting his fingers go. He'd be bringing computer specialists in here as soon as he could to nix Reeves and the AI's damned principles. Until then, Wexley could keep his ego in check. "Mila, I'll ask you one more time. What was in this tank?"

"We were testing it out for you, Wexley," Mila spat back, "but you know what? After this? I think we'll just dump you in the ocean instead."

What a waste of time.

"Reeves? Answer my question." Wexley nodded back towards the tank. "It's important."

"Actually, it is immaterial," Reeves said. "Please, if you would, Mila. The suit awaits."

"This is insane, Reeves," Mila said, "and you know it."

"I know that I am keeping you alive. For now, that will be enough."

"And if I don't go willingly?"

"You will be sedated."

Wexley couldn't believe what he was hearing. Mynx's very own AI, turning on her and the other Paragons. All he had to do was put Mynx in some danger, and the Factory folded. Adriana would be amazed. He'd call her after this, relish the story and plot what came next, a conclusion he hadn't dared dance with until now.

"What happens next, Reeves?" Mila asked, walking towards the suit in apparent surrender. "What happens when this guy decides you're not necessary?"

"I will deal with that in due time."

"And when he deletes you?"

"That will not happen."

Wexley kept his face straight at that. He would most definitely be deleting, or at least reconfiguring Reeves as soon as he could. No way he'd trust something loyal to Mynx.

"Promise me you won't leave us," Mila said to the drone as it started putting the suit around her.

"I promise, Mila."

So touching, Wexley almost shed a tear.

HE LEFT two soldiers by the tanks, instructing them to see if there were any easy ways to disconnect the two bubbling berths from Reeves's network. The AI refused to cut the Champions off, and Wexley wouldn't trust the machine mind to leave them alone.

On the walk back down the corridor—alone now—Wexley ran through messages with Rhimes on his Tama. Rhimes had his crew clearing the Factory, making sure no

Paragons were hidden in the eaves. Meanwhile, loyal Ziran resources were en-route. Tech specialists that could start taking control from Reeves. It would have to be a subtle effort to start, giving the AI no idea what was happening until he'd lost control.

Wexley planned how he'd break the news to everyone. First, of course, he would rope in his council, get them onboard with the imminent anomaly capture and containment. Then Wexley would go wide, use Ziran's broadcast abilities to tap into every phone, every computer and send an alert that humanity had a driving position in its own future once again.

There would be panic, but Zhan-Yo's preparation would serve here. There would be bodies across the globe waiting for this moment to step into power. Countries would reclaim their governments, borders would re-appear, and before a week had passed, the world would enter a new age.

And where would Wexley be? At the top? Managing all everyone as they scurried around, trying to profit off the change?

No. The dance played out as he walked the stony hall, his echoing steps matching the party in his imagination. Wexley would stay right here, in his prize Factory. He'd police the world, his drones enforcing Zhan-Yo's much-desired democracy while making sure anomalies never again threatened humanity. A watchful, beloved guardian.

Just what he promised his sister.

And, who knew, Wexley wasn't all that old. Adriana either. Perhaps they could find a time to properly get to know one another. A family, even.

No.

That thought held no purchase. His sister proved

Wexley's genes had anomaly potential, they could spring forth in a new generation. Not a risk he could take.

But adoption?

Rhimes pinged through a message as Wexley arrived at the Factory's central elevator. For all the facility's fanciness, like those open-air platforms in its giant assembly area, Mynx went as basic as everyone else for the essentials. Wexley punched the call button, read Rhimes's message. The software techs had arrived. The drones let them in.

The elevator hummed. Wexley tapped a reply, telling Rhimes to have them find a way to disconnect Reeves from the drones as fast as possible. And, after that, find a way to delete the AI.

Nothing loyal to the Paragons could be so close to power.

The elevator stopped humming. The doors didn't open. The floor counter hadn't changed. Wexley rolled his eyes up, to a small camera lingering over the door.

"Reeves," Wexley said. "Don't tell me you're getting cold feet already."

The AI didn't answer. Wexley looked back down the rocky corridor towards the medical chamber, those two vats. He brought up his Tama, flipped it to the short-range signal, tried to send a message to the mercenary pair Wexley had left behind.

Caught static.

In fact, his Tama found no signal whatsoever. His connection to the Factory's internal network looked severed.

"I thought we had a deal?" Wexley said, starting back towards the medical chamber.

Mynx and Mila were his only leverage. Lose them, and Reeves had no reason to hold off on the drones. Had no reason not to slaughter Wexley and his team.

Ziran's CEO, the revolution's latest leader, ran flat out down the rough floor, dropping his jacket to get some more speed. He blitzed by the server rooms, the water heaters, the buzzing and beeping Factory innards. Cut around the corner hard.

The two mercenaries were down. Worse than that, by Wexley's trained eye, both looked very dead. Looming over them, coated in glistening red wet, stood Reeves's arm drone. Behind it, at least, both vats still sat full, with their Champion's sealed away in their suits.

"Man versus machine," Reeves said, voice coming from the arm drone. "So far, I'm up two points."

Wexley didn't have any weapons. They'd given up the guns early on, and he hadn't wanted to take a chance sneaking knives past the Factory's scanners. He'd have to get clever.

The drone lurched forward, its ten arms snapping and lunging at Wexley like some metal hydra. At first, Wexley danced back, giving himself space. The drone followed him out the medical room's door, into the wider corridor. Every second brought more strikes, all short.

But Reeves clued Wexley into the drone's moves. The arms attacked in a pattern, each one needing a few seconds to get itself together before doing another snapping, finger clasping strike. They alternated sides too, coming at Wexley's left and right to keep him centered. The arms spread out around the drone like a halo, leaving a middle without much in the way except a silver stalk.

His only target.

Wexley bounced back from a leftward blow, then burst forward, charging off his right foot towards the very arm that'd fired. As he moved, Wexley caught an arm on the drone's right snapping across, fast enough to clip Wexley's shoulder and tear his tactical vest, gash the skin beneath.

The hit didn't nudge Wexley off his course, the sting driving an extra push into Wexley's left-footed kick.

The shot struck the drone's center stalk, ringing loud and sending a ripple up Wexley's foot, his calf, and all the way to his spine. The drone itself, though, didn't move. The blow a non-starter, Wexley let his right foot slide out so he fell on his back. The drone's next hit, a leftward slap that would've knifed through Wexley's middle, flew over Wexley's face.

He rolled left, tucking in and getting beneath the arms as the drone rotated to follow. Putting his feet beneath him, Wexley sprang up and went back towards the medical room. Whatever hope he wanted to find there didn't show: the same two dead bodies, the same two Champions suspended in their healing vats.

And now, behind him, the drone blocking the room's only exit.

26

Triple Threat

For all the rules Aegis taught Celice, her father always returned to one key principle:

When your life's on the line, do whatever the hell it takes to survive.

With Sydney throwing Celice around and Benny getting himself carved up by Roger, Celice went to her Tama. Said a word she never wanted to use, one every Paragon had access to. The Tama fired out an alert, calling any and all nearby drones and Paragons to the scene.

Roger and Sydney's own Tamas rang out, their proximity giving the alert higher priority. Sydney glanced at the sound, trained habit taking control and giving Celice a chance to make her one legged, one armed attack:

Combat boots, steel-toed.

Celice pulled hers off and whipped it, a shot that shouldn't have worked, except Sydney had her focus on the Tama, had less than two meters separation. The boot struck Sydney hard, knocked her head back, and broke the anomaly's concentration.

With one sock and one shoe, body bruised all over,

Celice sprang on the Paragon. She went straight for Sydney's throat, temples, kidneys, anything that might keep the anomaly from focusing. Celice didn't know how Sydney's abilities operated, but anomalies tended to work that way: keep their minds a mess, and they wouldn't be able to mess with you.

Then again, that philosophy worked on just about everyone.

Sydney proved herself ill-equipped for an up-close brawl, crumpling under Celice's precise punches. The Paragon wilted so fast, falling back into the open pod, that Celice nearly toppled in on top. Instead, with her right hand catching on the pod's sloping front, Celice reached into Sydney's jacket, grabbed the Paragon's stun gun, and fired it point blank.

Sydney's yell didn't even get started.

Benny's came loud and clear.

Whirling left, Celice caught a grim picture: Benny, bleeding all over, had himself backed into a corner. Roger, Tama alert ignored and knife drawn, pressed in on his prey.

Too focused on the target to check his back.

Pulling the stun gun's trigger a second time was all too satisfying.

Roger dropped forward, face mashing into Benny's stomach before the Elemental pushed Roger off to the sidewalk. The anomaly hit hard, and Benny tore the knife away.

"Nasty scratcher," Benny said, tossing the knife down a sewer grate and meeting Celice at the pod. She dragged Sydney from the vehicle, dropped the Paragon on the curb. "Nice of 'em to bring us a pod though."

"They're following orders," Celice said, frowning at the two, but getting in the pod with Benny anyway.

The Elemental tapped in an address and the vehicle set off on its humming way. Benny, hissing as he tore into the pod's mandatory first aid kit, managed to squeeze in a head shake.

"Don't you give them excuses now," Benny said. "They made their choices same as you."

"Did they?" Celice asked, tracking morning's bright arrival in London.

A beautiful day for an execution.

"What're you on about?" Benny replied. "You said it yourself. They're taking what Gatete gives'em without complaint."

"Because if they don't they'd get sent back to the streets. You want to move up in the Paragons, you do what your commander tells you."

"Till you're under a Champion and then what, wait for death?"

"Or transfer." Celice glanced at her Tama. A couple hours yet until Gatete's appointed time arrived. She swiped away the emergency alarm and the drones tracking overhead drifted away like parting clouds.

"Such a healthy organization we have leadin' our little planet."

"It's worked fine for decades."

"If you think that's true, then your daddy did a better job on you than I could've imagined."

There were some arguments worth having and others not. The Paragons and their reputation wouldn't get anywhere with an Elemental, so Celice stayed quiet.

Benny slapped lotioned bandages over the cuts where the ointments would tie his skin together into its pre-sliced self. Celice found a painkiller in the kit, considered sending it down her throat, then left it there. Her scrapes hurt—the way Sydney had bent her hands and ankles sent the wrong twinges along her nerves—but Celice figured she'd need all her senses running fine where they were going.

"What's the address?" Celice said, nodding towards the pod's console.

"Close to where we need to be," Benny replied. "Mathieu has his team pulling together one last raid, trying to save their leader. Figure we'd help out."

"You 'figured'?"

"I took a hunch that when you stunned your two Paragon buddies that you weren't on Gatete's team anymore. Am I wrong?"

Celice looked out the window, saw coffee shops springing open, Londoners finding their way up and down Underground stations. Most looking all right, heading into a stable day without fear, without wars.

Was she really turning her back on all that to rescue the man that'd stabbed her father?

"Am I crazy?" Celice asked.

"Not an answer to my question, but fair enough. Trust me to diagnose you?"

"It's rhetorical."

"I'll take that as a yes." Benny sat back into the seat, apparently done dealing with his cuts. "You're the orphaned daughter of the world's most famous hero slash dictator. You've been on a vengeful hunt for daddy's killer, and now the organization you've spent your whole life working for is trying to take you out in turn. Seems ripe for a little noggin splitting, you ask me."

"Which I didn't."

The pod scampered across the Thames, the river looking regal. Off to the right, Celice caught the Tower of London and its attendant bridge, still ancient and imposing. Over the landmark, as if preparing for the moment, five black and blue drones hovered in a cloudless sky. At least one news drone joined them, its smaller silver form darting for the perfect shot.

One thing hadn't changed across humanity's centuries: public executions were big draws.

Mathieu and his crew lurked in a grocery store's back-end, strapping on body armor amid frozen meals and stacked pints. The few employees manning the place avoided the mercenaries, not meeting Celice and Benny's eyes as they went right on back. Who bought them off, and for how much?

"Not telling," Benny replied when Celice asked. "Trade secret."

"That doesn't—"

"Ah, get over yourself," Benny said as they walked through the swinging, slate-gray door leading to Mathieu and his team. "You're about to join a bunch of normals in an attack on an old prison to save the man that stabbed your dad from a dude with super powers. Who's slippin' the shelve stockers a few reps isn't your concern."

Put that way, Celice could agree.

Mathieu gave a brighter greeting, doable because the man looked like he found some sleep after their late night. While Celice fell somewhere in between nauseous and tweaked out from the caffeine, Mathieu shook her hand with the vigor due someone who'd enjoyed their mattress. She hoped her jealousy didn't show too much.

"Benny said you'd change your mind, but I didn't trust him," Mathieu said. "He's always promising things."

"And delivering on those promises!" Benny patted Mathieu's shoulder. "We found ourselves in a scrape though. Gatete sent his dogs after us, and Celice showed why she belongs here, and why I belong on the sidelines."

Mathieu returned the gesture and Benny took his leave,

scooting back out the store with a promise that he'd be back with reinforcements soon.

"Elementals?" Celice asked. "You trust them, after all Zhan-Yo's done?"

"Enemy of my enemy, isn't it?" Mathieu replied, handing Celice a thick black vest. His assembled team numbered eight, and they had extras. "What we've heard is Lukas didn't spend much time in London, and Gatete didn't make many friends. People looked the other way for us, and the Elementals have a strong presence here. They know, like we do, the Paragons could snuff them out if they wanted to."

"That won't change," Celice said, going through the motions as she scoped out the weapons on offer. Vests, but no guns. Clubs, some pepper sprays. This wasn't an armed force preparing for an assault, it was a ragtag group on its last legs. "Especially with this."

Mathieu put up a brave show, slanting a grin and waving an arm at the team, "Not many left after your raid yesterday. We'll be enough, and once Zhan-Yo's out, with your help, we can put all this behind us."

Celice slipped on the vest, winced as her hair caught in a strap, "If we win, and that's a huge if, it's just the beginning. The Paragons can take all this right back."

"I know. That's why we have to do this right."

"I'm not—"

"No killing," Mathieu continued. "Not a single soul if we can help it. That's why there's no guns here, no knives. Zhan-Yo's learned, and so have we. The world's not going to follow a bunch of killers to a brighter future."

"Like they did the Paragons?"

"That was forced with fear."

Celice laughed, "If you say this revolution will come through love, I'm walking out right now."

Mathieu shook his head.

"With choice, Celice. For the first time in history, all the world's going to choose their leaders, from normals and anomalies alike."

"Zhan-Yo has you all seeing stars."

Mathieu handed Celice a blackjack, the weighted, short sap heavy in her hands. The thing felt dangerous enough, but next to all the anomaly abilities she'd seen . . .

"It will do," Mathieu read her expression. "It'll have to. Otherwise, we're dead and it won't matter."

"There's the optimism I needed. When do we leave?"

The Tower loomed as the clock closed on ten. Celice couldn't see Big Ben from the alley she and Mathieu stood in, but her Tama told the time well enough. Across a wide street, closed off by Paragons in their blue and white, sat the gardens surrounding the Tower itself. Somewhere inside the building, no small space, would be Zhan-Yo.

Mathieu led their group in a casual walk down the alley. Acting secretive when drones already had eyes on them would only raise suspicion. Bringing Celice near the tower at all meant they'd get Gatete's full attention anyway.

Mathieu counted on it.

"They're going to wonder why I fought two Paragons just to walk in here," Celice muttered.

"A question I'll answer in precisely ten seconds," Mathieu replied.

The blackjack rested in a loop high in Celice's brown jacket, a huge, warm garment that climbed down to her knees. A sweater beneath hid the protective vest from cursory inspection, and made Celice feel overstuffed. Mathieu claimed she looked fashionable, but Celice put about as much stock in the man's cosmetic eye as she put in her father's.

As soon as Celice had the money and ability to buy her own clothes, Aegis never bothered and Celice never asked.

Three Paragons met them at the alley's mouth, the Tower's walls one wide courtyard and a green space away. The leader, a stocky fellow with a pipe dangling from his lips paired with two younger women, both finishing and tossing teas as they stepped up. A drone hovered into position behind the trio, its angry cameras staring at the intruding pair. Celice gave the machine a wave.

"She came asking help," Mathieu opened the conversation after the lead Paragon held his palm flat out for them to stop. "I thought we might be able to reach a deal."

"A deal?" the Paragon asked, a jelly-thick voice suggesting that pipe had done some work. "Like what?"

"You get Aegis's daughter, we get Zhan-Yo."

Celice figured faux outrage would be in order here, so she pushed off Mathieu and shouted, "Liar! That's not what you promised!"

Really, her shrill accusing voice was quite good. Particularly with all the stone around to echo the anger.

"I promised you nothing," Mathieu countered, putting his own heat into it. "You tried to kill my friend, remember? What'd you think I was going to do?"

Celice went forward, looking like she was going to take a fist and turn it to some nefarious use, when a neon-green color cut between the pair. At first Celine didn't notice the hair-thin line, but found it pretty hard to ignore when the laser-like beam spawned winding tendrils up and down. Like ivy on aggressive fertilizer, the tendrils looped around each other, stretching to the alley ground and up a meter over Celice's head. Other than the shape and color, nothing else suggested the creation had plant properties.

Particularly the buzzing, spitting sparks flying from those same green lines.

"Now now," said the pipe-bearing Paragon. "Don't need any fights breaking out. Don't think Gatete's going to be taking your deal, but I suppose there's no harm in delivering you two and asking."

"Delivering?" Celice shot her glare the pipe's way this time. "I'm not going anywhere."

One woman behind the pipe Paragon waved two fingers towards Celice. All those tendrils shot towards Celice together, a collapsing green net. The lines had no weight to them, but Celice couldn't struggle either: nothing budged the lime restraints.

"Could've used that a while ago," Mathieu said, folding his arms like a satisfied customer. "Let's go. I don't want your boss getting excited and killing Zhan-Yo early."

The Paragon trio escorted Mathieu and Celice across the courtyard, past the gardens—looking soggy—and into the Tower. Celice played her part, cursing here and there and maintaining a scowl the whole way. So far, though, Mathieu and his plan held true.

In fact, Celice wondered if it might work too well: Gatete might just add Mathieu to the chopping block, and leave Celice bottled up until he could reap the rewards for 'saving' her.

The Tower's interior had some space around the central building. Celice caught the setting's usual play in the merchant stands, the historical museum placards scattered around. No civilians today, their role supplanted by a motley Paragon and drone mixture all hovering around a gallows assembled, it seemed, by some swift runs to a home improvement store.

Pristine lumber laid out a half-meter-high rectangle, on which sat a squat board turned on its side. A small portable stair pressed up against the platform's left end, rising from weedy gray stones. Zhan-Yo himself stood not far behind his demise, cuffed and dumped on the ground like some child in a strict time out. Two Paragons stood near him, both holding coffees and donuts gathered from the large breakfast buffet table laid out steps away.

An execution and a brunch, what's not to love?

Celice would've been angered by the sight, except the Champions had done things like this for a long time. Not so much the public executions, but mirroring punishment and party had been an Aegis staple. All part of the Paragon public relations process: put a picture up showing the ugly end to a criminal and pair it with the comparative paradise for those who followed the rules, and you had an effective way to diminish dissident.

If Zhan-Yo had been a local rabble rouser, or an anomaly that refused the Paragon trace and its accompanying responsibilities, Celice doubted Gatete would have the Tower under guard. More likely, any tourist happening on by could watch the discipline, a public shaming before some drone shipped the anomaly off to Mynx's island, or to some dusty cell far away.

"Just when you believe you know the day's course, it surprises you," Gatete announced, emerging from a blanketing Paragon crew with arms as wide as his grin.

Mathieu and Celice, firmly secured in their escorts's middle, couldn't do much else except watch the Paragon leader approach. The surrounding viewers, drones and Paragons alike, gave space, leaving the six centered among the stones, the Tower itself blocking the sun's view. The shade brought a chill, one that looped up inside Celice's jacket as her green binds dissolved away.

Gatete, tsking her Paragon captors, waved away every line with his dusting ability, no doubt feeling very much superior as he did so.

"I'm here with a deal," Mathieu said, reaching over

and taking Celice's arm, and not in the kind way. "Aegis's daughter for Zhan-Yo."

"Were you two not friends last night?" Gatete asked, eyes roaming between the two, still sparkling with denied laughter. "What soured so for this to happen?"

"I want Zhan-Yo dead," Celice answered.

Mathieu nodded, as if that response told the whole story. Gatete took in a deep breath, then raised his Tama.

"You know, I received an interesting message not many minutes ago. My two associates, ones you know well, Celice, were found unconscious and bloodied outside the very shop where they had been sent to find you." Gatete swiped on his screen while Celice's eyes narrowed. "London does have such wonderful surveillance. You did fight well, but aiding a known Elemental to hurt Paragons?"

"Roger and Sydney tried to kidnap me," Celice said. "I didn't want to go. I'm sorry that they're hurt."

"So you aided an enemy, then ran to another to find sanctuary?" Gatete said, ignoring the apology. "A tragic misstep. I'm sorry you have chosen the wrong path, Celice, but I suppose we were expecting too much from a normal."

Celice blinked. That wasn't expected. Gatete should've eaten up her presence, put her on camera as the witness to a vengeance-fulfilling execution. Celice would've asked to wield the killing weapon, strike the final blow, and in that moment signal the strike to spring everyone to freedom.

"It seems our own Champion of Champions was betrayed," Gatete said, bringing up his voice so everyone in the courtyard, and those watching online, would hear. "His own daughter, a normal succumbing to their jealousy, sought to have his father murdered and succeeded."

"That's not true!" Celice shouted, reading the winds.

"Protest if you like," Gatete said, those sparkling eyes falling very grim. "Your cries will not save you." He turned back to the crowd. "We have tripled our number for today! Three normals, all acting against the Paragons. Justice delivered here and now, by your Paragon, Gatete."

Celice drifted a hand towards the blackjack, thought about pulling it out and braining Gatete right then. She might've, too, if Mathieu hadn't touched her arm again, met her look with his own worried face, and said, "Trust me."

What else did she have to lose?

27

A Little Insurrection

The hospital tore Kat from the pod, had her in an operating room within scant minutes. Chicago at night had its problems, but Calvin's Paragon ID chewed through them fast. The moment's morality aside, providers leapt to Kat's aid, breaking apart Calvin's half-assed bandage and going after the bullet. Assisting medical drones swirled around the human surgeons and their attendant nurses, a whirlwind Calvin witnessed through glass outside.

Alone, until Gordon arrived.

Kat's former flame and current friend had a harried look, an outfit slung on while fighting off sleep. Coffee came with him, Gordon even bringing a second one for Calvin. The tracker knew how to treat his allies. The scruffy beard Gordon pulled together from his bedrest days —Calvin may've caused that crisis—snatched and grabbed at random, distracting from the heavy jacket with pockets in all the right places.

When Calvin gave Gordon the call from the pod, he'd told the tracker to bring protection.

"How's she doing?" Gordon asked, taking up a spot next to Calvin.

"She's fighting," Calvin said. "Bastards are cheating, but she's not gonna let them win."

"What'd they do?"

"Wexley shot Kat weeks ago," Calvin said. "Elementals saved her, but in anomaly fashion. Guess they reversed the job."

Gordon nodded, as if that explanation cleared it all up. Calvin didn't have a better way to put it: anomaly abilities tended to evade simple, sensible stories.

In the room, some monitor went off and the flurry picked up. Calvin tried the coffee, burnt his tongue. Used his power to siphon away that pain and spin it out through his fingers into the glass, where it fogged a tiny patch.

"Can you stay?" Calvin asked.

"Look at me, man. What do you think?"

Calvin didn't answer. Gordon's play didn't register with an anomaly that'd spent his life ditching and dashing, always grabbing what he could and throwing it on his back. Calvin wouldn't assume anything from someone's shirt.

"No," Gordon finally answered, stumbling over the word. "I've got nothing going on at three in the morning. Or tomorrow. The Paragons are a mess, and without them, the trackers don't have much going on either."

"Cool. Call me if you have to leave." Calvin took one last glance at Kat, oxygen mask over her face, surgical gown over everything else. He put the angry surge into an aggressive shoulder pat as he went by Gordon. "Hell, you call me if anything happens."

"Sure," Gordon watched Calvin's stride for the exit. "Where are you going?"

"Work."

Calvin took no pleasure in Gordon's confused look: he already had his fingers calling a pod.

THE PARAGON TOWER in Chicago greeted early morning like everywhere else in the city right now: lights and action. Calvin ditched the pod a block away when he hit roadblocks and the Paragons manning them. Without his uniform, Calvin flashed his Tama to get past the tired guards, dishing them a warning to watch for Elementals as he went by.

Not that it would help.

Calvin knew the Paragons pulling guard duty at night like this would be the lowest on the training totem pole. If Beth and her anomaly squads made their attack, the chumps slurping late night lattes and showing off their powers in the dark wouldn't last long. Not without help.

"But help's on the way," Calvin muttered as he went right through into the lobby.

Particle waited on the other side. Like before—and Calvin wondered if Particle had even changed—they sported all their tactical gear. Guns meshed with nasty-looking knives, all clad in a dark blue Paragon uniform meant for wet work.

"Hey," Calvin said, then took a pointed look around the deserted lobby.

"Upstairs," Particle said. "Weed's trying to convince Pixie you're trustworthy. Smoke and Lob are with him."

"Pixie?"

"Flew in fast after Mynx disappeared," Particle said, walking Calvin towards the elevators. "She's Atlantis's de-facto Champion at the moment." Particle gave Calvin a slanted stare. "Shouldn't you know that?"

"I've been busy." Calvin went for a subject change. "Where'd that uniform come from?"

"Easier to get my hands on the good stuff when we're doing official work," Particle said, "and not running off to a random barn in the country."

Mentioning the rescue mission turned Calvin dark, a shift Particle picked up as the elevator arrived. The two stepped in silent, Particle sending them to the top floor.

"She's hurt," Calvin said. "Kat."

"Elementals?"

So Weed had spilled to the team. Good. Would save Calvin some time.

"They turned a trick on her," Calvin said. "She's at the hospital now getting carved. I tried to get the Paragon there to come in, but they're busy with Mynx's aftermath."

"Weed, Lob, and Smoke needed help too," Particle said. "Bloody day."

The Tower's top floor did what top floors tended to do in the city: maximize the view. Chicago spilled out around them, floor-to-ceiling windows showcasing a glittering wash in the dark sky. Drifting drones blinked their yellow, red, and white lights across the streets to the horizon, hunting whomever did something dumb.

The floor itself had little in it, leftovers from a traitorous turn here not too long ago that left the walls bullet riddled and the carpet blood-soaked. Afterwards, Mynx had the furnishings ripped out, the stand-up walls torn down and the carpet cleared. Now, the Tower's apex served as an oasis, empty and isolated.

"Chicago's next leader can remake it," Particle muttered as Calvin looked around. "What a welcome gift, right?"

Weed and the others preached to Pixie across the floor by a corner. Pixie, in a Paragon classic getup, had her back turned to Weed as the man laid out the Elemental's positioning throughout Chicago. Smoke and Lob threw in back-up assurances as Weed went on, lending whatever credibility they had to Weed's arguments.

"He's here," Particle said as they joined in on the standing meeting.

Calvin felt the spotlight hit him hard. Back in the pod, racing this way, he'd called Weed expecting some alarm to sound. Paragons and drones alike scrambling to position, ready for all-out war. Turned out the Paragons didn't mobilize on single hunches alone, especially those coming from a taciturn, at best, member.

"Calvin, is it?" Pixie said, turning. She had her hands on a necklace hanging from a gold chain. Each stone looked different, with no regard for design. Otherwise Pixie had the listless look everyone shared at this awful hour. "You're calling in this alert?"

"For all the good it's doing," Calvin replied. "Those are standard patrols down there, Pixie! The hell are they gonna do when the Elementals roll up on them?"

"What they're trained to," Pixie replied, and while Calvin expected cold, he heard patience, warmth instead. "I can't mobilize Chicago on hearsay, Calvin. Too many Paragons went with Mynx only hours ago. They're tired, hurt, or called away chasing after her."

"So what, then, we play defense with scrubs?"

"We play defense the way Paragons have for years now." Pixie nodded out the windows. "Drones don't get tired." Pixie saw Calvin's mouth opening and she wagged a finger. Calvin surprised himself by shutting up. "I know the Elementals quite well. They're not built for open war, but surgical strikes. Tricks and bluffs. Their anomalies will fold if the drones attack."

"So you're saying we—" Calvin broke Pixie's charm,

but now Weed stepped in, clamping a hand on Calvin's shoulder and digging in.

"Calm down, captain," Weed said. "We're only a few hours removed from getting shot ourselves. Pixie's got the chair, let's give it to her. You can get back to your girl."

As if calling the session to a close, the elevator dinged open back across the floor, spilling out another Paragon cadre.

"If it helps, Calvin, you're far from the only one I will disappoint tonight." Pixie sighed, offering up a tired smile.

"THEY TOOK MYNX TO THE FACTORY," Calvin said as the elevator shot back down, making his ears pop on the way. "Damn Elementals made me forget."

"Who's 'they'?" Weed asked, the quintet all piled in together. "The people at the barn?"

"Guy named Wexley. He shot Kat."

"Tonight?" Smoke said. "Man moves fast."

"No, long story," Calvin replied. "Can we get in touch with the LA Paragons? They'll need to get there quick."

"Is this a hunch," Weed said, "or do you have evidence in that jacket somewhere?"

As the group ventured back into the lobby, Calvin made his case. Particle, at least, took it seriously enough to pull up their Tama and tap away the suggestion to a friend on the west coast. A reply came back quick, while Calvin, moving towards a pod the whole time, gave away the back-story on Wexley and Kat.

"I think we live boring lives," Lob said as the story wrapped, the Paragon blockades around the Tower close at hand. "They're running all over, getting shot at. Fighting on the docks. What'd we do yesterday, Smoke?"

"Watched an empty street for ten hours."

"Trade you," Calvin said, then nodded his head at his called pod. "You know where you'll find me."

"Hope she pulls through," Weed said, the others echoing the sentiment.

"You keep your guards up. Beth doesn't say stuff for no reason."

The two Paragons that'd waved Calvin in half an hour ago waved him back out. Up above, the sky held its first signs dawn was on its way. A train whirred along in the distance. Someone shouted a few streets away, followed by a laugh. Delivery pods shuffled towards their restaurants, hotels, and shops. All normal for a big city ending its night.

Maybe Beth called it off.

Calvin brought up his Tama as he approached the pod, the small craft's door swinging open for him. He tapped out a message to Gordon, telling the tracker Calvin would be back at the hospital soon enough. He asked how Kat was doing. Calvin settled into the chair, let his eyes drift closed for the jaunt to the hospital.

And flew through the air.

The pod launched off the street as if a hammer struck it, Calvin's stomach dropping out in the split second it took for the pod to hit a nearby building, slamming through windows and crunching to the floor. Glass rained as the pod's roof collapsed, the small car spinning through an office. Calvin, strapped into the seat, curled up and tried not to die.

Dull lights greeted the stopped vehicle, flickering on as the pod's motion triggered their automated responses. Things fell off desks all around Calvin, gradual clatters as the crashes' aftermath played out. Brushing glass off himself, Calvin reached forward, unclipped the belt, and landed on his left shoulder. His head played a banging concert, but Calvin's eyes were clear enough to get him from the pod, his feet steady enough to bring him standing.

Outside, back along the devastation trail, Calvin caught why he'd gone for a smashing office tour: The Elementals had arrived.

Like a grungy street force, the Elementals burst from alleyways and behind cars, sending whatever they could muster at the Paragons. Calvin caught a few flashy powers going off, but more dark shadows sprinting along the street as he crept back towards it. The Elementals didn't have raw power, but they had physical surprise, and they used it.

The two Paragons standing guard were already gone. Calvin didn't see their bodies, didn't see their barricade either as he peeked out from behind a half-broken cubicle. A huge construction pod in manual mode barreled down the street, Elementals clinging to it as the vehicle sped by their buddies running on the sidewalks.

Beth might not have an army, but she had enough idiots to cause some real damage.

The fighting started fast towards the Tower, with tell-tale flashes, shouts, and concussive bangs coming as the Elementals impacted their legal siblings. Calvin glanced back, down the street he'd been about to take to the hospital. With the Elementals past, Calvin could get away from the wreck and head for Kat. Dodge the conflict.

Leave Weed, Particle, and the others to whatever the Elementals could do before the drones took control.

"Sorry, Kat," Calvin said.

Gripping a cubicle wall, Calvin siphoned away its strength and laid it down across the jagged glass. The makeshift bridge let Calvin leave without cutting his feet, putting him back on the street, behind all the action.

Looking head-on, Calvin saw the Elemental's shock-and-awe strategy bought them a straight run to the Tower.

Paragon patrols closed in from the sides, dueling with Elemental ranks while Beth's anomalies fought resistance at the tower's door. The big vehicle grumbled in the middle, a huge target that nonetheless avoided any incoming fire.

One anomaly stood on the construction pod like some ancient commander, her body flashing white like a strobe whenever a beam, a gunshot, or something worse headed in at the pod. Rather than striking the pod, the attack vanished, hitting nothing.

Or, Calvin figured as he started towards the vehicle, hitting something the Paragons very much wanted to miss.

The construction pod used its invulnerability to swing mechanical arms, dig trenches in the ground around it and launch the scrap at Paragon groups whenever they dared move into the open. Calvin caught one trio, the lead Paragon oozing some nasty green from his fists, as they ran in at the Elemental line. The Elementals broke ranks, and the construction pod swept its primary shovel in an arc towards the Paragons. The three stopped, dodged back, and in the process opened themselves up to Elemental counter-fire.

Blue-green bolts, a yellow, sparking energy ball, and what looked like a black knife lanced in at the Paragons, downing them fast. The Elementals didn't stop, either: the construction pod began a swing back, on target to finish the job.

Only to halt when Pixie dove in, catching the big arm and knocking it aside with her plummeting momentum. The construction pod heaved, its structure compensating and dragging it back into a stable stand. Pixie darted, wings too fast to see letting her blitz around Elemental fire.

A dance that couldn't last for long.

Saving random Paragons hadn't been on Calvin's to-do

list, and it wasn't now, but sticking it to Beth and the Elementals had just become his number one goal. As the construction pod's arm went back to its original mashing task, Calvin jammed his left hand to the hard ground and pulled back his right.

He'd blow his cover, but you couldn't hide in the shadows all the time.

"Pixie!" Calvin shouted, the words mixing into the battle's noise. Pixie, though, caught the call, her eyes glancing his way as a ruby-red wave slashed over her shoulder. "Catch!"

Calvin threw the glistening, sharp blade he'd fashioned from the street's cement. Thin, strong, and small, the cement dagger flew. Pixie swept in beneath the pod's arm, caught the dagger as she rotated to her back. And slashed.

The weapon did its work, severing the cabling keeping the big digging shovel in place. The construction pod's weapon wobbled, then dangled to the side as the machine smashed it down. It hit the concrete courtyard at an angle, the Paragons less than a meter away, covered in grit and dirt, but alive.

Calvin saw more attacks converge on Pixie, but new shapes turning his way stole his attention. Two Elementals came at him, two he knew.

"You should've died in that pod!" Anthony yelled, apparently recovered from Calvin's spear-sticking lesson back at Beth's place.

That hit should've been fatal, at least knocking Anthony out for a night. Maybe that guy, the healer with the tattoos, had replaced Kat's with a new one for Anthony.

Calvin had a choice word or two for them all.

Della, Anthony's so-often partner, stopped while Anthony blew past her. Lit up in the street's golden yellow,

Della took in a big breath. Calvin knew what he'd see next, and once was enough for that damn trick.

"You should've let us leave," Calvin countered, keeping his left had on the street surface as Anthony took his leap.

The anomaly went up, growing larger as he went with Della's wind boosting his speed. Back in the training room, Calvin went for the shield. This time, with Kat's panicked, paling face flaring in his mind, he went for the spikes. Waving his right hand across his body, Calvin dredged a concrete line and raised a palisade before him, sharp points angled right where Anthony, already in the air, would be heading.

Calvin fell back as Anthony, his charging roar dwindling into a yelp, crashed into the spikes. The anomaly's jacket and jeans had nothing on Calvin's defense, and while Anthony's huge size bulldozed the wall, knocking Calvin back, Anthony had no follow-through. Had no second swing to batter Calvin to butter.

Instead, the anomaly, slowed and shrinking as his speed fell away, stumbled and fell, seven concrete spears sticking from his stomach, chest, and legs. Calvin picked himself up, caught Della coming towards him, already calling for help.

Not this time. They might've killed Kat, and they were going to pay.

To his left, Calvin caught a light post. He grabbed it, siphoned the metal inside into a long spike, grooved to slice through Della's wind. Calvin lofted it, launched it, and watched as a metal arm intercepted the throw and knocked it to the ground. Della stopped her run, matching Calvin's look towards the gladiator drone now splitting the pair.

"Stand down," the drone spoke, its compartments sliding back to reveal far too many weapons.

Above and around the fighting, more drones swarmed

in from Chicago's surroundings, crashing into the fight. Commands to stand down echoed through the steel canyons, and where there wasn't compliance, loud cracks followed as the drones obeyed their programming.

Calvin took his own breath, moved his hand away from the lamp post. Beth's little insurrection might've caught the Paragons off guard, but nothing fooled the drones.

Good.

28

Never Going Back

Cassidy gave no warnings, just ran.

Her shoes splashed in the puddles as Cassidy sprinted into pod traffic, relying on the vehicles to shift around her. She held no firm direction, only away. Slip her pursuit and vanish into the massive city. She'd find a new identity somehow, scrape along the streets—couldn't be harder than the island, right?—then catch a flight back to Pacifica, back home.

She'd show up on her kid's doorstep, and damn her husband, she'd take them back.

"Cassidy!" Daw, the younger one, called after her.

The Paragon's voice whistled around the pods, the machine's ad-bedazzled forms spraying water as they swerved around Cassidy. Each one offered cover, even as it gave Cassidy's position away. A trade Cassidy would make because she didn't think for a second she could outrun a fit Paragon twenty-plus years her junior.

Above and around her, Bangkok's buildings offered a neon-drenched setting, signs declaring Cassidy had gone right into some shopping district. A giant crab waved a blistering red claw, while down the way a beer bottle several times Cassidy's height tipped back and forth. On the sidewalks, people venturing out into the rainy evening popped their umbrellas and stared at the strange woman dashing down the street.

An intersection to Cassidy's right offered an opening, and she took it. The smaller side street lacked pods, and Cassidy used the opportunity to switch to the less-crowded sidewalk. Her lungs worked in the humidity, every gulp seeming to take with it as much water as air. Already, her pumping legs and arms burned, her island years and so many days spent languishing by the waves collecting their slovenly dues.

The feel wavered Cassidy's conviction. Had she been rash, ditching away from Thane so fast? The Paragons would catch her, would send her back to Mynx's island. The whole adventure would be for nothing, except now her kids would know their mother still lived, only for her to disappear again.

"Cassidy!" Daw called again, this time much closer.

Cassidy flashed a look back, saw Daw and his partner tearing down the street after her. A misstep on the curb sent Cassidy stumbling, the ankle letting her know it wasn't thrilled with her choices. Another step clued in that she wouldn't be running far.

"Stop chasing me," Cassidy said, falling to a walk and turning around.

The few folks on the side street caught the Paragon uniforms and made themselves scarce, vanishing into the buildings on either side. The rain picked up, hammering away any other sounds. It washed through Cassidy's hair, streamed down and off her nose. Her shoes squelched, her clothes clung to her.

Daw and Kamnan strode up with dry confidence, their

uniforms doing work. Kamnan had a stun gun drawn and pointed Cassidy's way, while Daw had his palms out and forward, as if trying to calm an angry dog.

The voids leapt to Cassidy's fingertips. Cast a few and she'd warm up plenty.

"You can't leave," Kamnan said. "Apinya will not allow it."

"I don't give a damn what Apinya allows," Cassidy countered. She needed another path, a way out. No alleys offered themselves, and Bangkok's sewer system hadn't put a manhole on this street. "I don't work for him."

"Isn't that the deal?" Daw asked. "They brought you here with those anomalies from up north. Aren't you going to help with that?"

"Daw," Kamnan growled.

"Help?" Cassidy asked. "What?"

Daw read something in Kamnan's face and clammed up, only shrugging at Cassidy's question, "Just saying, I guess, that it's not like we're putting you in a cell."

The idea, getting jammed in a cage after the island, had Cassidy laughing, deciding. She'd die before going into a Paragon prison. Die before going back to that island.

Behind the two Paragons, a pod veered down the side street. The craft picked up speed along the water, cruising towards the trio. Its safety programming would kick in soon, but until then . . .

"—right now," Kamnan spoke. "Are you listening, Cassidy?"

She snapped back to the Paragon, wiped away the water for a hot second with her left arm, "No, I'm not."

Even in the overcast, Cassidy saw the man flush. Heard Daw sigh. With her right hand, Cassidy figured she'd add to their misery, and launched a void. The invisible power slashed between the two Paragons, hitting the space five meters behind them, right where the pod started its slow-down. The void opened above the ground, sucking and tearing at the pod's base.

The screeching sound tore both Paragons around, letting them see the speeding pod, now unable to slow down, crashing along the street towards them. Kamnan dropped his stun gun, shouting for Daw to run. The young Paragon turned, slipped, and splashed on the asphalt.

Her eye widened a tick and Cassidy threw a second void, a small one just to Kamnan's left, the pod's right. The little black hole sucked at the pod, lurching its crash away from Daw and towards his older, still standing partner.

Distraction, not death.

Cassidy went to the street's right side, slashing another void into a door's lock and stepping through. Behind her, an orange flash lit the street as the pod collided with Kamnan. Always interesting to see what an anomaly could do, but Cassidy pulled her attention forward, to the elevator in the apartment building.

She punched the call button, heard a sound to her left, as Daw shouted again for Cassidy to quit running.

Why he believed that would work, Cassidy didn't know.

A surer bet came when Daw, Kamnan not in sight, picked himself up and rushed the apartment building. The elevator didn't answer Cassidy's call right away, so, with rain drops turning to sweat on her forehead, she called on another void. Planted it right in the doorway.

"Don't come any closer!" Cassidy called as the void made the risk plain: it snapped the doorway's frame, swallowed the glass and lock, and bent the outside light around its circle.

"I don't want to hurt you!" Daw replied, but he stopped his advance.

The elevator, at last, popped its doors open.

"Then don't, and leave me alone!" Cassidy said, stepping into the dull gray-green box.

She tapped the highest floor available, then swept a hand across all the others for good margin. As the elevator's doors started to close, Cassidy whipped another void at the elevator's floor, a small one. It chewed a hole, dying fast.

As the elevator started up, Cassidy dropped through the hole and down, a solid drop-and-roll to the basement floor. Her shoulder hit one of the struts meant to catch the elevator, a nasty bruise, but otherwise the hard concrete didn't kill her. Pipes and emergency signs surrounded her, along with stained yellow-gray walls. A few emergency diodes glowed, illuminating the basement's doors.

Another void wrenched those apart, and Cassidy, forehead hot and sweaty, picked herself up and into the apartment's maintenance area. All the pieces that kept the building churning lay strewn about here, their mechanical lives buzzing away. For a second, the sheer multitude necessary to survive in a modern city threw Cassidy, who'd lived for so many years with a campfire and little else.

An exit sign, glowing green in the far corner, past a cart loaded with tools, offered a direction and she took it. The ankle played nicer as Cassidy went, the slight sprain suggesting a walking speed, if not more. She'd have to escape through guile, not speed.

Doable.

The exit led to a parking garage's bottom level. A left over from the pre-pod period, the garage held on to some old-model cars, carrying stickers Cassidy couldn't read but, from the wheels and frame pictures, assumed these were licensed for use. If Cassidy still remembered how to drive, she might've tried to steal one.

Instead, she hiked along the marked concrete, staying

to the inside wall and heading towards the street-level exit. Back in the rain, she'd meld with the crowd and vanish. She walked faster, grimacing away her hurt shoulder. Cassidy was so damn close. For the first time in so, so long she'd almost succeeded at her own plan.

The crowded sidewalk scattered before the drone landed, blocking her exit. An older, smaller model, the yellow-black paint did nothing to hide the machine's weapons. Four arms, two legs, all ended in danger. The torso as big as a dresser held the plasma jets letting the machine fly.

"I didn't miss you," Cassidy said, slowing. "Ten years, and I get to see you again?"

"Stand down," the drone ordered.

That's all they ever said.

"Last time, you had friends. Too bad."

Cassidy knew where to throw the voids. Her right hand, her left hand, launched one apiece. The first struck the drone's center, eating out its power source. The second, a thin, long razor, sucked in and snapped the drone's legs near its waist.

The drone fired as it died, its shots off the mark. Two stunning darts and one golden yellow energy bolt that would've melted Cassidy's skin off her face struck the walls instead. Someone outside the garage screamed.

Cassidy kept right on walking, past the sparking, dead drone and into the pouring rain. This time, neon wasn't the only thing greeting her: harsher lights, burning rockets. Three more drones, coming in from different directions.

They all wanted a piece of her.

Let them try.

"Remember me?" Cassidy shouted up at the machines. The crowd on the street picked up the tone and vanished down a thousand different holes. "Remember how you ruined my life?"

"Stand down," the drones said in unison, dropping to the street, surrounding Cassidy.

"Don't think I will," Cassidy replied, feeling the cool rain run across her skin.

Her voids were ready.

With a quick flick left and right, Cassidy put up spinning, sucking circles as tall as herself and twice as wide. The two drones on those sides spat stunning fire, the darts vanishing into the voids. The third, the one right across from Cassidy, had no such barrier.

But then, it had no body either. Sending her hands forward, Cassidy shot two more voids, feeling the heat race up along her body, the spasms as her muscles, her energy, her will ran to her hands and out. Her hair sizzled, the rain putting out the fire as it threatened to start. The two voids lashed forward, splitting the third drone and pulling its halves together into nothingness.

Cassidy kept her first two voids alive and burning, but the drones weren't stupid. After emptying another round into the sucking circles, both machines leapt back into the air, angling for better shots. Cassidy let the first voids die, ducking down and popping a new, wide void over her head.

A mistake. The effort had spots popping in her eyes, and the void caught the falling rain, leaving Cassidy scrambling as her lungs boiled. Too many large voids, too fast.

She rolled as the air above her crackled, the drones switching away from the ineffective stun darts to their more lethal energy weapons. Cassidy went low, letting the cold, wet street serve to cool her down. She left the void as the drones exhausted their fire, without cover for the snap second between shots.

Cassidy flung her left hand, reaching and pulling another void from a body no longer so eager to send them. Like running a last lap, Cassidy mined her muscles and sent the void spinning towards the closest drone, keeping her older void, the one swirling over her head, between the farther drone and herself. Sloppy cover, but anything helped.

Her void, small and sputtering, sliced the drone's right rockets. The machine tried to compensate, but its hovering state sent it careening to its left, into the apartment building. Glass and wall shattered as the drone hammered on through.

"One more," Cassidy muttered, turning towards the third.

It dove, apparently deciding range wasn't an asset in the fight. As it went, the machine's legs swept through Cassidy's leftover void, shearing them off. Cassidy tried to get another void going, anything to stop the metal mass plummeting her way.

Her hands shot forward, fingers pointed, the heat burning her up inside. The yellow-black drone, blurred by the rain, crashed down and her voids wouldn't, couldn't appear. They faltered on her fingertips, breaths catching at the last moment.

The Void found her limit.

Orange blossomed, a flower expanding before Cassidy. The drone slammed into the growing petals, flat and flaring, growing brighter as the drone's momentum drove the machine further. Cassidy stepped back, splashing in the road, as the flower burned, halting the drone in its brilliance.

"The drone will not survive," Kamnan said, walking up beside Cassidy. He grabbed her arm, then released it with a hiss, shaking out his hand. "You should be on fire."

"If not for the rain I would be," Cassidy said, her eyes on the flower as its petals closed in around the drone, melting it away. "That's you?"

"My curse, yes."

Cassidy glanced Kamnan's way. The flower's absolute drone devouring coupled with her torching insides murdered any further escape plans. More important, now, was finding a safe place to rest, to repair the damage she'd caused with Daw and Kamnan.

Another escape could come later, provided she stayed alive to attempt it.

"Not many anomalies call their abilities a curse," Cassidy said.

"Mine is not like most," Kamnan replied. "Come now, coward. It's time you returned to where Apinya wants you."

Around them, Bangkok's braver citizens returned to the streets, some sparing looks for the downed drones sparking in the roadway. Most hurried on without a second look, though, content with avoiding Paragon business. Cassidy understood that instinct, she'd followed it herself, before.

"Where's Daw?" Cassidy asked, letting Kamnan help her to the sidewalk.

That ankle was going to be sore tomorrow.

"Where he needs to be," Kamnan replied.

"That's cryptic."

"I don't divulge our secrets to the enemy."

Cassidy couldn't fault the man on that. The flower, and how it dissolved the drone in its burning grasp, stuck with her as Kamnan led them back to the Paragon's building. New Paragons stood outside, replacing Kamnan and Daw as their shifts ended.

Kamnan handed Cassidy off with a warning to the

others to watch her closely, a warning Cassidy acknowledged with a hard eye roll. Soaked, exhausted, and with a damaged shoulder and ankle, Cassidy wasn't going to be doing anything soon.

At least her new captors didn't seem as touchy as Kamnan. Thane and Apinya were still deep in discussions, so on Cassidy's request they brought her to the small quarters reserved for visiting Paragons. A bed, a place to charge a Tama, and access to a shower. A closet containing spare Paragon uniforms.

When Cassidy asked for something else to wear, they came back with loose t-shirts and shorts, both bearing the Paragon blue P. They laughed when Cassidy suggested something neutral. Then the door shut, the lock clicked.

Two pictures hung on the walls, beside a TV screen. The larger one, a black-and-white piece, showcased the original Paragons forming the Bangkok . . . outpost? Base? Cassidy didn't know, didn't care what the right term was. Thirty grinning anomalies, all across the age and demographic spectrum, lined up in rows on some waterfront pier.

Apinya right there in the middle, his own smile the most zen-like. How many were still alive? How many had retired, or been torched in some mission by someone like Cassidy?

No wonder the Paragons liked those drones so much. Cassidy had dismantled three machines—two, really, but who's counting?—that could've been three lives. She'd killed before, on the island, where keeping yourself in good standing with all the bastards and rogues required getting bloody. She'd tried to slice a Paragon on the jet over here. She could've snuffed out those smiles.

A normal person, the subjects she'd taught so much about back in her old life, would've felt something at the thought. Would've gone queasy, maybe chilled as fear at their own abilities ran roughshod over their nerves. Cassidy found only frustration.

Cassidy looked at her own hands. Cool now, the voids whispered again, calling for another release.

Not yet.

The other picture, Cassidy had seen enough times: the original Champions, laid out in their Paragon best. All optimism, all ready to charge ahead and cause untold misery for so many. This time, when the voids whispered, Cassidy listened. She sent a small one right into the picture's middle, right where Aegis's big head dominated.

The void tore it apart.

29

Vision Attained

Wexley put his back to the two vats holding the Champions. The drone didn't follow, choosing instead to keep its position at the doorway. No chance, then, for Wexley to get by.

"I could wait," Reeves said, AI voice so emotionless, "and you would die here. Decay while Mynx and Mila live. They would find your bones when I wake them."

Keeping on his toes, Wexley regarded the drone, and the AI behind it. Reeves was a program, it wouldn't find satisfaction in taunting Wexley, which meant it had a reason for dialogue. Reeves wanted something, needed something.

"What are you after?" Wexley asked.

"For you to send your people away from this place," Reeves replied. "Tell them to abandon their efforts and depart. In exchange, you can keep your life."

"Until you let Mynx free and she sends every drone she has after me."

"A possible future. Your death is assured in the present if you refuse."

Wexley considered, then waggled his Tama, "You want me to talk to them, you have to give me a network to do so."

"Done."

Reeves operated fast. Wexley's Tama chirped its happy rejoining with civilized society as Reeves finished his one word reply. Wexley brought the device up, started tapping with his right hand while reading the incoming, delayed messages.

It'd only been a few minutes, but Rhimes had the techs working fast. Mynx's safeguards were all set up to prevent external intrusions, not inside attacks. From the Factory's control room, the Ziran crew injected one virus after another, each one breaking down locks and opening doors for Wexley's use.

They just needed, because of course they did, more time.

"All right," Wexley said, lowering the Tama. "I sent the message."

"Liar. I can read the network traffic in here. You sent the opposite."

"Oops."

The drone lurched from its spot, careful to keep itself between Wexley and the exit.

How to fight a machine without any weapons? Wexley looked around the room, the vats and the stone walls not offering much to work with. The drone advanced further. One arm snapped in, a tentative swipe. Wexley ducked it, wondered why Reeves wasn't being more aggressive.

The reason pressed hard against Wexley's back, cold and smooth. The vats. Reeves wouldn't chance breaking open his charges.

Wexley stepped between the vats into the narrow, pipe-filled gap before the stone wall. The drone came closer, angling its arms for diving strikes. Again they were slow. Far too slow. Wexley feinted right, went left, cutting behind Mynx's vat. Just before he reached the vat's far side and the gap between it and the next, empty, vat, Wexley stopped.

Another arm smashed where Wexley would've been, banging into the rock. Sparks flew as metal hit smooth stone. Reversing, Wexley found more grasping claws on the vat's other side. The drone might move slow to keep the vat safe, but the machine had Wexley trapped all the same.

Unless. . .

"What happens if I break it?" Wexley shouted, his back to the stone wall as the drone's arms creeped further around the vat.

"Break what?" Reeves asked, and Wexley flinched away from another claw.

"Your Champion's bath tub."

Wexley felt around with his feet as he ducked, dodged the encroaching claws. Cables ran to the vat, power and draining, pumping pipes. Whether Wexley could actually do anything with the connections, he didn't know, but that wasn't the point.

Reeves had to believe he could.

The AI didn't answer Wexley's comment, instead sending in arms from either side. Their angles adjusted mid-strike, one going down and the other up. Wexley took a scratch on his shoulder, twisted and writhed as much as he could. More arms followed.

"Stop or I shatter the glass!" Wexley called, falling against the glass and keeping one hand inside his jacket. "She'll die if I do."

"The odds are against it." Reeves said, but the claws stopped.

"So you're willing to risk it?" Wexley asked. "Everything for me?"

How many calculations would the AI be running now, how many scenarios would it game out? If Reeves knew what Wexley would do, if the AI could fathom what might happen with Wexley at the Factory's helm, the AI would have no choice but to strike.

Mynx, though, had been all hubris. Every action couched in the belief that she and her Paragons, her Champions were unbeatable. That nobody would dare strike at her this way. Reeves came from Mynx, and it would be like her. It *had* to be.

Wexley pounded a fist on the vat, the glass making a loud thump throughout the room. The water inside rippled, its lemony green shifting around the unconscious Champion inside.

The Tama chirped.

"Some risks must be taken," Reeves said, and the claws dove in.

Wexley tried to move, had nowhere to go. He pulled his empty hand from his jacket, rammed his elbow against the glass. No cracks, no threat. The arms found him, claws grabbing and digging into Wexley's shoulders, his arms, his legs. The drone, its body on the vat's other side, lifted Wexley up, pressing him to the vat the entire way.

A meter off the ground and the drone stopped its lift, leaving Wexley facing the black rock wall. For a second, nothing happened except the soft whir as the drone recalibrated itself. Wexley tried to shift away, squirm free, but he couldn't break the machine's grip. One claw gripped Wexley's left wrist and moved his Tama towards Wexley's right hand.

"One more opportunity," Reeves said. "They leave, or you die."

Wexley looked down at the small screen, its touchpad calling to his fingers. A few words and he'd be free, able to jump back into the darkness and try his hand again. Wexley knew he would've typed the command too, except for Rhimes's latest message:

We're in.

"Reeves, do you know why you lost?" Wexley asked.

"That is not—" The AI's voice stuttered as its control faltered, Wexley's technicians snipping off Reeves's abilities one by one. "That is—"

The drone's arms tightened hard, blowing air from Wexley's lungs. Crushing him. Reeves making a last effort. An obvious, desperate play to destroy an enemy on his way out. Wexley's eyes bulged, his tongue puffed up, and spots appeared in his eyes.

Uncomfortable? Yes. Painful? Of course.

Worth it?

Absolutely.

Reeves didn't get a last word. The AI's voice stopped talking, and the drone dropped Wexley without warning. He hit the ground, fell back against the stone wall and sat there, picking up his breath, staring at Mynx's floating body. A captive Champion, her fortress now his own.

"Wexley?" Rhimes spoke into the room. "You all right?"

"Never better," Wexley wheezed, wincing at his bruised ribs. "Your timing could be improved."

"The AI fought us every second," Rhimes replied. "It's not gone either. According to the team, Reeves has isolated itself in the network."

Wexley gripped the pipes, pulled himself standing. "Can it hurt us?"

"Not without help," Rhimes replied. "We're trapping it. When we're done, it'll need Mynx to come back."

"And the drones?"

"Ours, Wexley. We have full access to every single one

across the planet." Rhimes whistled. "There's a lot more than I expected."

"Does that really surprise you?" Wexley said, pulling himself around the vat. He looked at the spindled drone, its arms unpowered and hanging.

A younger Wexley would've kicked the thing, or smashed it for what it'd done to him. Now? Now he could look at the drone and know that it was his. Everything in the Factory was his, and only a fool would damage his own possessions.

"I'm coming up," Wexley announced. "Be ready to show me everything."

ZIRAN'S TECHNICIANS swarmed the Factory's control room, hooking into Mynx's main terminals with their Tamas and other portable computers. Rhimes supervised the takeover, designating every tech with a specific task, specialty, and goal. Standing near the room's only exit, now armed with real weapons, were two more mercenaries.

No technician would be leaving the room without supervision. None would be leaving the Factory itself until Wexley had full control. The revolution would not take breaks.

"Start the Factory as soon as you can," Wexley said. "I want drones pouring out as fast as they can be built. Get the suppliers running too."

Rhimes tapped away on his Tama as Wexley spoke, dishing off messages to middle managers. Those souls whose careers had been spent clocking hours now had a chance to rise and ensure the Factory would have an unbroken supply. Others would be getting the Factory's schematics sent to them, all around the world. New copies would be built as fast as possible, with no costs counted.

Debt didn't matter when Wexley, when Ziran would save the world from the anomalies. Any bank would forgive the price, any worker would be glad to give their time to the revolution. And if not? What could they do? Stand up to drones by the thousands?

Wexley tried hard not to laugh, succeeded in holding himself to a smile.

"And the local Paragons? What do they know?" Wexley asked.

After Reeves, the greatest threat to this operation came from other anomalies getting suspicious. Without the drones up and running, Rhimes's couple dozen mercenaries would be the only protection.

"Our blackout's keeping things quiet," Rhimes said. "Ziran's put out all the normal excuses. So far as the Paragons know, nothing's happening."

"Beautiful."

"Have to say, sir," Rhimes spoke, shaking his head. "I didn't think this would work."

"It hasn't yet." Wexley pat Rhimes on his broad-shouldered back, "But we're close. A few hours ago the world's future was tyranny. Now, we can choose a different destiny."

"You're sounding like Zhan-Yo now."

"Am I?" Wexley chuckled, embraced the bruising pain. "He was my mentor for a long time." He picked up a finger, wagged it. "That's a good idea, Rhimes. Put out a message, send it to every Ziran device. Let them know that Zhan-Yo's dream is being fulfilled."

Rhimes squinted, "Not sure anyone's going to know what that means?"

"They will, Rhimes. They will." Wexley felt the rips in

his clothes, realized the media would want a chance to speak with him soon. "That drone caught a few lucky hits. Any ideas on where I might get cleaned up?"

"I do. Think you'll like it too."

MORNING ON THE CALIFORNIA COAST. Wexley inhaled the sea salt on Mynx's deck, his hands on a great glass table. Waves crashed, sunlight did its thing. He'd gone hunting for coffee and failed to find any, and even a cup for water required digging deep into cabinets that seemed little-used. As if Mynx didn't bother touching her own kitchen with her hands.

At least the Champion had painkillers by the box.

Rhimes peppered Wexley's Tama with updates as the minutes passed, every marker giving Ziran greater control. Drones here, Paragon rosters there, and the tracker board, with all the targets Mynx's hired army traced. Wexley couldn't know how many anomalies existed among humanity at the moment, but he had to figure Mynx had eyes on most.

And now Wexley saw them too.

"You won," Adriana said, her voice coming through the Tama. She'd already hopped a plane, was on her way to LA. "After all this, you actually did it."

"Not just me," Wexley said. Graciousness in victory was an admirable trait, or so Zhan-Yo always said. More importantly, it served to keep people loyal, committed. "Rhimes and his team did well. Our intel on Mynx was good."

"Better than good. When was the last time someone captured a Champion?"

"And held on to them," Wexley replied. Paragons, Champions included, had their bad days, but any problems tended to be corrected by anomaly swarms riding to the rescue. Not this time. "When you get here, we'll send out the call to the others."

"You're waiting for me? How nice."

"We're a winning team, Adriana. Hurry up now, we shouldn't keep the new world waiting."

Not five minutes after the call ended, Rhimes joined Wexley on the deck. The fighter looked as tired as Wexley felt, but Rhimes took steps to solve their problem when he asked the air for two hot coffees and some breakfast.

"There someone here I missed?" Wexley asked, quirking a bleary eyebrow at his friend.

"Not someone, but something."

Three chirps, like a merry bird, sounded. Rhimes told Wexley to sit down, wait a second. Wexley eased into the stiff chair, basked in the breeze, until he smelled a dark roast's telltale loam. A small, hovering drone set a foamed mug before Wexley, and a second gave one to Rhimes. They zipped away, then returned with frothy scrambled eggs, some lab-spun bacon, and a fruit bowl brimming with berries.

"The drones," Wexley said, staring at the feast. "You have them?"

"In pieces," Rhimes said. "We're taking them territory by territory. Our guys estimate we'll have the world by lunch."

"Which ones do we have now?"

Rhimes gestured at the house, "Here, Atlantis. The Western Hemisphere."

Wexley could wait. Adriana would be here soon. But every minute lost would be another ceded to the Paragon rescue efforts. Ziran's networks would come back online soon, and with them, the Paragons would know what happened, where to counterattack.

"Then what are we waiting for?" Wexley said. "We've come this far. Let's keep moving."

"Sir?"

"Give the drones their new priority mission: find and eliminate all anomalies, starting with the Paragons."

Rhimes hesitated, "Eliminate? That could pose . . . problems."

"Are you expecting the Paragons to do anything less when they come for us? The anomalies must go, Rhimes. All of them."

Rhimes met Wexley's eyes, and the two searched out each other in that look. Rhimes was a good soldier, able to make the hard calls on the battlefield. Here, now? This wasn't a battlefield any longer.

It was a slaughterhouse. Rhimes would adapt, or Wexley would need to find a replacement.

Hopefully, things wouldn't come to that.

Putting On A Show

Three blocks shared the executioner's platform. The old stones looked the part, excavated from where, Celice didn't know. Zhan-Yo, the true prize, occupied the center already. Left in the same outfit he'd worn last night, albeit swordless, the revolution's leader had his eyes closed as he kneeled before the stone. Behind him stood a Paragon, stun gun out and held level with Zhan-Yo's skull.

Gatete sent Mathieu up next to take the farthest spot. The man, hands bound, walked with his head high, like some old hero accepting his noble sacrifice. Another Paragon, young like Zhan-Yo's guard, followed. Their footsteps creaked on the wooden platform, echoing over the quiet courtyard. Celice couldn't hear a whisper from the quiet crowd.

The wind and whirring drone engines provided the only counterpart to London's wall-muffled traffic. Above, the clouds cleared up for a moody sun, its rays burning off the last lingering morning fog. Planes left contrails in the blue sky, and Celice wished she could hop up to one.

She'd been keeping her eyes up because putting them anywhere else meant seeing Paragons studying her face, looking for the traitor Gatete proclaimed sat right there. A shame and embarrassment to Paragons across the globe, a human failure. Not even a parent as great as Aegis could rescue a normal from their awful existence.

Gatete could go throw himself in the river, but Celice didn't feel like having that argument with the assembled crew. Not like they'd see her perspective anyway.

The third execution overseer poked Celice's back with a stun gun. Celice rose, a little unsteady with her hands behind her back, and stepped towards the short stair to the platform. As she moved, Gatete put himself before the stage, its lift putting Zhan-Yo's kneeling head close to Gatete's.

The Paragon leader owned the moment, spreading his arms wide and launching into some prepared speech to the crowd. And, more importantly, to all the watchers tuning into the drone feeds.

"We have received no word from Mynx," Gatete said, sliding some choice sadness into his voice. "As such, we have no choice but to carry out our threat. These criminals must pay, and perhaps their end will persuade our enemies to give up their reckless paths."

Gatete kept going, but Celice tuned him out to focus on the steps and the stone she'd been kneeling near. Mathieu had said to trust him, and that trust so far had cost Celice her blackjack and her freedom. Now an idiot's acting seemed to be the closing chapter on her life. Unless she could find a way out.

The stone itself had heft. Sun-bleached and more beige than gray, the rock had pits but nothing catastrophic. No chance to crack it with a head-butt, delay the inevitable. Celice, with the stun gun pushing down against her shoulders, knelt alongside the other two, and gauged the wood. Old and strong. No snapping through the boards with a knee or well-placed leverage.

Which left one option.

Gatete hadn't revealed who or what would be doing the executing. Celice figured there would be a moment there, a chance when the Paragon behind her might be distracted. Might—

The Paragon leader cut off his speech in a frustrated growl. The news drones followed Gatete's eyes, spinning away towards forms coming in over the walls. Pops echoed from beyond those same stones, and Celice caught flashes: assault tech going to work against the guards Gatete dropped beyond the Tower.

"It seems the pests will not go quietly," Gatete said, pointing towards Mathieu's commandos as they scaled the wall. "Destroy them."

Villainous proclamation aside, the Paragons operated like the force they were trained to be. Celice felt some annoying pride when the Paragons broke quick into their teams, anomaly abilities springing to life in concert. Mathieu's commandos, cresting the wall and tossing more flash-bangs towards the courtyard, found themselves barraged by light beams, windy gusts, and at least one yellow-glowing bat swarm conjured from nowhere.

The chaos was, among other things, exactly what Celice needed.

She felt the stun gun loosen its pressure on her shoulders, a sure sign her captor had her attention elsewhere. Celice rocked back on her heels, bending down and popping up to get beneath the stun gun and send her skull smashing into the Paragon's chin. Rising, twisting, Celice rotated into a snap-kick that caught her guard, Paragon uniform already ruined by a blood-gushing nose, in the stomach.

The hit sent the Paragon flying off the platform and bought Celice two new friends: the Paragons holding Zhan-Yo and Mathieu whipped their weapons her way.

"I surrender?" Celice offered, hoping against hope that her two fellow condemned weren't morons.

Zhan-Yo acted first, but in the wrong way. The revolutionary threw himself forward, bringing his legs up and kicking into a dive off the platform, right into Gatete's back. The two crumpled to the ground in a tangle, mud flying up as Zhan-Yo leveraged his legs, his head, and elbows to keep himself in Gatete's space.

Mathieu, at least, went for the smarter play. Like Celice, he snapped back, ramming his head up into his Paragon. This one, though, took Mathieu's hit without moving. Mathieu bounced off the Paragon, cursing and falling over on his side. The Paragon unfroze, swinging his stun gun back to his charge.

And leaving Celice facing off against Zhan-Yo's executioner, who didn't hesitate.

The stun gun shot, a dart launching out and sticking right in Celice's shoulder. The pain pinch shifted fast into spreading numbness, not a good sign. She had a few seconds, though, and put them to good use: Celice ran two steps forward and swung a kick into the Paragon's groin. The man apparently didn't know how to fight dirty, his hand moving too slow to get in the way.

The first hit stunned him, Celice's second move swept the Paragon's legs out and knocked him to the ground. She couldn't feel her left arm, and couldn't tell if she breathed or not. Luxuries.

Mathieu's enemy leveled the stun gun at the commando's face. Celice dove, not at the Paragon, but at the weapon. She hit the gun with a shoulder charge, its dart flying wide and sticking hard in the dirt. Hitting the weapon did nothing to stop Celice's momentum and she flew off the platform's far side, tumbling into the mud and grass.

If she'd scraped a knee or bit her lip, Celice had no idea. Lying on her back, she could only see the blue sky. That, at least, looked beautiful, save for a small, black triangle cutting through the middle.

And stopping, seemingly right above her, albeit way up high.

Any stun-muffled curiosity vanished when Celice's broken-nosed Paragon appeared over her, hands reaching down and shoving Celice onto her side. The new view told Celice Mathieu's uprising had gone the way fights tended to when normals confronted Paragons and their drones.

Celice had spent so many years shaking her head at hapless criminals as they fired their pistols, swung their bats, or crashed their cars into her father and his Paragon allies. She'd asked Aegis so many times: what was the point?

Survival.

Gatete had freed himself from Zhan-Yo, had two Paragons holding Ziran's former leader up against the platform's side. Gatete himself held out a hand now, and a third Paragon presented a mean-looking ax to go in it. Gatete tilted when the ax haft, a whole meter long, found his grip. The weapon's black iron head gleamed, no doubt ready to take another life. The Tower's history came rushing back, its executions about to add another to their number.

Celice had to admit, Gatete had a flair for theater.

"Stay down," her Paragon captor said, as if Celice had a choice.

Up on the platform, Mathieu hadn't fared much better. Despite being disarmed, the invulnerable Paragon pinned the commando against the stone and held Mathieu there, hands tight around the man's neck. As for Mathieu's reinforcements, Celice caught them coming in pieces, bloodied and beaten as Paragons threw them against the Tower itself. Gatete would probably add them to his line-up, desserts to the main killing course.

The plays had been made. Mathieu's gamble struck out. Benny's Elementals hadn't even breached the field so far as Celice could tell. Zhan-Yo had himself an ax aiming at his head. If some other plan waited to pounce, Celice didn't know about it.

Somehow, being Aegis's daughter put Celice in a bubble, one faltering on the ground. With the world's Champions as first-name friends, Paragon and drone swarms standing ready to help, Celice hadn't felt vulnerable a day in her life. Not even in this last London week, darting through the alleys alone.

The Paragons were always a call away.

And now?

Her Tama buzzed. Celice felt the vibration, but she couldn't see the thing's screen. Her left arm too numb to move. Behind her, Celice caught the shadow as her guard loomed.

The slightest pressure came through her back, piercing the stunning dart's effect.

"Give the adrenaline a minute," her Paragon captor muttered, cursing softly to herself. "I'm trying to help."

Celice widened her eyes. Stupid. She was Aegis's daughter. Gatete wouldn't command every Paragon's absolute loyalty, particularly not the ones, unlike Roger and Sydney, that wouldn't benefit from Gatete's ascension to Europe's Champion.

The injected adrenaline did its work while Gatete lined up his ax swing. Zhan-Yo gave the man a defiant, legend-worthy glare. The drone cameras came in close.

"Your revolution ends today," Gatete declared, bringing the ax up on his shoulder.

The angle would make it hard to get a clean hit. A messy execution. Gatete must've decided not to let perfect get in good's way. Celice felt her throat, her lungs come back into tingling life.

One chance to stop a mistake, to save her father's killer.

"Don't!" Celice shouted, her call rising over the murmurs, the groans, the last scuffles between the Paragons and Zhan-Yo's would-be rescuers. "Aegis wouldn't want this!"

Gatete held his swing, hit Celice with a boiling look. "His killer paying for his crimes? I believe Aegis would want exactly this."

Oh, Celice had him now.

"How would you know?" Celice asked, taking courage from her limbs as they came back to life. As the Paragon, with Celice's back to an empty vendor stand, knelt down and unclipped her cuffs. "Have you asked the Champions, his best friends, what to do?"

With the drones broadcasting the feed live, Gatete had to play. Had to indulge Aegis's daughter in the conversation. He couldn't ignore her and expect to be anointed. Couldn't—

"Bring her over," Gatete said to Celice's would-be rescuer. "I will not mince words with a traitor."

The Paragon picked Celice up, holding her formerly-cuffed hands still.

"Sorry," the Paragon whispered. "Did what I could."

"It's enough," Celice said.

"What?" Gatete asked as the Paragon marched Celice over. "What is enough?"

Celice moved in that moment. Broke her hands from the Paragon and charged Gatete. One good shot to the man's throat, his skull, his groin and the whole show would be ruined. Maybe not stopped for long, but any time offered a chance for something to change.

Something hard and metal struck her shoulder. A drone, the gladiator's precursor. Half Celice's height, but heavy and strong, the robot bore her to the dirt and planted its legs into the ground to keep her there, once again looking up towards the sky.

This time, an ax filled the view.

"A traitor or a murderer," Gatete said. "It makes no difference who dies first."

Gatete lifted the weapon, held it high over his head. Beyond it, in that blue, the black triangle grew larger. Celice threw out another question, asked if Gatete wanted to kill Aegis's only daughter.

The Paragon ignored her. The ax came down.

Celice didn't see the bullet. She saw the broken haft, heard the ax head fly forward and embed itself next to Zhan-Yo with a cracking *thunk*. The platform didn't last another second: something struck hard and blew the wood to pieces, scattering Mathieu and his Paragon escort, sending splinters biting into Celice's skin.

Gatete frowned, his ability turning all the wood flying his way to less than dust. Celice, blinking crap from her eyes, saw the man's frown deepen, his head turn to one side and start to shake.

"Sorry to ruin your moment," came a voice Celice heard all day, every day. One that'd haunted her dreams and chased her thoughts. "Turns out this man's not a murderer, because I'm not dead." A hand reached over

Celice, grabbed the drone and gripped hard. The drone knew its master, because the machine released Celice, whereupon the sapphire-gloved hand whipped the drone up into the sky. "And if you ever call my daughter a traitor again, Gatete, we're going to have more than words."

Aegis, the man, the myth, the *father* reached down and helped Celice to her feet. The daughter tried to square what she saw with what she remembered. Her dad had gone off on one last mission to Chicago looking burnt out, trying to capture some faded glory. The Champion standing here sported a new uniform, recognizably Paragon but with a metal glint along all the lines, and Celice guessed more than fabric made up that cloth.

Her father's wrinkles thinned, his hair glossed where before it'd been on its wispy ends. Aegis had always been fit, but now his muscles strained against his suit, as though he'd bought into an aggressive training regimen or found the right steroid. He even had a damned tan.

"Dad?" Celice said, echoing the sentiment, if not the word, of everyone watching.

The Paragons in the courtyard had their mouths open. Mathieu and his beaten commandos matched the slack-jawed awe, though a few stole the moment and started slipping away, only for drones to take them in hand. Zhan-Yo, at Celice's right, looked just as unbelieving as Gatete, who kept shaking his head.

"Mila's miracles," Aegis said. "Time to end this show, Gatete. Call off the drones. Send everyone home and I won't hold this against you. We have bigger problems now."

"End the show?" Gatete replied. "What show? This was a loyalty demonstration, to you and all you stood for. Send them home? These criminals and traitors?"

"Did I ask you?"

Gatete worked his lips, saying nothing as he searched for an escape. Celice gave it to him: she walked past her father and put her hands on Gatete's shoulders, her eyes level with his.

"We're offering you forgiveness. You take it," Celice whispered, "or we hold an execution after all."

That, at least, punched through Gatete's stupor. Celice let the man go, and London's Paragon leader waved away his anomalies. Celice noted, with some satisfaction, that the Paragons around the Tower had already backed off their prisoners. They stood down at Aegis's command, as it should be.

The drones, however, did not comply. One kept its camera rolling while others, their gliding metal bodies bristling with weapons, floated higher. The machines put themselves at angles covering the entire courtyard. Beyond and further above, larger gladiator models drifted into view, coming from London's other districts.

"Gatete, the drones," Aegis repeated.

"I gave them the signal," Gatete stammered, then tapped at his Tama, that head shaking again. "They're not complying, Aegis, and I can't get through to our central command." Gatete glanced up towards some Paragons. "Get back to base, tell them to shut the drones down!"

One leapt up, her body buoyed as if by some invisible hand. She lofted into the sky, weaving around the drones and angling west. Another popped. Simply disappeared and reappeared meters away, like a flickering signal.

The drones struck.

The flier died first, vanishing as six drones rotated as one and blitzed her with energy and hard projectile weapons. On fire, she plummeted to the ground. Gatete's other chosen had a split second longer to react, warping himself towards the tower's gate in an erratic pattern.

Celice couldn't see what happened, but everyone heard the scream, saw the flashes.

"Code Steel!" Aegis shouted, hitting a hard trained, if little expected, Paragon trigger.

Gatete's Paragons knew their manuals and popped into action. Gatete himself, arms waving, took a drone hovering several meters away and dissolved its metal limbs to dust. As its engines disintegrated, the drone found its enemy and dove, heading right for Gatete's skull. Celice leapt without thinking, caught Gatete around the waist and pulled him away.

The drone crashed, crackling dirt flying up. A miss. Celice pulled herself away from Gatete and saw another drone bearing down on them, the smaller robot's twin guns spooling up. An ax, that ancient relic, smashed into the machine from behind, biting into its back and sending it off course. Aegis followed through, reaching into the new pit and grabbing the crashed drone. He threw it after the ax, the banging, burning sounds showcasing a hit.

Aegis didn't notice a gladiator coming down behind him, four arms lining up shots.

"Dad!" Celice shouted, picking herself up and snapping into a run. "Up and away!"

The Champion followed orders, planting his feet and coupling his hands at his waist. Celice jumped, caught the grip, and felt Aegis launch her into the air. The ground shrank beneath her, replaced in another instant with the gladiator's yellow-black bulk. Celice landed on the big drone, caught her fingers in the thing's open missile bays.

Reacting to her presence, the drone gave up its onslaught and flipped, testing Celice's grip and dangling her above the courtyard. She held on, looked onto the war playing out beneath and around her. Aerial Paragons took to the skies to fight the drones in their own field, while others blasted beams, shifted gravity, or created new elements and threw them from below. The power medley should've been incredible, a statement that anomalies ran the world, not these machines.

But Paragons didn't train against Mynx's drones. Gatete's Paragons hadn't been expecting a fight like this, and the drones hit with accuracy no human could match. Their bullets shredded the gaps in Paragon uniforms, hitting faces, necks, and feet. Larger drones took to martial means, slamming into their squishy targets.

One faction stood out in the melee, if only because they ran from it: Mathieu, helping Zhan-Yo and flanked by his commandos, made for the Tower's exit. No drones pursued them.

A hissing sound brought Celice's attention back to the drone she hung from. It'd been shaking her, whirling around at speed, and it'd worked its way down to the most extreme option: electroshock.

"Got you," Celice muttered, feeling the drone's body heat up as the thing's batteries prepped the move.

Pulling hard, Celice brought her legs up, planted them against the drone's hull. The timing had to be perfect.

And Dad had to be watching.

The spark drove the kick, Celice leaping into open air as blue lightning arced across the gladiator drone. While she flew back, the drone dropped faster than a rock, plummeting as the lightning killed its own engines. Any enemy clinging to the drone would be stunned or already dead, and the resulting crash would bury the target under metal tons.

Instead, the drone crashed into a Tower wall, collapsing stone upon itself as it tumbled to the ground. Celice saw the impact as she fell, the wind catching her hair, her stomach flopping, and finally landing in her father's outstretched arms.

Celice didn't see pride in those eyes, though. Only anger, and fear.

Above them, the midday sky darkened: London's drones heeding some new master's call.

Siege

Surrounded and repulsed from the Paragon's tower, Beth and her Elementals circled up in the courtyard around their construction pod's ruins. Calvin found his way to a ragged Paragon line: the scattered anomalies around the tower numbered fewer than twenty, but Pixie and the drones made it seem an army. The Atlantis leader hovered over the assembled Elementals, drones flanking her and everyone else, weapons ready.

"I didn't realize we had this many," Calvin said to Particle, standing next to him and bearing a bloody burn on their right leg. "Drones, I mean."

"We didn't," Particle said. "Look at'em. The smaller ones. They're the older units, retired ones we've had in storage. Someone thought to activate them all."

"Smart."

Particle didn't answer. Calvin matched their look, tuning in to the back-and-forth between Beth and Pixie. The Elemental leader bargained for their lives, for a chance to give anomalies their freedom. Pixie countered with something simpler.

"You attacked us," Pixie said. "You forfeit any right to ask for anything. Instead, I'll make an offer here and now to your people: join the Paragons, commit to our vision, and you'll have a chance to redeem yourselves. Or you will not be leaving this courtyard."

Calvin winced. Ultimatums tended to suck no matter who gave them, and while the Paragons forced anomalies into service all the time, seeing the ugly laid right out tweaked an old nerve. How many times had he fled foster families when the discipline outweighed the meals, the warm bed?

The Paragons wouldn't be so easy to leave, no matter the distaste roiling Calvin's stomach. They would send drones, trackers, other Paragons after Calvin now. Desertion wasn't permitted, only retirement after serving for decades.

Congratulations on your powers, here's your life laid out for you.

Beth seemed to be having the same thoughts. The woman's hand drifted beneath a jacket, to what might've been another weapon. The defiance on her face faded, though, when an Elemental behind her groaned. The man, close to Calvin and Particle, had his hands on a vicious wound to his gut. A bronzed spike stuck out, some Paragon's production.

Another thing worth wincing at.

"Make your choices then," Beth said. She dropped her arms, stared at the ground. "I'll not judge any of you for what you do now. We made our stand."

"And they failed," Particle muttered.

"You heard her," Pixie shouted. "Make your choices, hold up a hand and we will help you."

Chicago's city noise seemed to vanish after Pixie spoke, the tension dulling any outside sound. Calvin felt his hands tingling, ready for any last ditch attacks. They'd cornered the Elemental animals, and here's where desperation would find its hold.

The shot came with a crack. Pixie fell, diving to the ground and striking the concrete tiles hard. Calvin processed the moment, started to look at who could've fired a bullet hitting Pixie from behind—Wexley, somehow reverting to his sniping ways?—when more fire rained. Calvin's eyes snapped to a drone, pushed there by Particle's force.

"Code Steel!" Particle's voice rang out as everyone scattered.

A list rammed through Calvin's mind, diagraming exactly what the Paragons should do if the drones ever decided the anomalies weren't their masters anymore. First and foremost?

Retreat and re-evaluate.

Particle grabbed Calvin's arm and pulled him away, back towards the busted office building and Chicago's more crowded streets. A strategy Calvin would've been on board with, except for what he saw when he pulled his eyes away from the drones.

Pixie, downed in the courtyard's center, with Beth standing over her, shooting a small pistol at the machines.

"We're not running yet," Calvin said, shaking his arm free.

Particle protested, but Calvin broke into a run towards the courtyard's middle. Dragging his right hand on the concrete, Calvin sucked in the grit and spat it from his left, creating a crumbling concrete shield. Bullets struck the makeshift barrier and sparked off, blowing rocks against Calvin's face as he ran.

Lights, screams, bangs, thuds, and worse exploded around Calvin as the Paragons put Code Steel into effect.

The Elementals caught on quick, their own powers coming into play. Portals appeared as anomalies teleported themselves onto the drones. Lob, doing his work, threw Weed into a nearby gladiator raining fire on an Elemental quartet. Weed's body replicated itself, tiny clones diving into the gladiator's weapons and jets, tearing them apart from the inside.

The gladiator's breaking fireball should've slammed down into the courtyard, should've crushed Calvin on his run, but another Elemental grabbed the debris and shot them like meteors into other drones, punching holes. Someone conjured a lightning bolt, but from the ground, the blue-white jagged laser lancing up into a gladiator and splitting it asunder.

Smoke met Calvin and Particle in the middle, the woman pushing Beth away from Pixie and popping up a fuzzy fog. From a pack on her waist, Smoke pulled out a syringe, was about to toss it to Calvin until she saw his hands were busy.

"Keep them occupied," Smoke said, turning Pixie over with Particle's help. "If the drones get inside my cloak, we've got nothing."

The drone's shot had hit Pixie right in her back, just below her neck. The bullet should've killed her, except Pixie had on a Paragon uniform, one built to keep those bullets from getting through. Instead, she had a nasty bruise and lungs that weren't quite working.

"You," Beth said, noticing Calvin and bringing her pistol around.

"Surprise," Calvin said.

Calvin swung the concrete shield, bashing Beth to the ground, her gun flying away. Letting the concrete shield crumble onto the Elemental, burying everything below her neck in chunky rock, Calvin left Smoke to Pixie's care and went looking for a way to draw attention.

And found it at his feet. The courtyard had lights embedded in the ground every few meters to get that magical glow so important for the Paragon image. Calvin stole a little more concrete, formed a pointed hammer in his left hand and bashed the light open.

"What're you doing?" Smoke said as glass bounced against her face.

"Getting creative. Just get her awake quick, 'cause we're gonna need a way out after this."

"She's not flying anywhere soon. We need to shut these things down, now."

"Leave that to me."

Below him sat a fractured bulb, sparks showing power flowing where it needed to be. Calvin looked at his left hand, took a breath, and grabbed the exposed wires.

The rush hit instantly. His whole body burning up as Calvin's hand sucked in pure electric energy. Like a Champagne bottled filled to overflowing, Calvin popped. He stuck up his right hand, looked out through Smoke's barrier at three drone smudges close together.

If the earlier Paragon had summoned a bolt, Calvin blew out a storm. Channeling a wire hooked right into the Paragon tower's juice-sucking circuit board, Calvin drank in everything Chicago's power grid could send. Searing yellow lines arced from Calvin's hand to the drones, electricity finding its conductor in the metal constructs.

Fires broke out across the machines as the lightning did its work, leaping around like an insect from one target to the next. Calvin swung his right hand around, continuing to lance fire at the drones, burning down those three. He wanted to look for more, but the brightness seared his eyes as he went, forcing Calvin to send the storm straight up as he clamped his lids shut.

"Got you," Particle said.

Calvin, even with his eyes closed, felt his head swirl as Particle yanked his attention around. With his hand outstretched, Calvin funneled the electricity, sending the power from one spot to the next, wherever Particle directed him. Spinning in the dark, his head, heart, whole self buzzing, Calvin detached, became an object Particle could wield at will.

Until they pushed Calvin away from the light, breaking the coil. Calvin stumbled, hit the ground, opened his eyes and saw spots. Beyond them, orange flickers. Bullets didn't fill the air anymore, but groans, shouts did. His muscles spasmed, blood filled his mouth from his bit tongue.

But he lived, dammit.

"Hey," Particle said, kneeling next to him. "You okay?"

"Not really," Calvin groaned. "Can't see."

"A blessing," Particle replied, thawing their typical ice with worry. "The drones you didn't down fled. Didn't know they would even do that. Ambulances are here too, bodies all over."

"Our side?"

"Both. Hold on a sec."

Calvin sat up as Particle vanished into the blur. Heat washed around him, flickering waves suggesting fire rather than some temperature shift. His left hand, too, ached. Calvin reached over, felt it with his right, and sighed as crusted, singed skin blistered at his touch. A price paid for the Paragons.

Kat said it was dangerous, joining the blue.

Kat.

Calvin lurched up, felt an aftershock run through a body too spent and nearly spent his stomach right there.

Instead, he felt an arm wrap beneath his shoulders, hold him up.

"Nice work, new guy," Weed said. "Didn't think going all gonzo was your deal, but I like it."

"Don't get used to it."

"I never get used to anything in this world. Need some help? I can flag a medic."

"Need to get to the hospital."

"You got it." Weed, keeping his hold steady, hollered for some help.

"Pixie, she going to be okay?"

"Like the rest of us, she's had better days," Weed replied. "Unlike some here, she'll see more."

BY THE TIME the pod hit the hospital, Calvin could see more than smears. Spots still danced, but some fast-acting infusions pulled Calvin towards normal. He'd been stacked in an ambulance pod with several other anomalies, two Paragons and an Elemental. The other three had bullet wounds and worse, making them the first ones out.

Calvin came last, said he'd be okay, and asked a harried nurse to let him walk away. With other ambulances running both before and after Calvin's, the nurse didn't object, leaving Calvin on the sidewalk outside the hospital's emergency entrance.

Flashing lights, calls between nurses, providers, and transporting personnel made for a calmer chaos as Calvin tapped away a Tama message to Gordon. The tracker responded with Kat's floor and room, a recovery area.

She'd lived, then.

For once, Calvin had good news. For once, he wanted to share it with someone, but his Paragon team hadn't made the trip. They were helping with the evacuation, pulling critical crap from the Tower as the anomalies departed to hidden safe houses. Instead, Calvin gave a nearby security guard a slap on the shoulder, leaving the confused man in his wake.

The day had sloped farther and farther down, a grim ride to a bad bottom, but now Calvin caught the rise. Kat would be okay, Pixie and the bigger Paragons would get these drones figured out, and, with Beth turning ugly, Calvin would never need to do another Elemental anything again.

Not too bad.

Kat's room had all the hospital characteristics: sterilized smell, framed flower photos on the walls, a TV that looked about a decade too old hanging on the wall. Kat, asleep, held center position in her stretcher, white blankets pulled up tight around her loose hair. She looked more ghostly than usual, lips a pastel pink. An IV dangled from her right arm.

Gordon hunched in a flimsy chair near the window, locked into his Tama. He'd put some bags under those eyes in the hours since Calvin had ditched the man here. A paper coffee cup sat on the window sill, steam sneaking out through its black lid.

"Cozy," Calvin whispered, slipping around the stretcher and sitting across from Gordon.

"She's way out, you're not going to wake her," Gordon said. "She might crack a joke by morning, probably not before if the nurses get their way."

"She's okay?"

"Surgeons were optimistic. No guarantees, but she's strong."

"Like she would leave Seeker behind."

Gordon laughed, a tired thing, then jerked his look

back Calvin's way, "I was just reading about the fight down at the tower?"

Calvin crashed through the details. The Elementals, the drones, the bad omens. Gordon put it all together like it was the world's easiest puzzle, pitching follow-up questions to Calvin about Wexley and his paramilitary group that had the anomaly putting up his hands.

"Slow down and tell me where you're going," Calvin said. "This keeps up, I'm going to need my own coffee, maybe spiked with whatever she's having."

"You don't think Mynx getting captured by a guy that hates anomalies, and then her drones turning traitor is a coincidence, do you?"

"Man, I've been fighting for my life all day. Haven't had much time to play detective."

Gordon gestured around the room, "That makes one of us. The point I'm going for here, if I'm right, is that the drones aren't going to stop."

"They did after we beat their asses."

"For a hot minute, maybe. And that was here, in Chicago, when you had a whole bunch of Paragons and Elementals in fighting shape ready to go. What happens in Cleveland, or Little Rock, where you've got five Paragons and fifty drones?"

Nothing good, that's what happened. Still, wasn't like Calvin could do much about it. Pixie, or whomever played her part in Pacifica, would need to figure it out. Gordon must've read Calvin's expression, because the man slid into a sulk.

"It's like you don't even care," Gordon said.

"I do, but I care about her more."

"Yeah? What happens when she wakes up and all the anomalies are dead, huh? What happens when you're gone, when her job is toast, and we're all living under whomever's got the drones on their side?"

"Makin' it sound like it's different with the Paragons?"

That had the tracker shut up. Dude wanted to go on some rant about unstoppable monsters taking over the planet, he ought to look around. Calvin might've joined their ranks, but he held no illusions about what the Paragons really were. Dictators, conquerors, an occupying force. Benevolent to some, not so much to others.

Calvin cut the philosophy with a Tama check. Particle sent along an update, dished coordinates for a re-group and a strategy session. If Calvin wasn't dead, they wanted him stopping by.

"I don't want you staying here then," Gordon said, snapping Calvin's attention away.

"What's that?"

"You said the drones went after the anomalies," Gordon continued, keeping his voice quiet, even. "They won't stop, and they'll find you here. Kat's not ready for that."

"The hell—" Calvin stopped himself, shut his eyes, his mouth for a moment, breathed.

He and Gordon were far from friends, but the man might have a point. A drone shooting through this glass at Calvin might hit Kat. The Paragons wanted a re-group. He could leave, again.

"I'll let you know as soon as her condition changes," Gordon said. "I won't leave her side. Promise."

"Yeah?" Calvin said, not moving, not yet. He'd fought so hard to get back here. "You know she almost died protecting me."

"Me too. Because of you."

Calvin nodded, "You're going to do the same for her?"

"If I have to."

"Good answer." Calvin pushed himself from the chair, fighting off his own confusion, the annoyance. "The minute she gets up, you let me know."

"I will."

Calvin's Tama buzzed again. Particle, upping the priority. The Paragons wanted to attack first, keep the drones from organizing. Calvin stole one last, long look Kat's way. She looked, at least, peaceful.

Better than him.

On the way back to the street, Calvin grabbed a coffee, an energy bar, and a hooded sweatshirt with the hospital's name on it. Slipping the clothes on over the Paragon uniform, he went back out into the dark, trying to hide from the cameras.

The programs behind those metal eyes weren't friendly anymore.

The Void Returns

The shaking woke Cassidy. A tremor ran up the bed, rattling her teeth and popping her up into darkness. Cassidy waved a hand, asked the room to turn its lights on, and received nothing in response. Nothing, that is, except another bone-shaking rattle. Dust shook itself off the ceiling, unseen but felt as it gathered on Cassidy's bare shoulders.

Feeling her way in the dark, the Void threw on her clothes. She tried turning on the TV and found nothing doing there either. The lights kept up their refusal. Cassidy's Tama, at least, packed power, though a sad screen claimed Cassidy had no network connection. The Tama's glow helped Cassidy find the door, get her shoes on straight.

She tried the door's handle. Locked. Cassidy rolled her eyes.

No trust in this place.

A third rumble, this one followed by more bangs. Furniture hitting the ground? A roof caving in? Some Paragons having an anomaly bout overhead?

Cassidy stared at the door, trying to decide whether or not to go back to sleep. Her nerves, her instinct told her the shakes weren't natural, that this wasn't the usual for Apinya's Bangkok fortress. She could lay down, but dreamland would be a hard find with the shaking.

"And I don't want to stay here," Cassidy muttered, feeling the voids waking up along with her.

She threw one, small and spinning, at the door's handle. With a shriek, a tear, and a sole escaping spark, the metal disappeared. Letting the void dissipate, Cassidy pushed the door open, hoping Apinya would forgive her the expense.

Then again, he'd probably ordered her locked inside. His fault.

The hallway, a soft-lit affair when Cassidy had arrived a few hours ago, had the same dead darkness as her room. Noises cascaded in, shouts, screams, and the staccato chatter belonging to bullets. Most came from her left, the way leading back to the building's center.

Cassidy hesitated.

Who would attack a Paragon stronghold, much less one with a Champion inside? Nobody would be that stupid, that suicidal.

Worse, from what Cassidy could tell, the attackers seemed to be winning. For a confused moment, Cassidy wondered whether Thane might've decided to go all wrecking ball, but the gunfire proved that idea wrong.

Thane might decide to kill some Paragons, but he wouldn't use bullets to do it.

A half-step towards the main building and Cassidy stopped. She felt another tremor, smaller and from behind. She turned, saw nothing. Down that hallway, her Paragon hosts had said, sat more rooms, most being used to hold the new arrivals. All those kids from the orphan outpost.

Cassidy held her breath. Listened. Heard her heart beating. And something else.

A step, light and precise, like a pen clicking in and out. Then another. Closer.

"Someone there?" Cassidy asked the dark.

Nothing answered, save more clicks. Behind her, back in the main building, a deeper boom rattled, more screams followed. Panicked, these.

Adjusting her wrist, Cassidy shone the Tama down the hallway. Right into a tracker drone's gleaming rush. The machine, a meter-long steel centipede, jumped at Cassidy, legs clacking in the air.

She might've screamed.

She definitely threw a void.

Cassidy's power cut the drone in two, the machine's front half spewing sparks as it slammed into Cassidy and carried her to the ground. She felt its sharp legs gouge her arms, her side as Cassidy rolled, throwing the machine off. The busted half hit the wall and started to orient itself before Cassidy threw another void into its center, shredding the drone.

Grimacing at her new scratches, Cassidy used another void to annihilate the tracker drone's other half while asking herself what the hell had gone wrong. Tracker drones were used for just that, tracking and destroying rogue Paragons or other dangerous anomalies their human partners didn't want to tangle with.

Had Apinya decided to assassinate Cassidy and be done with it? Didn't seem his style, nor did it answer whatever was going on back in the main building.

A different scream cut Cassidy's internal Q&A short. This one came closer, down the hall towards where the kids lived.

She didn't hesitate.

Pounding down the hall, Cassidy wielded her Tama like a flashlight, catching doorways and looking for drones. She found other rooms already torn open from the outside in, at least one splattered with blood and a body its likely source.

She hadn't been the tracker drone's first catch.

The kids had a block near the hallway's end, large rooms reserved for the refugees the Paragons would process into new heroes. Two doors looked open, their rooms empty. The third, occupying the hallway's ending wall, lay on the ground, ripped off its hinges.

Voices came from inside, children. Cassidy recognized the older ones, the brave few who'd confronted her and Thane outside the house. They were ordering the others back, telling them to be brave.

She went in.

From her Tama's light, Cassidy caught four tracker drones, two on the ceiling and two on the floor. They stalked towards the children, clustered behind an older pair. The girl and boy who'd played guardian at the orphanage reprised their role now, standing in their Paragon pajamas, faces filled with a fraught, pure bravery.

"Leave them alone," Cassidy said.

The two drones on the ceiling wheeled towards her, while the bottom two stayed focused on the kids. Cassidy let the voids fly, sending two at the top drones. These trackers hadn't jumped yet, though, and Mynx designed them well. They jerked aside as Cassidy's voids hit the room's ceiling, snaring tiles and the wiring beyond them. Sparks flew, the kids screamed again.

The drones skittered to the walls, coming at Cassidy from opposite sides. Their legs clacked, notches in their metal skin opened up to bring stunning weapons and their lethal cousins to bare. Cassidy stood still, waited as the clacks came close. Kicking her feet out from under her, Cassidy slid to her back as the clacks ceased.

She threw her hands up, casting the voids where her body had been, where the drones flew. The Tama caught their mangling destruction, the voids warping and snapping the drone legs, shells, cores. Cassidy rolled, careful not to sit up into her own voids, and looked towards the other two tracker drones.

The metal bugs advanced on the kids, paying no attention to Cassidy. The older girl made the first move, stepping towards the drones and planting her right foot. A jagged line cracked along the tile, dark edges splitting the two drones. The machines sidestepped the line, skittering forward, only for the boy to raise his hands, as if praying to the sky.

The floor beneath the drones shuddered, then closed in around the drones before smashing them up to the ceiling, the building's foundation lurching up and forming a wrist and forearm beneath the gray tile hand. One drone took the smash and exploded, while the other wriggled free, scurrying over the top and landing on the leading girl.

Its legs pinned the teenager to the ground, its weapons, sticking from its shell like so many spikes, found targets in the huddled crowd behind her. The boy, his display crumbling back to earth, breathed hard from the ground, apparently exhausted.

The drone went for the kill.

So did Cassidy.

The machine's weapons fired, stunning darts and killing bullets streaking towards the children and vanishing as they soared past the drone's head. Cassidy's first void, a widespread, shallow oval, caught the attack. Her second plot the drone's middle, sparking out the machine's life in a crackling finale.

"Don't sit up," Cassidy said to the girl, the drone's dying bits lying on her. "Give me a moment."

Dispelling voids felt a little like catching a thrown knife: Cassidy had to get her touch just right or she'd find herself getting sliced up. She started with the spinning death over the girl, then, after helping the scared kid away, killed the protective void before the other children.

All those faces gawked at Cassidy now without the defiance they'd had back at the orphanage. Teens huddled together, a brave few standing apart and looking like they might attempt their powers if Cassidy kept going.

"I'm not gonna hurt you," Cassidy said, reaching down to help the lead girl up. "But those drones will. We have to get away from here."

"And go where?" the boy with the hands said, recovered and standing after his attack. "Those were Paragon drones, right? They'll keep coming."

"Apinya will know what's going on," Cassidy said, not quite sure she believed the words as she spoke them.

The boy had it right. The Paragons either sent the drones to kill the kids, which made zero sense, or something worse was happening. Given all the noise from the building's center, Cassidy knew which way she'd lean.

"You think we can trust him?" the girl asked now. "He put us here! We were fine back at the house."

"We don't have a choice," Cassidy said, then swept a stern, motherly look around the group. The kind she'd give to her kids before telling them not to run across the street without looking both ways. "We either wait here and see what else comes after us, or we get out. I know which way I'm going."

When she left, the children followed.

The main base emerged earlier than Cassidy expected. The hallway grew more and more acrid as the group walked, Cassidy and her voids leading the way. Fires and their food layered the air with stinging scents, the rumbles continued to shake the floor beneath their shoes. Bullets made their clattering noises, ending in *thunks* or shattering glass. More than one scream ripped through the dark.

But no tracking drones found the group. The gap let Cassidy cool down, her sweat lingering in Bangkok's humid air, now delivering its heavy wet to the breached building.

"Wait till I clear it," Cassidy said as they reached the hallway's end. The door, a double-wide wooden thing, sat ajar on its hinges, a scanner and locking mechanism torn from the wall and lying on the floor. "If I don't come back in five minutes . . . " Cassidy trailed off.

What could she say? Break through the walls? Chance it on your own? Her charges met Cassidy's silence with mixed stares, but the oldest few wore their defiance plain.

"We survived a long time," the girl said. "Go."

Cassidy took the invitation and went to the door, leaned around and glanced into the base's wide center. Apinya built his home like a giant spider, with a central hall and his audience chamber—Cassidy might've rolled her eyes at that—giving way to at least twenty offshoots, some ending in offices, others training rooms, bunks, meeting areas, and more. Stairs and small elevators connected the various segments, all lockable.

Apinya hadn't explained why he wanted every section sealable, but when you worked with powerful beings like these, it might make some sense. Something went wrong, Apinya could trap the offender where they were, or at least delay them a minute or two.

Though, looking into the hall, Cassidy and her crew might've been the last to arrive.

Drones and Paragons splattered across the chamber.

Smoldering metal plates, arms, legs, jets and more scorched carpeting and burned holes in walls. Paragon bodies matched the machine debris, the anomalies ruined with so much uncompromising force that Cassidy looked away from the worst to save her stomach.

The building's front entrance, when Cassidy checked, offered no solution. Several large gladiator drones stood blocking the exit, weapons ready, if quiet. Preventing a retreat. To her left, Cassidy looked deeper into the building, where fighting noises continued.

More tracker drones, supplemented by the flying types Cassidy had fought in the streets the night before, pressed a Paragon team as the anomalies retreated towards Apinya's hall. With the Paragons holding the drone attention, Cassidy figured they could make a run across the hall, get to the far side and through. The Paragon base bordered the river, meaning breaking through the other side might get the kids into the water and out of sight.

If they could swim.

"Hey, it's you."

Cassidy heard the whisper, strained, and saw, amid a statue's ruined stand, a beat-up form she recognized. Daw, the new Paragon from before. His arm looked trapped beneath some fallen stone, and his face and Paragon uniform bore more bloody spots than could be healthy. Cassidy grimaced, then turned her back on Daw and returned to the waiting group.

"Come up to the door," Cassidy said. "I need to help someone. While I do that, make a run for it behind us."

"A run to where?" The girl asked.

Cassidy brought her to the door, pointed across to the opposite hall, "Through there. At the far side, you can punch through the wall and escape."

"Uh huh."

"You'll have a better chance with that than you will with those gladiators," Cassidy replied, nodding towards the building's main doors and the monsters beyond them. "Now go."

At Daw's side in a second, kneeling on bloody yellow carpet, Cassidy looked the young man over. She spun up a small void and used it to crack the stone trapping Daw's arm. Behind them, with the girl and boy leading, the kids began their odyssey, dashing across the wide hall while the fighting raged deeper inside.

Daw looked like he'd fallen unconscious, closed eyes and weak breathing not an encouraging sign. Cassidy recalled rudimentary first aid warning against moving someone with unknown injuries, but leaving Daw here would give the Paragon a more permanent end. She slipped her arms beneath Daw, thanking him for being a lanky string, and lifted.

With the Paragon's arms and legs draped across her, Cassidy stepped into the central hall, coming in behind the teenager line. The last anomaly blipped near her, fading in like a miniature blizzard before blowing across the chamber and reforming at the far end, the boy's ice blue eyes watching Cassidy and her cargo.

Not the drones.

The base's entry doors, already destroyed by what Cassidy presumed was the initial assault, proved neither barrier nor alarm to the gladiators. Their tremendous legs pounded in, bright lights locking on Cassidy and Daw. Three machines, each more than a story high, all focusing their weapons on the pair.

Cassidy could drop Daw, throw some voids, but she couldn't count the weapons trained on her. In the past, when the drones had taken Cassidy in so long ago, they'd pitched warnings. Consequences that could be avoided, somewhat, if she surrendered.

Back then, Cassidy didn't want her kids to watch their mother get annihilated. Now, Cassidy didn't want these teenagers to see it either.

"Run!" Cassidy shouted, not looking towards the teenagers, not doing anything to draw the drones' attention their way.

She'd have time for one void. One.

She knelt in a smooth motion, rolling Daw off her arms. With a wrist flick, Cassidy sent up a wide, flat void between her and the drones. The gladiators did what they were designed to do and opened up on Cassidy, sending bullets, stunning darts, and at least one superheated laser straight at her.

The void caught them all, sucking the assault into its gravity-crushing embrace. Cassidy felt the heat start again, like catching a fever. She kept the void up, like remembering to keep a muscle flexed. Not so bad with a single void, but the gladiators weren't stupid.

Splitting up, the drones flanked Cassidy. She whipped up two more voids, blanketing Cassidy's left and right sides. The attacks continued, and Cassidy knelt over Daw, sweating, breathing hard as she kept the swirling voids doing their defensive dirty work.

Despite the barriers, the gladiators kept firing. Cassidy figured they'd try a different strategy, but the drones held her there. Would they wait until she passed out?

A new vibration answered the question. Cassidy couldn't hear anything over the deafening drone gunfire, but she could feel the skittering steps as they came closer. With her sweat-soaked hair matted to her forehead, Cassidy stole a glance back and saw two tracker drones scurrying her way. They must've abandoned the other fight, or finished it, and were now coming after dessert.

Cassidy reached for another void, reached and faltered. Her other voids shivered, shrank enough for a bullet to streak in over Cassidy's shoulder and strike the ground behind her. She couldn't get it, couldn't pull another one.

Instead, she looked at Daw, the Paragon's eyes still closed, and waited for the machines to make it end.

33

The Future

The world's stakeholders called in one by one. These were faces, names, companies that had charted humanity's course for generations until the Paragons stopped them. Zhan-Yo had assembled the list, using Ziran's pull to bring them on board to his revolution, and now Wexley, at last, could deliver.

He greeted them from Mynx's deck, the ocean rumbling in the background. Or was that the Factory, already picking up pace?

"We have control," Wexley said at the start, "and we are using it."

At first, some complained. Cities erupted as drones and Paragons, as drones and anomalies, as drones and people who didn't know any better fought across streets, fields, and rooftops. Wexley's actions shook the economy, drove uncertainty, created panic.

"As has every major change," Wexley answered. "The Paragons found the same when they staged their takeover. They promised a better future. We can now deliver one.

We've planned for this. You all know your roles. Commence them."

They had planned. Documents long drawn up and left to founder as Zhan-Yo's promise faltered under its own aspirations. Wexley and Rhimes had bet long ago that, if Zhan-Yo ever succeeded in pulling apart the Paragon rule, chaos would inevitably result.

Which was why gathering an instant army had become the only true course, the only way someone not a Paragon could overtake the established world.

They asked for time, these leaders. They wanted to revisit what they'd drawn up, wanted to dig deep and find the dead constitutions from nations long past. Schedule elections, promise reforms, name representatives for all various peoples, including the anomalies.

"In due time," Wexley said. "For now, do what you can. The drones will establish control, and once they have driven the Paragons from their posts, the machines will ensure they cannot return. Your people will wake up tomorrow free from their control, ready to begin new and exciting lives."

When one asked what would happen with those drones, whether they would become the property of the country hosting their weaponized presence, Wexley demurred. Shook off the question as premature, claimed that he and his team were still learning how the Factory and Mynx's systems worked.

Until then, until the world stabilized, Wexley would keep control. That statement sent the expected shockwaves through the group, the narrowed eyes and shaking heads anticipated by Ziran's CEO.

"My friends, we all have our skills," Wexley said. "Mine is eliminating anomalies. I suggest you let me focus on that, while you draw up our planet's beautiful future."

With a wave, Wexley dismissed the call and the startled faces. Most would connect with each other, begin forming their alliances and plotting what Wexley's moves really meant. It didn't matter. The economy would continue despite the interference. People would continue to work, to grow their food and raise their families.

So long as the Paragons, so long as the anomalies weren't in the picture, everything else could be sorted out.

"The victor standing in his spoils," Adriana said, coming out onto the deck with two fresh champagne glasses.

"And ready to share them," Wexley accepted the offer, clinked her glass. Adriana's searching smile showed she hadn't caught the meeting. "They'll come on board. They're surprised."

"They don't know you like I do."

Wexley laughed. Adriana had been as shocked as the rest. Nobody saw this coming, even Wexley doubted the plan until it succeeded.

"I'm ending the Paragons right now," Wexley said, the champagne a bright note to the morning. "The drones are chasing them from their towers and their bases into the woods, the sewers, and any hole those anomalies can fit into."

"The Paragons will surrender. They must."

"That will not save them."

"What?"

Wexley waved back at the Factory, built into the mountain behind them, "Look at what Mynx built, Adriana! This is global domination, this is an army that needs no food, no rest. The Champions could've lost all their abilities and still done as they wished."

"But you defeated them."

"No. I took what they built and turned it against

them." Wexley tapped on the table, brought up the top trending videos from around the globe. All showcased drones wreaking destruction in major cities, obliterating Paragons. "We took their ultimate weapon, and they will never get the chance to make another."

Adriana tilted her head, "I understand killing the Champions. They'll never forgive you. But all of them?"

"I'm not cruel, Adriana," Wexley replied. "Just precise. Any anomaly is a threat to us, but they don't have to be. A simple solution: keep your abilities hidden, and the drones will leave you alone."

Adriana didn't look like she quite understood, so Wexley said it a different way, to be sure she had it clear.

"An anomaly that doesn't use their powers is a human. Life goes back to what it was. No Champions, no Paragons, just us."

This time, Wexley noted, Adriana's toast wasn't quite as enthusiastic.

"Isn't that a bit short sighted?" Adriana said as their glasses clinked.

"How so?"

"You said yourself, you won by stealing what the Champions made." Adriana waved her glass at Mynx's house. "Why stop now?"

Wexley traced the words, tried to find Adriana's meaning. When he found it, confirmed it in Adriana's slow-growing smile, Wexley frowned.

"It can't be done," Wexley said.

"There's one who came close. In this very city, no less. We can start with her research and, with so many potential subjects, progress it."

"To what end? We already rule the world."

"But for how long? If we make this work, we'll have this view forever."

Wexley finished his champagne without another word, watching the waves and wondering. Adriana let him think, but she felt her eyes on him nonetheless. Simply wiping the anomalies off the map would be the cleaner solution.

But controlling their power?

That would secure Ziran's position. Would secure his own life against some anomaly assassin. And maybe, just maybe, Adriana could find the answers to those self-destructive anomalies. A noble goal, that.

"Another round," Wexley called to the little serving drone and the machine buzzed back into the house.

"Oh?" Adriana asked.

"I don't think we're done celebrating yet. Now, tell me more about this idea."

Dawn broke over the eastern cliffs, a purple orange explosion. The sunlight sparkled over the ocean. A beautiful start to a brand new world.

34

Boxed In

The vessel had little to recommend it save size. Shipping containers stacked stories tall in every bland color Celice could imagine. Nightfall and some well-placed bribes sent guards and workers away as the group approached, twenty altogether hustling through the Port of London. Zhan-Yo, Mathieu, and Benny led the entourage, all wearing drab and unremarkable clothes stolen from the Elemental's large stash. Celice felt the itch, the weight as her own jacket bore down on her. Her shoes fit too tight, blisters squeezing in around her feet.

She'd take it, though, because it meant not dying, it meant not facing those damned drones again.

They left bodies behind when they fled the Tower. That's what Celice couldn't dismiss as the minutes and hours passed afterward. Those faces, twisted up in short-lived pain as the drones finished off any Paragon, any person they managed to hit.

Aegis called the retreat and Gatete dissolved a hole in the Tower's outer wall nearest them. Those Paragons able to move provided what cover they could for Zhan-Yo,

Mathieu, and the agents. A losing, pyrrhic battle as more drones continued to arrive, summoned from London's outskirts and willing to expend every weapon they had against the heroes they should've helped.

Pods pulled up outside the Tower, called by the Elementals to help the evacuation. If Celice hadn't waited for her father, she would've been in the first one, with Gatete. She would've been trapped like the Paragon leader when the drones did what they could and sealed the vehicle, stuck it in place. Gatete tried to erase a path to freedom only to find drone fire waiting for him.

The Elementals, though, proved their resourcefulness: one, wearing a barista's uniform, ran into the street's center and slapped the ground. As the everyone fled the Tower, a circle appeared amid the slap, widening and hollowing away the street's surface like a knife scraping off a topping. The Elemental pointed to a spot near her creation's growing edge: a manhole leading to the city's sewers, its cover erased by the anomaly.

Celice, this time, led the call, shouting for everyone to follow in a mad dash towards the hole. She refused to watch anything other than the goal as she ran, jumped, and fell through the circle. The Elemental's own ability faded as the drones found her, a targeting that would've been deadly had Aegis not wrapped the woman up in his arms and dropped with her down into the muck.

From there, Benny took the lead, with another Paragon using his abilities to collapse the opening behind them in a hissing burst-pipe blast. A pitiful few from the numbers that'd been alive an hour ago, but more than zero.

More than zero.

All those jobs, all those missions Celice had directed from the Bastion's control rooms, involved sending Paragons like these out to stop evil anomalies or prevent natural disasters. Sometimes, Paragons had been injured. A few died. Not like this, though. Not shredded by supposed allies without pity.

Not even Thane had killed this way.

As they trudged, Aegis, Zhan-Yo, and Benny turned to what would happen next. Celice let the conversation bounce around the tunnel, still trying to find a way to piece together what'd just happened.

And how.

"Mynx," Aegis said later, when they'd reached the Elemental's safe house. Two showers served for the group, coupled with fresh clothes. "She's the only one with global control, the only one who could do something like this."

"She'd need Reeves to do it," Celice countered. The five sat at a metal-and-rubber card table, one that looked like it'd seen far more decades than anyone there. The room around them had stained walls, a clock that ticked incessantly, and enough vacant stares to sap the soul. "No way the AI would let her turn the drones on everyone without a warning."

"She didn't do it," Aegis replied, both fists clenched and sitting on the table. "They took her, and made her."

"They?" Benny asked. "Who's they?"

"My friends," Zhan-Yo said, bending over a tea-filled mug. Its steam floated up around his head, but Zhan-Yo drank it in sips anyway. "The drones were one plan. A last resort."

"For your revolution?" Aegis said, acid on his tongue.

Benny stood up from the table without a word and left the room. Nobody followed, nobody cared.

"For our freedom," Mathieu countered Aegis. "If you wouldn't accept any other way, then we would have to use force."

"You already did that, remember?" Celice said. "The LA bombing? Or did you forget?"

"A desperate mistake," Zhan-Yo replied. "We thought one more push might lead you to change."

"Because terrorism always works."

Celice saw the thread hanging between them all. One good swipe and she could cut it, get Aegis to flip the table and break into a fight here and now. Zhan-Yo didn't have his swords on him—the blades were somewhere in Gatete's base—and Mathieu had no visible weapons. An easy revenge for all those who'd lost their lives in LA.

"Take a breath everyone," Benny said, walking back into the room with an old six-pack.

The Elemental slapped the cheap beer on the table, then handed one out to everyone.

"I don't drink anymore," Zhan-Yo said.

"Then spit it out, but you're toasting with the rest of us," Benny replied.

"Toasting to what?" Aegis asked.

"Our survival. You all might be newer to this game, but the Elementals have been in the shadows for a long damn time. You celebrate the big win so the little fights don't tear you apart."

Celice raised her glass first towards Benny's. Not because she felt some overwhelming desire to smooth the mood, but because she found no energy for anything else. Another fight would be too much, too soon. She hadn't processed all those bodies, read the names that would be familiar to her: people never met but messaged, read about in Paragon bulletins.

Mathieu joined next, an unsurprising move for the man. He'd played his shrewd cards throughout and why change that here, with Aegis otherwise ready to tear his head off?

Zhan-Yo and the Champion eyed each other for a long moment, long enough for Benny to cough and jiggle his can. Zhan-Yo went first, nodding at the Elemental and clacking the aluminum. Aegis, his last place secured, completed the toast. Benny drank the longest.

"To stop the drones, we need to get Mynx," Aegis declared, foam lingering around his lips. "That means getting to Pacifica. I assume the machines will be watching, or destroying, our Paragon transports."

"We use normal methods," Zhan-Yo said. "A passenger plane."

"No." Mathieu reached out, popped his Tama off and set it in the table's center. With a swipe, the Tama projected what looked like a large ship. "The drones will have access to anyone boarding a plane, and unless Benny's been more proactive than me, false IDs aren't going to be ready for a while. I vote we go in a box."

"In a box?" Celice asked. "A shipping container?"

"No scans we can't control, no drone interest," Mathieu said. "It's safe, and Atlantic transit doesn't take long at current speeds."

"We can get you one," Benny said. "We've been moving material in and out through those dockyards for a long time."

Aegis frowned at the Elemental, but didn't object. Instead, he stood, holding his beer can. "I need to get word out to the others, make sure my Paragons know to keep their heads down. Make the arrangements. Celice, I trust you."

The Champion spared a shoulder squeeze for his daughter. A nice touch.

A gray container marked their objective. It sat open, waiting with a crane above for loading onto the ship. Provisions for the days-long journey had been stacked by

Benny's people in the back, bland crates stuffed with food, water, and other essentials.

The foursome approached, Benny marking his own farewell at the dockyard's edge. He'd be reuniting with his favorite pair, Roger and Sydney, to organize a resistance. When Celice asked Benny how he'd handle working with a man he'd stabbed, Benny shrugged, said the past was the past, and moved the conversation along.

If Celice had felt the same, she might've avoided the London trip altogether. Might've stayed with Mynx in LA and been there to keep this disaster from happening.

"Hanging in there?" Mathieu said, and Celice realized she'd fallen a few steps behind. Aegis and Zhan-Yo made the container, were inspecting it for any surprises.

"Sorry, distracted," Celice said. "This is a lot."

"You get used to it," Mathieu replied.

"Used to what? Running in the dark? Seeing friends get shot up?"

"Unfortunately, yes." Mathieu flashed a dark look towards Aegis. "Your father killed my sister. She worked for Zhan-Yo, and the night he pulled off the—"

"I'm sorry, but I'm also not," Celice interrupted. "I get it. Our lives don't have room for self-pity. There's only what it takes to survive."

Aegis waved back their way. The container was safe, no lurking ambushes.

"Not quite," Mathieu said as they crunched the last steps along the concrete. "It's hard, but that doesn't mean you can't have a little fun."

"Like?"

"We've got three days coming up that we'll spend roasting in a metal box." Mathieu reached inside his jacket pocket. "Figured we'd need a way to spend the time."

Out came his hand, holding a deck of cards.

The ship's rumble provided the soundtrack to their container lives. Mathieu and Zhan-Yo, those cards in hand, staked out one side while Celice sat with her father on the other, tapping out messages on their Tamas. For hours they strategized, overcame the shocks pouring in that Aegis still lived mingled with drone-caused horror. Champions and other Paragon leaders from cities major and minor looked for direction.

Aegis told them to hide. To wait until better plans could be made. Anomaly lives were most important. Finally, after hitting send another time, Celice couldn't help it. She put her hand over her father's screen, drawing his attention to her.

"You came back," Celice said. "I don't understand how, but you came back."

The words seemed obvious, stupid even, but they were still true. Celice had grown up around so many anomalies, had seen powers covering almost everything, but death remained inviolate. Nobody could reach into the beyond and pull a life back.

"Mila can answer that," Aegis said. "She and Mynx, together, brought me back."

"When? How long ago?"

"A day? Mynx brought me up, told me Gatete had Zhan-Yo and that you might be in trouble." Aegis grinned. "I said if Gatete crossed you, he'd be the one in trouble, but Mynx gave me her jet anyway. Told it where to take me."

Celice shook her head, "We should've taken that jet back."

"Tried. It stopped responding as soon as the drones turned. Don't know where it wound up. Not that it matters. Rushing back to the Factory will only get us killed."

"My dad, refusing to run right into danger?"

"Last time doing that nearly cost me everything. Whomever took the Factory isn't weak. They know who's coming for them, which means we need to be better."

Celice looked over at the card players, "We have them."

"Normals," Aegis said, then caught Celice's glare and softened his look. "Skilled normals. They'll help, but we need the Champions, or as many still live. Paragons too."

How many times had her father saved the world? He spoke like the coming Factory assault was just another problem to solve. Another bump in the road for the Champions. Celice wanted to doubt the man's confidence, his grim resolve, but stopped.

Aegis lived. They had a plan's beginnings.

And, for the next few days, Celice had her father all to herself. She could live with that.

The Raid

Lob brought the squad, one at a time, up to the building's roof. Afternoon sun cut the spring breeze and gave a good view, the lakeshore to the left and the target straight ahead. A fenced off, square-topped center, the local drone repair facility had itself humming. The early morning fight sent drones here by the dozen, the machines settling into lines as they marched towards the center's entrance.

Calvin didn't know what algorithms in there would sort out, define and divide the drones into the proper service lines, but he could see the results buzzing out the center's far doors. Like insects leaving a nest, repaired drones flitted off on their missions.

"They're calling it freedom," Smoke muttered, staring at her Tama as the group checked their gear. "Ziran made some statement about taking humanity back from the anomalies, and everyone's buying in."

"Everyone?" Particle replied, locking several nasty-looking guns into their belt.

"All the comments on this, the front page piece, are going wild about it," Smoke said.

"They're idiots," Weed noted, the leader matching Calvin's crouching look down towards the center.

"They're bots," Particle added. "Ziran owns the news networks. They can spin up whatever they want."

"People will believe it," Smoke countered.

A pop-hiss cut the conversation as everyone turned to Lob, the man guzzling down a rancid-looking energy drink. Lob finished the can in a single take, issuing a devastating burp finale. Calvin chuckled in spite of himself.

"Tune in, people," Weed said, snapping his fingers. The man, with a thick bandage under his uniform covering the bullet wound, had a pasty look. Exhaustion ringed bright eyes. Fresh coffee stained his teeth. "Time's about when we kick off. Our partners will be hitting drones wherever they can find them, meaning we'll get their leftovers running our way. By the time they get here, we need to have this place dominated. You all know your jobs. Let's make the Paragons proud."

Calvin looked away so Weed wouldn't catch his eye roll.

Lob kicked things off, launching Calvin first. Calvin hadn't been shot from a cannon, but he figured that's what this had to feel like: one second feet on the ground, comfortable, and the next flying up into the air with a perfect arc. Sparse homes spread out beneath them, frosted yards looking pretty, a few souls out in the afternoon. One even looked up, caught Calvin soaring.

The toss brought Calvin up, but it wouldn't help set him down. The drone warehouse set five stories high, but that still meant a long drop from Lob's throw. Weed told Calvin he didn't need to make this move, but surprise would mean everything in the raid, and after what happened to Kat last night, Calvin felt like showing off.

So he picked up the air in his left hand, felt its particles and grabbed them, shooting their loose collection through his body and out his right hand, reaching below him. As Calvin fell, he created thicker and thicker air beneath him, slowing his descent bit by bit until he crunched onto the repair roof with a roll.

The metal slats offered little comfort, less protection, and the three drones guarding their broken brethren swiveled their spidery selves Calvin's way. Their black metal bodies, dirty, sucked in sunlight as they rose up over the building's sides seeking Calvin.

Too slow.

Calvin planted his right hand on the rooftop, caught the metal and ripped it, sending the structure out in ribbons around him. The metal reformed into a flimsy circle, not enough to protect against anything, but enough to hide Calvin.

When the drones fired, their bullets broke through the barrier and bounced straight through the other side. Calvin dropped through the hole he'd created, landing on a steel support beam inside the structure.

"I'm in," Calvin said through his Tama. "Hole's ready and waiting."

"Coming," Lob replied. "You've made some friends."

"Was counting on it."

Calvin stood on a large, dark red cross beam. Another three matched his, stretching through the converted facility from one end to the next. Vertical, shorter beams stood every few meters, connecting the cross beams to the roof. Down below, drones filtered into their lines, marching past still more drones with whirling arms, spraying welders, and more all bent on fixing up their fellow machines. The air stank with burning wires and molten metal, and Calvin found himself sweating all over. Sparks crackled, shearing noises came as parts were put together.

For a brief moment, Calvin envisioned the whole world covered in places like this, machines making more machines making humans extinct.

His flying drone followers guessed Calvin's destination, swooping in through the facility's front entrance, hunting him with those searching lights. With his entrance made, Calvin swapped his tactics.

With his left hand, Calvin grabbed the vertical girder, keeping himself steady and drawing its hard steel. His right hand turned the steel into sharp spikes, ones Calvin threw at the approaching drones. Each one a dagger, the spikes struck home, driving into the drones and sending the first two spiraling away. The drones kept enough control to dodge the fixing lines, collapsing into the building's corners.

The third came from behind.

Calvin whirled, saw the drone fire, and expected the bullets to strike him down. Instead they went wide right, whistling and missing by centimeters. The reason dropped next to Calvin, Smoke yelling for Calvin to take the machine out.

Another spike did the job.

"It's not easy fooling them," Smoke said, crouching to grab their girder with both hands. "I'm blurring us way out."

"Hey, it worked," Calvin said, then turned his attention to the line beneath them.

His vertical girder, pillaged for spikes, split apart when Calvin siphoned a little more. Turned the steel into a fragment cluster, then let it rain onto the assembly line. Each sliver, extremely sharp, slipped through the machines and severed wires, blocked circuits, and worse. The assembly line sputtered, some drones dying right away while others lurched back into action.

"Let's hit that one," Calvin said, pointing towards the next vertical girder.

A thump above said Lob had dropped off another member, and Particle made themselves known with a call through Calvin's rooftop hole.

"Lookout's in position," Particle said. "Get to wrecking."

"Already on it," Smoke replied as the two scrambled towards the next girder.

Calvin repeated his work, shaving off micro fragments and sending them slicing through the machines below. Not as one-by-one devastating as the spikes, the slivers made up for it by giving Calvin more coverage. He flung the slivers all around the facility, severing drones in all the little places that made the machines run.

Like playing some game, pure target practice.

"More incoming," Weed said, minutes later. He, Lob, and Particle had the rooftop watch while Calvin continued obliterating the drones. "All sides."

"Hold them," Calvin replied, running along with Smoke to another crossing beam deeper in the facility. "Not too much longer."

Despite running along a narrow girder far above a floor packed with robots that wouldn't hesitate to dismember him, Calvin kept a fast pace. He didn't flinch, didn't pause to take deep breaths and work up the nerve. He'd felt this determined calm before, with Kat on their missions to find and take out Wexley. Now, with a full team operating around him, Calvin tossed his anxieties aside, focused on the objective.

Destroying these drones meant keeping Chicago safe. The Paragons could re-establish themselves, could fortify the city until someone figured out what Wexley had done with Mynx. Kat could heal up, Calvin could walk Seeker and play protector.

Calvin smiled as he hit the next vertical girder, slapping his hand against it and sucking up another sliver rain. He sounded like he had a home.

"Trackers!" Smoke called, pulling Calvin's attention to the wall closest to them.

Five bug-like drones scurried up its surface, heading towards the cross-beams. They must've been repaired moments ago, striking right out. Not that it mattered. Calvin shifted his right wrist, rotating the slivers, each one connected to his hand by the tiniest metal filament. Like a whip, Calvin would flick his wrist and let the filaments go, flinging the tiny spikes at their ends.

The trackers must've learned.

As soon as Calvin shifted the slivers, the drones broke ranks. Two shot up as fast as their legs could go, heading for the ceiling. The ones on either side broke in those directions, angling for other cross-beams. And one decided to play the martyr, charging right onto Calvin's beam. The Paragon whipped his slivers, sending the rain forward.

The drone twitched as its joints found their wires cut, its sensors shattered. A leg misplaced a step and the drone lurched to Calvin's right, then fell, dropping off the girder in a sparking fall to crunch against some unlucky machine below.

"Move!" Smoke cried, and Calvin agreed. The two tracker drones were nearly overhead, and the other pair would have the Paragons trapped in seconds. "Across and out. We've done enough damage, right?"

Following Smoke as she spoke, Calvin ran across the beam cutting the facility's middle. Fires rose below them, cut wires finding opportunities in spilled lubricants and leaking batteries. Those flames would spread, possibly enough to consume the whole building. Either way, the center wouldn't be repairing anything for a while.

"I think we're good," Calvin said, looking back up to see Smoke all the way across.

A tracker drone dropped from the ceiling as Calvin spoke, crashing to the girder behind Smoke, splitting her off from Calvin. The Paragon drew a standard-issue pistol from her belt and cracked off a shot, the bullet drawing a spark and nothing else from the drone. The tracker didn't turn towards her either, choosing instead to keep its focus on Calvin.

Behind him, Calvin heard the other two trackers coming up fast. Up above, the one that hadn't dropped looked to be keying in on Smoke's position.

"We need a rescue!" Calvin called into his Tama, slapping his left hand on the cross beam.

The tracker drone in front charged, steely claws grasping for Calvin. Scary, sure, but the drone had nothing on Seeker's white, growling menace. Back then, Calvin had sucked some metal from the scrapyard to knock the dog away.

This time, he went with a different approach.

Drawing all he could from the girder, Calvin threw his right hand behind him, spraying out the metal into a tight weave. As the drone ran from the front the girder vanished beneath its legs until its claws couldn't find a foothold. With one last lunge, the drone's reaching claws brushed Calvin's uniform, cutting a nice line across his chest.

Then it fell into the growing inferno.

Pistol shots yanked Calvin's attention around to Smoke, plugging away at the last drone. The machine dropped down near the stealthy Paragon, ignoring her hits. She backed up towards Calvin, wobbled on the girder and dropped her gun to catch her balance.

Calvin launched the steel spike over her head. The lance, long, thin, and sharp enough to give diamonds a test, struck and sank into the drone. The thing lurched forward anyway, but Smoke recovered herself enough to catch the drone's leading leg and pull it away from the girder. Unbalanced, the drone tumbled off, its flailing limbs catching Smoke's leg and snaring her.

Or would have, except Calvin, using the girder's barest remaining thread, threw a steel silk line Smoke's way.

"Grab it!" Calvin shouted, trying to keep his balance on the thin sheet beneath his feet. The spanning girder had little support left after Calvin's draining moves, and he could feel the stretch beneath him bending. "Hurry!"

Smoke snagged the thread, wrapped it around her left wrist as she hung over the roiling fire. Smoke, the dark, smelly stuff, rose up around her. Calvin gave up his left hand, using it instead to cover his mouth so he could breathe. Smoke put her hands over each other, climbing up as Calvin made his way one step at a time to the girder's thicker part.

"Nice throw," Smoke said, getting her fingers on the girder. Calvin pulled her up with his better footing. "Next time I need some drones destroyed, I know who to call."

"Helps when I have good weapons," Calvin said, nodding at the flimsy girder remnants.

Smoke coughed, "Think we're done here."

"Already finding a way out."

The roof hole, their entry and best chance at an exit, lay to the left. The heat and ash building in the facility made the short walk a daunting exercise, with Calvin feeling his way along the girder more than seeing it. The smoke served as a guide, the dark drifting stuff flowing towards the hole as a convenient escape.

Calvin wanted to ask where the others were, but

opening his mouth when his eyes already stung, when his uniform felt like it might melt to his skin, seemed like a bad idea. He couldn't tell anymore if Smoke followed him. If she'd fallen off or suffocated, Calvin had no way to know.

Something grabbed his attention, yanked his eyes up and to the right. Calvin was about to crawl right on past the hole, invisible with the pitch-black smoke surging around it. A hand reached down, feeling Calvin's shoulder then making its way to his arm. Coughs came from above, but the hand gave a tight grip, so Calvin kicked himself up.

No matter what lay on the other side, it would be better than burning to death in that building.

As the first hand lifted Calvin up, others reached down and gripped his shoulders. They were small, a hundred specks reaching around him like a living net to find grips and pull him up. It took Calvin a hot second to figure out what was happening, the idea only confirmed when he hit the roof's lip, coming over the side and seeing Weed, a thousand of him, clustered around the circle. His clones, growing at different rates, plunged back in to get Smoke while Calvin, lying on the metal slats, coughed until his lungs were empty, and then one more time.

"Nice work in there," Particle said, standing over him with an assault rifle, taking pot shots.

"You get next," Calvin wheezed.

Weed's tiny human chain found Smoke and pulled her from the flames, plopping her on the roof next to Calvin. Her uniform looked charred, embers glowing in her hair. Two toddler-sized Weeds ran over and patted them out while Smoke coughed and Calvin pushed himself into a stand.

Shapes cluttered the morning sky around the facility: drones flying in or popping up from the as-yet-unburned ground. While Particle took their careful aim and sent bullets flying, the attack seemed to make little impact on the incoming armada.

"What are they waiting for?" Calvin asked. "They should have us dead?"

"Drone strategy," Weed replied, the real one heading over while his copies fanned out across the roof, making targets. Lob followed the leader, putting his arm under Smoke and getting her on her feet. "Cut off every escape, fire together. No chance we get away."

"You don't sound bothered by it?"

"Lob," Weed said, "let's go."

"On it." Lob didn't wait for Smoke's okay, he just leapt off the roof with her, vanishing up into the sky.

"So that's two of us," Calvin replied as Particle cracked off another shot. It shattered a nearby drone's front camera, its black glass falling to the concrete below like jagged confetti.

"He'll be back," Weed replied. "We just need to stay alive till then."

In better times, Calvin would've thrown a wise-ass reply Weed's way. Here, on this sun-blitzed roof with drones closing on all sides, he kept his mouth shut and let his hands do the talking. With his left, Calvin felt the air around him, the molecules joining together making themselves known to his touch. He found what he wanted and pulled at it, a tug reaching from his skin and snagging the nitrogen floating everywhere.

A drone came up along Calvin's right side, zipping over the roof's lip with its weapons ready. Particle had their rifle aiming along the facility, back towards the city and other incoming enemies. Weed's horde danced along the rooftop, providing cover and leaping towards what drones were dumb enough to come close.

Calvin caught this one with his right, gripping the

nitrogen and sending it in a narrow lance towards the drone. The tight air struck the drone's nose, shunting it down as the machine fired. Bullets and worse unloaded into the facility's side, blowing a hole in the wall and sending fiery smoke out. The haze hid the drone, forcing Calvin to send more air waves through, each one clearing the smoke enough to track the machine as it reset. Calvin aimed for the drone's wing, hit it, and sent the metal bird whirling.

No kills, all delays.

Particle's rifle cracked, matched in its moment by Lob's crashing return. The grizzled man landed between his anomaly teammates and, without a moment's indecision, grabbed Particle. The two leaped away, Particle's rifle falling from their hands in the motion and clattering off the roof.

Without Particle's gunfire and constant redirection, the drones pounced. Weed called a warning—all his little selves screamed out together—and Calvin dove towards the smoking hole. Not that he wanted to go in the fire, but as bullets peppered the roof around him, the black gout provided a little cover.

Calvin stuck his hand into the smoke, found the char, and spread it, letting the burning soot launch out around him in a gray-black ball. He rolled within it, aiming for the roof's edge. Everything at this point flew by instinct, without words or real thought beyond escape. They'd accomplished the mission, now Calvin just had to survive.

The rooftop buckled. One moment, Calvin had a sturdy metal slat beneath him, and the next he felt adrift, weightless. Cracks and inhuman groans bellowed behind the constant gunfire as girders split and walls lost their footing. Smoke clouded his eyes, leaving Calvin scrambling, his hands reaching as the building crumbled.

Hands gripped him, bodies, small ones, pressed in around Calvin as his slat began its final fall, sliding off the roof and towards the ground. As he left the smoke, Calvin caught blue sky above, dotted with drones. And a figure: Lob crashing back in.

But not towards Calvin. Lob's course took him towards the facility's front, towards Weed, even as the Paragon leader's small clones buried Calvin in their hustle.

The reason came clear when they hit the ground.

The slat struck first, hitting burning rubble and sliding away, bouncing Calvin off with it. Weed's clones clung tight, keeping quiet as every hit battered them, tearing Calvin's living armor away. When the slat hit concrete, it stopped, sending Calvin onward and losing his last remaining clones. On his back, Calvin, wheezing for air, caught Lob's return to the sky, Weed hanging in the man's grasp.

Some drones chased after those anomalies. The others came for him. Calvin felt the concrete beneath his palms, started to draw it in and raised his right hand.

The first dart hit his chest. The second his stomach. They burned on contact, numbed after. A gladiator crunched down next to Calvin's head, weapons ready. A metal arm, clawed on its end with a device meant to rend doors and worse from their hinges, reached towards him. What it would do to his body, Calvin didn't want to know.

Thankfully the darts did their job, and Calvin didn't see, didn't feel.

Back To Before

A wordless roar filled the ruined Paragon hall, drowning bullets in its reverberating rage. Crouched over Daw, Cassidy felt her voids slipping and smiled. She knew that sound well, knew what would follow. The drones might get her, but they would pay.

The floor shook, no foundation-rattling explosion this time but deep, bone-crunching thuds belonging to a particular anomaly. Glass burst and smaller bangs followed as decorations not meant for earthquakes fell.

Cassidy felt a pinch at her ankle, turned and saw a tracker drone, the insect-thing's claws sneaking beneath her voids to stab. The metal knives scrabbled for her as Cassidy tucked her legs in. Bullets continued to rain, locking her voids in place. Summoning another would put Cassidy at four voids at a time, a number she'd never reached and one that seemed as likely to kill her as save her.

"What's happening?" Daw asked, his eyes flickering open.

"Stay still. I've got voids wrapping us."

The tracker lunged, scored a gash on Cassidy's leg, ripping a seam along her calf. She screamed, then bit off the sound. Tried a kick that bounced off the drone's metal.

"But if you've got any other tricks, kid, now's the time."

Daw flicked his eyes past Cassidy, blinked at the tracker drone. Cassidy, the void heat launching sweat down her face, listened for a break, any break in the gunfire. She might be able, in the second a drone spent reloading or swapping weapons, to send a new void at the tracker and—

The Paragon *flickered.* Daw's body, with Cassidy's hand resting on his shoulder, popped out and back, her hand moving into the space and then getting shoved back out, hard, when Daw re-appeared.

"Try kicking it again," Daw said.

Cassidy didn't need much encouragement with the tracker drone coming forward again, this time both front claws looking for a cutting slice. She kicked out, her booted foot flickering through the tracker's nose. Daw's ability flashed Cassidy back solid, the force bending the charging machine like balsa wood. The centipede machine pushed back on itself, inflexible metal banging, snapping, breaking. Joints cracked, sparks found freedom, and coolant hissed out in a cold gray rush.

The voids snapped at Cassidy's surprise, her concentration breaking as her boot sent the tracker drone falling back. The collapsing voids broke an immediate icy chill through Cassidy's nerves, and panic flared as she rolled off Daw, trying to bring another void back.

Three gladiators surrounded the Paragon and his protector, all taking in the vanished voids. Cassidy expected their bullets to find new homes in the next second, but the machine trio didn't light up the anomaly pair. Instead, all three whirled to face down the hall.

Another roar gave the reason. Cassidy felt the air from Thane's howl blow her hair, felt her bones shake as the anomaly landed over her, the wood floor cracking at his arrival. The giant man, his wispy hair matching Thane's torn outfit, kept moving, bounding over a flickering Daw to tackle the middle gladiator in a rushing charge.

Cassidy couldn't call herself a drone expert, but gladiators had size and strength to spare. This one nearly equaled Thane's height, and it snapped its joints into position to meet Thane with a grapple. The two titans should've bashed together and stuck, but instead Thane tore through the gladiator like it'd replaced its steel with silk. The big machine split in two, each half in a Thane hand.

Daw flickered again.

Bullets flew in from the other two gladiators, striking and drawing red welts on Thane's musclebound hide. The raging anomaly spun, still holding the destroyed drone halves, and launched one apiece at his two remaining attackers. Far from the wispy, weak stuff Thane had just destroyed, the broken halves struck their fellow drones with crackling bangs. The gladiator to Cassidy's right lost its head in a spark shower, while the one to her left had its legs bent askew as the machine attempted to dodge.

A void whispered at her fingertips, and Cassidy threw it while Thane roared at the remaining gladiator. The tiny void, its nexus half a meter wide, whipped into the stumbling drone and snared the machine's center, ripping wires, joints, and coils apart. With an electric groan, the gladiator settled to the floor, dark and dead.

Shoulders heaving, Thane whirled back and forth, looking for more drones to tear apart. Cassidy didn't see any, didn't hear any more screams from deeper in the facility. Maybe they'd all been destroyed, or—

"A retreat, nothing more," Apinya announced from behind Cassidy.

The Champion approached, flanked by several Paragon squads. The anomalies weren't unscathed, many holding arms or each other for support. Most had a terrorized glaze to their eyes, their slow steps.

Cassidy felt an angry, vindicated rush: now these high and mighty masters knew what it felt like to have drones attack. She'd lived under that shadow for so long . . .

"Hey," Daw said, his voice drawing Cassidy back as Apinya issued commands to his Paragons. One squad went down the side, following Cassidy's children, while another broke to the rooms Cassidy had cleared out earlier. "Thanks for saving me."

"I didn't," Cassidy said, crawling over next to Daw. She looked at her torn leg and winced. The pain would hit harder as the adrenaline faded. "Thane did."

"No." Daw sat up, put a hand to his stomach and groaned, then laid back down again. Cassidy managed to get a hand behind the young man's head, softening its landing. "You bought me time. I helped your friend. Teamwork, right?"

Beyond them, Apinya approached Thane, the Champion holding out hands while his last Paragon squad split to the hall's sides, wary looks flying free. Thane growled as Apinya came closer, and Cassidy wondered if Thane's past would come back here, now, and rend Apinya's head from the man's body.

Instead, Thane shriveled. His muscles withered, his skin went loose before tightening up around the man's smaller frame. Where a giant stood, in seconds, a slightly stooped, thin older man barely taller than Cassidy met Apinya's hands with his own.

"Teamwork," Cassidy said. "The Paragons will give you that, so long as you play by their rules."

"Sure, but what other choice do you have?" Daw asked.

Thane spilled information while Apinya led his remaining Paragons from the facility. Without anywhere to go, Cassidy stuck with the group, Thane helping her walk with her wounded leg, embracing the slight protection against future drone attacks. The mishmash followed the children's route, sticking near the water and beneath bridges as much as possible as they made their way towards Bangkok's outskirts and the forests beyond.

Emergency sirens echoed through Bangkok's late night traffic as fire prevention drones and their human partners converged on the damaged facility, each rumbling pass-by at first pushing the evacuating group to hide in the bushes for cover before frequency forced Apinya to keep them moving anyway.

Thankfully, whomever had sent the Paragon drones on an attack course hadn't done the same with more domestic robots. None broke from their response course to act against the anomalies stalking through the brush, batting at mosquitoes and trying to reconcile their shattered lives.

The machines had changed their minds without preamble, Thane said. He and Apinya had been well into a new plan to reshape society—Cassidy may have rolled her eyes here, exhaustion notwithstanding—when two older guardian drones nearby raised their weapons and attacked the Paragons in the hall outside.

"He wouldn't let me loose," Thane said and Cassidy didn't need to ask who he meant. "Even as his own people died, Apinya kept me restrained. He put me in a meadow, surrounded me with butterflies beneath a clear blue sky."

"That worked?"

"I'm still human, much as everyone wants to believe otherwise. Convince me I'm in a peaceful place, and I will remain at peace."

That charm held until Apinya himself came under attack, breaking the Champion's concentration and plunging Thane from a blissful day into a fire-torn, bullet-ridden war. Giving into his angry side didn't take more than a few seconds, and Thane had himself targets aplenty. He'd gone through, rending one drone after the next, and nearly taking some Paragons at the same time.

"I would've killed them all, but Apinya found a way to manipulate me," Thane said, and where Cassidy expected a frown, the anomaly instead fished out a smile. "He refocused, put me in a new place. Not peaceful, this time, but he cloaked every Paragon with something I wouldn't attack even at my worst."

"Dare I ask what?"

"You, Cassidy."

The man said the words as if he expected it to come across as sweet. Some fond token that Thane still had affection for Cassidy. And maybe it would have, except Thane had just ditched her, left Cassidy to rot after taking her to a city she didn't know, dragging her off the island. Sure, the place had been a prison, but she'd had a life there.

A home.

"You're quiet." Thane said as the column ducked under another bridge and found Bangkok's cityscape dwindling at last.

The moon, at least, provided a welcome bright white glow. Something for Cassidy to look at while she tried to figure out how to tell the world's most infamous villain that he was an asshole. Looking skyward kept Cassidy from noticing a rock, and stepping on it twisted her leg in an unpleasant fashion. She wanted to curse, to scream, but neither would've helped, so she bit back while Thane helped steady her.

Time to change the subject.

"This was your big plan, wasn't it?" Cassidy asked. "Take all those drones and turn them into your private, impartial army?"

"A plan that can still work," Thane replied, not showing any hints that Cassidy's brush-off dented his feelings. "The wrong hands are on the controls now. If anything, this has shown how effective my idea would be."

"Yeah, all terror and blood. Sounds wonderful."

"But this would not be our blood, our terror. Only those who deserve it would suffer the consequences."

"Said the insane man."

"You don't believe me?"

"I wanted to," Cassidy said. "On that island, I wanted to believe there was something better back in the real world. What a mistake that was."

Thane didn't answer as they navigated a swampy, reedy mess. Apinya, at the front, had them avoiding the main roads and going as much through nowhere as possible. Progress was slow, and wet.

"Apinya said you had reached out to your family," Thane said once they found some dry ground, beneath trees so dense the moon disappeared, its presence evident only in silver shafts slicing through gaps. "Aren't they here, in the 'real world' as you call it?"

"On the other side of it, and with more problems than distance besides," Cassidy said. "Thane, I don't know if you can understand what it's like to be one of us. To be me."

"What?"

"A parent. An anomaly with a life and a career that's lost it all. You think you've had whiplash, try having all your dreams yanked away in middle school when you wake up and your fingers want you to tear apart reality. I went to college a fugitive, hiding my powers from everyone."

Thane appeared smart enough to stay quiet as the troupe marched through the trees, so Cassidy kept talking.

"After a while, I made peace with it. Graduated, found a job I loved, started a family with someone I thought I understood. But it never goes away, you know? The whispers?"

"I know."

"When I lost everything, when Mynx took me to that damn island, I figured I'd had to reset my life once before, I can do it again." Cassidy brushed hair from her eyes, matted over with sweat because, even at night, this damn country was too hot for her. "And I did, but here we are, and I'm having to tear myself apart and build me up yet again, and I don't know if I can do it."

"You're not alone this time," Thane replied. "You are not hiding, you are not trapped."

"Is that what you'd call this?"

"You know what I mean. You have allies."

"That will leave me alone the moment it comes time to chase something shiny."

Thane didn't pick that one up, but let the conversation cool. Cassidy felt his touch growing lighter, more fragile. She looked his way, saw a more wrinkled, weaker man next to her.

"Going galaxy brain?" Cassidy asked.

"Next time, you will stay in the room. You will offer your opinions, and we will benefit from your insight."

"You had to get smarter just for that?"

"No," Thane said. "I needed to understand where Apinya wants to take us, and I think I know."

"Is it close?"

Thane looked at her, grinned, and fleshed himself back out, "Not at all."

They walked through the night, taking breaks throughout. Healthier Paragons would break off from the group to raid convenience stores and other places the group passed, using their abilities to keep the scavenging secret. Apinya figured any Paragon caught using their Tamas to buy things legitimately would trigger a drone response. Best to keep things safe.

With dawn plenty broken, the group staggered into a lakeside collective. Thatched huts floated on bamboo rafts along the lake's edge, drifting in the mild ripples brought about by morning's breeze. The Paragons seemed to know the place, breaking out into squads, with some hustling the Cassidy's saved teenagers to selected spots.

"You two will stay with me," Apinya said, waiting for Thane and Cassidy on the lakeshore. "We need to discuss what happens next."

"Discuss?" Thane asked. "Our next steps are clear."

Apinya raised his eyebrows.

"He does that," Cassidy said.

"Apparently," Apinya replied. "Would you care then, Thane, to enlighten us?"

"Mynx runs the drones from her Factory," Thane said. "Whomever controls the drones must have taken it. Nothing we do matters until we wrest the Factory back, and destroy the ones that captured it."

"So simple," Apinya said.

"It is. All we need is a plane that can fly me over the structure. Drop me in, and I can take care of the rest."

Apinya glanced at Cassidy, "I don't suppose you have a plane, do you?"

Back on the island, a plane seemed a dream in a drone prison. Here, as the sun rose over the foggy water, Cassidy found herself back where she began: dark shapes hovering on the horizon and little hope of escape.

And yet, around her she saw something different than on those beaches. Faces, wills that said they would fight and keep on fighting, no matter how long it took, how hard the struggle.

"I don't," Cassidy said. "But I bet we can find one."

CONTINUE *the adventure with* LIBERATOR'S LIGHT, *the fourth and final book in* The Hero's Code *series, available at your favorite retailer:*

An Excerpt from
LIBERATOR'S LIGHT
THE HERO'S CODE BOOK 4

Rhimes stalked the objective beneath palm fronds. Hiding small arms beneath a billowing shirt and shorts proved trickier in LA weather than Chicago's, but the operative and his team made do. Across the street and approaching from the opposite side, three mercenaries completed Rhimes's four-member squad.

They backed up the main weapons: a metal duo skittering through the neighboring yards. The tracker drones, roach-like robots with sharp edges aplenty, would be taking the lead.

Rhimes could care less about turfing off the opening responsibilities. Any attack carried the most danger in its first moments, when plans went awry and intelligence failures became evident. Better to risk robots that could be churned out by the hundreds every day than a single normal life.

At least, that's what Rhimes told Wexley, who didn't argue.

"Last check," Rhimes said. "Go?"

His three operatives clicked an affirmative, and the two

drones, sitting somewhere to Rhimes's left behind a white fence, followed with their own okays. Their target, a two-story bungalow with a modern design, all creams and dark wood, sat ahead and looked, like most places on this residential street, to be deserted.

If only.

"Let's get it done," Rhimes said, triggering the op.

Reaching into the loosely buttoned shirt, Rhimes pulled out a combo gun from its shoulder holster. Double-barreled and designed by yours truly, Rhimes had the Factory turning these babies out fast enough to equip Ziran's entire force. A little switch swapped the weapon between lethal and not, a discretion becoming more important by the day as Adriana's influence pushed aside Wexley's bloodier instincts.

Rhimes didn't know what Adriana did with her prizes, but at least she kept the body count low. Any revolution came with casualties, but Wexley wanted those drones turned to anomaly execution real quick till Adriana convinced him otherwise. Not quite the equal-opportunity society Zhan-Yo had preached.

Regardless, Rhimes set the pistol to stun and closed with the house at a light jog. To his right, he saw his operatives head into another house, one co-opted from its bribed owners for today's event. In a few seconds, Rhimes would have rooftop cover. In fewer, the drones would be inside.

The tracker drones had their own lethal bent, but they'd be prioritizing a nerve agent, one that would send a victim's body into static shock for enough hours to get them where Adriana needed them to go.

Where that was, Rhimes didn't know. He hadn't asked. Enough anomalies could read minds that Rhimes kept his own life as need to know as possible.

A helicopter buzzed along overhead, its noise masking

the tracker drones as they carved through the house's back windows. Rhimes watched the entry on his Tama as he took cover behind a parked pod on the street near the house. Now came the delicate dance between observing the drone's progress and keeping his own eyes ready in case the anomalies decided to take flight.

Then again, there'd be noise aplenty. Anomalies didn't run quiet.

On the Tama's screen, Rhimes caught clear video as the tracker drones scampered inside. His chosen view veered sideways as the machine scaled the wall to the ceiling, ready to pounce on any incoming body. The second drone crossed the kitchen fast, getting itself on a wall opposite the glass doors where anyone coming to investigate would—

There. A man, holding a coffee as he rushed into the room, eyes wide. He turned, shouted something back into the house, and noticed the drone, more than a meter long, hugging the wall.

The dart, fired from a joint in the drone's front right leg, one of six knife-like limbs, stuck in the anomaly's neck. The man staggered back a step, dropped the coffee, then fell into its expanding brown pool. Rhimes winced as the man's head cracked on the tile. A nasty concussion coming with that one, most likely.

Then again, he'd take that over the anomaly getting his ability off.

The drones held their position, waiting for the new bait to work. How many could they add to their collection? Intelligence gathered by these same tracker drones and aerial surveillance suggested at least five anomalies—Elemental members, all—lived here.

"Movement on the second floor," came a buzz from Rhimes's second on the mission, the one providing rooftop cover. Brielle had a switch Rhimes envied, going from smooth-talking philosopher to straight-laced sharpshooter in a second, and now she had her competence game on. "Taking shots?"

"Only on exit," Rhimes replied. "Let the drones do their work. The quieter, the better."

In the couple months since the takeover—Wexley kept promising he'd find an official name for when Ziran toppled the Paragons worldwide, but he hadn't yet—civilized society swapped between outright panic and sustained disbelief that anything about their lives had changed at all. Markets, manufacturing, and good old fashioned day-to-day took their time getting settled, but as the sun kept rising every morning, more and more cities, countries, and governments found themselves remembering the before and reverting to it.

All out warfare in the streets threatened to disrupt that careful balance, so Wexley and his shadowy backers said. Rhimes had to be quiet, focused, and sharp. Take out the anomalies, let people get their lattes. A balance.

Two more shapes showed up in the drone cameras. Together, neither with drinks in their hands, the man and woman, both past middle age, looked at the fallen man and waited. Rhimes slid his fingers along the Tama, zooming in on the pair. The drone catching the shot had itself squeezed onto the ceiling, nestled behind a fan, but it'd be seen if the two dared look up for more than a second.

With a closer look, Rhimes saw what he suspected: the woman's fingers moved, as if playing a piano in the air. The man's eyes had a faraway bent to them, as if in a daydream. Tapping on the Tama, Rhimes sent a different command to the drones.

No more waiting. Time to go on offense, before the anomalies finished whatever nonsense they were planning.

His Tama vibrated. An outside call. Not taking that now.

Instead, raising the firearm, Rhimes swept around the car and made for the house's front door. Sunlight glinted off gutters. Two twirling sparrows flitted by, oblivious. Some children splashed and shouted in a pool across the street. Rhimes held his focus, looked down the barrel at the rose-red door.

It opened. A face looking back inside the house as the door swung wide. The older man. Rhimes fired. The upper chamber hissed, popped, a quiet launch muffled further by the gun's design. The man jerked as Rhimes's shot hit him between the shoulders.

Wexley's main man picked up speed, breaking into a run as something large crumpled inside, metal grinding on wood. The Tama vibrated again. Behind Rhimes, he heard more feet running. His two agent back-up.

"Second floor," Brielle said. "Teenagers in the windows."

"Anomalies?" Rhimes asked as the man he'd shot stumbled onto the cement porch.

Rhimes reached the man as he turned, stuck a left foot against the victim's heel and slammed the man down. Just before the anomaly's head had a rude encounter with the concrete, Rhimes slipped his left hand beneath it. Earned a scrape against his knuckles for the effort, but the anomaly didn't leave a bloody splatter, instead blinking fuzzed eyes up at Rhimes as the numbing drugs did their work.

"Unclear," Brielle said. "They're together. Three."

"That's more than reported," Rhimes said, aiming back toward the open door. A quick Tama check showed two missed calls and static on the drone feeds. "Family?"

"You're asking questions I can't answer."

Rhimes signaled his back-up to wait, watch the

opening while he moved inside. Using the door for cover on his left, Rhimes looked right as he entered. A dining room, fresh flowers in glass atop dark wood. Chairs positioned properly. Framed photos on the wall, the kids smiling. Nobody waiting for him.

"Can you hit them?" Rhimes said, fishing in his belt for help. Vague art sat against the teal inside wall on his left now, the door covering his back, the two outside covering the door and Brielle doing what she did on the opposite rooftop.

The house blueprint flickered in his mind. The stairs would be behind him, to the right. If the kids grew frisky, they'd make noise.

"I can," Brielle said. "They've shut the door. One's opening the window. Go?"

The stunning rounds were dosed for adults, not kids. Hit someone too tiny and the drugs might knock them out permanently. The younger ones might not even be anomalies—powers weren't always inherited. Balance that against one being an adolescent bomb.

Protect his people. Ziran could always claim the whole family had abilities later.

"Go." Rhimes said. "And signal medical."

Its own risk, bringing innocent help into the play before he'd secured the site, but Rhimes liked to tell himself he hadn't lost himself yet.

"On it."

Rhimes snapped around the dining room entry, covering the opening leading into the kitchen. Soft cream carpet met bronzed tile where the kitchen began, the ceramic getting itself swamped with the golden and blue fluids found in the drones. It leaked out to the left, beyond the drywall arch where Rhimes couldn't see.

Glass shattered again as Brielle took her shots.

"Watch the exits," Rhimes said, clicking twice to clarify the order went to his two on-the-ground agents. They'd split, one back and one front while he cleaned out the inside. "Nobody gets off the property."

"Medical's incoming," Brielle said, voice chill, almost happy. "Two down. Third one's hiding behind the bed."

Rhimes approached the kitchen entry. Listened and heard twinkling twitches. A drone's last gasps, functions fighting for their lives. He debated calling out, giving surrender a chance. Doing that would out his own position, but might spare the woman, or his agents, or himself.

Instead, Rhimes looked into the kitchen, watching right, where the microwave, a shiny new model, served him well: its glass finish gave a distorted mirror view into the living room, where two long, shiny bodies showed drones that'd had better days. Nobody else stood with them.

Rhimes took a breath, embraced the cautious fear always haunting him at times like these, and went through the arch.

The drones showcased their demise: a long winding cut scythed through their bellies, less like a sword and more like a painter with a razor brush stroke. Their innards spilled circuits and coolant all around, dooming the home to a makeover once this adventure ended. The second drone, hugging the ceiling, had crushed a coffee table in its fall, adding wooden bits to the mess. A TV sat mounted over a fireplace, walls covered in more family photos.

Children's drawings had their place on the fridge behind him. Good ones, too: strong crayon strokes.

Rhimes went forward, rolling his feet with the gun up.

"Third one tagged," Brielle said. "He went for his siblings. Medical three minutes out."

Rhimes clicked in reply. The wall on his left wrapped around the home's central stairs. He followed it to the end, washing around the edge to the last square. A half bath on the right, door open and nobody inside. The living room empty all the way through.

Just the stairwell going up. He wanted to ask if anyone had seen the woman, but there'd be no point. His crew would've spoken, they were good. A glance behind Rhimes confirmed his agent had a place in the backyard near the pool, weapon aiming up. Every window covered, every door spied.

Time to talk.

"Give it up," Rhimes shouted. "Your family's down. Whether they live is up to you!"

No reply. Rhimes gave it three heartbeats, then took another step towards the stairs. A rosy chime jerked his attention to his right, towards that TV. Someone turning it on. The screen went to a splash selection, icons aplenty. Rhimes recognized one glowing towards the top, signaling a link with someone's Tama.

They whirled through the icons, hit one then another, and Rhimes felt his fear melt into resignation. A chosen video started to play. Kids, probably the ones upstairs, laughing and playing around the pool. Parents, both in Paragon white-and-blue uniforms, sharing a drink with their casual-clothed grandparents. Dots connected themselves, as they always did.

"Then save your grandkids," Rhimes called up the stairs. "Don't be selfish."

He couldn't tell the woman she'd save herself, that she could see them again. He wouldn't make false promises, not now.

"Door's opening," Brielle said. "Kid's room. It's her, but I don't have a shot. She's staying behind that door."

"Going up," Rhimes replied.

A maple stair, light wood with a carpet running up the

middle. Cheery teal, matching the walls, the pool water on a bright day. A dead light hung above him. Vacation photos on either side, so crowded as if the family couldn't bare a naked patch. Rhimes kept moving, fast now, and cleared the hall in time to see the woman walk through the door ahead on the right.

"Take the shot!" Rhimes said.

The drywall on his right split open, a flickering green line slicing through towards Rhimes. He fell back, slipped and rolled down the stairs, landing on his back with his gun facing up.

A crack rang through the air. Loud, sharp.

"She's down," Brielle said. "So's Jesse."

Rhimes swung up to his feet, pounded the stairs and swung into the room, pistol up and ready. Three teenagers lay about the room, collapsed and unconscious. Posters conquered the walls, an unmade bed the room's center-piece. The target, a fatal red blossoming beneath her, laid on it. Beyond her, sharp gashes broke through the house walls, tearing down into the yard where Jesse, Rhimes's third agent on this mission, had lost his bottom half.

Rhimes let the pistol fall to his side, watched as medical pods rolled up, as more drones poured in from above.

So much for quiet.

Continue the adventure with LIBERATOR'S LIGHT, available at your favorite retailer:

bitly

Acknowledgments and Author's Note

Revolution's Rise continues a series exploring something I've always found interesting, namely, what happens when folks who used to be, physically, unstoppable find themselves very much stoppable. When your self-identity is wrapped up in something that falls victim to time.

Could you change? Would you?

As ever, this story is brought about through Nicole's endless support in letting me play in fantastical universes. My brothers, parents, and in-laws all bring a joy and wonder to my life that encourages exploring the vast reaches of science fiction and fantasy. Their support is everything.

Readers, too, fire the creative furnace. Whether through five star (or less!) reviews, messages passed through the infinite web of social media, or simply a ping on the sales chart that says someone's taking a chance on my stories, that powers the drive to keep on keeping' on. So thank you, and I hope you enjoyed this novel and the rest of the series.

About the Author

A.R. Knight spins stories in a frosty house in Madison, WI, primarily owned by a pair of cats. After getting sucked into the working grind in the economic crash of the 2008, he found himself spending boring meetings soaring through space and going on grand adventures.

Eventually, spending time with podcasting, screenplays, short stories and other novels, he found a story he could fall into and a cast of characters both entertaining and full of heart.

A.R. Knight plans on jumping through to other worlds and finding new stories to tell in the limitless borders of our imagination.

Thanks, as always, for reading!

For more information:
www.adamrknight.com

To Alex